Rod and Tod

Richard Gough

Nocterna Books

Rod and Tod

First Edition

First published 2020

Copyright © Richard Francis Gough

All rights reserved

All the characters in this book are fictitious, and any resemblance to actual persons, living or dead, is purely coincidental.

Thank you to Melissa Spence for your hard work with the illustrations. Thank you to my family for your endless support.

Also by Richard Gough:

Nocterna Book Of Chasms

Nocterna II The Band Is Back Together

Plant Warriors *(Graphic Novel)*

Nocterna Books

Chapter 1

Crude Creations

"What do you make of it, Rod?"

"Very little if I'm being totally honest, Tod." Tod grimaced slightly before he continued, "It's a weird looking planet, isn't it Rod?"

"Yes Tod and I suppose it is a perfect place to relieve our boredom for the moment."

Tod's facial expression slowly morphed into a grin. He had a massive face, you see, being a purple cloud; no legs, just a perfectly bouncy, soft as a cushion, cloud. Actually he resented the last part. If anyone were to sit on him there would be major trouble and pain. Mustn't forget the pain part now, Tod reminded himself.

Rod remained floating just opposite Tod. His shape was similar, yet his colouring was closer to pink than purple. He didn't share his friend's exuberance for chaos, but he was more than interested in a little bit of trouble here and there. That was only normal for entities in their position.

The two clouds were surrounded by white, quite literally the colour white. There was nothing else around them and this white colour seemed to reach as far as the eye could see and then on a little bit further for good measure. Predictability was something neither would tolerate, so stretching out that little extra yard was always worth it, no matter the cost nor the situation.

"I do not wish to sound foolish, but isn't Earth often chosen for acts ranging from annoyance to sheer destruction? We aren't being predictable are we Tod?"

"No, I don't think so Rod. The reason that Earth is chosen with such frequency is that its dwellers always react either through amusement or violence, but little else in between. It will make the perfect spectacle for us. Shall we record our findings?"

"Yes Tod. We could record it on the ground. What do you propose we make our show about?" Rod was feeling somewhat lethargic now and wished to get on with the experiment. This was supposed to be fun, I mean this was recreational time for both of them.

Tod pondered for a moment and it was evident that he was thinking hard about the subject. It needed to be original, yet familiar, even odd and certainly, most definitely, sad yet funny.

"Let's release a golden one. Purple and red will be too cold or warm so I suggest we go with gold." The confidence in Tod's voice was there for all to hear, or just Rod, seeing as he was the only other being present in the room, well, white area, whatever anyone wanted to refer to it as.

Rod agreed with this and confirmed the stance, "Yes okay, I'm happy to agree with that. Shall I get one then?"

"No need Rod, I have already taken the liberty." Tod closed his eyes and appeared to be focussing on something with great concentration.

Rod was happily smiling as he usually did when Tod was thoroughly in control of a situation. He was well aware of what would happen next.

Slowly, but quickly, Tod could never decide on which way to go so he did both, a golden rock materialised in front of the clouds. It was roughly the size of a tennis ball, but far more jagged at the edges as it was not perfectly round. It floated amongst the white with the two clouds.

Tod opened his eyes to review his handiwork. "They did have

other ones, but I preferred this shape and size. We can fit this into smaller spaces. Actually, Rod, there was one particular nugget that was the size of Earth itself. Not ideal for what we are trying to achieve today, but something that could be extremely useful if we want to wreak havoc on some of the giant planets."

Rod nodded at Tod with glee. Well he sort of bounced. Clouds didn't really nod.

All of a sudden, Rod's pink features became more prominent as he asked a question that he had obviously been mulling over for a considerable period of time. "May I drop it? Please Tod, you know I can do this. Surely now it is my turn. Please Tod, please may I?"

The usually casual Tod was slightly perturbed by this request. He had foreseen it coming at some point, but this was not in the manner he had predicted. In truth, Tod had felt that Rod would have wanted to deliver a drop on a far more important target. The fact that he wanted to perform one on somewhere as irrelevant as Earth meant that this was an ideal opportunity to test him.

The purple cloud let out a brief yet wry smile, "Very well then Rod, we will see how you handle the situation. I do hope it's something obscure but regular though."

Rod was now beaming with delight. Obscure but regular would be fine – a breeze even, but he must not get complacent with it.

Rod closed his eyes and Tod drifted back away from the golden rock to allow his friend the space to carry out the activity. The expression on Rod's face did not alter and the same broad smile remained.

The rock jiggled a bit, then shot through the white shade of colour beneath them. Silence enveloped the area the two clouds occupied. Rod looked longingly at Tod, desperately seeking approval.

Tod gave him a menacing stare at first, which made Rod feel uneasy.

"Just kidding, you did great. I believe that is an earthling expression. Now let's enjoy the ride."

Rod laughed aloud and both clouds began to circle each other in what resembled some form of ritual dance. Both hollered, screamed, cackled and generally made as much noise as they possibly could. Undeniably the operation had already been deemed a solid success.

The rain continued to pour down over Central London. It was of course a typical summer's day in the capital and whilst the temperature was not low, the rain was doing its best to saturate everything it could. It seemed to possess a mind of its own and was purposely harassing those who were dry. People scrambled with waterproofs, coats and hats, desperately seeking cover.

Oxford Street itself was still well populated and business was thriving. Stretching further into Soho left a little more to be desired. It had become a proverbial ghost town. There was not a soul in sight.

Tucked away down a small alley off Wardour Street lay a toppled-over wheelie bin, with its contents strewn around the confined area. A trail of ants was attempting to brave the hurricane like weather and to make its way inside a white pizza box searching for the treasure within.

Just beside this lay an encyclopaedia. The page was open on a definition of the mainland of the United Kingdom. Adjacent to the encyclopaedia and resting against it, was a pile of what could only be described as green sludge. It was not a clear or bright green, but rather a mishmash of various colours that had all been mixed together. It was not unlike the appearance of plasticine after everyone has had a turn and all the colours have gone and merged into one dark, murky-green colour.

One ant moved towards a small gap in the pizza box but was quickly blown away by a voice. "These ants are ruining my rest. I don't have any slices left. Go away."

"Sssshhhhh. The last lot of people who heard you sprinted away from us. You need to be quiet," said the encyclopaedia.

The sludge was fast to comment on this, "Calm down. It's not as if those people didn't have a choice. They could have carried on about their business as normal. What's with the ants? They are attracted to you, or to your interior I should say."

The pizza box sighed and blew away a couple of ants that had become far too intrusive. "It's not me they want, it's what's inside me."

"Old pizza I assume?" said the encyclopaedia.

"No it is not pizza scraps. It's some old apple crumble. My guess is that the people who ordered me could not finish their dessert and simply dumped it on me."

The group was fine with this perfectly logical explanation, but only momentarily. The sludge was the first to speak and one could easily sense the scepticism in his voice.

"Wait a minute, what do you mean by guess? Why don't you know?"

The pizza box pondered on this and if he possessed a hand he would surely have clutched his chin to portray his train of thought. He did not have a clue of course, which naturally led to the next line of enquiry, this time coming from the encyclopaedia.

"You don't know do you? Come to think of it, I'm not entirely sure how I got here either?"

"You're out of date," said the sludge, "It says so on the cover that is flapping at me. You're a 2014 encyclopaedia, hence your now former owner probably purchased a new one and threw you away. It's a simple deduction really."

Both the pizza box and downtrodden book now focussed on the murky sludge.

"Okay then, that would make sense regarding our knowledgeable friend over here, so I suppose there is only one important question left. How did you get here?"

The sludge answered instantly, "I've been here for ages. I mean I don't have any evidence to support this statement, but if one looks at my complexion and colour, it would suggest that I have been here for quite some time. To counter your question, pizza box, why is it that we can suddenly talk and why is it that we have no recollection of our past and that we have only been sentient beings for about ten minutes. Either that or we are incredibly shy because we were not speaking to one another earlier, or perhaps we are very rude for the same reason I just gave."

"Well I haven't been rude. I started talking as soon as I could," said the encyclopaedia.

"I don't doubt that for a second," said the sludge.

The three entities were silent once more, although only

fleetingly, as they were mulling over the sensation of being alive.

The pizza box lid flapped once more, "Shall we go then? I assume we will have to stick together, as the humans who occupy this world will not take kindly to our existence. I am of course basing this on the fact that my first meaningful memory is of a pair of people sprinting away from me in terror whilst I uttered my first words."

"How do we even know what humans and this language are? It is like all this information has been shoved into our..." The encyclopaedia ceased momentarily before continuing, "Brains I suppose."

The three chuckled at the prospect of having brains, but all considered the danger of some trickery at play here. Finally the sludge broke the laughter, "I propose we see what else we can do. If we can talk and think, some humans are incapable of that, then we attempt to move. Besides, I'm not keen on all this rain that keeps hammering down on us."

The pizza box and encyclopaedia shook around indicating that they were nodding in as best a fashion as they could muster.

"I'd better go first then, as I suggested it. I don't want to be seen as a wimp – how I even know about that term is a mystery."

The pizza box and encyclopaedia grumbled at the sludge.

Slowly the goo began to lift off the ground and take shape. At first it resembled a dog, then an oversized ant, a giraffe and lastly the sludge settled for a humanoid form. It now resembled a plasticine figure that had been made in a primary school classroom. It had no features whatsoever, that was until the sludge used its hand to carve in some eyes, a straight nose and a line for a mouth.

"No. You look like something out of a cartoon show, make yourself cooler than that," said the pizza box.

The sludge saluted and within seconds had grown a series of spikes on his back.

"Now you're a walking hedgehog!"

"I haven't finished yet, book. Take a gander at this."

The body shuddered until the head popped back inside it. Eventually the entire figure transformed into the shape of an egg. Arms and legs popped out of each side, and strangely enough, some blue eyes appeared on the front of the egg, followed by some red lips.

"I had just enough colour to produce my eyes and lips. What do you think?"

"You're a walking egg. What happened to the spikes, I thought they were cool?" said the pizza box.

"Oh I still have them. I shall merely use them when necessary. I happen to like my form. I'm an egg because I'm just so intellectual and clever and the spikes are my secret weapon that I may unleash in the blink of an eye." With that the egg shot out the spikes from behind and then popped them back in. The egg/sludge was grinning wildly now, "From this moment forth I shall be referred to as 'Eggo Maniac'. A name that will strike fear into the hearts of thousands."

"Why do you want to strike fear into the hearts of thousands?" said the encyclopaedia.

"I don't know, it just sounded good. Anyway you're detracting from the point. Perhaps it is your turn to rise up and take your true form, old book."

The pages of the encyclopaedia flicked back and forth as it

decided what it would be. The book now hovered over the saturated paving stones and the pages continued to sway from side to side.

Eggo Maniac watched keenly, as did the pizza box. Eventually the pages stopped.

"What country are we in Eggo Maniac?"

"England, part of the United Kingdom."

The encyclopaedia bent in half and then folded itself once more, then again and again until it was too tiny to be visible to the naked eye. It spoke briefly, which was mildly disturbing, as it was not currently visible.

"I'm afraid that's not my homeland mates."

Eggo Maniac leaned forward to study the space where it had been. He glanced at the floor and could hear a tearing sound coming from within. He darted back, clearly alarmed by this. The volume of the tearing increased, as did the speed of it.

Silence finally ensued and out of nothing the book fell to the ground. The expansion commenced. The book grew to at least the size of a sixty-inch plasma television screen, but far thicker to accommodate the numerous pages within. It shivered briefly and moved on to stutter.

As it shook, it became clear what the tearing of pages was all about. On either side of the hardback blue cover there were two perfectly round holes. They were opposite each other and were positioned with such precision that if one was to look through a hole, then it would have been like looking straight through to the other side, with not even a jagged edge or miniscule torn bit of paper obstructing the view.

It gave the impression that these two holes had been professionally cut using some sort of expensive milling machine.

Quickly, the holes began to fill with some white liquid. There was far too much of it for the book to retain, so it leaked out of the sides. It did not drip onto the floor however. No, this was a controlled movement and it merely extended outwards, stretching like an arm on either side and this is what it became. The liquid at the end of the arms moulded itself into hands and, underneath the now constructed arms, two more perfectly aligned holes appeared. The same process started again, with white liquid oozing out from the sides.

This time it did drip onto the floor and moments later this encyclopaedia had a set of arms, hands, legs and feet, all in the same matching white colour.

"What about your face? Surely you require a face to see and eat amongst other things," said Eggo Maniac.

The now limbed book laughed. "Ha ha, that's coming mate, don't you worry."

Within moments a green eye sprouted on each cover above the arms and a red lipped mouth that stretched oddly across the fore-edge of the book materialised.

Eggo Maniac nodded politely in response and was about to ask one more question regarding why the book had suddenly taken on an accent, one that sounded Australian in fact, when he was rudely interrupted by the pizza box talking to the book. "What's your name then?"

"Bruce, mate. I mean just Bruce. Bruce, but I was calling you mate."

Eggo Maniac rolled his eyes in acceptance. The two then turned to inspect the only remaining member. Eggo Maniac examined the pizza box curiously. "Well I suppose we have had some strange transformations and we are due another. The floor is yours my friend."

The lid of the box flapped and the pair who were watching could not decide whether it was the wind or not.

They did not have to wait long for their answer. Out of the now open box slid the remains of the apple crumble. The green of the apples had liquefied as it oozed onto the floor. Intermittent bits of streusel crust moved underneath the box and lifted it from the floor.

The apples and crumble merged together and continued to push the pizza box into the air. It was now at least six feet in height. The apple crumble acted as a pillar beneath it.

"He won't move about very well like that," said Bruce, who had opened himself up and was casually perusing his own pages, as he leant up against the walls of the alleyway.

"I don't think he's finished yet, chap," said Eggo Maniac.

The pillar of crumble rumbled and shook. Gradually it formed arms and legs and a physique of which an athlete would have been proud. The pizza box was now sitting on top of the body of an Adonis, made out of apple crumble. It was green with bits of strudel mixed in. A pair of green eyes then sprang into life on the top part of the box. It flexed its new muscles briefly, showing off the odd bicep and pectoral before stopping and taking in a deep breath.

"My name is… Howard."

"Needs work, mate, I reckon," said Bruce.

"Now, now dear Bruce, if that is what he desires to be called then that is what we shall call him. Good to meet you Howard."

"Thank you Eggo Maniac."

The three then shook hands, which was initially difficult for Bruce due to the fact that he had firstly to close himself before performing the act. Then there was a pause, an extremely long pause. Indeed this pause seemed to last for an eternity. The quick realisation set in that, whilst they were now sentient life forms, they had no idea what to do?

Howard was the first to speak, flapping his pizza box mouth, "What now then guys, where shall we go?"

Eggo Maniac immediately showed Bruce the palm of his murky hand, indicating to the book to wait until he had spoken before interrupting. He was unsure as to whether Bruce had something to say, but he was not going to be interrupted this time. Bruce was not impressed by this gesture.

"Chaps, I think we have a slight conundrum on our hands. We have no home, save for this alley and I for one do not find it to my taste. Yet worry not, London is a thriving metropolis, home to much wonder and vast experiences. Surely we will find something to do if we just roam."

"No way mate, think about the state of us. We don't look like your normal, everyday humans do we? We need to hide away otherwise we're gonna get locked up," said Bruce.

Howard was the next who wished to intervene, but was rudely cut off by Eggo Maniac, who quickly raised his hand once more as a sign that he would speak and all others must listen, "Chaps, we are over-thinking things at present. We are fortunate that we are in Soho, a very colourful area, where nothing is out of place. We will fit in. Trust me."

Before Howard could say anything, Eggo Maniac had marched out of the alley and onto Wardour Street. The general public had returned and the road was bustling with people wandering up and down, entering and exiting shops, whilst others packed the restaurants and coffee houses, all chatting the day away.

Eggo Maniac glanced left then right and as he did a number of people nonchalantly trotted past him, not batting an eyelid. He smirked.

"Come out Bruce, Howard. It's perfectly fine."

Bruce exited the alleyway. He did this quickly, possibly because he was keen to test out how nimble his new legs were.

Howard was far more reluctant. Creeping up to the edge he stuck his head around the wall. On the last occasion he had spoken, a horde of people had run away from him in horror. Perhaps he should test the water.

"Eggo Manaic I'm still unsure of this. Last time I spoke, everyone…"

"Are you speaking now Howard?"

"Well yes Eggo Maniac." He stopped and reflected on this. He moved himself onto the pavement and his impressive physique was now in full view of the general public. He laughed, not just a tiny giggle though, but a roaring scream of amusement at the situation. He had known, although he did not fully understand why, that humans were peculiar creatures. This was serious confirmation of that fact. Why were they frightened of a talking pizza box, yet a hulking great Goliath of a body, made out of apple crumble, complete with a pizza box head and green eyes that popped out of the top was absolutely fine.

"People are strange," said Howard.

"Indeed they are Howard, indeed they are. It's just like the song that bears the same name," said Eggo Maniac, "Well shall we do the off then chaps?"

Both waved at the walking egg and almost skipped down the road in delight. The trouble was, none of them knew their destination.

Chapter 2

Interview Nerves

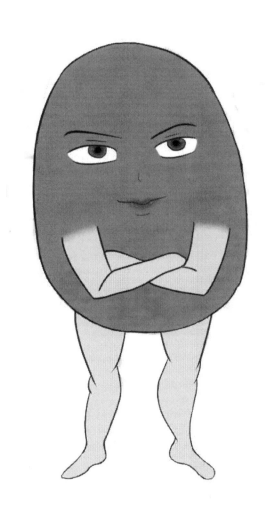

"Well they're on the move Tod."

"Yes they are Rod. Do you know what must be done now?"

The pair of clouds floated directly over a circle in the floor of all the white that surrounded them. Within this circle they watched all the action unfold in London. It was not unlike a giant television screen in the floor, 8k of course.

"I think I do Tod. We must set up an opponent?" Rod was pretty sure he knew what must happen, but he was not one hundred percent confident, hence the hint of uneasiness in his retort.

Tod laughed at him, naturally.

"Of course that is correct Rod. Come now, how many times have we done this, hundreds, possibly even over one thousand? You should honestly know by now. Anyway, technically you got it right, so I shall forgive you. Which one do you like best?"

Rod pondered on this. He did not want to seem as if he lacked confidence in front of Tod and he most definitely did not want to get anything wrong.

He observed the purple cloud, in an attempt to analyse him. It was impossible. He had truly mastered looking happy, yet sad and therefore was completely unreadable. He would have to go for it.

"I like Howard the best."

Silence ensued once more as he watched Tod's facial expression. Tod did not look impressed. Concerned that his answer was wrong, Rod opened his mouth to speak but was instantly cut off.

"Excellent Rod, very good indeed, I was using a face of caution to attempt to destabilise you, yet you stuck with my ideas and principles and saw it through to a correct answer. So now that we have decided whom we like best, what is the next step in the process?"

"Why, it is to pick an opponent Tod." Rod gleamed with pride as he said this. The two were about to embark on the 'fun' part of the task.

Both began to hover up and down, not unlike bouncing, overexcited children. Gradually Tod returned to his usual floating state. Rod followed suit immediately. The screen in the floor now showed the trio of oddities in a café. They had stopped to get some coffee and Rod could only wonder how they would have any money to pay for it.

"They won't," said Tod.

Rod faced the floor once more. He detested Tod's impromptu mind-reading sessions and was not looking forward to another one.

"Worry not Rod, I am not going to conduct a lesson with you, at least not yet. The emphasis of this mission is on you. Please do not forget that. The relevance of their ability to pay for some coffee is neither here nor there. We must be on the lookout, unless…"

This was unusual. Tod never ever paused in his speech. He was too arrogant ever to reflect upon his actions. Could this be an opportunity for Rod? He would have to finish the sentence and if he failed to deliver, then Tod would shun him for sure. Tentatively, Rod voiced his opinion, "Unless we make the opponents the coffee…"

The bit about coffee he said very quietly. So quietly that it was improbable that Tod had heard him. He was oblivious as to why he had communicated in this way. Tod was reading his thoughts so he knew precisely what he was going to say.

"Yes that's right Rod. We shall use the coffee - and ants."

"Ants?"

"Yes ants Rod. If you recall our first meeting with the trio, Howard complained about ants invading his mouth. They would surely be a wonderful nemesis for him. What better way to create a super villain than by using the very thing that upsets one of them. A natural dislike for ants will result in a natural dislike for his opponents. It's brilliant really."

Rod bounced in recognition, despite being unsure about the direction of the mission. It was common practice to introduce only one villain, not two. Admittedly the more experienced practitioner would comfortably utilise between four and twenty villains and, at the very least, some giants. This was a big ask for his first task.

"Relax Rod. I am with you. We shall complete this together," said Tod.

Contemplating this briefly, he understood that his friend was right. Together this would be no problem whatsoever. Tod shut his eyes and focussed once more. He quickly lost his train of thought however, as Rod was tapping his arm repeatedly.

"Tod, Tod, I have an idea! May I conduct this part?"

"Well I…" No sooner had Tod uttered his reply than Rod closed his eyes and out of nowhere, what could only be described as a golden boulder appeared in front of them.

An alarmed Tod yelled at his friend to stop, but to no avail. Rod was deeply involved in his experiment now and his concentration was so great that he could hear nothing. Had he been in the centre of a thunderstorm or the epicentre of an earthquake, he would have still heard absolutely nothing.

Tod lunged forward attempting to shift the boulder before it fell through the white floor and down to Earth. He managed to get a couple of fingers to it, but that was all. It was just far too fast. The boulder slipped away, hurtling to its destination – a small alley in the West End of London.

"Rod you have just caused a real situation down on Earth," said Tod.

Rod's eyes slowly opened. He yawned, that sort of thought process was hard work after all. He could see the concerned expression on his friend's face. Perhaps Tod was playing another mind game with him and he was pleased, no, ecstatic, about how the whole mission was moving along so smoothly.

"Thanks for the compliment Tod. You don't have to mask your emotions and pretend everything went badly when we both know that this was a huge success. I seriously do mean huge, by the way." Rod began to circle the screen jumping up and down and shouting in delight.

His fellow cloud did not join him though. Underneath his breath he spoke to himself, "What have you done Rod? What have you done?"

"I'm finding this drink rather odd Howard. What do you make of it Bruce? Is coffee the liquid of choice for you?"

"I'm a fan mate. I also like these sofas Eggo Maniac. It means I can actually spread out and relax. It reminds me of home." Bruce was able to release his full body across the couch on which he sat. London was a fairly awkward place for him. For example he had to walk through the coffee shop door clutching his sides to ensure that his hardback cover did not get jammed. He didn't mind this though, it was a small price to pay considering all the knowledge he contained.

Eggo Maniac continued to sip away. Howard was slightly more concerned, "This hot stuff makes my mouth soggy. It will dry, of course, but it seems to make it soggier than normal water. I can't help but feel that I am sagging."

Eggo Maniac and Bruce found great amusement in this. It was logical of course. Having a cardboard pizza box for a head was not the ideal place to put boiling hot coffee.

"Chaps, I think it's time that we…" Eggo Maniac paused. Something had caught his attention, yet he did not know what. He surveyed the room. The two bored members of staff stood behind the till in as relaxed a fashion as they could muster without being asleep, so it was not them.

The people from the table next to the group had left, which was strange, as they had been seated after them. Come to think of it there was no longer a queue. That in itself was odd considering they were in one of the busiest areas of London. Where had everyone gone?

Bruce was oblivious to this, but Eggo Maniac could sense that Howard was getting worried with the situation. "I see you share my concerns, Howard. This entire coffee house has emptied out. However, there were no screams or signs of hysteria. It was a silent exit. What could have done this?"

Howard placed one of his green and crumbly hands on the lid of his pizza box and scratched it. He was at a loss too.

Eggo Maniac and Howard stared at each other, both equally as baffled as the other. "Ow," said Howard.

"What is it? Have you discovered the solution to this riddle?" said Eggo Maniac. Not being in full control was something he simply could not manage.

"No I haven't, but something just burnt my arm."

"Guys," said Bruce, "I'm going to need some help over here." The two swivelled around to lock eyes on the reason for the instant evacuation of the venue. Standing by the window, was an enormous coffee mug. It must have been the size of a cinema screen and just as round to boot.

It was a white mug and had brown eyes and a gaping brown hole for a mouth that was shooting out hot coffee at all who were in its path. It had no legs or arms, but rocked violently from side to side spraying its liquid at anything that moved.

Despite its lack of limbs it was able to move through levitation and then crashing down onto its victims. Eggo Maniac and Howard had figured this out by the fact that Bruce was squashed underneath it. He was flapping his arms at either side of the mug, trying to hit it and throw it off him.

As the mug rocked, drops of coffee fell out and were staining Bruce's pages. It opened its mouth and out shot a small hurricane of coffee. This black, swirling menace engulfed Eggo Maniac, who was now forced to spin with it.

Howard on the other hand had managed to sneak behind the menacing mug. He had a quick glance through the window into the street and saw row after row of people standing and watching. They thought it was some sort of show – a promotion for the coffee shop perhaps.

Quickly, he placed his hands underneath the mug and attempted to lift it. It was heavy, but not too heavy. Bruce slipped out from underneath it and immediately assisted Howard. Between the two of them they now held the oversized cup in the air.

"After three then, mate?" said Bruce. Howard nodded and the pair counted in unison.

The cup of coffee crash-landed into the far interior wall amongst a pile of debris. There were shattered cups, bits of wallpaper, concrete and broken bricks surrounding it. The mug's eyes were closed and it was clearly unconscious.

Eggo Maniac fell to the ground as the caffeine ridden hurricane that held him now disappeared. Bruce proceeded to wring some of his wetter pages out onto the floor near the counter. He noticed that the two members of staff behind the tills still looked bored and he wondered whether they had actually paid any sort of attention to the showdown that had just occurred. Ignoring them, Bruce made his way over to the giant sleeping cup of coffee. "What shall we do with it?"

Howard quickly joined him and examined the debris. "I have absolutely no idea. What do you think, Eggo Maniac?"

"Well chaps, I have to be honest with you. I do not think we will have to worry about that."

Both Bruce and Howard shifted to face Eggo Maniac, who was now attempting to get rid of some coffee stains from his body. In truth the brown stains mixed in quite well with his murky-green complexion.

Quickly noticing the looks of scrutiny on their faces, Eggo Maniac proceeded to point at the mug, "Take a gander for yourselves. I do not think there will be any trouble whatsoever."

The pair took a step back and observed. The giant, sleeping cup of coffee was shrinking. Even its features were vanishing too. Where the brown eyes and enormous mouth once stood, the white of the cup had returned. It was now a normal size – in fairness the debris nearly covered it.

The scene felt slightly pathetic now. Three fully grown beings arching over a standard sized mug of coffee that was slightly cracked at best, and surrounded by chaos and destruction, left a lot to be desired.

"You haven't paid for that cup," said the closest cashier.

"Now he speaks," said a frustrated Eggo Maniac.

"We're going, so you can keep your cup mate," said Bruce.

Howard swiftly bundled them both out of the door and into the safety of the surrounding streets.

Upon their exit they could not move. They were cornered. The mass of people that were originally watching the fight had more than trebled. The group could not see for humans.

One dark haired lady in the front row started to clap. Then another person and another joined in. Within moments the entire audience was electric. Cheering, hollering, clapping and the odd scream greeted them.

Both Howard and Bruce nudged Eggo Maniac, clearly not understanding how to deal with their current plight. Eggo Maniac grinned. "Just follow my lead chaps, follow my lead. Smile, wave and, if necessary, shake hands."

Howard and Bruce waved awkwardly at their new fans. It was undeniably odd for them and their reluctance to enjoy the attention was there for all to see.

Eggo Maniac on the other hand relished the moment. He was like a conquering hero or a triumphant gladiator in the way he controlled the crowd. He worked them up into a frenzy and then brought them back down to silence, as they hung on his every word. He was like a conductor commanding the tempo and volume of his orchestra.

Howard and Bruce stood behind Eggo Maniac and allowed him to perform. Nerves had taken a hold of Howard and the lid of his pizza box quivered ever so slightly.

On the other hand Bruce was now leaning up against a shop window. He peered inside and noticed that it was a record shop and sold genuine vinyl LPs. He was terribly bored and wished that everyone would just leave them alone. Stepping forward, he grabbed Eggo Maniac's shoulder, "Come on mate, we've been here for ages now. I didn't think we wanted to attract attention to ourselves. It seems like you're doing a pretty good job of ensuring that we do."

"Nonsense Bruce. This is all part of the plan. If we become celebrities then we shall be able to live our lives in luxury."

"Listen mate, it was Howard and I who sorted out that big cup of coffee, not you. Stop taking all the credit and let's leave."

Eggo Maniac turned to Bruce, put his arm around the book and addressed the crowd, "This is Bruce, whom many of you will recognise as his resemblance is that of an encyclopaedia. Please understand that he is a valiant warrior and was absolutely vital to the success of our mission against the evil coffee cup. I mean, his presence was almost as imperative to the mission as mine was."

Deafening cheers from the crowd filled the street. Meanwhile the police had arrived on the scene, not to break up the celebrations, but to block off the roads so that no cars got stuck amongst the people.

Bruce smiled, somewhat falsely, and waved. Maybe he should just relax and savour the moment, he thought to himself.

A violent gust of wind blew down and forced the trio to cover their faces. The general public did the same, holding onto hats and pulling coat lapels and scarves around them. All looked up and could clearly see a helicopter hovering directly above the proceedings. A rope ladder unfurled from the side door and out stepped a blonde-haired lady wearing a grey suit-jacket and matching skirt. She grabbed hold of the ladder with one hand and clearly held a microphone with the other.

Slowly the ladder descended and a smartly dressed camera man followed. The smile on Eggo Maniac's face widened (which was almost impossible in itself) at the sight of what could only be a reporter. The pair of them glided down the ladder with ease and it was obvious that this was a regular occurrence.

Bruce could not fail to be impressed by the agility of the man, as he hauled a great silver camera on his shoulder at the same time. The reporter jumped the last few rungs of the ladder and landed perfectly about two yards away from Eggo Maniac. She pulled a comb from her suit-jacket and quickly adjusted her hair and ensured her grey high-heeled shoes were intact.

The camera man was the next to hit the ground and he did so at a far greater speed. His landing, too, was perfect as he took his place just behind his reporter colleague. He swept some dirt from the lapel of his jacket and straightened his tie. It was red and blue striped, which suited, excuse the pun, his pale complexion and carefully styled hair. Without saying a word he jumped in front of the lady and commenced filming her before the crowd.

This irritated Eggo Maniac as the attention of the general public had shifted to the camera and the reporter. He watched people shoving and pulling each other out of the way in a desperate bid to get their faces onto television.

"Good afternoon, I'm reporter Anne Weavers of Channel CBA bringing you the breaking news live from Central London." Cheers were clearly audible after her introduction and it was easy to deduce that she was clearly some sort of minor celebrity in her own right.

Bruce nudged Eggo Maniac once again, "Listen mate, I can see that you like this sort of public outing, but this isn't good for us. Just look at poor Howard over there."

The egg-like performer peered over at the apple crumble body of Howard, which was now shaking with fear. Bruce continued, "We've got to get out of here. Once the media gets a sniff of us there will be no tomorrow mate. They will never leave us alone. We are too different from everyone else in this city to go into hiding and if we get our images on TV then we're cooked mate."

"Nonsense Bruce. We are celebrities now and this is a lifestyle we must embrace. It's not every day one gets a chance to bask in the limelight, so when it comes one must do the right thing and grasp the mantle and..."

"That's what you're gonna do when the authorities and their scientists get hold of us and test us to the maximum because we're not human? Think about this for a minute. Put your ego aside and consider the consequences here. If we're all mates then we need to protect each other and right now I'm protecting you from yourself and Howard from them." Bruce pointed directly at the reporter.

Eggo Maniac looked down at the pavement. He knew the encyclopaedia was talking sense and that they really had to care for each other. Howard was standing petrified behind them, and all he was doing was playing to the crowd. Bruce grabbed Howard and tried to muscle his way through the endless sea of people towards Oxford Street.

The reporter caught wind of this immediately and rushed at Eggo Maniac. She plunged the microphone in front of his face and before he could even contemplate her next move the camera man had his lens fully focussed on him.

"Very nice to meet you, sir. My name is Anne Weavers and I just have one or two questions that your new adoring UK public would like to ask you. Firstly the show was great and the effects were like nothing we've ever seen from a live performance. How did it feel to be working with such a high level of theatrics?"

"Well erm…" Eggo Maniac struggled to answer.

"Also I notice you're still in costume. What's the relevance of your body being an egg and your face being in the centre of your body or egg as we like to refer to it? I enjoyed the way your two fellow actors threw the cup and then shrunk it down to size. How did they achieve that? Who and where is the director of this feature? I guess he's pretty pleased right now?"

The questions continued relentlessly and Eggo Maniac could not have answered them even if he had tried, such was the speed of this reporter's delivery.

What would he do now? He could not see Bruce or Howard as they had disappeared out of sight, probably barging through as many humans as they physically could. He was stuck in the middle with this Anne Weavers, who was not going to let him leave easily, that was for certain.

Eggo Maniac ran for it. He attempted to sneak around the reporter and stealthily duck amongst the folk behind her. This seemed like a sensible plan as the shock element of his swift movements should buy him the time to escape.

He was wrong.

That was not the surprise at all. He could not move. This reporter had grabbed his right arm, not that this should be a problem of course, but it was. He literally could not even waggle a toe or wave his hand. He was under some sort of temporary paralysis. Anne Weavers was far more than met the eye. She dragged Eggo Maniac back into the spot where he had been standing initially and gestured to the camera man to cease filming.

She pulled him closer to her, "I don't know if you can hear me, as I can't locate your ears, but this is how it is going to play out. Your lack of movement is not permanent and once you have answered my questions and given me the story that I want, then I shall release you. Do you understand what I am saying?"

"Yes, yes of course," said a more than concerned Eggo Maniac.

Chapter 3

Publicity

"Why won't these humans get out of the way, are they insane?" Bruce's words fell on deaf ears. The loud and at times raucous behaviour of the crowd saw to that. The encyclopaedia could not hear himself think and was carrying Howard over his shoulder, not unlike a fireman.

He had tried a plethora of different holds, but had found that many were inappropriate when dealing with the masses that kept swarming them, and this was what he could not work out. Why were all these people approaching them and attempting to touch, grab, hug and on some occasions, kiss them? It was sheer lunacy. They were not heroes, well they sort of were as they dealt with that overgrown cup of coffee, but that was all they had achieved.

Howard was a quivering wreck. Surely that was evident for all to see, yet they still went for him. One fan had attempted to open his pizza box mouth and pour a soft drink into it, as if anyone would do that to a human.

Bruce couldn't decide whether he would rather face the people or the giant cup of coffee. Another bystander squeezed Bruce's arm and from the corner of his eye he noticed a second fan approaching with a marker pen. Goodness only knows what his intentions were.

Bruce had just about reached the police barrier, which had cordoned off Wardour Street from Oxford Street and moved to cross it.

"I'm sorry sir but I'm afraid I am unable to let you pass." It was the police. This particular officer was short but broad and Bruce imagined that he would pack quite a punch. He wore sunglasses, despite the lack of sunshine, and did not show even the remotest sign of a sense of humour.

"What's the problem, officer?" said Bruce.

"The problem is a simple one sir. I don't have your autograph." The madness continued. This policeman had switched from calm to hysteria in a matter of seconds. He now produced a small hardback autograph book with a picture of a blue book with eyes on it.

"I'm your biggest fan. Please sign it, will you, will you, will you?" His speech was now like that of a toddler, who had resorted to repeating himself in order to obtain his goal.

Bruce dropped Howard who landed on his feet beside the officer. He was calmer now as other police officers on the scene were keeping the general public away from the two heroes.

The pizza box leaned in, "It's definitely supposed to be you Bruce. They've got the eyes right, but the actual likeness of an encyclopaedia isn't very good."

"Let me see that." Bruce had dived in front of Howard and snatched the autograph book away from the hands of the policeman. A pen was shoved in his face and he duly grabbed it and signed the first page, 'Bruce... Nice to meet you mate.'

He lifted the cover up closely to his face for further examination. Howard and the policeman watched him, eagerly awaiting his response. His eyes closed slightly, widened again, then finally he grinned. "This isn't an encyclopaedia, it's a dictionary. It clearly says that on the front."

"What, I'll have that street seller arrested," said the officer.

"No need to book him officer. I can make things better," replied Bruce. He threw the autograph book back into the hands of the policeman and began to flick through his pages, slowly at first, but the pace soon picked up and his motion was so fast that Howard wondered how he could possibly know what he was reading.

Moments later a screwed up page unravelled itself and wrapped around the outside of the encyclopaedia, covering Bruce in his entirety. He was still a blue book, but now instead of encyclopaedia printed on his cover, it read 'Dictionary'. Once more his face, arms and legs materialised. "That's better isn't it officer?"

"Thank you, could I take a quick selfie with you now?"

Bruce shrugged as he was grabbed and had a mobile phone camera flashed in his face.

Howard was amused by this and it took his fear away momentarily. He simply had to ask, "What's the plan then, Bruce?"

"No time Howie, we have got to get outta here. Officer, can you keep these people back whilst we make a quick exit?"

The policeman nodded in response.

Bruce nodded back to him, pulled another page over him to revert back to encyclopaedia form, then grabbed Howard and stuck him on his back. "Sweet as, hang on tight Howie, I'm getting us outta here."

Bruce reached into his pages again and threw a great, white ball of fluff onto the ground and then another and another until there were five large balls of wool.

Slowly heads and legs began to pop out of each one. They were sheep, not small, average sized sheep, but sheep the size of lions.

"What are these things going to do?" said a more than confused Howard.

Before Bruce could answer him a member of the public had managed to get his way to the front of the police barrier. He was slim and wore a black, flat-peaked cap, matching coloured waistcoat and trousers. He also sported a white shirt, purple tie and a monocle.

"Get your sheep posters. Spectacular sheep posters. First on the market. There's nothing like these around anywhere yet. Get them here first. Five pounds a pop. Official merchandise."

"Hey we haven't authorised those, therefore they can't be official merchandise. You can't sell my likeness or the likeness of the Sheep Brigade either without notifying us first." said Bruce. He was clearly agitated by the situation and had seemingly forgotten about making a quick exit.

The seller turned to face him, "Sorry mate, that's not right. Your image rights are all over the shop. They sold out about ten minutes ago. I have an official licence." With that the man produced a photographic identity card that, sure enough, displayed the fact that he owned the rights to sell Sheep Brigade posters.

Howard inspected it, "I want to know how they get this merchandise released so quickly."

"That's the trick of the trade, mate. I'm Wheeler Dealer. The greatest salesman in the world," said the flat-peaked capped man.

Bruce grabbed him by the collar, "You may well be the best seller mate, but you've got no stock."

Wheeler Dealer looked at him clearly confused.

"Sheep Brigade, go to work," said Bruce.

In no time at all the five sheep set on Wheeler Dealer. The first grabbed his cap in its mouth and the second picked up a large cardboard tube of posters. The third and fourth took the posters that he was displaying to the crowd and the fifth, final sheep grabbed his licence.

The poor man had no idea what to do.

This Sheep Brigade was eating absolutely everything he had. He shrieked as he fought desperately to get back his tube of posters. It was to no avail. It was consumed with considerable ease.

"I thought sheep chewed things. They've ruined my stock in seconds," said Wheeler Dealer.

Howard and Bruce laughed, as did the policemen and the general public. Bruce gestured for the Sheep Brigade to return and they made their way back to his side.

Howard was still concerned though. They might have dealt with an irritating salesman, but they still had much to do regarding their escape.

"Worry not Howie, we will make our exit now, or rather the Sheep Brigade will."

Howard did not have any idea about what to think of this comment as he simply didn't have time. Before he could even contemplate what the Sheep Brigade would do, one had positioned itself underneath him and he was now seated like a jockey on a horse. He turned to check on Bruce, who was in the same position with another.

The Sheep Brigade then moved into an arrow formation with Bruce and Howard taking up the back left and right hand sides of the arrowhead respectively.

The sheep at the front raised a hoof. "Sheep Brigade, away."

A thunderous noise engulfed the end of Wardour Street as the hooves of the Brigade hit the ground hard and fast. The stamps left no mark on the floor and the pace of the movement was so quick that the legs of the sheep were nothing more than a blur.

It was at this point that Howard realised they were not stamping on the ground at all. No paving stone had even been touched. They were stomping on the air. Their frenetic pace and power meant that they were, in reality, taking flight.

The leader of the Brigade shot up further into the air and the rest followed suit. Howard hung on for dear life, but Bruce seemed to be savouring the journey and lifted his hands in the air like the earthlings do when they are on a rollercoaster.

"Where are we going?" said Howard.

Bruce could not hear him and it required his own sheep, which he was riding, to comfort him. "We are going somewhere safe. Don't worry. Sweet as."

The eyes on the pizza box closed tightly – to say Howard was not enjoying the ride would have been an understatement.

Yet another cheer erupted from the bystanders. Every single person present, and there must have been over ten thousand at the very least, was focussed on Eggo Maniac. They hung on his every word.

This is exactly what Anne Weavers had wanted. Pure, no holds barred questions met with unrivalled imaginative answers. This Eggo Maniac truly did think the world of himself and this made him an ideal candidate for interviewing. So far he had informed everyone of a close, life threatening encounter with the coffee mug, that had turned out to be real and not an expensive advertisement for the coffee house.

Eggo Maniac had recalled the story perfectly. Whilst his apple crumble/pizza box friend was trapped in a whirlwind of coffee and his other ally lay stuck underneath the sinister foe, he was able to sneak behind and surprise his enemy.

Using his biceps of steel he had managed to lift the entire thing on his own and cast it aside, as if it was a beach ball. He was making himself into a hero and everyone was lapping it up.

There was now only one more thing that Anne needed before she could release him and that was a name. Sure she knew that he was called Eggo Maniac and his two pals were Bruce and Howard, but she required more than that.

Headline after headline went through her mind, for this would be tonight's and tomorrow's main story, but still there was something more she craved.

Then it clicked, just like it always did for Anne Weavers. Individual names would not do; oh no, that would have been too simple. She needed a group name.

If she could bring these creatures, or whatever they were, together, then she could create her very own team of superheroes.

Eggo Maniac was still talking and it had occurred to her that he would have to be the leader and spokesperson of the group, simply because he was incapable of being quiet.

Anne inhaled deeply. She was about to break her number one rule of journalism. "Sorry to stop you from talking Eggo Maniac, but could I please ask you one more tiny question?"

It felt wrong interrupting someone she was interviewing. Usually she liked to let her victims, er, interviewees speak for as long as possible. That way they would, more often than not, talk themselves into trouble or reveal something about themselves that they shouldn't have; but this was why it felt wrong to her because she was breaking one of her 'special' rules. Still it was worth it, or so she hoped.

Eggo Maniac placed his hand on her shoulder and smiled, "Of course Miss Weavers, please do fire away."

"Thank you Eggo Maniac, but please do call me Anne. Anyway I was wondering what a group of superheroes like yourselves names their group. Surely you have a name that unites you all to your cause. Just what is it?"

At this point one could have heard a pin drop. There was absolute silence as all, including Anne Weavers and her camera man, waited with baited breath. What was this group of odd misfits called?

The tension was mounting. Eggo Maniac could feel it and was feeding from the raw energy of the crowd. He was absolutely loving his predicament. He cleared his throat.

"Well, to begin with, I must say that we did not take the naming process lightly. It took many hours of consultation and discussion, but in the end there was no compromise. There was no compromise because we will not compromise our crime fighting abilities. We are the…"

Eggo Maniac had dropped in a pause on purpose just to build that sense of excitement that little bit more. It was like overinflating a balloon. He would have to be careful because this crowd could pop at any moment.

"Anne Weavers, good citizens, we are the Hazardous Trio."

Nothing - not even a clap.

Eggo Maniac closed his eyes and smiled. He was certain the ovation would come and he would be ready with his victory pose. He outstretched his arms opening up a clear view of his egg shaped body/head.

Perhaps this moment of silence was an earthling custom and that his rapturous applause would be arriving shortly.

Instead he was met by the shrill tones of Anne Weavers, "You're joking, right? That's not seriously your name is it? Surely there's something else you have in mind? I mean a hazard is a negative thing. It's destructive and causes damage or problems to things. Worst of all is that the trio bit sounds very fifties. You can't use that. You need a much better name, in fact you need a publicist."

She shouted the final part of her monologue as her idea grew. This lot were not going to be her big break out story that would make her enough cash for an extremely early retirement.

They were too weird and kooky. Without someone handling public relations for them and ensuring that people only saw their cool traits and not their geeky ones, they were finished.

Then she stopped. She smiled. The crowd was generally losing interest in the situation. A few were discussing the prospect of leaving until Anne addressed them directly. She adjusted the lapel of her jacket to ensure she looked the part and managed to run her comb through her hair in what must have been milliseconds before she made her announcement.

"Good people of London, Eggo Maniac and I would like to

thank you all for coming out to witness some real crime fighting action today. We believe it is only good, fair and honest to let you know that I have successfully organised a deal with Eggo Maniac, Bruce and Howard to become their manager and publicist.

Don't be alarmed by the name Hazardous Trio, that was our little joke to illustrate why they need me to assist them. They fight the crime and I'll save them time - by sorting out their paperwork and interviews amongst other things.

So please, put your hands together and make as much noise as you can for Eggo Maniac and don't you worry, next time Bruce and Howard will stay for the whole show. Thanks once again for coming out."

The deafening celebrations that Eggo Maniac had been hoping for suddenly occurred. He waved and revelled in his glory until he heard the helicopter blades spinning above him. The rope ladder descended in front of them and Anne Weavers and the camera man took hold of it.

She looked down at him, "Well, what are you waiting for? Grab the ladder and hold on. We want to get some good footage of you waving to the crowd whilst being whisked away into the clouds. Don't stop until I say and then you can get in and show me where your base is. Oh, and we can take a little bit of time to discuss that ridiculous name of yours."

Eggo Maniac obliged and took hold of the ladder, it was all he could do.

Chapter 4

Nests and Ants

"Is everything alright Tod? It's just that you haven't spoken to me for at least one Earth hour. It's just a bit strange to me, that's all."

Tod did not move. He had positioned himself on the edge of the whiteness, adjacent to the screen in the floor, observing the happenings on Earth with greater interest than usual.

His expression was, as per normal, unreadable, but he was finally coming round to the idea that mistakes could be made, especially by Rod, and it was best to forgive and forget. I mean, there were worse, more troublesome planets on which someone could drop a golden boulder, Maosis for one. He could do without the Plant Warriors down there gaining extra powers, that was without question.

He glanced at Rod and it appeared that his friend was becoming genuinely upset. Perhaps he had pushed it too far on this occasion. These guilt trips that he pulled on Rod when he was aggravated with him were probably getting a bit harsh now.

"I'm sorry Rod. I didn't mean to hurt your feelings; it's just that you made a slight mistake by dropping such a powerful item on a planet like Earth. The creatures down there are not quite, how should I put this, civil? Therefore we could be in for a huge battle at some point."

"A huge battle – really Tod? Wouldn't that be exciting?"

Rod was smiling once more.

Tod contemplated this briefly. His friend was potentially correct. In fairness nobody had ever dropped one on Earth that was this size before. Anything could happen. Perhaps this could be fun. Perhaps it was time just to let things happen, to relinquish control. He licked his lips, "Okay then Rod. Let's just see what occurs. I agree with you that this is potentially intriguing and if things go too far we can always end the experiment."

"How do we do that then Tod?"

"Why it's easy Rod. We simply destroy Earth."

On the top of a terraced building overlooking Soho, Howard, Bruce and the Sheep Brigade all sat in a circle. If there was a fire and it had occurred in the countryside at night, it would have been a perfectly stereotypical camping scene.

All were slightly bewildered to say the least. They had been there for a good twenty minutes now and none of them had the foggiest idea of what to say, let alone what to do.

Howard scrutinised the leader of the Sheep Brigade. He was slightly larger in stature than the rest and had an air of self-confidence about him. Howard noticed he wore an eye patch over his left eye and this only served further to enhance his steel reputation. This sheep was a fighter, absolutely no doubt about it. The others clearly admired him and he bore the scars of countless battles.

It was hard to imagine how something that came out of Bruce's pages could be so battle hardened, as Bruce himself had only been around for a matter of hours. How could this sheep and his warriors have seen so much action?

The leader of the Sheep Brigade caught Howard's stare and the pizza box averted his eyes from the sharp gaze.

"I'm only messing with you. You can gaze at me all day long if you want to."

Howard continued to watch the floor despite the comments,

permitting him to carry on his analysis.

The sheep continued, "Well I'm Commander Winters. It's a reference to the manner in which I whiten the sky when my Sheep Brigade fly."

"And you're a poet and you don't know it," said another of the sheep.

"That's not funny. It's not even witty, Private Ostrich. I see you're still only showing your face and speaking up at the least opportune moments."

Howard noticed that this other sheep, Private Ostrich, actually tucked his head back into his wool. He now resembled a decapitated sheep.

Commander Winters moved to address Howard once more. "Don't worry about Ostrich over there. He only ever takes his head out when flying and even then that's not all the time. He's a good lad really, just doesn't know when to keep his trap shut. I suppose it's time you met the entire Sheep Brigade then mate."

At that point each member stood up and lined up in a perfect row next to Commander Winters. Bruce then shuffled round to sit by Howard, "You'll enjoy this."

"First up we have my second in command, Lieutenant Figs."

The sheep smiled from the corner of his mouth. He wore a red bandanna wrapped around his forehead and chewed on a toothpick.

"Secondly we have Private Lunatic. This lil' boy is as mad as they come. Don't ever underestimate his size. We certainly don't."

This sheep was the strangest of the lot. His eyes seemed to move in circles all the time, as if he was hypnotising someone. His tongue was sticking out and his wool was multicoloured. He looked like a rainbow sheep if there was such a thing.

"Thirdly, we have Private Cannon. Now I am aware we've got Private Lunatic, but this one's just as insane when it comes to weaponry. He's our very own walking, talking armoury."

This sheep stood straight and tall and saluted immediately. He wore a bullet belt around his wool, but did not appear to have a weapon. A green soldier's helmet rested on his head.

"Now you've already met Ostrich over there, who's probably one of the most formidable combatants you're ever likely to meet. He's always planning our missions in the minutest detail possible."

Commander Winters took a deep breath, "And that's the team. That is the Sheep Brigade – The fastest, craziest, coolest, toughest, strongest, greatest assembly of sheep flyers the universe has ever seen."

"No wonder he needed to take a breath, that's as long an introduction as I can remember," said Bruce.

"Virtually any introduction will be the longest you can remember. We have only been conscious for a few hours," said Howard.

Bruce grinned. At least their spirits were high. Now all they had to do was to locate Eggo Maniac and then… Well he didn't know, not a clue. This was hardly an ideal situation.

The wind swept any remaining dirt from an otherwise pristine landing pad. As the CBA News helicopter took its place perfectly on the concrete, Eggo Maniac stared out, looking over the city.

They were still in Central London, by the river, and quite how he knew that he was not sure, not that he cared anyway. He was far too overwhelmed by how much of London he had managed to take in from his impromptu transport above it. The sheer size and the amount of buildings and skyscrapers had impressed him. He knew they were there but, as with most things, until one sees them it is difficult to decipher their reality.

The co-pilot trotted out of the door and opened it for Anne Weavers. She jumped out quickly followed by the camera man.

"Come on Eggo Maniac, we have much work to do. I intend to market you and your friends to such a level that the whole of Earth will know you better than they know themselves. Now get out of the helicopter and let's go and work on some group naming ideas and you can call or contact the others so we can get them on board too."

Eggo Maniac followed Anne Weavers through a door and down a series of steps. The building they had entered was extremely high tech and the walls all resembled silver metal. There was the odd monitor spaced here and there, on which the pictures were regularly changing.

They showed a variety of different newsreaders but there was no sound so it was impossible for Eggo Maniac to hear what they were saying.

Occasionally he would pass a few buttons – normally red or green and for some unknown reason, he felt a great urge to press them.

At the end of a series of corridors (Eggo Maniac had been led through so many he was totally disorientated) was a lift. The building must have been incredibly large as there were over two hundred floors.

The camera man then took out a small spray from his inside

jacket pocket. In the corner of the lift was what must have been a close circuit television camera. He sprayed it. The entire camera was now black and he had obstructed any view it may previously have had.

Weavers then followed this lead by producing a credit card from her pocket. It didn't look particularly spectacular as it was plain red with nothing else on it.

By the buttons in the lift was a small, black rectangle. Weavers swiped her card through this rectangle and waited. Seconds later another one hundred buttons sprang out of the side of the wall underneath the current ones. There were now buttons spread down the entire wall to the floor.

Weavers knelt down and pressed button number two hundred and fifty seven. The lift then moved swiftly down the shaft. It was a smooth ride and Eggo Maniac had many questions to ask; the first of which related to his position. Had he been captured or had he come here of his own volition? Was he a prisoner or an ally? Just who was Anne Weavers anyway? How did she have all this power?

The lift clicked into place and interrupted his train of thought. The doors slid open and Weavers led the way into a darkened space.

Eggo Maniac trotted behind them. Where was he? This could be some sort of high tech dungeon or portal to another world. The thoughts and concepts of where he could be raced through Eggo Maniac's mind.

Click, light at last. Weavers was standing by a perfectly ordinary standard lamp that she had turned on. It had a brown wooden stand and a white floral lampshade. By this were two red sofas and underneath these lay a maroon carpet. In one corner of the room was a kitchen worktop, fridge and oven. In front of the sofas was a chipped, mahogany coffee table and a largish television, complete with stand and video game console underneath.

The whole room was fairly scruffy and there were no windows. The walls were a dull shade of magnolia and there were some reprints of several famous paintings that, inexplicably, Eggo Maniac was able to identify. This would serve as a good starting point for conversation.

"Are you a fan of René Magritte?"

"Pardon?" said Anne, who was now sitting, relaxing on the sofa.

Eggo Maniac pointed towards the painting, "Your picture, on the wall, the one with the apple over the man's face."

"Oh yes, that. I like the picture, it's excellent. It really suits the room don't you think? It brings out the redness."

Eggo Maniac nodded. He was still slightly surprised that such an ordinary living room was located in such an establishment of great technology.

"It's all about feeling at home if you must know," said Anne.

Eggo Maniac was stunned. "Did you just read my mind?"

"No, I didn't have to resort to that. The look on your face makes it fairly obvious what your current thoughts are. You are shocked by this place. I suspect you imagined that you were going to end up in some super futuristic lab or prison cell.

That's not how we work. You see you should feel privileged to be down here. No one else has seen this place save for us. I have let you into my home, Eggo Maniac. You would do well to appreciate this."

The green, murky egg bowed his head in response.

Anne Weavers stroked her hair. She was pleased that he had shown some humility – perhaps she could work with him and his allies after all.

"Excellent, Eggo Maniac, this is a wise choice. I must inform you that I released you from my control back in Soho where all the people were gathered. You have come here of your own will, which is a good start of course. Now it is time…"

"To find my friends, Bruce and Howard?"

Weavers was somewhat astonished by his perceptiveness. "Yes, that is correct. Do you have any idea where they are?"

"No, not at present. They ran away into the crowd as they did not wish to be filmed. I think it will be difficult to persuade them to come here. They do not crave the limelight and Bruce insisted that publicity for us would be negative and that we would end up in laboratories with scientists performing all sorts of tests on us.

I mean we are situated underneath an enormous television studio. There is no way they would wilfully walk in here."

Weavers scratched her chin. The egg was right. She did not want to resort to mind control but she would if she had to. It was imperative that she had these three with her – it was an opportunity which she could not afford to miss.

All three in the room jumped when the television burst into life. It was quite an old set, hence it was thick at the back and crackled as it switched on. A slim line, HD television this was not.

Both Anne and the camera man moved with such intent to watch that they almost had their noses touching the screen. It quickly dawned on Eggo Manaic why this was the case. They were not watching a standard television channel, but what was quite obviously some live camera footage.

In front of them was a giant ant, about the size of a house, running amok around Regents Park. The public were running for cover as it ripped out trees and threw them around. It was clearly fighting with something, but they couldn't see what.

Sitting back on the sofa, Anne seemed far more relaxed. She spoke into the grey lapel of her suit-jacket, "Change the angle for us please. This creature has a target and we need to know what it is."

Almost before she could finish her sentence, the screen had altered. On view was an oak tree hurtling towards a café. It smashed into the building and rubble spilled out of the sides into water and onto the surrounding grass.

A headless sheep, followed by a rainbow-coloured one, leapt out from the rubble and raced towards the ant.

"What are those?" said the camera man.

Anne Weavers sprang up from her seat, "It would appear that the old saying is correct. You wait for one bus for a long time and then two, in this case three come along at the same time."

"I beg your pardon?" said the camera man.

"Don't worry, it just means that we have been waiting for a few unique beings to surface and we now have a whole load who have come at the same time. We are getting closer. Now go and prepare the chopper."

The camera man ran to the lift. Weavers then spoke once more into her lapel, "JoJo, I want all of this recorded please."

She stopped and watched a bemused Eggo Maniac. "There's a small microphone in my jacket, not that that is any of your concern. Now, do you wish to come with me and do some investigating? Something tells me your friends might not be far behind this event."

Eggo Maniac nodded in response. He felt completely lost in this situation and perhaps the only way to solve his issues was just to go with the flow, or go with Anne Weavers.

Yet another tree smashed into the café in Regents Park. The ant was picking them up and hurling them around like a toddler with a packet of straws. It only launched them at anything that moved – which created problems, for obvious reasons.

Howard, Bruce and the Sheep Brigade were intent on protecting the public and so far had managed to achieve this admirably. The park was now deserted so they were the only remaining targets of course.

Bruce could not make his mind up about Earth. Initially he had enjoyed his short stay, but having to fight a giant cup of coffee and now an oversized ant was not his idea of a relaxing day.

Yet again another log landed on the café, which now was a pile of rocks.

The encyclopaedia sprinted to the left of the ant in an attempt to get behind it. One of its legs swiped out at him, but he was nimble enough to duck and run underneath it.

Bruce's size was quite misleading. Whilst he was a human sized walking encyclopaedia, he had the agility of a gymnast. All he had to do now was to find some cover and see if he had any more tricks in his pages. The Sheep Brigade had worked a treat last time, surely there was some way in which he could distract the ant.

He surveyed the landscape. Near the café were some deep lakes of water which were in the park for scenic purposes. If he could hold his breath underwater for long enough, then he could flick through his pages there and find something with which to combat the ant.

Bruce went for it. Sprinting towards the water, he noticed the ant twist its head and spot him. It hurriedly began to chase him. Bruce was hardly taken aback and decided the best advice he could offer himself was not to look back.

He accelerated again and the ant swiped out at him. He leapt for the water. The ant jumped for him, but it did not get off the ground. Bruce landed in a heap just shy of the man-made lakes. He closed his eyes waiting for oblivion, but it did not come.

"Just get into the water now. Lieutenant Figs and I can only hold him for so long."

Bruce opened his eyes and watched as two members of the Sheep Brigade desperately clutched the ant's back legs. Lieutenant Figs could not see as his bandana was now obscuring his vision because it had dropped over his eyes in the commotion. The other, Commander Winters, was biting at its leg.

The blue encyclopaedia gave them a thumbs up and dived into the water. It was surprisingly deep and there was very little sea-life in it, just a few plants and a bit of a muddy bank at the bottom.

Bruce flicked through his pages frantically, desperately seeking some sort of bizarre conclusion. It was difficult as he could not use the traditional sorting method of alphabetical order due to the numerous pictures, crossings out and new and often misspelled words that had been written in a multitude of different colours throughout the book.

His mistake immediately dawned on him. The pages in his book were now saturated with water. Many stuck together and were impossible to separate. Combine this with the fact that the ink on some pages was running meant that there was nothing he could do, as his ability to know what was written on them was fading. If the writing was not legible then he simply could not decipher the words. His plan had failed royally.

Rather than sit underwater sulking, Bruce swam to the surface and jumped out of the pool.

"That didn't work." He gasped as he ran for cover behind some trees. At this point the entire Sheep Brigade was all over the ant as it tossed and turned, throwing them off its black body and repeating the whole process upon their return.

Howard was standing just behind the beast and appeared to be in deep thought. Bruce wondered why this was the case. It made no sense to him. Howard was the most muscular and strongest of them all. Surely it would have made sense for him to get involved and start throwing the ant around, or at least to do something physical.

Yet he wasn't. He just stood there with his apple crumble hand on his pizza box chin. He side-stepped at one point when Private Lunatic was cast his way and the rainbow-coloured sheep shot back up to his feet and entered the battlefield again. Howard did not take a blind bit of notice at all.

"Stop," said Howard at the frantic fight scene in front of him.

No one listened.

"I said stop."

Again there was no reaction.

"STOP NOW! I HAVE A PLAN!"

This final racket persuaded Commander Winters to look up from his position on the ant's back and respond politely.

"What do you expect us to do mate? We're in the middle of hand to hand combat here."

Howard pleaded with the commander. "Listen, I have noticed that the ant keeps attacking the café. That must be what he wants. Think about it, there will be sugar, jam and sweets in there. Those are all things that ants love. That has to be what he is after."

Commander Winters continued to cling on, but it was easy to see from his facial expression that he was at least considering the idea.

"If it wants the café so much then why is it attacking every creature that moves?"

"Think about it Commander, if you have a picnic and ants get into your food you would swipe them away too wouldn't you?"

"I wouldn't throw trees at them that is for sure."

"You couldn't lift a tree, that's why."

Commander Winters chuckled at Howard's last response. He composed himself.

"Very well Howard, you have a point. Sheep Brigade stand down and shift to the rear of the beast. We are then going to use stealth to back away from the creature and into the woodland."

"Without being disrespectful, commander, there is no woodland," said Lieutenant Figs.

"Then duck behind those big oaks over there."

The Sheep Brigade saluted at their commander's orders and one by one crept away from the ant.

Bruce had heard the conversation, it would have been more difficult not to. He had snuck around to stand with Howard, who at this point in time was quite the genius in Bruce's eyes.

Slowly they made their way behind a set of five enormous oak trees and watched. His friend was spot on with his tactics.

Initially the ant looked around itself and eventually decided there were no more irritants around to interefere with its plans.

Carefully it let out a strange sort of smile and almost cantered towards the rubble pile formerly known as the café. Rocks and debris flew through the air as it dug out its treats.

First it pulled out a confectionary vending machine and made short work of the glass front before grabbing at least ten chocolate bars. The wrappers were of no consequence to it, as these were consumed along with the bars inside them.

"My goodness it can go some," said Private Lunatic.

The others grunted in acknowledgement.

Howard spoke to the group, "I would say that now is the time for us to strike. We need to construct some sort of cage or net that we can put around it and keep it subdued. What do you think?"

That question was meant for the entire group but all he received was yet another grunt.

"Good I'm glad you concur. Now we need to move very quietly away from the ant and make our way towards the..."

He could not finish the sentence. The deafening sound of the CBA News chopper had interrupted him. The group gazed up and watched the rope ladder unfurl from the side. Anne Weavers appeared, as did her camera man and they both clung to the rungs of the ladder.

It seemed the camera man was filming her as she reported on the scene with one hand on the ladder and the other gripping her microphone. The helicopter moved towards them. Anne Weavers had spotted them and was approaching eagerly.

Bruce nudged Howard warning him to be ready to sprint away at a moment's notice. None of them was prepared to give this intrusive reporter the light of day, let alone an interview.

Then, in a surreal moment, Eggo Maniac emerged at the door of the helicopter and joined the other two on the ladder. Howard and Bruce did not like to admit it, but they were happy to see the murky egg and his arrogant grin. He was waving profusely at them which surely indicated that he was relieved to see them too.

"We'd better stay here," said Bruce, "Something tells me that this newsreader has more about her than we think. If she's managed to convince Eggo Maniac to hang with her then she must offer something."

Howard stood strongly by his friend. He was not going to let a fear of public speaking tip him over the edge again.

The ladder touched the grass in front of them and Anne Weavers, the camera man and Eggo Maniac descended quickly, stepping gently onto the ground in front of them.

"What a great day for it guys, I'm Anne Weavers, your new publicist. We have got a lot of work to do, so let's get everyone together back at the CBA building where we can speak freely about our intentions and plans."

"What about the ant?" said Howard.

Anne Weavers turned to see the ant coming towards them. "I thought it was docile?"

Howard shook his head.

"We had just lulled it into a false sense of security through silence. It is the noise that irritates it, for the ant is simply attracted to sugar.

Everything was running swimmingly until your helicopter got involved and attracted its attention. You've ruined everything and now we have a creature that is going to revert back to being bent on destruction, or more specifically our destruction."

As he finished his sentence he dived out of the way, narrowly avoiding yet another tree that was being used as a missile.

Anne smiled. This would be the perfect introduction for her team. She hadn't managed to film the fight with the coffee cup, so this confrontation with a giant ant would be a fitting introduction to the world for them – providing they were victorious of course.

She signalled to the camera man who immediately ran for the rope ladder. She followed suit and the helicopter pulled upwards, ensuring its safety by remaining out of the ant's grasp. Anne shouted down to the group.

"You've got to stop it. If you can beat this ant, then you can beat anything. I'm going to film and report from up here. That way we can use this as a promotional video."

Howard sprinted towards Bruce and Eggo Maniac. The Sheep Brigade had once again surrounded the creature and was ready to attack.

Bruce attempted to flick through his pages, but they were still far too wet. "I'll have to go it solo this time."

"Don't worry Bruce. We are all going to have to go up against this thing. We won't be able to create any peace or quiet here due to that great chopper blade above." Howard was grinning as he finished his sentence. It seemed he had suddenly developed quite a thirst for combat in the last few seconds.

Eggo Maniac bowed to the pair of them and joined them by their side. The egg then tapped both on the back, "Well, we came into everything together chaps. Why don't we see just how far we can go."

Affirming grunts were the only retorts and that was the only thing he needed and wanted to hear.

Bruce manoeuvred himself in front and between Eggo Maniac and Howard. They were now in a triangular formation with Bruce taking up a position at the point nearest the ant. "After three then, mates. One, two…"

"Three," said Eggo Maniac as he raced ahead of his two friends.

Howard followed instantly.

Bruce shrugged and attempted to get their attention as he ran.

"Hey, I said I would count to three, not two."

Chapter 5
Friends in High Places

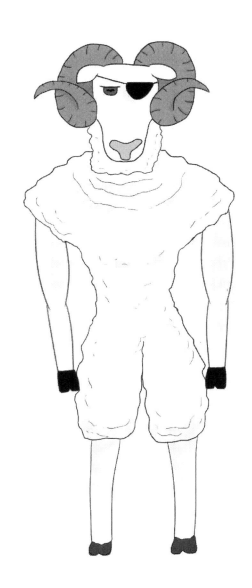

"Oh it's getting good now Tod. Look at all the action. That ant is pretty big and must be quite the handful."

Tod giggled at his friend, "That's because you made it too big Rod."

Both clouds were hovering above the screen in the floor of whiteness. The mood had altered significantly now that Tod had eased up on Rod. He was far happier with the situation and consequently with the results that Rod was delivering.

"I think it's interesting that the one called Bruce, the book, managed to release the Sheep Brigade so easily. Clearly he is tapping into his powers more quickly than the others. He is one to watch Rod."

"Tod."

"Yes, Rod."

"What do we do if one team is winning quite easily, or should I say one thing is winning quite easily."

Tod yawned, to be fair he was hardly paying attention now, as this was one of the first occasions that he had felt relaxed in a long time. Perhaps this was what he had been missing. He had been so wound up that he had forgotten how to release any tension he might have been harbouring. His response was calm.

"Well Rod, it depends on how long you want the experiment to go on. If you want a greater story, a longer battle or affair, then of course you have every right to intervene.

If you want a quick decisive victory for one side, then you can just let things unfold. That is the beauty of these assignments Rod. One can just let them progress as one sees fit."

Tod now had his hands behind the back of his head/cloud and

was lying horizontally, floating in the air. It was quite a bonus for clouds that they could simply lie down anywhere with no consequence and their bodies would continue to float. That was certainly one talent of which multiple creatures of the universe were jealous.

Rod peered over at his friend and then sharply back at the screen in the floor. The scene wasn't quite playing out as planned. Did he disturb his friend though?

It seemed that he had finally gained Tod's trust, which was no mean feat. The aftermath could be dire though. He would have to say something, "Erm Tod, I think there is a slight problem. The situation is…"

"Natural course, Rod, don't forget that."

"But Tod, it isn't that simple."

"Of course it is Rod. There are always multiple answers and conclusions. The correct one will play out in the end."

"No I'm serious Tod. The guys that we picked out… They're going to lose."

Now whilst Tod had managed to remain calm, this last comment had stirred his interest. At least he was floating up straight now. He stared at Rod.

The pink cloud shied away from his gaze even though he was well aware that Tod wanted him to divulge more information.

"Rod, I do not wish to pick your brains, but I shall if needs be. Generally your performance on this mission has been of a good standard. Yes, there have been a few blips, one that I thought could be major, but you have helped to teach me the importance of relaxation, for which I am grateful. Please do not ruin this moment as it is a rarity for me. So I shall ask you plainly and clearly, what is going on down there? Give me a full report."

The tone of his voice and the look on his face was enough to make Rod realise that his friend meant business. More worryingly was the fact that Tod had begun to change to a slightly deeper shade of purple than usual; a classic indication that he was getting irritated.

Rod was now in quite the conundrum. He knew that if he divulged the truth then Tod would implode and if he said nothing then equally he would have the same reaction. Evidently an explosion was on the way then.

Rod opted for the braver route of clouding up and telling it how it was, besides which, if he didn't then his mission was finished before the end of scene two.

"Tod, we agreed that we liked the creations of the alleyway and we even picked out specific ones that we thought would be great warriors. You yourself only mentioned recently about how impressed you were with Bruce and his ability to spawn the Sheep Brigade from his pages."

"Go on. I feel that you are detracting from the point."

"Well to put it…"

"Put it right Rod. Tell me precisely what is happening without dithering please."

"They're losing and if we don't intervene soon, then that ant is going to make short work of them all, especially Howard, whom it would appear he desires to eat."

Tod did not reply. He didn't even flinch. He just stopped and his purple shade continued to darken. He was nearly black now.

Rod was petrified. He had never seen Tod become a thunderstorm before. He imagined that the power of his lightning would be immensely destructive.

Desperately he pleaded with his friend.

"Now come on Tod. A thunderstorm is not going to help matters is it? You could badly damage the planet and then the humans and everything else on Earth will start to investigate. It might alert them to our presence."

Tod lightened ever so slightly. It was a fair point. They could do without human intervention.

"Come on Tod, you know it makes sense. Just think about how calm and relaxed you were earlier. You took pleasure in that. It was the first time in ages that you had been able to mellow. Surely you don't want to throw that away over a few made-up players and a big bug?"

This last bout of begging seemed to do the trick, as Tod's facial expression, for once, showed that he was debating the situation.

Gradually his familiar purple tint returned and he immediately made his way over to the screen. "We are going to need an item, a good prop to solve this. I do not want us to lose any of our creations down there and that includes the ant."

Rod breathed a sigh of relief. Tod was back to his old authoritative self.

A can materialised in Tod's hands.

"Prepare for drop. I shall deal with this one, Rod. Once this commotion has calmed, then you may take over as before."

Rod nodded and Tod dropped the can through the screen. It was silver and whilst it had appeared small in the hands of Tod, when it approached Earth it was far, far larger. It landed on top of the remains of the café, and due to its sheer bulk, crushed absolutely everything underneath it.

This can was the size of an ordinary three bedroomed house. It was as if the café had been replaced with this odd, silver can. The label on it was plain white and sported a series of bizarre symbols that resembled some sort of man with a cat's head shaking hands with another man, but this one had a dog's head.

The battle continued to rage on the screen with the large ant gripping both Commander Winters and Bruce, whilst everyone else approached it.

There were no signs of any battlefield tactics whatsoever from the rest of the group, just intermittent charges being met by fierce blows from any of the four remaining legs of the ant.

After this, the being that had been swatted away would leap up and strike again, to no avail. The repetition of it all was quite comical, not to Rod and certainly not to Tod of course. The troublesome aspect for them was that their new arrival had made no impact whatsoever.

"Why haven't they opened the blasted tin yet, Rod? It is a sure fire way of getting the ant into something in which it can be captured."

Rod remained silent, not wishing to answer Tod's question. He assumed it was rhetorical, until he paid slightly more attention to the white label and its imagery. In a more than jovial manner he spoke.

"I've got it Tod. It's the writing on the label. That text is Valerian and does not resemble any language from Earth. We need to translate it. That way the group will understand what they have to do with it."

"Quite right," said Tod, "I was hoping you would notice that, Rod. Just another part of the testing procedure, as I'm sure you're more than aware."

The pink cloud viewed his purple friend with an air of suspicion.

"No time for chit chat anyhow Rod. We must act and act we shall." He clapped his hands and the sound of faint thunder could be heard in Regents Park. It was so quiet however that it did not alarm any of those involved in the fracas with the giant ant. They were far too concerned with their opponent to worry about a spot of bad weather.

Both clouds watched the screen as if everything depended on it. As the action unfolded the can came into sight. Rod was the first to react in his usual excitable manner. "It's changed, Tod. Now it's written in English."

"Yes it is, Tod. This should turn the tide, providing they see it. If they do not take action then perhaps they are not the warriors we thought they were."

Howard found himself upside down, slumped at the base of a tree. This was becoming a familiar situation for him and he wondered how much more his apple crumble body could manage.

It was at least the fourth time he had been cast aside by the ant and as he rose to his feet he noticed a headless sheep, otherwise known as Private Ostrich, hurtle past him and connect with a bush. Perhaps he needs to use his head he thought to himself, but quickly came to the conclusion that this was hardly the time for bad comedy. There had to be something they could do.

He surveyed the area again and as he did, Private Ostrich rushed by, this time of his own volition, charging at the ant once more. This was the only strategy that the Sheep Brigade employed and he wondered why they even bothered with rankings. They had a commander and a lieutenant when all they truly required was someone to bellow 'charge' and that would have been more than adequate.

Carefully and quietly this time, he approached the ant that was still thrashing around. He could see that Commander Winters was biting on the leg that held him, yet Bruce was not fighting back. He was firmly in the ant's grip, yet seemed to be gesturing towards something.

Howard moved closer, this time slightly faster, but he was opting for stealth as opposed to all-out attack. He neared the leg that held Bruce and it swayed quickly towards him. Dodging the blow, he rolled to the ground. Howard quickly came to the realisation that this particular attack was not meant for him. The ant was obviously so distressed that he was just throwing his legs around in any and all directions.

Bruce had turned rather green, which is quite the feat for a blue book, due to the impromptu fairground ride he was receiving.

"Howard, Howard, the can, it's over there, where the café was, look at the can. Surely that can solve the mess we're in."

Sure enough Bruce was correct. Howard scolded himself for failing to see a silver tin, the size of a house that stood behind the ant. The fact that the word 'treacle' was emblazoned on it only made matters worse. The issue he had now, was how he could get the thing open and then it struck him.

During the introductions of the Sheep Brigade, one of them

was referred to as an absolute weapons expert. Just what was his name though?

"Private Cannon reporting for duty Howard, sir," said the sheep. How on Earth did he know that was what Howard wanted him to do?

Well there was no time to sit around and wonder why things were occurring when they had allies to save. He observed Private Cannon. He wore a bullet belt as before and his green army helmet was still gloriously intact. Howard could see a few bruises and cuts where he had engaged the ant, but that aside he wondered how he managed to keep his equipment so clean, even during combat.

Private Cannon was grinning insanely. It was quite clear that he was enjoying himself and he was in his element.

"Private Cannon, do you have a can-opener handy?"

"No sir. I do however have a katana." Private Cannon then produced a large, black and red handled samurai sword from his wool. It was so sharp that it glistened. The sheep's eyes ran over it and he held it above his head to ensure it was fit for purpose.

"Marvellous, Private Cannon, I think that will do nicely. We need to open the tin of treacle to attract the ant. Once it gets a whiff of the scent, it should leave us alone and move towards it. How are we going to do this then? Is it easier if I come with you and take on one side and you the other?"

"Negative, sir."

This puzzled Howard.

"You do not want any assistance, meaning you can cut the side off something that is essentially the size of a house, on your own with only that sword?"

"That is affirmative sir."

"Go on then." That was all Howard could muster. He simply could not think of anything else to say.

Private Cannon scuttled off into the background towards the tin of treacle and held out his sword.

Howard was intrigued to see just what this sideshow would deliver.

Private Cannon leapt onto a nearby tree and sprang off the side of it. This elevated him to such a height that he was now well above the can. As he came back down to the ground below he took one almighty swipe with the katana blade.

He landed.

Nothing happened.

Howard sighed to himself. He knew that he was expecting far too much and that it was preposterous to expect a sheep with one sword to cut open an object of such mass and size.

He ran towards Private Cannon, who had put his sword back into his wool and was standing in front of the can of treacle. As Howard approached, Private Cannon grinned at him. "Would you like to finish the job sir?"

"Finish the job, what do you mean?"

"Sir, please go and tap the left hand side of the can and then retreat as quickly as possible."

Howard shrugged and did as the sheep asked. He tapped the end very gently and swiftly stepped aside.

Nothing happened once again.

"Please do move back sir. If you come and stand by me then that will be sufficient."

Once again Howard obeyed the sheep and took his place, as requested by his side.

Immediately the can began to vibrate and rumble. The smile on Private Cannon's face widened and Howard experienced a slight touch of guilt for ever doubting the weapons expert of the Sheep Brigade.

The left hand side of the tin slammed into the grass below, as treacle oozed out into Regents Park.

"May I ask just one thing, Private Cannon?"

"Of course sir."

"It is clear from that display that you did not require my help in the slightest. You could have easily knocked the side of the tin off yourself. Why did you want me to do it?"

"You're the one who suggested we work together sir."

Howard chuckled to himself. "Quite the witty one aren't you Private Cannon. I like your style, now if I may…"

"Move out of the way sir."

Howard felt himself hit the ground as Private Cannon landed on top of him. He was about to ask the sheep why he had been tackled, but upon closer inspection the answer was there for all to see.

The ant had finally cast aside Commander Winters and Bruce and made its way over to the treacle. Howard took a deep breath.

"Thank you Private Cannon. Thanks a lot."

The sheep nodded, he had saved Howard and the apple crumble/pizza box was grateful for this.

The ant was devouring the treacle and had no qualms about

getting sticky. It had dived in and was having a wonderful time. Its whole body was covered in the stuff and its legs were submerged to halfway at a minimum.

The black substance was not confined to the ant though. Howard and Private Cannon found themselves coated in it as little blobs were flung their way. "It's probably time to go sir," said Private Cannon.

"I agree Private Cannon, but we must remember that silence is the key. We do not want to upset this creature. On the last occasion he could not hear us and we were able to keep him occupied, subdued even. Now follow my lead and we can get out of here."

"Please don't leave on my account."

The voice travelled through the entirety of Regents Park and then further on into the surrounding streets. The rest of the group looked around trying to see from where it had emerged.

It had echoed a great deal which made it all the more mysterious. Howard and Private Cannon, however, were shaking. This was for two reasons. Firstly the sheer volume of the voice had struck them hard, and secondly they knew exactly who the owner was and this filled them with a smidgen of fear.

It was the ant.

"Honestly, you do not have to go. I have no desire to force you into leaving such a wonderful park."

Private Cannon reached inside his wool, preparing to remove some kind of weapon in an attempt to nullify the situation. He immediately felt an apple crumble hand grab his arm and pull it back out.

"This is not the time Private Cannon. We have seriously misjudged this ant. Who gave the orders to attack it?

"Commander Winters Sir."

"Why did he do that?"

"It was a clear threat to our safety, Howard," said Commander Winters.

Howard was perplexed by everything now. He had a multitude of questions to ask, and as this ant was no longer an enemy, he actually had the time to ask them.

"So we arrived in Regents Park and just attacked this big ant. That is all that I can recall. How did we even get here?"

Bruce and the Sheep Brigade all looked at each other. They did not have a clue. It was an interesting point that Howard had raised and was one that demanded attention.

Bruce was the first to offer a response. "We were on top of a building - and then my memory is blank I'm afraid. I was just suddenly here."

Howard bowed his head, affirming that he, too, could not remember. An awkward silence embraced the scene. Suspicion now gripped everyone and all were eyeing one another, silently questioning why they were in this predicament.

The Sheep Brigade had managed to accumulate on one side and Howard and Bruce stood opposite. They were now facing each other as if combat was about to commence.

The tension was rising fast and neither side was willing to stop it. Private Ostrich had even taken his head out to have a quick peek to ensure he was ready for whatever might happen. He quickly added his two pennies worth. "If it helps, I don't have the foggiest how I got here either."

The impending battle ceased immediately.

The Sheep Brigade laughed. Bruce and Howard joined them. What indeed was the point of them fighting? The giant ant had spared them all some grief, merely by way of being in the same scenario.

Howard was about to address the ant as he wished to know why they had been fighting, but was unable to do so as a certain Anne Weavers had muscled her way into the picture. The CBA helicopter was hovering above the tin of treacle and despite facing the bottom end of the ant, Anne held her microphone out and proceeded to interview.

"Anne Weavers CBA News, reporting live at Regents Park, London, where there has been the utmost commotion involving a giant ant and some other strange creatures battling it out for supremacy."

"I'm no strange creature," said Private Lunatic.

Eggo Maniac was quick to put an end to any bad press, "Sssshhhhh, we need to listen to this."

"Mr. Ant, sir, madam, if that's what I can call you, could you give us a few words regarding why you were in battle with these others?"

The ant ignored Anne Weavers and continued to slurp down the treacle. "Sir, I am asking you as a member of the CBA broadcasting team, why you were brawling in Regents Park? I mean it is against the law. You understand that, right?"

The ant flicked a little treacle at the reporter. She was far too quick though and was easily able to dodge it and remain on the ladder.

Howard was impressed by her agility. Not many people would be able to move so quickly yet maintain balance. The same could not be said for the camera man, who was hit by the lump of treacle. It splattered on the top of his head and trickled down the sides of his face and onto his suit below. It now looked as if he was wearing a sticky, black wig.

Anne attempted not to laugh.

Everyone else on the ground was not so forgiving. They had broken out into laughter once again. Moments later the ant popped its head out of the tin and smiled at everyone present. Eventually the commotion calmed and once there was a lull in the noise the ant addressed all present.

"Anne Weavers, sir will do. To everyone else, I have been listening to your conversation whilst savouring my treat and it would appear that I am none the wiser than any of you. I, too, have no idea how I arrived here, although I do know that I have only had the ability to speak and think, in the manner in which I do now, for two hours at the very most.

I am also aware that I was far smaller than this. My growth rate has gone far beyond that of an ordinary ant. If you want to ask me why we were fighting, all I can say is that I woke in Regents Park and we were immediately launched into combat. I wished to talk it out and try and come to a resolution that would suit us all, but this was not possible because your Sheep Brigade, as you call it, was just relentless in its assault. Therefore I had no option but to defend myself, and now I find I'm here, like you and with you."

There was no reply. The ant had a point though, Howard

pondered to himself. All of them were in the same boat. They had only known Earth for a few hours and already they were fighting. This was crazy. There had to be something more to this.

Chapter 6
Background Secrets

Rod was angry and Tod wore a look of sheer exasperation on his face. This was not going according to plan and something would have to be done to save the situation.

Now it was Rod's turn to change colour and the darker shade of pink suited him. Tod had recognised that this would not be constructive and moved to calm him.

"Do not despair Rod. These things happen. No one would have predicted the change in behaviour of such a large creature, not even a Plant Warrior."

Rod's colour lightened slightly, which was fortunate for him. Tod was hardly the tolerant type and under any normal circumstance would not have indulged in this sort of behaviour from Rod.

This time though, for reasons he could not fully comprehend himself, he was willing to give him a chance. Perhaps it was the strange sensation of feeling relaxed that he had experienced earlier, or could it have been empathy on his part for Rod and his first mission. It wasn't going particularly well, so supporting Rod would surely be the right move.

"Listen Rod, this experiment can be rectified and you are the one to do it. Stay here and do not touch or do anything for the moment."

"But they are allying themselves with the ant. All of them, even the reporter. Why is she involved anyway? She isn't part of the cast and we..."

Rod took in a great breath of air, clouds need a lot for obvious reasons. He was so riled by the situation that he could not get any more words out.

"That is the way of humans, Rod. They do tend to interfere in things and you just have to accept that. Half the time they do not have the foggiest idea about what they are doing, they just do. It's impulse action after impulse action with little thought behind them. You'll get used to it. Just think back to your training module of improvisation."

Rod bowed as Tod floated off into the whiteness of the room.

He was soon out of sight and Rod was left alone to view his task, the first time he had been able to do so on his own. He had returned to his usual pink state now and was slowly accepting the situation.

It was often said that the more mistakes one makes on the first mission, the better one gets on the second. Rod desperately wanted that to be the case. Tod had always reminded him of his lack of wisdom; well, this experience should go a long way to making him wiser.

That news reporter, Anne Weavers and her camera man were a severe problem though. They kept on interacting with his characters and worse still, almost kidnapped Eggo Maniac.

If anything, they were now taking a starring role in the proceedings and this was totally unacceptable. He needed to get rid of her.

There were lots of methods at his disposal but for one's first task, subtlety was the key. Only the higher ranked officials were able single-handedly to eliminate outside influences with no reason at all. They had the mind control powers to back it up though. A few specific tiny memory wipes of a few million life forms would soon have them forgetting that something existed, yet they still retained all the other information to which they had been privy. That was one of the mastery techniques.

He had witnessed Tod use it before, only once though, as it undeniably was a last resort. Some odd pink piece of matter was wreaking absolute havoc on Quarnerior III and was simply ruining the peace. It had lived there for thousands of years and was a story passed down from parent to child and so on.

To cut a long story short, it was real and was released onto the unsuspecting inhabitants. He dealt with it and it was gone.

The bosses did not want that though, therefore he had to rebuild it and now it sits in a safe place where the bosses can play with it, or do as they see fit. The only issue that remained was that Tod had to go about and erase the very existence of this creature from everyone's minds.

That took some time, but he got there in the end. Now the inhabitants of Quarnerior III live in perfect harmony, well almost. It's as good as it's going to get down there.

Rod's reminiscing was brought to an end by the reappearance of Tod. He had floated in quite quietly through the white mist and was carrying a small, green device. It was rectangular and had what could only be described as a red blob on the end of it.

Rod was excited, he knew exactly what it was – a microphone, not just a standard microphone though; it was one that would allow them to give instructions to the dwellers of any planet within their range.

"May I speak Tod? May I speak Tod?"

Any composure that Rod may have had was gone as the

excitement was too great. He had never used a microphone of this sort before and he was quite keen to give it a try.

Tod waved his arms in a bid to get him to stop bouncing up and down.

It did not work.

"Listen Rod, I shall go first, just to ensure we get things back on track and then you can follow my lead; that way you still get a turn and we can fix this odd allegiance your players have found with the human, Anne Weavers."

Rod was happy with this. It still meant he would get his turn and that was the main priority in his mind.

Tod observed the screen, mic still in hand. He had not moved and, from the looks of things, was not planning on using the device any time soon.

Finally Rod's excitement died down and he positioned himself next to his friend to watch what was occurring.

Tod could sense Rod's eagerness and sought to explain why biding their time was the way to go. "We are not going to rush into this Rod. As you can see, at present, the news reporter and the others are heading back to this CBA (I believe that's correct) news building. That is where we shall strike. The humans hang onto great superstitions and this is what we shall use against them."

Rod nodded in agreement, despite not really knowing what Tod was talking about.

Riding on top of an ant was an interesting experience and one that Howard did not think would happen at the beginning of the day.

Mind you, he wasn't technically alive at the beginning of the day, so everything was a bonus. Bruce sat next to him and even the Sheep Brigade, who were capable of flight, had decided that this was an opportunity they did not wish to miss.

The ant was a bit bristly and therefore was a touch rough to mount. This was probably the reason that Eggo Maniac had opted to fly in the helicopter with Anne Weavers and the camera man.

Another distinct advantage was the lack of traffic, unheard of around the streets of Central London, but very much a reality now. This was of course due to the people not being used to seeing an ant the size of a house wandering down Baker Street with five sheep, an encyclopaedia and an apple crumble man with a pizza box for a head as passengers.

Anne Weavers had even got on the news and warned the civilians not to worry about the situation and that everyone was quite harmless. Perhaps people just hadn't tuned into the bulletin.

The helicopter hovered above the ant and kept pace with it. Anne Weavers kept on staring at the creature and Eggo Maniac could see that she was captivated by it.

The camera man who sat in the front seat with the pilot was just concerned with removing as much treacle as he could from his hair.

"How are we going to get the ant inside, then?" said Eggo Maniac.

It was a question that had been bothering him ever since they had all agreed to go back to the CBA News building. He had entered through a lift that would never accommodate such a creature, and as the actual room he had entered was underground, he could not fathom how this ant would fit.

"Worry not, Eggo Maniac, there is more than meets the eye regarding that room, in more ways than just size," was the reply from Anne.

Over the last few hours it had become quite apparent to Eggo Maniac that Anne Weavers was no mere reporter. The way that she had used her powers to control him and the fact that she was living in a secret underground area that had to be accessed by a special card, in a particular lift, were proof enough of that.

He wondered whether her place had any special controls or secret hidden vehicles or weapons that would spring out at the flick of a switch. Just what was her purpose though? What was she trying to achieve? This was the key information that he wished to discover. Mind you, Eggo Maniac was not yet aware of what his own goals were, let alone anyone else's. Perhaps this could be his objective then – to discover everything he could about Anne Weavers and then… Then what?

Who cares, thought Eggo Maniac, it was something to do. He would have to go about this by being as friendly as he could to Anne and gaining her trust. Perhaps a little idle chit-chat would be a good start.

"So Anne, what do you think about the weather? It's been raining now for…"

"Spare me this useless talk, Eggo Maniac. I'm a reporter, therefore if I desire to know about the weather I shall merely ask our broadcasting associate journalist who deals with the weather. He will then get it wrong anyway."

She even managed a scowl at the end to emphasise her point.

That was not going to work then. Just as the murky egg was about to open his mouth for a second attempt, Anne cut him off instantly.

"I just asked you not to bother with small talk. I will reveal my plans to you soon enough. I explained that I am now your publicist and I am going to turn you and your friends into superstars. You are going to have to live up to that billing though. Please allow me time to explain everything to you all. We are nearly at our headquarters anyhow."

Eggo Maniac slumped back into his seat. She seemed to know exactly what he was going to say before he did. Maybe it was her powers again. Was he still under her control? Is that why he had chosen to ride in the helicopter and not on the giant ant down below?

"Put your mind at ease, Eggo Maniac. I'm not a mind reader, well not quite, and I'm not tapping into your brain. Your facial expression is all I require to read your thoughts at this moment in time. Call it a trick of the journalist's trade."

She giggled to herself as she uttered the last part. Anne stepped out of the door of the helicopter and gripped the rope ladder tightly. She obviously had no fear of heights, as every time she did this it was not unlike taking a mini bungee jump.

Eggo Maniac knew what would happen next and sure enough, she whipped the microphone out and started giving instructions.

"Okay everyone, we are now at the CBA News building. I would like you all to wait outside the door to the reception and I shall meet you there in five minutes. We've just got to land the chopper and get the camera man cleaned up."

Bruce gave a thumbs up in recognition, whilst the ant lay down on the road. He would not fit on the pavement and there was no real threat to him, as word of their arrival had meant that all other people had left, including cars, buses and any other mode of transport imaginable.

The helicopter landed smoothly on the top of the building and Anne ordered the camera man off first. She gave him strict instructions to go and shower off, to put on a new suit and not to wear a striped tie with a striped shirt.

She then insisted that Eggo Maniac was quicker and ended up dragging him down the stairs and the corridor towards the lift. There was no need to use the secret card this time as they were only going to the ground floor.

Eggo Maniac barely had time to notice the décor of the lobby, but what he did see was particularly flashy and gave the impression of a high class, opulent building. It was the exact opposite of what he had seen in Anne's secret room below.

The entire front of the building was made of large, glass panels with an automatic sliding door in the centre, which was manned by two smartly dressed security guards. A third stood by the reception desk and all wore sunglasses, despite being indoors. Perhaps it was the glare of the sun reflecting from all the glass.

This was of no concern to Anne Weavers though and none of the guards batted an eyelid as she threw Eggo Maniac out of the door and followed swiftly behind him. She was so fast, that she managed to leap in front of him and catch him before his feet touched the ground. She placed him, upright on the pavement and then ran her fingers through her hair.

"Apologies for the bumpy ride Eggo Maniac, but I am never tardy in any way. It's one of my rules. Having assessed your abilities, I have come to the conclusion that speed is not one of your best attributes so I gave you a hand along the way."

The Sheep Brigade, Bruce and Howard applauded.

The ant cheered.

Eggo Maniac blushed.

To say he was embarrassed would have been quite the understatement. This woman seemed to be able to do everything. Eggo Maniac's suspicions heightened. Why on Earth did she need him or the others?

Anne laughed at her rapturous audience and raised her hands up in the air, hoping to quieten them down.

It worked.

She stood in front of them all now, as Eggo Maniac had joined them and was standing by Bruce and Howard, who were in the road along with the Sheep Brigade. The giant ant was stretching behind them and yawning. The journey had taken its toll on him.

Realising she had her audience precisely where she wanted them, Anne Weavers began.

"First of all I just want to say how pleased I am that you have all come with me to the CBA News building. Before I continue I must stress that I no longer have a microphone with me, nor do I intend to use one. What we are going to discuss shortly will be strictly off limits and none, aside from those present, will hear it.

You see, I am not just a mere news reporter, neither am I truly a publicist. I had to take on these roles in order to bring you all together and to get you here."

She paused.

Everyone in front of her was captivated. They were almost willing her to carry on. She was not going to let them down, "I think the key for us all is that we unite and work together to achieve a common goal."

"And what common goal would that be Anne?" said Eggo Maniac.

"I have explained to you all that there is much of myself that I must reveal. Once I have done that, then I feel that you will trust me. Please follow me into the building.

There are reasons for your existence and that goes for every one of you. In truth you have only been around for mere hours, but the information I have can help you understand why. Surely you wish to know your purpose in the grand scheme of things and..."

She took in a deep breath. What had started as a confident, verging on arrogant, speech had now spiralled into one that resembled begging.

She had no choice, she was so close now.

Fortunately for Anne Weavers, she had hit everyone where it counted. They all craved the meaning, the purpose of why they were in London, why they barely had any memories but knew how to speak and why they were different.

"Very well, we shall come with you," said Howard.

Bruce looked at the pizza box and was impressed with his quick turnaround from a coward fearing the public to an almost outspoken leader. He was nearly there, but not quite.

Anne grinned. It was the first time any of them had seen any real excitement in her eyes. All this was obviously important.

"Great. Now I need you all to follow me. We go left around the building and then up the street until we find the back alley of the Italian restaurant, Pierluigi's."

"What's all this for? Surely the quickest way to your building is through the front door and into the lift?"

The reporter sighed. She was growing tired of Eggo Maniac's consistent whining and complaining.

"It is meant for your average human beings, but you lot would draw attention from the security guards. Firstly it is true that they are lazy enough not to notice you, Eggo Maniac, or perhaps they must have thought that you were in a costume, but I think they would question a group of sheep and a giant ant, not to mention your other friends.

Secondly there is no way we would all fit in the elevator and thirdly, stop moaning, it doesn't become you."

The murky-green egg was rather sheepish now, as if the green had drained away and a fearful white had overtaken it. It was like a schoolboy getting a stern telling off from a teacher who had finally lost patience with him.

The other problem for Eggo Maniac was that everything that Anne had just relayed to him was logical and worst of all, true. He couldn't hide away from that. He did however have one more question, which he meekly posed. "Is that seriously why we rushed down through the…"

He couldn't even finish it.

Anne however did.

"Through the reception area so quickly? Yes of course that was why. It was so that the guards did not have enough time to form any sort of opinion or analysis of you. Now can we move on and get to this alternative entrance that will, Eggo Maniac, put us all into the building and will be far more comfortable and spacious?"

The group continued up the deserted streets of London. Howard was interested in looking into the various shop, café and pub windows. It appeared that the general public must have been in such a rush to escape that they had left the lights on and half downed drinks. One electronics shop still had the radio playing.

This dismayed the apple crumble man as it showed just how frightening he was to people; yet he himself had no interest in scaring anyone. Bruce, too, looked as if he was undertaking the same thought process.

The only option they had was to go with Anne and she could be anyone. She had already informed them that she was not a reporter nor a publicist, so what was she?

Howard then laughed quietly to himself, he was going to discover everything imminently, anyway no point dwelling on it. He might as well enjoy the walk, short as it was.

Within seconds they had arrived at an alleyway, not dissimilar to the one where he had entered the world. There were two large, green wheelie bins and between them was the entrance to a cellar. That must be it, Howard mused.

He was wrong, very wrong.

Anne opened the top of the left wheelie bin and jumped inside. She rummaged through the rubbish and pulled a small silver and black striped lever.

The group heard a click.

All stood in the mouth of the alleyway and watched as the pavement and tarmac slid away, save for the area where the bins were standing, to reveal an enormous, steel slide.

It dropped into darkness, but Howard accepted that this was due to the nature of it leading underground.

Anne smiled at all their stunned faces. She paused briefly, still sitting in the bin amongst the rubbish, before speaking.

"Please follow me to our new home."

The group smiled with her. This was exciting, as they all realised they too could potentially have somewhere to live. Howard hadn't even contemplated that he was actually homeless, but not anymore, so it seemed.

"NO, ROD. DON'T PRESS THAT BUTTON."

"What's the matter Tod? I'm going to talk to the egg one. He's the one we need to…"

"THE MICROPHONE IS ON. THEY CAN ALL HEAR US. GIVE ME THAT."

Chapter 7

Leap of Faith

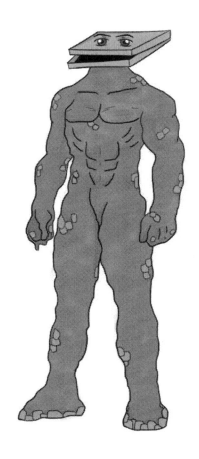

Tod had ripped the microphone from Rod's hands with some force. It was quite surprising that the green device with the red blob on the end of it had remained intact.

"What has happened is very serious Rod," said Tod, "I don't think you appreciate the gravity of the situation. I shall now be taking charge of the mission and you…"

"But Tod, it was not even switched o…"

"No buts, there will be absolutely no buts," Said Tod, who had once again taken his darker shade of purple indicating his anger – not that Rod needed that as a reminder of course. Tod gripped the area of cloud below his mouth, presumably his chin, in thought.

Rod did not dare to disturb him for fear of the repercussions. Unquestionably there would be some of those regardless of what happened now and he had no desire to add to them.

Tod cleared his throat before continuing his speech, which had been so inappropriately interrupted, "There is no time for childish arguments now Rod. We have a real situation on our hands. This play has gone out of control and I for one will not stand for it. You are to take your place as assistant and assistant you will remain until further notice, is that clear?"

"Yes Tod."

"I shall now lead this mission and get us out of this mess, understood?"

On this occasion Rod bowed. He just wanted the whiteness of the room to swallow him up, not literally of course, as that would hurt and he could end up on Earth, but he certainly wished to be as far away from Tod as possible.

The purple cloud sighed. He knew that Rod was trying his best and that it was his exuberance that had caused the mistake, but what a mistake it was.

As far as Tod was concerned Rod had let the beings down below know of their existence and worse still, he had mentioned Eggo Maniac. The whole world, the whole planet had heard their conversation. It did not matter where the living things were, they could have been on a plane, deep sea diving or stuck in a mine somewhere – they would have all heard the conversation. They would all have heard the words 'Eggo Maniac'.

The wiping of that many minds would take too long, so that was not an option. He did not want to discuss it with the bosses as this would get him into trouble and that was never good.

This was something the pair of them were going to have to fix there and then, but what could he do? He could hardly talk to that odd group on Earth and put it right. Opening up a conversation was the primary reason they were in this mess.

Gazing over at Rod, he noticed that his friend was upset. It was his error of course, but Tod felt some sympathy for him. He was only a junior, an assistant and Tod should probably have taken a closer, more proactive role in his development – whatever that meant. He had heard one of his superiors say it once when he was in Rod's position.

He approached the pink cloud and placed his hand on top of his head, like a brother ruffling a younger sibling's hair, except that it was a cloud, obviously.

"Listen Rod, I don't want you to feel bad or lose confidence over this matter. It is just a bump in the sky and we can easily iron this out. I have probably offered some harsher words than I should have and I accept that. So for that part of it I apologise to you.

You just need to be more careful. I am aware that the majority of this is down to your raw enthusiasm and I commend you for your approach. It is just your execution of specific areas that we must look at."

Rod was immediately grinning again. It was as if a switch had been flicked that automatically altered his mood. "So what do we do now Tod?"

"Now Rod, we wait and we watch. We scrutinise their every movement, every word, paying close attention to the human, Anne Weavers. I think it is fair to say that she possesses some interesting powers and I for one would like to know where and how she acquired these. At present the group trust her and she has stated that she will reveal all to them. I suggest we bide our time until she does that. Our problem, however, is that now they are going to be talking about…"

"About us and the odd voices they heard?"

Under normal circumstances Tod would have scolded Rod for cutting him off whilst he was speaking, but not today.

"Calm yourself Rod, but yes you are right. I would imagine our voices will be the major headlines across all types of media. Now we must try to regain our stealth before we strike."

The journey down that tunnel in the ground was swift to say the least. Howard had quite enjoyed it. The speed and the thrill of all the twists and turns were exhilarating.

He wasn't quite so sure that Eggo Maniac had taken the same

thrill from the journey however. A series of screams and then a tough landing on the red carpeted floor were unlikely to be his idea of a good time. The only odd thing was the lack of the appearance of the giant ant.

Upon closer inspection the majority of them had landed in Anne Weaver's homely living room, complete with small kitchen area in the corner, but neither the ant, nor Anne Weavers for that matter, were there.

The Sheep Brigade was fully accounted for and Bruce had made himself at home and was sitting on the couch. Eggo Maniac was rubbing his backside, which had taken the brunt of his landing and the camera man was in the corner washing his hands in the sink, sporting fresh, pink tie and pressed, white shirt.

Bruce picked up the remote for the television and switched it on. He flicked through a few channels and settled on a cartoon. He had no idea what it was, but it entertained him nonetheless.

The Sheep Brigade moved over and sat around him on various parts of the sofa. Commander Winters was on the main cushion along with Lieutenant Figs, with Private Ostrich on the arm and Private Cannon perched on the other. Private Lunatic had taken up a position on the top of the sofa, just above the heads of the others and was lying flat on his back viewing the television upside down.

Nobody seemed to mind this until Private Lunatic began to froth at the mouth and the rainbow sheep was quickly instructed to settle on the floor by the coffee table if he desired to carry on with this behaviour.

Eggo Maniac sulked whilst Howard preferred to stand. The

television was of no interest to him and he continued to peruse the room. He was quite surprised that none of the others were concerned about the whereabouts of Anne Weavers and the big ant.

Howard did not have time to dwell on this for long. The entire back wall of the room rumbled. The camera man backed away from the sink in the corner and casually joined the others by the sofa. He was not alarmed in any way and this put Howard's mind at rest.

The wall began to rise and disappear into the ceiling. Beyond it was what could only be described as an enormous garage. The floor was concrete and had various yellow and black markings that must have been car parking spaces. There were two large trucks that looked military in style, except they were black.

The camera man walked towards the opening and waved at the others insisting they followed him. They obliged and it was not until they stepped out of the lounge, that they could truly appreciate the magnitude of this new room – if one could call it a room at all.

This was a base, almost a military base and its floor space was far greater than that of the CBA News building. Howard imagined it was at the very least the size of ten football pitches, whatever they were.

There were stairs, ramps, numerous black vehicles spread out and all neatly parked in their spaces. Howard counted motorbikes, cars, trucks, tanks, a couple of helicopters, two jets and a bicycle and this was all that was in view.

Of the two walls that Howard could see, the others were too far in the distance, there were stairways that led to multiple levels and balconies. In these walls were computers and screens with the occasional random set of coloured buttons. Everyone was taken aback by the grandeur of it all.

"It's some sort of futuristic base," said Bruce, who had started flicking through his pages in an attempt to gather more information.

Anne appeared along with the giant ant and gently grabbed Bruce's hand to stop him.

"That won't be necessary Bruce. There will not be any records of this place. Let's just refer to it as our secret station. Apologies for not meeting you in the more comfortable surroundings of our lounge, but unfortunately the ant could not fit in the alleyway, never mind the entrance. We took an alternative, much larger entrance.

Before I go on I must inform you that you are some of the first beings I have allowed in here for years. It is, as I said before, a secret station of operations and whilst it is attached to the CBA news building, all be it underground, the folks at CBA News have no clue of its existence and I wish to keep it that way.

I did warn you that I was not just a reporter and I think it is fair if we get to an explanation quickly, so do please follow me. We are going to ascend."

Howard had not even thought about looking up. He didn't think any of the group had, as they all stared at the ceiling.

They couldn't see it.

The metal wall panels, stairs, lifts, gantries and platforms ran endlessly until they submerged into darkness where Howard assumed there would only be more. Just how deep were they?

For this kind of height in an underground building they must have been close to the Earth's core. It was a good job that it didn't feel too hot.

The group followed Anne over to a grey platform with yellow and black markings that ran around the edge of it. Interestingly the ant was already there and must have been waiting.

The platform itself was huge and was situated in what was probably the centre of the base. Howard came to this conclusion because of the way that all the walls fell into darkness when they were on it, hence he assumed it was in the middle.

He examined the ant and could not think for the life of him why he did not know his name. He hadn't asked of course, nor had the ant introduced himself. The only thing they knew was that this particular ant was male, as he had agreed on being referred to as 'sir'.

The group stumbled slightly as the platform clicked into gear and gradually rose up the base. It was an interesting ride and was slow enough that the group could see all the control panels, screens and various levels of the base as they passed them by.

It did strike Howard as being odd that there were no people operating them. The only living creatures in the base seemed to be this group that were all standing on the platform.

The group stumbled once more as the platform reached its destination and jolted to a halt. Howard peered out over the side and the depth was so great that it was difficult to see the bottom where they had stood moments ago.

The Sheep Brigade had also moved to the edges to take a look, but Eggo Maniac and Bruce did not share the same desire to have a peek. It then struck Howard that there was nothing around them. The walls were black and all that he could see was a purple doorway. The problem was that this doorway was at least one hundred metres away and it had no platform or even a ladder underneath it. How did one get inside it?

"Surely there must be a bridge of some sort?" said Eggo Maniac.

Anne Weavers nodded and knelt down on the platform. She flipped up a small, grey flap and underneath it was a purple button. She pressed it and a beam of purple light shot out from underneath the door and stopped at the black and yellow edges of the platform.

"It's a light bridge. Far sturdier than the ones you have on Earth and far more practical. Please after you." Anne gestured to Eggo Maniac encouraging him to be the first to step on the bridge.

Private Lunatic was the closest to it at this point, as he was sniffing it.

"Probably his method of checking eh?" said Bruce to Howard.

Eggo Maniac shook his head, well body, as this is where his face was located. He was not amused.

Anne placed her hand on his back, "Come on, you've got to trust me Eggo Maniac. Would it help if I went first?"

Eggo Maniac breathed a sigh of relief. He was not interested in trust exercises of any sort.

Anne shrugged and gestured towards the camera man to come over. He complied and stepped out onto the light bridge. It was firm and did not move a millimetre beneath his weight.

Anne then followed him and both stood in the middle. The group looked on intently.

Anne then moved to the side of the light bridge and pushed the camera man off the bridge over the side.

Everyone gasped.

To the group's amazement, the purple light then materialised underneath the camera man and he landed softly on it.

He then got up and jumped over the side again, yet the light caught him once more.

Anne Weavers then performed a cartwheel into a somersault over the edge, but the light bridge generated beneath her and she landed safely.

Anne stood up and adjusted her jacket, "I told you to trust me. This bridge is set to safety mode, so it is impossible to fall to the land below. You don't really require the platform on which you are standing, as the light bridge will simply appear underneath you. Now come on over and give it a try before we leave this place."

Private Lunatic was the first to have a go and have a go he did. The rainbow sheep jumped so high into the air that he came down onto the light bridge in slow motion.

Bruce was out next and he decided to use a roly-poly technique although this was only due to the fact that he tripped over Private Ostrich, who was not looking where he was going, as his head was still firmly stuck in his wool.

Commander Winters ordered the rest of the Sheep Brigade out. They all obeyed the order and ran out onto the purple bridge. This left Eggo Maniac, Howard and the ant. Howard was the first to try, as he tentatively stepped out onto the air.

"Why don't you just step directly on the light bit?" said Eggo Maniac.

Howard shrugged. Earlier on in the day he had endured so much fear and anxiety, but now this was his opportunity to try to be a little more daring. A small flicker of light took shape underneath his apple crumble foot.

"Oh forget it," said the pizza box as he dived into the air. Sure enough the light caught him. As he landed on his front he could feel that the surface beneath him was indeed strong and firm. He waved back at the ant and the egg, "Come on Eggo Maniac. It's fun. Honestly you have to try this."

Eggo Maniac shook his head fervently, "No I shall just walk the normal route."

"Where's the fun in that?"

Eggo Maniac turned around sharply to confront the owner of the voice.

It was the ant and he wore a wry smile to boot.

Eggo Maniac did not like the clear mischief in his eyes, as it looked as if it could be trouble.

He was correct.

Before he could even reply Eggo Maniac found himself hurtling through the air into the oblivion below.

The ant had whacked him, quite hard too, and he was powerless to stop it. He was not heading into the oblivion of course, the purple light bridge caught him comfortably, but his screams sounded as if the end was nigh.

Howard attempted to conceal his amusement until he heard everyone else. There was laughter, a lot of laughter. Howard observed everyone in the room and all were in a state of hysterics. He joined them.

Suffice to say Eggo Maniac did not see the funny side of this. Anne Weavers made her way over to him and attempted to get him to lighten up by slapping him on the back. This did not work either of course, but it was worth a try.

Eventually the laughter subsided and the more pressing matter of entering the doorway was at hand. The camera man went through first, whilst Anne Weavers stood by the door ushering everyone over.

Somehow Howard had been shoved to the front of the queue and was expected to enter immediately. The first thing that struck him was the fact that one could not see through it. It was just purple light, a similar colour to that displayed by the bridge.

Anne could sense his nervousness and reassured him quickly, "It's a door nothing more, the camera man's just been through."

Howard nodded, though he was still unsure. He contemplated briefly, placing his hand on his pizza box chin, as he always did this. At that point it occurred to him that he had picked up his first habit. At least it wasn't a bad one.

He placed one apple crumble hand out and touched the purple light with his index finger. It did move through and when he pulled it back everything was fine. His expression changed to one of amazement, Anne's eyes met his stare and he chuckled.

"This is no ordinary door is it Anne Weavers? This is a portal."

She curtsied in response.

Howard stepped through instantly. It was the intrigue of where this portal would take him that spurred him on.

Bruce was next and followed immediately. Private Lunatic then dived in, whilst the remainder of the Sheep Brigade marched through. Eggo Maniac was ready to complain, as per the norm, but was quickly flicked through by the giant ant.

He screamed.

The ant poked one of his front legs through and then withdrew it. He just required one more tiny piece of information, "Anne I am willing to go through, there is no question about that, but I cannot."

"And why is that may I ask?"

"Well it is simple. I won't fit. It does not take a rocket scientist to see that I am too large for the door or portal, whatever it is you call it."

Anne giggled once more. Her character had altered from a stern, harsh cut-throat reporter to that of someone quite cheerful, since she had revealed to the group that she was something more. It was as if she lifted a great weight from her shoulders, or was in the process of doing so, she still hadn't told them who she actually was or why she had gathered them together.

In truth she had neglected to share any information regarding where they were going. They truly were a trusting bunch, she mused to herself. Her task could possibly be easier than she had anticipated. Perhaps this was the group that could help her.

Chapter 8
The Door of History

The screen in the middle of the floor went black and then faded into white, like the rest of the space. Rod floated with a confused look on his face.

Tod on the other hand was alarmed. He did not say anything, he didn't need to, his facial expression told the whole story. Fear was not something he was used to and quite frankly if this is what it felt like, he could do without it.

Rod, still clueless of Tod's demeanour, asked his friend, "Why has the screen switched off Tod? Is it a malfunction? Would you like me to go down to repair services and see if they can fix it?"

Rod awaited a response, but unusually for Tod it did not come instantly. Even Rod could now detect that something was wrong.

Tod was deep in thought.

Finally after what seemed like an eternity, the purple cloud spoke very quietly.

"I think Rod we have an issue that is quite serious now. This human Anne Weavers has caused us a massive problem. We were absolutely correct to keep an eye on her and perhaps, in hindsight, I should have made her expire earlier, rather than let her unite the group."

"Is that so they wouldn't have all been together and the conflict would have raged on?"

"No Rod, this has gone far beyond an entertaining battle. As I explained, this situation has now taken a turn for the worse. The screen is not broken Rod. This Anne Weavers has taken our creations off Earth."

Rod scratched the top of his head/cloud. He did not see why

this was a concern. If Anne Weavers was taking them into space then they could still be easily tracked and they could carry on their story there.

"No Rod I'm afraid that will not work. Anne Weavers and her odd camera man have taken them out of our universe. They are in another dimension and…"

He stopped.

The gravity of entering another dimension was enough to allow Rod to understand the seriousness of the situation. Rod had been taught about the Dimensional Wars, as all students were and the rifts that existed were closed, by both sides. Many of his ancestors had fought in these battles that lasted a millennia.

If life from the other dimensions was crossing over then, he could not even finish his thought process before his mouth opened once more, "That means that this Anne Weavers is from the other…"

"Dimension, yes that must be right Rod. Somehow she has crossed over and not only that, she is taking living entities from our worlds to hers. We have no idea why, although having studied the history of that lot, it will undoubtedly be for nefarious purposes. There is only one thing we can do now."

Rod's mouth dropped open. Surely Tod could not mean that?

"I'm afraid I do Rod. I shan't apologise for opening your mind there, but we must act with haste. We must go and inform the bosses."

Beyond the purple door was interesting. It was the most surreal thing that Howard had ever encountered, although this was not too hard as he had only been around for a day.

The ground underneath him was red and slightly slimy. It moved very gently, swaying back and forth. This actually assisted with balance and it was far easier to stand up here than where he had previously been. The texture of it was akin to a tongue. Aside from this there were no walls.

Everything around them was black and he could see that Private Lunatic had trudged out far beyond where the rest of the group had assembled. It seemed that the darkness ran on for an unlimited length.

"Private Lunatic return to the Sheep Brigade immediately," said Commander Winters.

Anne comforted him instantly, "Do not worry about him Commander, this is only because we are parked. Once I start the ship, the walls will shift back to their original place and bring Private Lunatic back with it. He is quite safe."

"So this is where we are. We are on a ship?" said Eggo Maniac.

Bruce opened himself and began to flick through his pages, desperately seeking out some more information on their whereabouts. Of course he could find nothing, absolutely nothing for that matter. He felt a hand touch the sleeve of his cover, gently and calmly.

It was Anne, "Calm down Bruce, don't be so concerned. Your information is not based on where we are going, and on that note I think it's time to tell you all what is going on."

A small, red pillar rose up from the ground. It appeared to be made of the exact same material as the tongue like floor. Water dripped off it and Bruce could see that on the top was an indentation in the shape of a hand.

Anne Weavers walked to it and placed her right hand into the grooves. It fitted perfectly and Bruce wondered whether the pillar had been cast specifically for her, as it was so perfect.

Once she had made contact the pillar glowed bright yellow. The floor that had been red was now the same yellow too. Gradually the walls retracted and with it, Private Lunatic was gently pushed back towards the rest of the group. A squelching sound, a bit like stepping in thick, soggy mud, indicated the walls had now fallen into place.

The group sat within a small yellow box-room. The walls, ceiling and floor all maintained the similar wet and gooey tongue like quality, yet it was comfortable. They all swayed too, as the floor had done upon their arrival.

Even Eggo Maniac, whom Howard was certain would not cope with the surroundings, seemed pleasantly surprised. Howard then recognised the fact that they were all sitting down. He supposed that the shock of the new dimension had caused him to forget this. The interesting aspect was that all the seats were different. The floor had moulded itself to lace each member of the group in a perfectly comfortable chair that suited their needs precisely.

Howards was long and thin and allowed him the space to lean back and relax. Eggo Maniac's seat was short, stout and wide which gave him the freedom to rock casually back and forth. Private Lunatic's chair was, different. It was essentially a bowl that he could roll around in amongst other bizarre actions that only Private Lunatic could account for.

Howard noticed that Anne Weavers had opted to remain standing. He wondered if she was somehow controlling the floor and the walls. He would not have to wait long for an answer to all his queries, as Anne Weavers began, "Well we are now airborne and making our way through the Adamantium dimension. We are travelling through space and our altitude is off the planet. The weather is calm. Isn't that how they do announcements on flights on Earth?"

"I wouldn't know I've never flown before," said Bruce, "Can you now tell us why we are here and where we are please?"

Anne Weavers nodded. Her smile disappeared and she looked each entity in the room directly in the eye, ensuring that she had the attention of all. Once she felt that everyone was focussed on her, she grimaced.

"As far as we are aware or should I say scientifically proven, there are two dimensions. The Ignacium and the Adamantium. You are all, my camera man aside, part of the Adamantium dimension. I am from the Ignacium.

Since the beginning of our records we were not aware of what a dimension was, let alone that another one existed. Many years ago, so many that it is difficult to put a number on it that is relative to Earth, by chance, we discovered the Adamantium.

To say we stumbled upon it would be overly ambitious. It was neither skill nor scientific genius that got us there, but a young, clumsy warrior that fell down a hole and popped through a rift that ultimately led to him landing on Earth.

There was little life on Earth at that point, as the majority of it was covered in water. Anyway he was quickly picked up by the clouds – a highly advanced species who live for entertainment. They were fascinated by this warrior and had not been exposed to the concept of battle before.

Through their own intelligence and hard work, the clouds managed to open a portal so that the warrior might return home. It was at this point that they revealed their true reasoning for assisting the warrior.

Being the most advanced race of their dimension meant that the clouds had never been asked to compromise or negotiate and they merely entered into our space and began to take over. They were not used to having to use force or to fight and genuinely thought that they would be welcomed as new rulers.

They were wrong.

They had never experienced combat before as their technology and intelligence had always got them through. The inhabitants of all the known planets and systems within the Ignacium took to arms and thus began the Dimensional Wars.

They lasted a millennia and the losses to both sides were high. At times the clouds were on top and at others we were. At one point we had almost swapped homes as we had much control of the Adamantium and they, the Ignacium.

A stalemate was all that anyone could muster, and slowly, gradually we all went back to our homes, sealing off the various portals that had been created around the different planets.

This tiny portal on Earth is the only one we are sure still exists and we are confident that the clouds have yet to discover its existence. I have been monitoring their actions for about twenty Earth years now and whilst it does seem they are not attempting an invasion, their cruelty still knows no bounds.

The clouds are currently filming wars on various planets and sitting back and selling the rights for these to their television broadcasters. It appears that they understand conflict as sport and boy are they getting high numbers.

Earth was of little significance to them as they viewed the creatures as a highly aggressive young species. Yet after the Dimensional Wars ended, they felt something missing.

Much millennia later they took an interest in your planet, you see they could sell your natives fighting as a sport and make big money from it. Every war, every conflict, be it a massive battle or a quick scrap in a playground, is broadcast to their citizens.

They even sell trading cards and sticker albums amongst a plethora of other merchandise relating to some of the greatest generals of Earth. Alexander the Great and Napoleon are particularly good sellers even now.

Forgive me for I am digressing.

You see mankind is perfect for them. Your naturally aggressive ways mean they require little work to make things begin. For the majority of your history they have sat back and watched. There are more cameras and microphones dotted around your planet than in a film studio.

However recently, 'Season One' as they dubbed it ended. In order to produce higher ratings and to add some twists, the clouds have now started to create fights on your planet. Your clash with the coffee cup earlier was instigated by them. They dropped the creature down onto your planet for you to fight and you obliged.

You see you're all the main cast of 'Season Two' and have been created specifically with this in mind. When I said I needed your help, it was to bring you here where you will be safe.

The rescue part of my mission is all but complete. My next step is to take on the clouds directly and stop them from interfering with Earth and any other planets for that matter."

Anne Weavers inhaled deeply and a small, yellow stool rose up underneath her and seated her gracefully.

Howard scratched the top of his pizza box head. He was about to ask a question, but Bruce beat him to it. He had developed quite the habit of doing this.

"So you're telling us that you rescued all of us and that we were created in order to fight each other."

Anne Weavers waved in confirmation.

"Well okay then, I just wanted some clarification," said Bruce.

At this point Howard did not have a clue as to what he should think. Oddly it all made sense. That was the only logical way they could all have known so much yet have been around only for a day. The question was…

"So what now then? What do we do now?"

Bruce had butted in again with the exact question he was seconds away from asking. Not that it mattered anyway. He would still hear Anne Weaver's retort.

The answer was instant, "You will take refuge on my home planet of Chordona. There you will be treated well and not unwittingly forced into conflict. Once we have reached Chordona, the rescue element of my mission will be complete."

"And then what?" This time Howard was not beaten to the punchline by Bruce. His question was asked as Anne was still finishing her sentence. The concept of being rescued was the last thing Howard needed. He had only just begun to adapt to life on Earth and now he was in another dimension, being hauled off to a new planet of which he knew nothing.

Anne's lip trembled, but not with fear, this was anger.

Howard remained at ease. He could not quite put his finger on why, yet somehow he was comfortable that this anger was not directed at him, or any of the others for that matter. These clouds must have really got to her.

Anne clenched her right hand tightly into a fist. Slowly she released her grip and one by one raised each finger up until her palm was fully visible. Inspecting it, she began to lick her lips, relishing what was about to transpire.

"So what happens next then?" said Bruce. Clearly he did not share the same amount of patience as the rest of the group.

Anne stood up once more and the yellow stool shrunk back down into the floor. Her eyes were alive now, as if there was fire burning in them.

Howard considered that perhaps underneath her pupils that was the case.

Quietly she responded to all present.

"After that my friends, after that I go back and destroy the menace of the clouds."

The seemingly never ending white space had vanished and now, unusually for any member of the clouds, Rod and Tod floated down a dark corridor. There were no clear walls as such, but as everything was black they felt enclosed.

Rod reached out with his hand and it pushed through some of the darkness surrounding him. It faded from sight and he quickly pulled it back to ensure it was still there. Fortunately for him, it was.

"Don't do that Rod. These tunnels that lead to the bosses are claustrophobic for a reason. They make us feel uncomfortable so that we only disturb them when things are absolutely necessary."

Rod bowed to confirm his understanding.

"You were really quite lucky not to lose your hand there, for what lies on the other side of these walls is anyone's guess. Some believe there are creatures that thirst for clouds and others say there is nothing there – a void if you will. Personally I think it's nonsense."

"So what do you think is there then Tod?"

"Oh I think if you go out there then you will be trapped and never enter a cloud city again."

Strangely Tod had replied cheerfully as if this was an acceptable fate. He giggled slightly and Rod could feel that Tod was once again prying into his mind.

"Put it this way Rod, if the bosses are angry with us, then the fate of not being able to enter a cloud city again might be more of a reward than a punishment compared to what they could potentially do to us."

Still Tod remained light-hearted, perhaps through nervousness mused Rod.

The corridor stretched onwards and eventually the pair came to a small opening that led in a downwards direction.

Tod now stepped in front of Rod as there was no longer enough room for the pair to continue moving side by side. Tod placed his hand on Rod's shoulder in an act of reassurance.

"Now this next part may seem out of control, but it is not. We have merely reached the second stage of turning back. The first we have passed, as neither of us were put off by the lack of space surrounding us. This next step is more about speed. If necessary close your eyes and you will remain on course."

Naturally Rod was unsure of this. "So Tod, if I close my eyes how will I know when I have arrived?"

"I shall inform you Rod. Remember I shall be in front of you. If I was in your position I would view this next step as an experience in itself. It is very similar to the large tube shape water slides they have on Earth. If it wasn't so dark you might even find it fairly exhilarating."

Rod remained unsure and had one further point for which he sought some clarity. "How many times have you done this then Tod?"

The purple cloud grinned. "Just the once, but as I stated previously, closing one's eyes worked for me. Now would you please let go of my arm?"

Rod examined his left hand. It was gripping Tod's arm tightly and shaking. He had not even realised that this was occurring. Before he had time to dwell on Tod's relative inexperience regarding the situation, the purple cloud was gone.

He had leapt down the shoot and despite it being dark, Rod could make out that it was a straight drop and the height of the drop was too great to allow a cloud to float down.

He shrugged. He had no choice anyway. The bosses would soon discover what had happened and there would be immeasurable trouble if he was not honest and did not inform them.

He sprang through into the shoot. The drop was considerable and Rod desperately attempted to keep his eyes open. All he could see was a blur of darkness and upon shutting his eyes it felt no different anyway.

He had no control whatsoever and he quickly found himself spiralling in all directions including a spell where he was certain that he had been twisted upside down. All this was of no consequence to Rod anyway; as Tod had said, he may as well just close his eyes and attempt to enjoy the ride.

His body was like a rag doll. Rod had absolutely zero control of himself and his destination and was tossed and turned to such an extent that he was now not aware of whether he was upside down or standing straight. Any idea of the direction in which he travelled had long since passed.

Eventually all went still.

Rod was sure he was no longer moving. He listened at first, recalling some of his training with Tod, in relation to unusual environments.

Silence.

Gradually, as he grew more comfortable he opened his eyes and propelled himself to a reasonable height for floating. Rod's eyes lit up as he was finally surrounded by an open space once more. It was similar to the endless, white room in which he had overseen the mission with Tod, except this place was purple. This would be an ideal location for Tod, he giggled slightly as he thought.

Surveying the room he speedily located his friend, who was floating at around the same height, slightly further in front of him. Rod ambled over and noticed that as he got closer, the room seemed to get smaller. He took his place beside Tod.

In front of them stood a rather large and imposing, rectangular door. It was black in colour and was at least fifty metres tall. Pictures of various historical battles from a variety of cultures and planets were engraved within the wood. Oddly enough they were all mixed together, thus creating an image of one colossal battle, filled with soldiers from all over the galaxy.

"Don't worry about this room Rod. Almost everything in it is an illusion, hence the issues with the constantly changing size of the room. This is our final stop. Through the door are the bosses. Hopefully they're happy to see us and…"

"Bosses, bosses, bosses, I must speak with you. Something has happened which you must know about."

Both Rod and Tod rotated to discover who was the owner of the interrupting and quite frankly loud voice.

Behind them, having just landed from the tunnel was a bright yellow cloud which was moving as fast as any thing Rod or Tod had recently observed on Earth and that included vehicles.

It rudely barged through them and positioned itself in front of the door.

Finally it stopped moving in order to gather some breath.

Rod and Tod sighed, they both knew exactly who it was. Rod

decided that this time he would be the one to address the situation.

"Excuse me Yod, we were here well before you showed up. Please let us get on with our task at hand."

"You don't understand Rod, this is a matter of the highest urgency and that is why it is imperative that I see the bosses before you."

The yellow cloud continued to pant as it was clear that he had overexerted himself.

Tod moved forward and confronted Yod, "Listen Yod, in a moment we are going to explain ourselves and seek entrance through that door. We were here well before you and, as Rod said, you will have to wait your turn. All matters that are put forward to the bosses are of urgent attention. That much is obvious, hence why we are all here. Move aside and allow us to go first please."

Yod grunted and briefly spun sharply left and right – indicating that he was shaking his head in disagreement.

Tod was about to follow this up when the room began to rumble. Gently at first but soon it became quite volatile. Suddenly it stopped. A booming voice echoed through the room.

"I am ready now. You may discuss the nature of your visit." It paused for a moment before continuing, "I notice there are three of you. Who is first in line?"

Both Rod and Tod attempted to move to the front, but it was too late.

"It was me. I was first and I shall air my issue," said Yod.

Rod was about to launch himself into the argument but felt a hand firmly grip his arm. He glanced back at Tod, who shook his head.

Calmly Rod moved and stood, or rather floated, by his friend once more. The door shook, as if it was thinking to itself.

"Is it alive?" said Rod to Tod.

"Of course it is. It is the first guardian of the bosses. It will decide who will get an audience with them and who will not."

The door ceased its movement and a pair of red eyes and a red mouth quickly bulged out of it. The face was examining Yod carefully. Eventually it cleared its throat.

"I have come to a judgement regarding your situation Yod. I do not need to hear anymore from you. In my opinion I don't even need to listen to you about your problem."

Yod looked happy, the tone in the door's voice was quite cheerful, as if there was nothing to worry about.

"Yod you will get exactly what you deserve. You were first after all."

Yod nodded profusely.

Seconds later the purple floor underneath him parted leaving a gaping hole below. "No please listen to me," said Yod as he tried desperately to stay afloat above the hole.

His resistance was futile. Yod shrieked as he was sucked into the vacuous hole beneath him. His yellow hand gripped onto the edge of the purple floor but it was whisked away. The floor then closed over the hole, returning the room to its usual state.

Rod looked at the floor beneath him. That was certainly not something he wished to experience.

The red face glared at its two remaining visitors. "May I help you?"

Chapter 9
Like a Rainbow

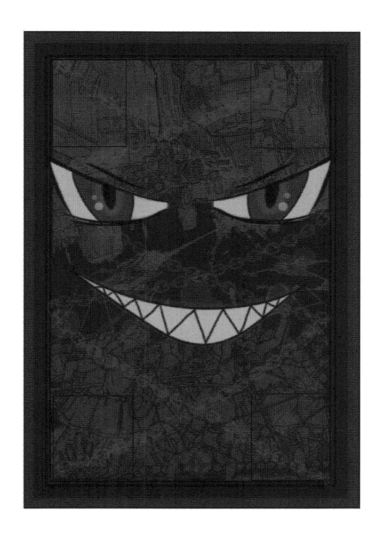

Chordona was nice. Howard knew that he could think of a far superior adjective to express his feelings, but nice seemed to do the job.

It was multicoloured for starters. This meant that every road, every plant and every building was similar to a rainbow-coloured spectrum. That was another thing, the buildings – these were huge. Every single one was a skyscraper of at least two hundred floors.

Howard had asked Anne about this and she had responded by informing him that they were actually staying in a village. The reasoning behind this being that it would be obvious for anyone attempting to seek them out to begin searching in major cities as opposed to a tiny, rural village.

He had to wonder just how large the cities were in comparison. This village, or Plazennta as it was called, had hundreds of streets and on each one, hundreds of buildings.

Howard, Bruce, the camera man, the ant and the Sheep Brigade were all sitting in a rooftop garden on top of one of the skyscrapers. The area of the roof was at least the size of four football pitches, hence why it made a logical place for them to stay as it comfortably accommodated the ant.

The rainbow colours had taken some getting used to for all of the group, save for Private Lunatic who had adapted to them extremely well, sharing the same colour wool, of course.

Anne had popped out to get some supplies for them and the camera man was inside the building, working, whatever that meant. Howard assumed that they must be dreaming up some sort of plan to deal with these clouds.

Moving over to the edge of the rooftop Howard examined the area below. He could hardly see anything and the residents that were going about their everyday business below were like insects.

Howard quickly turned around and stared at the enormous ant sitting behind him. Well perhaps they are like ladybirds then, tiny ladybirds, he chuckled to himself. He wondered why that was the first tiny creature to pop into his head.

"So what are we going to do? We can't spend all our time just sitting up here in this rainbow filled town or whatever it is." Bruce was lying on a sun lounger, flicking through his pages, "I also can't find anything about this place at all. The only thing that comes even remotely close are prisms, rainbows and Newton wheels and that only covers the colour aspect."

"That's because you are an encyclopaedia from Earth and not from Chordona," said Commander Winters.

Howard nodded in affirmation of this.

Bruce just sighed and continued flicking his pages; this time not even stopping to read them.

Howard rubbed the underside of his pizza box chin. He had to come up with something to alleviate the boredom at least.

"Well perhaps we could go for a wander through the streets. I'm sure that neither Anne nor the camera man would object to this."

No sooner had he finished speaking than the camera man reappeared, although this time he was multicoloured like the colours of the rainbow; like the colours of everything on Chordona. Even his clothes had been affected, as his suit, shirt, shoes and tie all bore the same rainbow like effect. The group paused and watched him carefully.

He smiled.

This was something that Howard had not yet seen the camera man do before. It was an uneasy smile and did not fit in with his usual persona.

Bruce had made his way over to Howard now and echoed his friend's opinion, "It's weird isn't it. I didn't think he was capable of good will or niceties or humour for that matter. I presumed that Anne Weavers had beaten it out of him."

Bruce's whispers caused Howard to smile, but he was quick to mask this. He wished to know what the camera man was going to say after all.

Adjusting his tie, the camera man grinned even more. The Sheep Brigade backed away from him and even the giant ant was taking notice.

"Please do not be concerned. I can detect that my change in disposition might be a touch strange for you, but I can assure you there is no problem, no problem at all. You must all understand that when I am back here on my home planet of Chordona and in the village Plazennta, where I grew up, I am far happier. Surely you can all afford me that luxury?"

The group all mumbled in agreement and uttered some brief apologies for their lack of trust.

The camera man nodded and his grin grew even wider.

Howard though, was still not entirely convinced.

"In all honesty chaps I have come up to see if you would like any refreshments, or anything you can think of for that matter. Anne and I want to ensure that you all feel completely comfortable here on

Chordona and my village Plazennta is renowned for its kindness and willingness to please. So do ask for everything, absolutely everything you can think of to make your stay here better – be it food, drink, chairs, televisions, games or beds; there really is no limit."

The group looked at each other. This sounded too good to be true.

Bruce was the first to test the camera man's hospitality. "So could I have a large margherita pizza with red peppers, onions and mushrooms then please? No offence Howard by the way."

"None taken Bruce. Remember my head is only a pizza box, not a pizza itself. Please do go on."

The camera man saluted oddly and waited for more orders.

"Well I would like some sparkling mineral water found only on the south island of New Zealand please," said Commander Winters.

Once more the camera man saluted. "Both those orders are but simple matters. Is there anything more complex you wish to have?"

"How about a swimming pool with a rapid wave system and a gallon of peanut butter flavoured ice-cream," said the ant in a sarcastic tone. Clearly he was as sceptical as Howard.

"Not a problem at all. I can have that here within the hour," said the camera man.

The group stopped to listen in disbelief once more.

Minutes later it suddenly dawned upon everyone that this man was serious. He genuinely believed he could get all of these things, no matter how large, costly or obscure. At that point the orders came pouring in.

The camera man had to back away as the group crowded him,

shouting and spitting out request after request. Even Howard had found himself wound up in the fervour of it all as he shouted out for a cappuccino and a reclining armchair.

Rod was trembling. Despite his best efforts, his body continued to shake. If he possessed bones like a human then he would have been rattling, but fortunately for him clouds did not, so at least he was silent.

The door guardian, if that was its name, was scrutinising them.

He had never envisaged that he would find a black, engraved door so imposing; but at this point Rod could not think of another time when he had felt so helpless. Their lives were in the hands of this red face that adorned this gateway to the bosses. Attempting to avoid the gaze of the guardian, Rod concentrated on the floor where Yod had once been floating.

The power beneath it must have been immense in order to suck a cloud out and into whatever was below. This was why so few clouds ever bothered to see the bosses – it was a matter of life or death.

Rod then concentrated on the purple ground beneath him. It was firm enough, of course. He could only judge this through the use of his eyesight; it was not as if clouds often touched the floor beneath them.

Next he focussed on his friend Tod. Perhaps he could find some sort of solace within him that would help to calm him.

Strangely this worked. He noticed that the face on the door was staring at Tod, directly into his eyes.

Tod reciprocated and the door appeared to raise the level of intensity in his eyes. Tod followed suit.

Rod was amazed at the sheer courage of his friend. He had not even flinched.

The expression on the door's face gradually altered from one of intensity to that of curiosity. It looked confused, then happy, then upset and back to confused again. In a less than aggressive manner, for once, it spoke.

"You have been here before Tod have you not?"

"I have."

"And if I recall correctly, which I always do, I let you in did I not?"

"You did."

"Excellent, I see you have also taken my advice since our last meeting."

"I have."

"This is most pleasing. It is nearly as pleasing as the way that you opted to alert us immediately of the problem you discovered on Earth. It is simply all that is asked of you as a cloud after all."

Tod nodded in response to the door.

Finally its red face smiled.

As it did Rod could hear the sound of clinks and clunks; these he hoped were the sounds of the door unlocking.

Gradually the face faded and as it did it let out a friendly giggle along with, "Do come on in. You are most welcome."

The face faded from view and the door began to rumble.

Instantly Rod checked on the ground, but was reassured by way that it was still there. He felt a hand slap him on the back followed by a friendly tone.

"Worry not Rod. We have been permitted access to enter. We have achieved our task of obtaining a meeting with the bosses."

Rod cleared his throat before replying.

"How were you so calm back there with the door? He seemed to try to intimidate you, yet you did not even flinch. How did you manage it?"

"Ah you see that is the test Rod. The calmer and tougher you are, the more the guardian will respect you. He also senses truth. That is why Yod was disposed of. He lied in order to gain access to the bosses. It would never have worked, the door is too intelligent and wise and saw through him easily."

Rod reflected on this briefly.

"Tod, what did the door mean when it said that it was happy you had remembered its advice from your previous meeting?"

Tod's laid-back façade ceased as he contemplated his answer.

Rod struggled to guess his friend's mood. He hadn't altered in colour so at least that meant he was not entirely angry. Instead Tod chuckled, a little at first, but then a great deal more very quickly.

Seconds later he was howling with laughter. He slapped Rod's shoulder multiple times as if he was trying to pull himself out of his comical hysteria. Rod just watched. There was little else he could do as he was not privy to the joke.

A couple of minutes passed before Tod was able to wipe some of the tears from his eyes and compose himself. It was rare for the purple cloud to lose himself, but this last day had enabled Rod to see a different side to Tod; one that he never dreamed existed. It seemed

Tod was indeed susceptible to emotions and did, believe it or not, make the odd mistake here and there too.

"Apologies Rod, I don't know what came over me. You see I was going to maintain a pretence of being cold and calculated but I cannot. I'm just not that cool."

He giggled again, but immediately stopped himself and continued, "In all honesty, the first time I met the door I was far more frightened than you. I noticed from the corner of my eye that you were trembling with, well let's not beat about the bush, fear. You did a far better job than I did of hiding it. That's why the door asked me to be calmer. Anyway we're wasting time. In we go Rod."

The pink cloud hurtled through the door as Tod had slapped him slightly too hard on the back. Rod did not have time to react however, nor did he wish to. The surroundings had instantly taken his full attention.

He was floating in what could only be described as a grand hallway. The flooring was made up of a variety of different shades of purple marble slabs. There were statues of all sorts of colours and sizes featuring many famous clouds that ran around the circular walls of the room.

The ceiling which towered above him was dome-shaped and had no one particular colour due to the fact that it was adorned with an enormous painting depicting a great battle scene between the clouds and some rainbow-coloured creatures. Some of these colourful beings were human. Others looked like dinosaurs, various insectoids from a multitude of colonies and many entities that he did not recognise.

The walls of the room were purple and had various pink

columns that stood directly in front of them keeping the ceiling in place. There were four archways, none of which contained any doors. There was nothing in them, but it was impossible to see through them. All the spaces within these arches were black.

Rod then turned back hoping to see the area that he had left behind to get here, but it had vanished.

"Do not be concerned about that Rod. You see the door we just went through has teleported us to the hall of the bosses. Beyond one of those arches are the bosses. The other three contain more guardians, except these guardians will just attack us instantly. There will be no conversation or reasoning as there was with the door."

Rod sighed; with every single step he floated, a new problem reared its head. "Go on then Tod, who are these guardians?"

His friend grinned as if he was excited at the prospect of filling Rod with yet more dread.

"Well you have already met one guardian, but the other three are far more powerful than the door. Firstly there is Slimax, quite literally an oversized piece of red slime. Do not let that fool you though. He is a bearer of plague, illness and disease. If he was to infect you, then that would be the end.

Next we have Eator, a gargantuan beast that is allegedly a sort of cross between a Tyrannosaurus Rex and a gorilla. I say allegedly because no one has seen his complete form as Eator is capable of growing new body parts whenever he wishes. His voracious appetite also means that usually all you will encounter is his head. This is down to the unusual quality allowing him to consume his own body when hungry, if there is nothing else around on which to feed. His face and head are always safe as his tongue and teeth cannot reach them. Eator is truly a monster to behold.

The third and final guardian is called Miss Terious and she is deadly."

Rod gazed longingly at Tod, waiting for some more details about this Miss Terious.

Alas they did not come. What Rod had assumed was a pause for dramatic effect had just changed into silence and an awkward one at that. "So what does she do then?"

"Who?"

"This Miss Terious; what powers does she have?"

"I don't know Rod. No one has a clue about her."

"Is it fair to say she's deadly then?"

"Just an assumption Rod. She must be dangerous as all the others are. It's the way of the bosses. They surround themselves with power."

Tod scratched his chin. Rod was clearly being naïve.

The pink cloud browsed the statues peering over at the black space within each arch as he passed it.

Tod watched Rod as he inspected everything and was pleased that his friend was trying to work out which path to choose.

Slowly Rod floated back to the centre of the hallway where Tod was waiting for him. He resumed his original position and placed himself directly adjacent to Tod. The two clouds looked at each other and then rotated themselves in unison, analysing each door together, yet without uttering a word to each other.

"You are more informed than you are letting on Tod. I do not know why I think this, but I do believe it to be true. Why are you withholding information from me Tod?"

"For this very reason Rod; I want to be adamant that you are learning, becoming more in tune with your feelings, predictions and dare I say it, mind reading. You have just shown me that this is the case. Technically you just read some of my thoughts. Well done. Now which one would you pick?"

Rod grumbled for a moment. He was getting tired of these games. Had he been told that he had managed to pick his friend's brain a few hours ago he would have been celebrating as if it was his birthday. Now though, everything had taken such a serious twist that he did not wish to be tested.

Rod and Tod found themselves in a scenario where if they were to select the wrong entranceway they were goners. There was only a one in four chance that they would get it right - twenty five percent. Rod was not keen on those odds that was for certain.

All of the doorways were identical. In fairness he could only tell which was which by using the picture painted on the domed ceiling as a marker. The rotations that he and Tod had just conducted had not helped either. He was confused and disorientated.

He spun himself round again and stopped. In front of him was one of the doorways. Above it was a picture of a rainbow warrior that sported long hair and was riding an oversized wolf.

Taking note of the picture as a marker, Rod spun himself around again, stopping randomly. He faced the same door with the rainbow soldier and wolf above it.

This time he rotated so quickly that he disorientated himself to the point where he could no longer see properly and everything became a blur.

Eventually, as his vision returned to normal, he found himself in front of the very same illustration. It was apparent that whichever way he moved he would always end up at this doorway.

He peered over at Tod, who had distanced himself from Rod, probably so that he wasn't hit. The speed at which Rod was moving was terribly fast, so this was logical.

There was no emotion on the purple cloud's face. He looked completely indifferent. Another test surmised Rod.

"Well Tod, after multiple attempts at deciding which archway to select I have reached the conclusion that the only choice to make is this one here."

Pointing at the doorway with the rainbow man and wolf, Rod inhaled a deep breath. All this assessment was hard work.

His statement was met by a brief, but slow round of applause from Tod.

Rod couldn't work out whether or not it was through sarcasm or was a genuine act of congratulation. The wide smile on Tod's face portrayed the latter, which Rod of course hoped was correct.

"Well done Rod, well done. You have made a choice and it did not take you too long to reach your decision. We shall go through the entrance you have selected at once without question."

Rod felt the familiar grip of Tod's hand on his and before he could offer even the faintest amount of protest or question, he was hauled through the black space that filled the entrance underneath the archway.

The pink cloud shut his eyes. After all he had only opted for that particular door based on the fact that he kept standing in front of it. There was no other rational or reasonable thought behind it.

Rod was terrified. All he hoped was to be confronted by the bosses, not by any of these guardians. In truth if one were to analyse his selection process honestly, Rod had essentially played a large game of spin the bottle, using himself as the bottle to decide randomly on a destination and more worryingly, had gone with the results.

Chapter 10
Visitors and Tourists

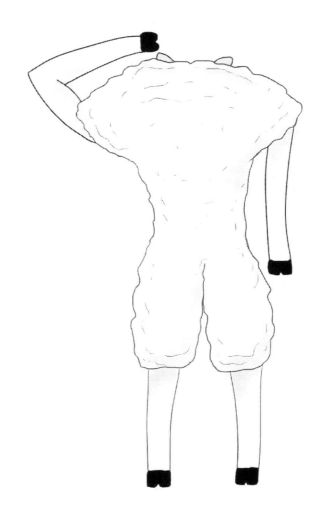

Howard reclined in his brand new, rainbow-coloured armchair, whilst sipping away at his cappuccino.

He gazed out over the rooftop garden and watched some of the Sheep Brigade splash around in the pool along with the ant, who was floating calmly from side to side.

He was certain that the actual area of the rooftop garden had expanded dramatically in order to accommodate all the requests that had been put forward to the camera man. True to his word though, the camera man had delivered even more.

Bruce was already munching his way through his third margherita pizza and each time he finished one another would appear brought by the camera man to replace the one he had previously eaten.

There was a water cooler which dispensed sparkling mineral water from the south island of New Zealand for Commander Winters and a large roller coaster, which wrapped itself around the sides of the building, for Private Lunatic.

This was unquestionably the best time Howard had experienced since his existence and he was happy to partake in all the fun. Anne Weavers could deal with these clouds if that was what she desired and he could stay in Plazennta on Chordona and relax. This was way better than conflict, that was for sure.

Howard and the group had been guaranteed their safety here whilst the differences and problems between the clouds and all the other folk from the other planets and dimensions were sorted out.

"Howard I have taken the liberty of having some green and black olives prepared for your consumption. There are cocktail sticks for you to use so you do not get your hands sticky."

Howard sat up to see the camera man standing over him, in all his rainbow-coloured glory, holding a small, white bowl filled with olives. It was just what he was going to order, so this was convenient to say the least.

"Thank you. I appreciate this, but how did you know?"

"It is merely intuition. Olives go very well with cappuccinos do they not?"

Howard beamed through his pizza box and nodded in agreement. The camera man vanished once more and left the group to it.

All Howard could think of now was taking a brief nap and then continuing to indulge. He shut his eyes and sank back converting his armchair more or less into a bed.

All was well until he was rudely interrupted by Commander Winters who, for whatever reason, was screaming and shouting at the top of his voice and he was not barking orders at his men. These were shrieks of fear.

"My leg, my leg, it looks weird what's happening to it."

The group all rushed around him, scrutinising his back, right foot. Instead of the usual, black hoof, it had changed colour. Just like everything else on Chordona, it now possessed all the colours of the rainbow, in hooped stripes across it.

Howard was the first to speak. "Just calm down Commander Winters while we assess it. Bruce can you see if there is anything, anything at all that can assist us?"

The encyclopaedia grunted and began to rifle through his pages.

"Eggo Maniac what do you think?"

No reply.

Howard attempted asking once more but in a louder voice, "Eggo Maniac what do you think?"

Still nothing.

He jumped up from the floor and scanned the rooftop. The murky-green egg was nowhere to be seen. He was about to begin searching for him before being brought back down to reality by the continued howling of Commander Winters.

Grabbing his shoulder, Howard attempted to settle him.

"Commander Winters, Commander Winters, I need you to calm down, otherwise I won't be able to figure out what to do about this incident. I need to ask you a few questions that will require very honest answers. Are you capable of this?"

The hysterical sheep controlled himself and stared at Howard directly in his pizza box face and nodded.

"Good," Howard continued, "I suppose the first question and arguably the most imperative to the situation is does it hurt?"

Commander Winters looked down at his foot. It was rather fetching in all honesty, then it struck him. His face turned from black to a deep shade of red. The extreme reaction he had held to having a multicoloured foot had got the better of him.

If there was one thing that Commander Winters took pride in, it was his appearance. He was a commander for crying out loud. Looking one's best was essential and that meant clean, black hooves and a prim and proper white coat of fur. This new 'image' was a travesty.

Slowly Commander Winters answered Howard in as meek a voice as anyone had ever heard him use.

"Well no it doesn't actually."

The group burst into laughter, which was short lived, due to the re-emergence of the camera man. He had rushed out onto the rooftop having listened to the painful sounds emitted by Commander Winters. He, too, was in a panic.

"Is everything okay out here? I heard shrieks and cries. What is going on?"

The camera man stood, still dressed in his suit, holding a tray (multicoloured of course) from which he was about to serve some more drinks. Bruce approached him and rested his arm on the camera man's shoulder.

"There's no terrible problem, only the ever so slight issue that the hoof of Commander Winters has turned the same colour as everything else on Chordona. It looks like a mini rainbow. I've been searching through my pages, which are pretty useless on any planet save for Earth, and have managed to find nothing. Surely you must understand how it works? Any assistance would be appreciated."

The group watched the camera man.

He adjusted his tie. He had developed quite the habit of doing this noted Howard. He wore a serious expression on his face and the group moved closer to him to listen intently.

As they did, he cracked completely.

The noise was almost as bad as the racket made by Commander Winters except this camera man was laughing, well he wasn't just laughing, he was splitting at the sides. Having lost control of his usual formal self, the camera man fell to the ground and literally rolled around.

"Clearly he doesn't get out much," said Howard to Bruce.

The encyclopaedia rolled his eyes. This fit of laughter had lasted long enough.

Gradually, the cluster of staring eyes got its wish and the camera man grew slightly more self-conscious about the presence of an audience.

Jumping up to his feet, he cleared his throat, straightened his tie again and attempted to mask his amusement through a serious expression.

"Do forgive me for that outburst. It is rare that I find anything humourous so when the occasions do arise I have to take them. I hope in some way I have put your minds at ease through my perception of the lack of gravity in the situation."

The group did not say a word, they merely shook their heads at him in unison.

The camera man, who by now had finally regained his composure, asked to see the affected area.

Commander Winters stepped forward sheepishly and revealed his multicoloured hoof, whilst the camera man knelt down ready to inspect it.

He touched it gently at first, but quickly gripped it firmly and began to rub at it with his hand. No matter how forceful he was with it, the colour would not come off. It was as if it had become the natural colour of Commander Winter's back right hoof.

Suddenly he stopped and sprang to his feet. "It is absolutely nothing to worry about Commander Winters, it is a perfectly normal adaptation to life on Chordona. It will not affect you in any way apart from the aesthetic aspect of course. It happens to us all," he said with a smile whilst pointing to his own multicoloured complexion as a way of referencing his point.

"What do you mean - *happens to us all?*" said Private Ostrich in a more than suspicious manner. This was one of the first times he had pulled his head out of his wool since they had been on Chordona.

Howard assumed that he must be able to see everything from inside; this would explain how he did not bump into anything when he moved around.

This question was met with warmth again from the camera man.

"What I mean is this; if any of you were to go on holiday on Earth, to say, a hotter climate than London and you were to sunbathe, what would happen to you?"

"We would get a tan I suppose, although I would use a lot of sun block, I burn very easily," said Commander Winters.

The camera man was quick to follow up.

"Right so that is the same here, except there are no negative aspects of turning multicoloured. You cannot be burnt as there is no sun that is fierce enough close to the planet. Here the planet assimilates everything on it naturally. Essentially what this means is that if you are here on Chordona then eventually your body will turn to the colours of the rainbow as it adapts to the planet.

It works at different speeds, so Commander Winters here is adapting far faster than the rest of you. It is completely harmless and we, as residents of the planet, like to view it as a bit of fun. You will have noticed that I changed colour instantly. That is because I have completely adapted to the planet. Anne also turned instantly, although I can appreciate you did not see her once we made it to this building.

The good news is that once you leave Chordona your normal colours will come back."

The group all sighed with relief at this in depth explanation. It made sense to them. Everything on the planet was the same set of colours, from paving stones to chairs to its inhabitants. There was no getting away from that.

The camera man observed them, they were all fairly cheerful about it and this made him feel better.

Howard, however, had one more question, "So if this is the case, is it the same for objects?"

"Of course it is. You will have noticed that my clothes, too, have altered in colour. Everything that comes onto Chordona changes temporarily whilst it is on the planet. We even have rainbow parties where everyone jumps into rainbow-coloured water. They are great fun. Perhaps I could take you to one if that sounds of interest?"

All nodded in agreement and a sense of joy and enthusiasm spread over the group, the likes of which had not been seen before. Howard joined in until the camera man left. He did not want to seem untrusting to someone who had given them so much, but he really was concerned about the whereabouts of Eggo Maniac.

He could not have gone far.

There was no way to leave the rooftop apart from the door which the camera man used, another thing that bothered Howard.

Were they trapped up there?

The shade had provided some much needed darkness and cover. It was unlike most beings to actively seek darkness, but the rainbow lights and rainbow everything had quite frankly been too much for Eggo Maniac to handle.

The murky-green egg had retired to the shadows, which, whilst he knew they were still bright and colourful underneath the dark, at least it was dark, if that made any sense at all.

He had been watching though the entire time. He had no wish to change colour, although he accepted from what the camera man had said that this was an inevitability. At least if he was hidden away he would not be able to see himself.

The peace and quiet afforded him some rare tranquility which he enjoyed. In his short life span he had not been on his own at any point and becoming conscious in the middle of Central London was hardly a quiet entrance into the universe.

A stone landed close to him and he flicked it away over the side of the roof. He had found a small corner, which was extremely shaded near the door that the camera man used to enter the rooftop.

Essentially Eggo Manaic was slumped up against the back wall of the small, brick, rectangular part of the building that hosted the door through which the camera man travelled.

The egg had been listening to absolutely everything and was pleased that someone had finally noticed that he was missing, not that he was attention seeking of course.

Another stone dropped in front of his knee. Quickly perousing the area, he could see that a few more were heading towards him. Eggo Maniac slowly rose to his feet as some landed behind him, where he had originally been standing.

He picked one up to examine it. Strangely, unlike everything else on Chordona, this particular piece of rock was blue, a light shade of sky-blue no less, if he was being precise, something in which Eggo Maniac took great pride.

He flicked it up into the air and noticed that it did not immediately crash back down onto the floor. Instead it hovered briefly, before slowly floating down to the ground. It was a very particular motion, as if the stone was in control if its descent. It certainly defied the laws of gravity back on Earth.

Perhaps things on Chordona were different he thought.

"Only one way to find out," said the egg to himself and with that he leapt into the air and instantly came hurtling back down to the floor.

As he did so a few more blue stones fell, then some more and then a lot more.

Looking up, Eggo Maniac could see what was now a shower of stones heading for him. Naturally he jumped out of the way, but quickly noticed that no matter where he moved, the stones altered their direction and remained on course for him.

Evidently there was no escape, so Eggo Maniac did what any brave warrior would do, crouched down in the shadows, shut his eyes tightly and hoped for the best.

The impact never came.

Granted it took Eggo Maniac a good five minutes to come

around to this and to have the courage to open his eyes and look, but at least he did not scream. That was progress in his eyes.

Once he had stumped up the guts to open his eyes he saw that he was completely surrounded by blue rubble. He was squatting within a circle of sky-blue rocks and remarkably felt quite pleased. Perhaps it was the fact that he had finally seen something on this wretched planet that was not a fountain of colour. The sky-blue was a refreshing change in an overly bright village.

He stood and went to pick up another stone to inspect it. Strangely he could not dislodge it from the rest of them. He attempted to pick up a different one, but again was met with the same problem.

Eggo Maniac tapped his foot in thought and then it dawned on him. He moved to kick the pile and see if he could shift them that way. As he swung his foot he stopped, just before the point of contact. This was not of his own volition of course and he adjusted himself in order to have another go.

The same thing occurred, except this time he could not return to an upright position – actually he could not return to any position whatsoever.

He was frozen. Someone or something had taken control of him.

He tried to shout for help, a regressive step, but he could not even mutter a sound.

A flash of light temporarily blinded him.

Once his vision was restored he could see that the pile of blue rubble was gone and standing in front of him now was a blue figure. It was a slim, but well built rock figure and was of course sky-blue. It possessed the physique of an athlete and had chiselled features making it a strangely captivating rock.

Its eyes were green and the only item of clothing it wore was a tattered old robe with a hood.

The wind fluttered slightly at it and blew the hood off its head revealing the rest of its striking, sky-blue, rocky head.

Eggo Maniac did not know what to do and simply remained in position, but with his jaw open in awe.

An awkward silence ensued until this was quickly broken up by the rock man speaking.

"You can move now. I only froze you so that you did not kick me. Hopefully you will have noticed that you have managed to open your mouth to quite a large degree, but that should be enough for you to realise that you can physically move. I mean you are balancing on one leg, which must be more uncomfortable than standing normally."

Eggo Maniac blushed and quickly changed his position so that he was now standing. He was about to giggle at his own stupidity, but it seemed that this man-made of rock lacked a sense of humour.

Once again silence had enveloped them.

Oddly enough, Eggo Maniac could no longer hear the noise from Howard, Bruce and the rest of the group. This did not concern him for the moment though, but what stood in front of him obviously did. He was being analysed and scrutinised by the rock figure's green eyes. He was not keen on this so attempted to reciprocate the gesture by glaring back.

This did not faze the rock man at all.

Obviously amused, he almost cracked a smile at Eggo Maniac's attempts.

The rock figure broke the silence, "Well that's fine Eggo Maniac, I can see that you are in good health, just as was expected. That means we can move on and begin phase two."

As he spoke, shrouds of black smoke shot up from the ground around them and covered everything, save for a small rectangle of air where Eggo Maniac and the rock man stood.

A wall and floor of smoke had surrounded the pair and the height of it was such that Eggo Maniac could not see his feet.

Above him the sky had dramatically changed to produce a dark stormy night. A harsh wind blew around the pair, although it was not powerful enough to shift any of the smoke.

Once the bleak picture had painted itself the rock figure addressed Eggo Maniac.

"First of all I must apologise for the dramatisation of these events. It is necessary in order to shield our meeting from 'some' other prospective enemies.

I am Emereldon, an ambassador for a secret sect of creatures that we refer to as CL8. Now I appreciate that, during your short existence, things have been particularly hectic for you. Since your inception you have encountered bizarre being after odd entity and frankly have discovered more of the unknown in this universe than most will in a lifetime.

Back on your home planet of Earth everything is running smoothly and as normal. Are you okay so far or do you have any questions at this point?"

Eggo Maniac presumed that Emereldon had asked him this

because he was twitching – something he had only just developed when he was anxious it seemed. He did have questions, many questions, but there were two key ones that he just could not get away from, "Well I would like to know two things. Firstly how you came across my name, although the whole universe appears to know it anyway and…"

"We have been paying close attention to you and your allies, particularly as soon as you met Anne Weavers and the camera man. We have been monitoring your movements and behaviour. In some instances we have been impressed with what we have seen; in others, not so much.

Do not fret though Eggo Maniac, unlike others we shall be open with our plans and designs for you and your group. It is unfortunate that you have been caught up in the middle of quite a large, universal dispute. It is still possible to escape it though, if you listen to us."

Emereldon paused, he sensed that this would be an ideal opportunity for Eggo Maniac to lodge his second and final request. He was correct.

"So if that is the case and I do not doubt you Emereldon, your points raised are the same as all the other folk I have met. Everyone wants to help us yet we don't know why. In saying that, that is not my second question, it was more of a statement really."

Emereldon nodded in agreement, urging the egg to continue.

"You said earlier 'we'. Who are the others that you are referring to?"

Emereldon's sky-blue face lit up with a short, but sweet grin.

This question had pleased him. It was something that he obviously wanted to answer.

"Of course Eggo Maniac, I shall be transparent with you as promised earlier. Reveal yourselves."

Out of the fog, stepped three figures. All wore black, tattered robes, similar to those worn by Emereldon. The difference was that these three all had their entire bodies covered as their garments were wrapped tightly around them.

Eggo Maniac looked to identify their faces; alas this too was an impossibility. As opposed to faces, the hoods of the robes hosted nothing. They were empty. No one could even decipher a feature.

Thick, black smog was all that was there in place and quite frankly Eggo Maniac quivered. It was times like these when he wished he could have had an ordinary life. The only noticeable difference that Eggo Maniac could decipher were their body shapes.

The first one to come into view sported a sleek and slender physique. It was highly likely that she was female.

He glanced at the second one and its body could not have been further from the first. If the first physique was impressive, this was quite the opposite. It was huge and resembled a lump of lard. It was intriguing, as, whilst the size was undeniably large, the shape of the body kept changing. It moved in all directions and shifted back and forth. Surprisingly the robe managed to hold it all in.

Finally Eggo Maniac set his eyes on the last, possibly the most mysterious of the bunch, if that was possible seeing as they were all covered up. This figure was odd because it gave Eggo Maniac the impression that it had no body at all. The garments seemed to just float around amongst the smoke. It was strange because the other two wore their robes tightly against their bodies, obviously to conceal them, but this one did not bother for logical reasons. You can't hide something if you do not have it in the first place.

This was the final straw.

Eggo Maniac could take it no more, "Th-th-they're ghosts."

The group laughed in unison. It was so slick that it appeared rehearsed.

Regardless of this Eggo Maniac remained fearful. It was difficult not to when you were engulfed with smoke and had four figures dressed in robes, three of which you could not see, surrounding you.

Gradually the laughter calmed down, once again eerily at the same time.

After a brief second of silence Emereldon spoke in a very clear but firm tone, "Do not worry Eggo Manaic. My associates here are alive and well, in fact you can refer to my associates as guardians."

Chapter 11
Trust Issues

Rod awoke.

Well at least that's what he thought he had done. He was unsure whether he had been conscious or not. He predicted it was more like a state of limbo when one is half asleep and half awake.

Regardless he was refreshed and bounced up instantly to take in his surroundings. The prospect of a guardian being there to meet him, or rather destroy him, was all he required to ensure that he was alert.

Fortunately for him there was no such problem; well not yet anyway.

He was in a navy-blue room that was about the size of an average earthling living room. Surprisingly it was very colourful and upon closer inspection he could see the four walls were adorned with socks; yes that's correct, socks. They were all of different shapes and sizes and featured a variety of patterns. In many ways it was the patterns and not the array of colours that were problematic. Stripes, polka dots, chequered, whatever one could think of was there for all to see. Bizarre was not the word for it.

"At least they are clean," said Rod to himself. He switched back to maintaining his alert stance as there could still be a guardian lurking somewhere, although not in this room. He searched for a door and sure enough, behind a load of fluorescent pink and green socks with stars on them, one was hidden.

Rod opened it without thought and continued into the next room.

This particular place was far larger than his previous surroundings. It was more akin to a hall where folk would go to watch concerts and the like.

Within it were, as before, socks, except of course there were more of them as the wall space was greater. The walls were blood-red in colour, although it was tricky to see that, as the plethora of socks made it difficult to look through to the plaster underneath.

Rod's attention was immediately taken away from the décor when he heard something emanating from the far right hand corner of the hall. It was a sort of muffled sound, as if something was trapped.

He rushed over and low and behold in front of him was an enormous stocking – far bigger than any of those that some earthlings put up in December. It was at least the size of an average door.

Relatively plain in appearance, it did not look menacing at all. Blue and green, hooped stripes ran down it, but it was the motions from within that were concerning.

Rod could see very clear hands that were punching around inside it, desperate to break free. The sounds were impossible to decipher as it did not resemble a language of any sort.

Rod pondered on this for a fleeting moment. Was this yet another test? He was getting sick of them by now. He had heard stories about how difficult it was to gain an audience with the masters, but this was ridiculous.

He put himself in the position of whoever or whatever was trapped inside. He would want someone to rescue him without question. That's what he would do then.

He prodded the stocking at first, touching the captive, which actually seemed to calm it down as it did not thrash around so much. He then floated upward ever so slightly, mindful that he should not exceed his floating range, to grab the top of the stocking.

"I wouldn't do that if I were you," said a voice.

It was the stocking.

Rod clung onto the top of it anyway.

"Why have you trapped something inside you?"

The stocking shook itself and Rod tumbled down to the floor below.

He sprang up and confronted the oversized sock. It had red eyes and a red mouth, much like the door guardian.

"You're a feisty one aren't you? Usually when I speak to anything that makes it this far, they run a mile, don't they folks?"

As the stocking finished his sentence, the entire hall erupted with laughter.

Rod performed a fast rotation to see that all the socks now had little red eyes and mouths and all must have been sentient beings.

"You though Rod, you though, I like you. You have some guts."

The voice of this stocking was still inexplicably loud. Obviously it only possessed one volume setting which was full blast.

Rod was getting fed up now. He had just about had enough of this and the expression on his face portrayed this.

"Listen to me, just release whoever is in there. I am done with these tests and I think I'm nearly at the point of being done with meeting the bosses. How insane is this procedure just to speak to some mysterious ruler? It does not make any sense at all. If I want my voice to be heard then should it not be straight forward?

Even the humans have managed freedom of speech. Are we

that far behind? I have been forced down a big slide, made to bargain with a door that incidentally is capable of destruction; made to pick a door that, if I should get it wrong and the chances are that I would, forces me to meet my doom at the hands of a guardian, either through illness, being eaten or goodness knows what?

Is this really the manner in which a society should be governed? We don't even have elections. These bosses, whoever they may be, are protected for what? They run this cloud kingdom through fear and that is it. The other citizens are terrified to approach them.

Poor Yod met his end because he was in a state of panic worrying that he would be punished, and guess what, he was punished anyway…"

"Yod is over there," said the stocking.

Rod quickly swivelled around and faced the opposing corner of the hall. There were just socks, lots of different coloured socks, all with red eyes and faces. The pink cloud scrutinised the area, but all he saw was the same. Convinced that this large stocking was wrong, Rod had to ask.

"Where? I can only see more socks. It's hardly likely that Yod is underneath them now is it?"

"You are mistaken Rod. Go over there and check the small sunshine-yellow sock, fourth from the bottom and third from the left of the wall," said the stocking.

Rod complied and floated over to investigate the sock. As he moved he continuously checked back over his shoulder. He did not trust this stocking for a second.

All of the socks found in this corner of the hall were

significantly smaller than the rest. Rod noted that, as he surveyed the room to the far right hand corner where the huge stocking was hung, the socks got progressively bigger. Perhaps it was some kind of pattern.

The sunshine-yellow garment that he had been asked to look at carefully just stared blankly at him. It didn't speak nor did it show any real expression.

There was something oddly familiar about it and Rod felt that he had a stronger connection with it, although it was still small. Slowly it raised a brief, fleeting smile at Rod and then slumped back to its ordinary, emotionless expression.

A shiver ran through Rod like one he had never experienced. The gravity of the situation had set in.

"Yes well the new recruits are the smaller ones, they hang in that corner and as they move through the ranks and grow they are granted to move and place themselves further up the wall. It's a very fair system."

He could hardly pay attention to the rambling of the stocking now. He moved closer to the yellow sock.

"Yod, Yod is that you?"

The sock did not answer through speech, but desperately wriggled itself up and down in an attempt to create a gesture of agreement. A tear fell from its eye.

"I shall get you out of this," said Rod.

"What are you saying to it Rod? There is no time for idle chit-chat with a fallen one. You must return to me and learn of your next test and step that you must take to meet the bosses."

This time the stocking's words echoed through the room more

than usual as if it had raised its voice, if that was possible.

Rod faced the stocking. The creature inside it had started to move and throw itself around again. Its cries were more audible this time and it must have been convinced that Rod had abandoned it.

Rod touched the stocking and whatever was inside began to calm itself again, as it knew that Rod was indeed still present.

The pink cloud looked up at the red face of the striped stocking. It was cheerful now, showing off an arrogant façade, as if it had Rod precisely where it wanted him. As opposed to being intimidated, Rod was determined not to toe the line.

"How long have you been here?"

The stocking was slightly confused by this. It was rare for anyone to question it and yet this cloud seemed to be showing it a certain amount of interest. Hastily it responded.

"I have been here the longest. You can see that by the fact that I am the largest and most powerful of the others here." It beamed with pride at this statement.

Rod chuckled.

This upset his counterpart, "What are you giggling at? I am by far the most powerful here. That is without question. I already have one prisoner within me and I could just as easily take another."

The threats made no difference to Rod's amusement and, if anything, spurred him on even more. Between breaths he spoke, "There is always great pride before a fall."

The laughter continued and Rod could see that the stocking had gradually been getting angrier and had now reached the point where livid would be the only fair way to describe it.

"In all my years of guarding this place I have never met such an insolent and petulant fool as you. You cannot be well studied in our history can you? You're supposed to have a rant and then we barter for your exit and if you lose you end up like this cloud who sits inside me now. I'll begin the process of eliminating him shortly, perhaps that will have to wait briefly as I intend to take you first."

"So it is a cloud inside you then?" said Rod, who was still, despite the harsh words of the stocking, finding the whole situation very humourous indeed.

"That's it Rod. I am going to take you and I shall love it. Don't you have any respect? Don't you know who I am?"

At this point Rod stopped laughing immediately. His eyes ceased smiling and focussed on the face of the overgrown sock. His lips were straight and expressionless. He allowed his arms to drop by his sides and he stood as straight as possible.

He moved towards the stocking so he could stare straight into its eyes. He had invaded its personal space and was now floating directly in front of it. There was no way that the stocking could have averted its gaze if it had wanted to as Rod was simply too close.

For the first time in its living memory the stocking quivered, only slightly, but it was enough for Rod to notice and more importantly it was enough to further empower him, as he knew he had it where he wanted it. Rod spoke slowly and in an extremely clear manner. There was absolutely no mistaking his words.

"No is the answer to your question. I do not know who you are."

He stopped.

He observed.

The expression on the stocking's face ran through every possible emotion one could imagine. It was like an actor attempting to show a full range of feelings during an audition. As this occurred Rod moved backwards and waited.

The stocking began to plead, but not with Rod, with itself.

"I don't know who I am. Please tell me who I am? How long have I been here? I don't even know where I am from. How did I get here? How do I get out?"

It repeated the same questions over and over again until finally it let out a scream, not unlike that of a banshee. Some of the socks, including the yellow Yod, were blown from their place, such was the sheer velocity of it.

Interestingly enough a door just to the right of it was blown open too. Clearly an exit of some sort mused Rod as he continued to observe the stocking. His plan was working perfectly.

Suddenly it stopped. The red face faded from view. Rod dashed to the striped sock and opened the top of it. He could see a hand thrashing about and he grabbed it, hauling it out in the process.

A couple of bumps later and Rod was on the floor along with the other cloud he had managed to rescue.

It was Tod.

This surprised him no end, yet he did not have time to dwell on it. Tod was about to thank him, but Rod cut him off instantly.

"No Tod, there is no time for that. I am going to grab Yod over there and you are to make your way through the door that has conveniently opened next to your lovely stocking friend."

Tod was about to question the fact that he was being given orders by a subordinate. Having quickly realised that he did not have a leg to stand on, well he was a cloud, he obeyed and rushed through the exit.

Yod was easy to locate due to his bright, sunshine-yellow colour and also because he was one of the few socks to fall off the wall. There were only a couple more, a grey and a pink, and Rod thought that perhaps these had a bit more character still left in them and had managed to help themselves off in a bid to escape.

Seeing as it would be unfair to abandon the two others if they had made such an effort, Rod picked them up too and made his way through the door to reunite with Tod.

He had no idea where this new attitude was coming from, but he didn't have any time for reflection anyway.

Racing through the door he could see Tod up ahead, making his way down a narrow passage. It was silver in colour and was well lit, as the previous room had been. Unlike the previous area however, traditional flaming wall torches adorned the walls and the surroundings were quite plain.

Rod even found himself looking into any nooks and crannies to ensure there were no more socks or stockings about as he caught up with Tod.

Initially neither wished to speak to the other regarding the previous incidents. Rod did not want to upset Tod's ego and make him feel inadequate and Tod felt particularly embarrassed that his inexperienced friend had had to rescue him. They both made a mutual decision not to mention it; of course neither told the other this and they tried to carry on as usual.

"What comes next Tod?" said Rod. He was still clutching the three socks he had rescued. None of them bore a face anymore and to the odd passer by, not that there would be any around this area, they would have appeared as standard, run of the mill socks.

Snapping back into his normal, confident persona Tod replied, "Well Rod, for starters there is good news because the room filled with socks that we ended up in meant that we chose the correct archway and therefore means that we have avoided the guardians."

Well that was positive thought Rod, although it wasn't as if the stocking was an easy thing to handle. Rod could sense himself beginning to settle back into his previous role of acceptance. Earlier he had become quite enraged with regard to the very make up of the cloud society and the reign of the bosses. Now he just wished to speak with them again.

At the end of the corridor was a small, indiscriminate, brown, wooden door. It would not have looked out of place as a simple front door for an earthling cottage. It did contrast with all the shining, silver walls and floor, almost as if it was not supposed to be there.

"You are quite right Rod. This simply is not meant to be here."

Rod squinted squeamishly at his friend, "Not another trick Tod?"

"Yes I'm afraid it is Rod, but this time it's a good one. It means that the bosses are willing to grant us an audience with them."

An enormous smile graced Tod's face. Rod could not recall another time that he had seen his friend so happy.

"So we can see them?" said Rod.

Tod gave him a thumbs up and then reverted to one of his short but sweet, history lessons.

"Now Rod, you will understand that this is a trick. Had this door not materialised when it did, it would have suggested that the bosses had no desire to admit us entry to their domain. One must prove one's worth first. That is the whole point of all these tests and encounters with various guardians and... stockings, I suppose.

We have qualified for a meeting fairly early. Under normal circumstances this silver corridor would have led us into a maze that is colossal in size. It is so large that we cannot truly comprehend its size. Many clouds are still roaming it now, desperately seeking an exit.

So we deserve to be absolutely elated that they have decided it is fine for us to see them."

Rod did not share in Tod's jubilation. Instead he put on a show for his friend to mask his lack of excitement. Those feelings of rebellion were reoccurring in his mind. This was perhaps due to watching his friend's acceptance of a system that was so clearly wrong.

Ensuring he held the three socks tightly in his grasp, Rod moved to stand in front of the brown door alongside Tod. It swung open towards them, forcing the pair to jump out of the way, narrowly evading it.

"That would have smashed me up against the wall," said Rod.

Tod held a far calmer opinion, "Worry not Rod. It was just another test. We have passed it so let's just go inside and hope they listen to us."

"Would you like some trivial information Tod?"

"If you must Rod."

166

"I have forgotten the reason that we wished to speak with them in the first place."

Tod grimaced at Rod, grabbed his hand and then marched him through the door.

Chapter 12
Recycling Choices

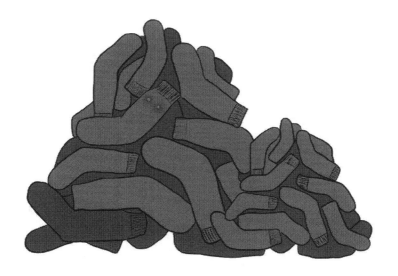

The guardians varied drastically in size, stature and basically everything.

Emereldon had asked them to reveal themselves to Eggo Maniac; well he had asked two of them. Strangely there was one that he did not ask.

The first dropped its robe onto the floor and resembled a large blob of red slime that moved continuously. This was the bigger of the group. It declared that its name was Slimax.

The second to reveal itself was the empty robe. Eggo Maniac instantly saw why this was the case. This guardian was merely an enormous mouth with brown eyes. He could see some faint bits of red skin accompanied by some harsh black fur, but that was all. This guardian was named Eator.

The third and final guardian did not disrobe. Instead she just whispered in a soft, almost tranquil voice. Eggo Maniac would have been content to just sit and listen to her speak all day. Her name was Miss Terious.

Guardians introduced and assembled, Emereldon once again took the lead and addressed Eggo Maniac.

"I think I need to make it clear that you have only been told one side of the story by this Anne Weavers whom you were oh so unfortunate to encounter.

You see Eggo Maniac, Anne Weavers, this camera man, they are all part of a nefarious scheme to topple the Adamantium; the dimension of the universe in which Earth resides.

We have been sent by the clouds, and yes I know that you have been told that we commenced a war between many planets and part of that is true. I did say to you earlier that I was not willing to lie to you.

However we stopped it. Seeing the damage that was done, the clouds pulled all forces back and sealed off the two dimensions. This meant that the gap between the dimensions could not be accessed by either side.

Anyhow it appears that this is no longer the case as this Anne Weavers and her camera man friend have been operating on Earth for a considerable time now. They are intent on rekindling the war with the clouds and we must stop this from happening. Can you help us Eggo Maniac?"

The murky-green egg looked bewildered for a short time and then quickly altered his expression to that of disdain.

In truth this was something that Emereldon had anticipated. Why should Eggo Maniac put his faith in them when they could just as easily be using him as was Anne Weavers.

The blue, rocky figure waved at the other three guardians. They all nodded and retreated back into the smoke, to a position where they were now out of sight; the less intimidation at this point the better.

"Listen Eggo Maniac, it is true that you have been created by the clouds and to an extent it is true that your purpose was for our television ratings. However it is certainly not the case anymore.

Through you the clouds stumbled upon a far more dangerous plot and as such have agreed to let you and your friends go free once everything is sorted. There will be no more enormous cups of coffee attacking you or weird entities hassling you. It will all be over and you can live out a peaceful existence. Surely that is what you want?"

The egg shook his head.

"Well what is it that you desire?"

After a moment of silence Eggo Maniac gathered his thoughts, "What I desire Emereldon is to be a super, no, a megastar. I want to be rich and famous."

Emereldon took a step back. This was not what he had expected. Perhaps he had misjudged the egg. A quick change of plan would not be too hard though.

"That will be tricky, but I think it is possible to work something out. First of all I must gain your trust. I am completely aware that I do not have it as yet, nor did I expect to have it this quickly, for you are of a higher intelligence than most of the clouds' creations."

"Flattery will get you nowhere," said Eggo Maniac.

"I simply wish to show you what is currently going on with your friends. Is this something you would be interested in? I am only asking for your time, nothing more. Is that an acceptable proposition?"

Eggo Maniac nodded.

"Very well then." Emereldon raised his arm into the air and the stormy clouds departed. Both were now standing in the shadows on top of the building in Plazennta, back on Chordona.

Casually Emereldon wandered out onto the rainbow-coloured roof and stood in front of Howard, who was lying back on his reclining armchair, reading a novel named Nocterna.

Eggo Maniac rushed to the side of the rocky man.

"Can't he see you?"

Emereldon shook his head, "No he cannot. We are both shielded from view and from their touch. It is quite possible that should your friend Howard wish to stand up and walk through the very space in which we are standing, he could and he would feel nothing. Neither would we. It would be like walking through thin air."

Eggo Maniac didn't bother asking how this worked, why it occurred or whether it was magic or not. Little shocked him now and this was no different. It was just another element added to the list.

One thing though that did spike his interest was the state of Commander Winters. The usually proud sheep had altered his appearance somewhat drastically. Instead of the usual, pristine-white, woolly coat that he wore, he now sported one that was rainbow-coloured, much like everything else on Chordona.

In fairness Eggo Maniac had listened to the camera man's speech regarding adaptation on Chordona and assumed that his friends were having a great time; hence the speed at which they were changing colour. Upon further inspection he saw that all the group had at least some multicoloured aspects to them. Howard's pizza box head, the front cover of Bruce, the hooves of the Sheep Brigade and even the giant ant's back legs had all shed their original look and moved to the planetary-standard, rainbow colours.

Quickly he stared down at his feet and stretched in all sorts of weird and wonderful positions to see whether or not he had begun to adapt.

Emereldon had remained silent for this time. He observed the odd positions that the egg put himself through before speaking.

"Worry not Eggo Maniac. You have not been tainted. This is why we came to find you."

"What do you mean tainted?"

Eggo Maniac swiftly returned to a standard position and glared at the blue figure. For once there was a slight look of shock on the rock man's face.

"You mean you do not know? The guardians and I assumed that you understood the seriousness of the situation and this was the reason that you withdrew from the group and went into hiding.

Evidently this is not the case. I brought you here so that we could quickly check on your friends and to show you just how bad the situation has become before moving on and explaining the next step of our mission. I see now that I shall need to enlighten you."

Eggo Maniac averted his eyes and gazed at the ground below him. He loathed it when he did not know something. It had become one of his pet hates.

Emereldon ignored his sulking and started his explanation, "Your friends have been tainted and to be blunt, many are further along the process than that. They are essentially being poisoned and the rate of their progress can be gauged by their colour. For example the large ant over there has only had the rainbow spread to its back two legs; Commander Winters on the other hand, whose whole body is multicoloured, is further down the road."

"What do you mean poisoned? We, I mean they, were told that it was simply adapting to life on Chordona. You can see that the buildings, plants, roads, citizens and everything are the same. Even the camera man is the same colour."

"And Anne Weavers?"

Eggo Maniac pondered on this for a moment. It was true that he had not yet seen Anne change colour, but then the last occasion he had been with her she was on the ship. If he was honest with himself, he had not yet encountered her on Chordona.

Under normal circumstances that would have been a perfectly sound explanation for Eggo Maniac and he would have been happy with that. Something bothered him though. There was something that was not right. If what Emereldon said was true then he needed more information.

"What do you mean poisoned?"

"I can sense that you are beginning to trust me, which is good. Your friends have been poisoned along with all the other inhabitants of this planet. You can see for yourself that this poison is so potent that it has affected even the very buildings too. Nothing has escaped it, even inanimate objects have fallen to it. That is everything except you."

Eggo Maniac brushed aside this fact, as for once he was more concerned about the welfare of others as opposed to himself.

"What do you mean by poison though? I know what poison is generally, but is it lethal, what are the effects? What does it do?"

"It controls all those that succumb to it. Whilst the poison itself is not physically harmful, it is a powerful mind controlling tool that Anne Weavers has used to enslave this world. The more you indulge in the so called paradise that she offers you, then the faster your journey to becoming one of her servants will be.

We believe she witnessed the fight between you all and the coffee cup and captured you to work for her. Her sole aim is to destroy the clouds and then, I would hazard a guess, to rule everything."

Eggo Maniac again paused to digest these next particles of information. It made logical sense. That was of couse, if he trusted Emereldon and these guardians though Anne could have been telling the truth also.

Sensing the air of caution surrounding the egg Emereldon recalled his guardians. They emerged within a flash yet Eggo Manaic did not take a blind bit of notice of them.

The blue figure spoke, "I cannot begin to understand how you must be feeling. Everyone or thing that you have ever trusted has, to put it mildly, screwed you over; that is aside from your group of friends out there, but believe me they have been poisoned.

They will act differently when you next meet them and please bear in mind that it is not their fault. Anything they do from here on in is not of their own volition. They are being controlled. I do not wish to pressure you so this is how we shall approach the situation. I shall give you this."

Lunging forward Emereldon grabbed Eggo Maniac's arm and clutched it tightly.

The egg tried to resist, but as he did the grip tightened further and he could see there was no escape, especially with the guardians surrounding him.

The body of Emereldon began to glow; it was a turquoise shade and to the average eye would have appeared to be a silhouette surrounding the rock like figure.

Gradually it spread from his hand and moved to surround Eggo Maniac. The pair of them were now engulfed by this energy. There was great concentration on Emereldon's face and it was quite apparent that this, whatever he was doing, required a great deal of strength, both physically and mentally.

He looked in pain.

There was no suffering on the other hand for Eggo Maniac. He quite enjoyed the process. He tingled at first and gradually became more relaxed. A state of tranquility consumed him and he did not want it to end.

A brief flash of light quickly brought him back to his senses and reality.

Emereldon waved his hand. Steam was coming from it, but it quickly died down as he shook it vigorously.

"We shall now take our leave Eggo Maniac and allow you to discover things for yourself. We are willing to give you a few hours and will monitor your actions. I can only hope that you make the right decision. Please remember both sides of the story when you inevitably cross paths with that camera man or Anne Weavers. Goodbye."

"No wait. What if I get poisoned?"

The guardians turned their backs and faded from sight.

Emereldon, who had also positioned himself to leave, grabbed Eggo Maniac by the shoulder and shook his other hand firmly.

"Worry not my friend. There are many issues that you will encounter shortly, but the rainbow poison is not one of them. When I took your hand earlier, I passed on some of my energy. It will act as an antidote when the toxins of the poison begin to come into contact with you.

I can only advise you at present, as you have yet to choose a side, but I would indulge and spend time with your friends. If you do not get involved with the debauchery taking place then I would fear that the camera man would suspect you. So go, order what you want and have fun, but remember what I told you."

He released his grip and walked away.

Before Eggo Maniac could even mutter goodbye, Emereldon was gone. What in blazes would he do now? There were still so many questions he had.

The facts he knew for certain were that there were two sides in an interdimensional dispute and he had to pick one.

His choices were either Anne Weavers and her lot, although camera man aside he had not met anyone else but presumed they would be some of the rainbow natives of Chordona, or he could side with Emereldon and these guardians who represented the clouds, that had created him and his friends. This was not going to be an easy choice.

"Eggo Maniac, Eggo Maniac, there you are. We have been searching for you all over this rooftop. Where have you been?"

The cries from Howard took him away from his train of thought. Evidently whatever had been keeping Emereldon invisible was not working anymore and he was clear for all to see.

Half of Howard's body was now covered in the colours of the rainbow from his head down to his stomach. Perhaps those guardians were right.

"Erm, hi Howard, it just got a bit too much for me so I went for a nap. I see you are all having a good time."

His friend grinned at him through his pizza box features, "Yes, yes, we are having a fabulous time now come and sit down and let's order some more food."

Eggo Maniac grabbed a chair and sat back into it. It was comfortable, as if the seat had been shaped specifically for him. It felt wonderful. He stretched out and as he did a glass of sparkling mineral water was placed into his hand.

He opened his eyes to see the camera man smiling at him. Somehow he had managed to predict the exact drink that Eggo Maniac desired. He chose not to think anything of it and replied to Howard.

"Sure I'll join you. I was getting a little bit peckish anyway."

The pair leaned forward towards each other and chinked glasses. Well Emereldon had told Eggo Maniac to enjoy himself. This was an opportunity which he was not going to miss.

Darkness shrouded everything around Rod and Tod. They could see nothing. It was pitch-black. Although Rod was aware that he was standing next to Tod, he could not see him. That is how dark it was.

The pink cloud held his hand in front of his face and struggled to see even its outline. Reaching out his left hand he touched Tod's shoulder, just to ensure he was still there. Fortunately he was.

"Worry not Rod. This is perfectly standard. As you have probably gathered the bosses are a touch secretive."

"No, No, Tod I would never have predicted that." Rod stopped quickly. This was neither the time nor the place for sarcasm.

As they had floated through the door there had been an odd buzzing sound and suddenly they were here, in the middle of wherever they were.

By Rod's estimation they had now been waiting for approximately ten minutes. This was hardly endearing him to these bosses; mind you if they were as powerful and as all-seeing as they were supposed to be, they would have been fully aware of this by now, following his rant with the stocking and his thoughts in general.

A tiny flame of bright, yellow light flickered in front of them briefly before moving to their left, right and finally behind them. As it circled them it grew in size until they were surrounded by a ring of fire.

Both Rod and Tod were unmoved by this and remained still. Eventually the circle of fire split into four huge fireballs, each one moving to a different area of the room.

The first moved in front of them, the second to the right, third to the left and finally the fourth behind them. Each fireball then morphed into a round, bright, yellow face.

Rod examined them all and strangely they all showed precisely the same expression. If one blinked the others did too. If one raised its lip, all did. At least some light emanated from them. Useful as candles then thought Rod.

"Why can't we just speak to someone? Everything is just smoke and mirrors. I am really starting to get…"

"Fed up, is that what you were going to say Rod?" said each of the yellow heads in unison.

Rod grinned at the face in front of him, "I understand it now. So you are all the same entity. That's why you do everything together."

"Incorrect, we are different but share the same opinion. It is an example of how close we are in our opinions," said the faces.

Immediately Rod felt a nudge in his ribs from Tod. His friend was livid at the lack of respect he had so far displayed to the bosses.

The heads spoke again, "Calm yourself Tod. We have acknowledged that you do not share the same opinions as your friend.

You have shown us that you have a sense of propriety even when others do not."

Rod yawned. "So you are the bosses then? May I ask why it is so difficult to speak with you? What would happen if someone needed to tell you about something that was incredibly urgent? They might not reach you and then you would not find out."

The faces all laughed. It was a horrendous noise and as they all chuckled away in unison, sounded quite eerie too.

"Worry not Rod and Tod. We shall discover it anyway. You yourselves have some urgent news for us do you not? I believe it involves some creatures you have created, who have crossed over into another dimension? Anne Weavers, Eggo Maniac, Howard, Bruce, a giant ant and a Sheep Brigade; oh and let's not neglect to mention the camera man."

The faces were smiling now. They were mocking the two clouds and were highly amused.

This time it was Tod who wished to answer them.

Rod noticed through the dimly lit room that Tod was changing colour.

His usual, calm purple shade was altering to that of a dark thundercloud. He was upset, extremely upset by the look of things. It did not even cross Rod's mind to attempt to control his friend. He was relishing the fact that the bosses were about to get a piece of his mind.

They were not aware of this as they continued to laugh.

Tod cleared his throat and began in a quiet but firm tone.

"Will you please clarify what you meant by informing us that you would discover it anyway? Are you insinuating that this journey to find you, not to mention all journeys to find you, are pointless?"

The faces ceased their noise immediately and answered the question with a very serious demeanour.

"As your bosses, we do not have to tell you of our ways. You have no right to ask us. We are secretive in our methods because we are better judges if we rule from afar. It means we do not get involved with any of you – it means there will be no decisions made based on emotion.

Every choice we make is a practical and sensible one that allows us to steer and guide the clouds in the right direction for success.

The reason it is so hard to contact us is that we would rather you did not. That's why few, if any, ever make it. We know exactly what has happened. You are all monitored carefully. Tod you are one of the only clouds to ever make it to us twice. Rod you were impressive in getting here and initially it was our opinion that you would not make it."

"So hang on then, every decision you make relates purely to the advancement of the clouds, no matter how harsh on particular individuals?"

"That is correct Tod. We are mildly pleased that you have figured this out. The clouds are the top species in this dimension and we intend to keep it that way."

Tod, who was still visibly irritated, raised his voice slightly. "So you're telling me that everything we have done was in vain, as you already knew?"

The four faces nodded.

"Yes and you will be pleased to learn that the situation is being dealt with accordingly. We have sent the guardians and one other significant entity after Anne Weavers to stop her and bring the others back.

We shall then take control of the show you were producing, finish it and air it on TV for the general public. You're quite lucky that the guardians were not present, as we were going to send you to them for recycling."

This was the final straw for Tod who was now seething, almost frothing at the mouth in rage.

Rod on the other hand was quite calm. He was intrigued to know what Tod was going to do next. He enjoyed unpredictable situations though he was slightly concerned about the recycling statement.

"What do you mean recycled?" said Tod.

"It means the end for whoever is recycled. It is a necessary option for us to have. It is what happens to the majority of clouds who seek an audience with us. We must maintain our secrecy."

Tod was about to yell at the bosses, but Rod grabbed him and held his hand over his mouth.

"Now is not the time to get angry Tod. We need to stay calm as I fear they have plans for us that we are not going to like," said Rod.

The pink cloud then spoke to the face on the right of him, "So what now for us? I mean you are fully aware of why we came to see you, therefore that is sorted. I presume we can leave now. Which way is it?"

The faces showed no emotion as they replied.

"We are afraid you know too much and are now scheduled to be recycled. We cannot have you returning to society and informing everyone about the fact that we know and see all that goes on. We must protect our secrecy."

"What. That's outrageous, why don't you tell the clouds that you know about everything that occurs? That way nobody has to risk a life by taking a perilous trip to speak to you."

Tod screamed the last line and Rod grabbed him once more to calm him down. He thought he should have stuffed his mouth full of socks, but that would have been harsh on Yod and the others that he had rescued, to be stuck in Tod's mouth.

The faces took a stern approach.

"It is to maintain our secrecy. That is all."

Tod lunged forward and attempted to grab the head in front of him.

Rod moved for the one to the right.

All four heads faded from view, throwing the room back into the pitch-black darkness it was before. A gust of wind blew through the room, then another and shortly after that another.

Rod had a moment of realisation and warned his friend. "Tod grab onto something, anything you can find. This room is about to become like a vacuum cleaner."

The two clouds scrambled around feeling and touching anything they could, desperately hoping to find something that offered them some grip.

Rod clutched on to what felt like a table and Tod was on top of what he thought was a chest of drawers, hugging it as if everything depended on it.

The air flowing into the room was fiercer now. Its intensity had risen dramatically and Rod and Tod were fully aware of this. The velocity grew and everything in the room was rattling.

Both pieces of furniture rocked back and forth and the clouds could feel the wind attempting to suck everything out.

Once more the wind rose in intensity. Rod began to lose his grip, Tod was stretched out, flailing in the air, his grip, too, was loosening.

A final, unstoppable burst smashed through the room. The clouds clung on gallantly but this was too much.

Chapter 13
Breakthrough

"Ha ha ha ha ha. That's funny," said Eggo Maniac as he gulped down some more mineral water.

Howard had undeniably become quite the comedian and he was thoroughly entertaining.

Eggo Maniac was relishing his surroundings and had never felt this rested before. At present he had everything he could possibly desire. If there was anything else he could think of, the camera man would simply bring it to him.

Perhaps Emereldon and those guardians were wrong and Anne Weavers and the camera man were just genuinely lovely people.

He quickly scanned his own body up and down to make sure that there were no rainbow markings on him.

There were not, so he sat back and continued to soak up the atmosphere. Everyone was cheerful and all were relaxed. He noticed that Commander Winters was now fully covered in the rainbow colours. Actually the majority of the group was almost there; that is everyone except for him.

He still maintained his murky-green colour and was beginning to feel slightly conscious of this. Fortunately none of the others showed any signs of being bothered by his lack of change which did help.

A tap on his shoulder caused Eggo Maniac to jump up and turn around, clearly his nerves were not quite at ease.

It was the camera man. "I am sorry to bother you Eggo Maniac, but would you please come with me. We would just like to have a little chat if that is possible?"

He smiled as he spoke which made Eggo Maniac slightly ill at ease. He couldn't very well refuse as he had been asked so nicely and that would instantly show his suspicion of Anne and the camera man. Instead he bowed and followed the camera man through the rooftop exit and down some stairs into a corridor.

There were multiple doors on both sides and they entered through the third on the right.

Inside was a basic, wooden chair in the centre of the room, an enormous, elaborate machine (rainbow-coloured of course) that took up an entire wall and was filled with lots of buttons, controls and switches and Anne Weavers, standing by the machine.

She was still wearing her usual suit, but now, like everything else, it was rainbow-coloured.

This was a relief for Eggo Manaic as he would have been concerned if she had not altered along with everything else on the planet.

A large face on the screen was observing him and upon closer inspection, Eggo Maniac noticed that on this screen was a digital pair of eyes, a nose and a mouth. It was a proper face.

"Hello Eggo Maniac, it is wonderful to see you doing so well. Please come and sit down in the chair, apologies for bothering you, we just wish to ask you a few questions about how you are doing. You could look at this as a well-being check if you like. It's a perfectly normal procedure here on Chordona," said Anne with a smile.

It didn't suit her – smiling. It made her come across as very insincere, or at least that was what Eggo Maniac made of it. Perhaps Emereldon was right. Maybe this Anne Weavers was trouble.

He had to maintain his front though, he could not allow Anne

Weavers to know about his contact with the guardians.

She moved towards him in a gentle manner.

"Now listen Eggo Maniac, I can sense there is some fear within you. Please do not be agitated. You must let go. That is the purpose of your stay on Chordona. You are here to rest and enjoy yourself.

I can understand to a point an amount of sceptical thinking towards me, as you have not seen me for a while and towards the lifestyle here on Chordona because it is so different from what you experience on Earth."

Eggo Maniac reflected on this briefly. Perhaps she was right. There were so many cynical folk and untrustworthy people on Earth. Was he being too suspiscious? He really didn't have a clue about what to think now. His mind was scattered and all over the place.

It was ironic to him because, whilst he had been someone who was so mentally strong, he had been brought to his knees in little more than twenty four hours. He wanted to speak now but couldn't. He was a mess.

"Stop treating yourself so harshly. It is understandable for some confusion to creep in. You are too hard on yourself Eggo Maniac. This is why you are struggling to release and let go of your problems. Here on Chordona there are neither issues nor struggles. This is why you and your friends have been brought here, to show you an alternative way to live. You're going to have to trust me. Put a little faith in us. We have your best interests at heart and I think you are fully aware of that."

Anne's soft voice was both calming and soothing. She leant over him and stroked his arm, then the side of his cheek. A tear trickled down his egg like face.

Shortly after that another fell and then another and another. He was blubbering now. Everything had taken its toll on him and he was at crisis point.

Anne hugged him to reassure him.

Eggo Maniac was not aware if this was a good thing or not. He noticed from the corner of his eye that the camera man had closed the door and was standing by it, like a guard. This was probably to stop the wailing noise travelling through the corridor.

Here he was being comforted and consoled by someone he had been told was supposedly the enemy. As he rocked back and forth Anne Weavers continuously spoke to him, "It's okay to cry here. No one is judging you. Let it out."

The repetition of those words seemed to have a positive effect and through the tears Eggo Maniac managed a little grin.

Emereldon and those guardians were wrong. This woman could not possibly be a dictator attempting to take hold of a dimension. She was too caring and understanding for that. After a bit of sniffling and counting to ten inside his head, Eggo Maniac calmed himself.

Anne Weavers gradually let go of him as the egg's composure improved. She listened carefully to his breathing and, as it calmed, she began.

"Please take your time. We had no intention of creating a stressful situation like this for you. The amusing thing is that you coming to see us now was supposed to help you settle in. I believe that we have failed in that respect and for that I am sorry."

Eggo Maniac gazed directly into her eyes. Strangely he now found himself captivated by her. She was being sincere, there was no question about that. Through a few more snuffles he managed to speak, "What is it you want?"

She smiled once more and waved the camera man away. He left the room but re-entered seconds later with a couple of chairs for Anne and himself.

The camera man seated himself by the enormous machine with the face and Anne sat far closer to Eggo Maniac. She continued to smile at him and again, in her soft voice, she spoke.

"I think what we really need to do is try to understand why you're not adapting to life on Chordona; why you're not assimilating. There have to be some good reasons and I feel it is imperative that we get to the bottom of this.

Believe it or not, we care for your well-being and we want to see you let go of all this tension. Something has upset you and we need to find out what it is. Would you not agree with that Eggo Maniac?"

He nodded in response; this sounded just right.

"I want to add that you may stop this meeting at any time and are free to leave of your own volition. I shall not stop you, nor shall my camera man here. So please do tell us if we may continue."

Anne fluttered her eyelids at him this time, which was odd as it didn't become her.

He waved to indicate it was fine to keep going.

This time Anne stood up and wandered slowly back and forth across the room, still maintaining her caring approach.

"The first thing my camera man noticed is that there are no rainbow colours on you, anywhere. This is strange because even the most adamant and opposing of creatures have succumbed to it; yet you have broken all our known records of resistance to the rainbow.

I suppose what we want you to understand is that letting the rainbow overtake you is a positive thing. Take a look at us for example. We would not allow this to happen to us if we did not think it was good would we?"

Eggo Maniac shook his head, "Well I…"

A bleeping voice then rudely cut in, "This is the problem area. You have found it Mistress Anne."

She nodded and sharply placed her index finger onto her lips indicating to the machine to stop talking.

It did not work.

"This is the avenue of interrogation you must pursue Mistress Anne."

"Can someone cut him off," said Anne.

The camera man fumbled around close to the side of the machine, searching for either a switch or a plug socket of some description.

"Negative I cannot be turned off. I can give you a moment of silence if that is what you desire Mistress Anne."

"Well do that then. Give us a few moments of silence in a row, now."

The face of the machine immediately vanished at Anne's order and was replaced by a series of numbers, letters and symbols.

Eggo Maniac tried to decipher what it meant, but it did not correspond with any languages, new, ancient or modern that he recognised.

Anne could not ignore the attention that her guest had been

showing the machine and was quick to calm his nerves.

"I must apologise for the behaviour of that machine. It is called Mylo and I'm afraid it would appear that manners have not been programmed into it. This would explain why Mylo is so blunt. His will is good and he means well though. Combine this with the assumption that he is usually correct and you can understand why we have him with us."

"No I can understand. Machines have been assisting people on Earth for centuries. It is only natural that they would be of equal help on other planets. Is he sentient?"

Anne was impressed with Eggo Maniac's courteous response. What Mylo had achieved was drawing the egg's attention away from his unstable state of mind. He was now back to using his logic – a far healthier position for Anne and the camera man to begin questioning.

Nonchalantly glancing at her nails Anne began, "There was some truth in what Mylo said though wasn't there? There's something you dislike or fear about the rainbow and that is why you are so reluctant to open yourself to it."

She looked up and stared directly into the egg's eyes as she spoke; her tone altering to a slightly more stern approach, "Am I correct Eggo Maniac?"

The weight of her stare caused Eggo Maniac to avert his eyes. He could feel the pressure and at this point all the thoughts of Emereldon and the guardians came flooding back.

Unfortunately for him, he was not able to mask his body language or facial expressions and this meant that both the camera man and Anne could read him like a book; no pun intended regarding his friend Bruce of course.

A pair of hands reached out and gently touched his shoulders, massaging them gently and calming him down. He was aware of who they belonged to, but he was willing to allow Anne to continue.

"Now Eggo Maniac, just let us in. Tell me why you fear the rainbow so much and I can put your mind at rest, if you permit me to do so."

Eggo Maniac observed her. Was this someone he could trust? Mere moments ago he had been blubbering like a baby and so this was obviously an odd scenario to be in. Perhaps more importantly he had to ask whether he trusted himself. Under these conditions the answer was probably not. He had to put his faith in something or someone.

Slowly he lifted himself from the chair and waddled over to the machine. He inspected the jibberish that it displayed on its screen. It meant nothing and whilst he did this he knew that Anne Weavers and the camera man were watching his every step.

He had an audience and he was pleased by this. He entranced them, at least he thought he did anyway. Finally after a dramatic pause he decided to deliver his opening line, "I thought it could hurt me."

"It cannot, if anything it enhances your already, special gifts. It is beneficial to you, not a hindrance."

Anne was immediate in her answer, as if she had been rehearsing for Eggo Maniac's impromptu performance.

"So what if I were to let it in?" said Eggo Maniac.

"I think you need to consider me and the camera man first. Would we honestly let anything happen to you? We allow the rainbow to take us, it is invigorating."

Anne stood up as she ended her line; a perfectly feasible thespian manouvre. Eggo Maniac questioned whether she was playing along and was fully aware of what he was doing. Now he was ready to drop his blockbuster line, the most important line in the play; "I heard it was like a disease."

He had whispered it to accentuate its importance.

He needn't have bothered. The reaction of his audience/players was all the drama he could have hoped for and then some more on top.

There were no more pleasantries, over the top actions or even any melodrama. Everything went cold. The jovial exterior of Anne and the camera man dropped out of them like a stone. If he had been searching for a range of emotions then Eggo Maniac had just taken them from cheerful to mournful in a second.

The icy silence that enveloped the room told him that this play was over. Seriousness had swiftly returned. Mylo, the machine, broke the silence, "The interrogation procedure must begin now Mistress Anne, either willingly or through force. Please inform me as to which method we are going to utilise."

There was no snapping back this time from Anne; a more conservative answer was the order of the day.

"It will be willingly, for of course we trust Eggo Maniac as he is a dear friend of ours."

This statement was delivered in her usual, non-descript, unemotional manner.

"Please do have a seat Eggo Maniac, I think it's high time we ended this charade and got down to business."

Eggo Maniac complied immediately. Fear had overtaken him

now. Through his own foolishness and arrogance, he had revealed the one thing, the only thing that he was not supposed to – that he had been contacted by an outside force.

Now Anne Weavers and the camera man were not stupid. They would be all too aware of what was coming. Anne moved her chair opposite him and swivelled it around so the front of the chair faced him too. She sat and leant her arms on the back of the chair, so she could rest on it. Before doing so she adjusted and straightened the lapels on her jacket. She clearly meant business.

"Let's start from the beginning. I would like you to answer my questions one by one, but the key thing is that you do not leave nor omit any information. This will be a step by step process and I shall allow you enough time to think about each question before you answer it. The more detail you can give us, the better things will be. Is all this clear so far?"

He nodded in response.

This was intense; it was as if she was reading the instructions to a test paper. It felt as if an exam was being administered.

"Excellent, now remember you have to trust us in this difficult time Eggo Maniac. There is every chance you have been tampered with and that could unearth the problem with your reluctance to embrace the rainbow."

What did she mean tampered with?

"Okay then, the first question is quite simply when were you contacted?"

"It was around two hours ago at a guess."

He noticed the camera man scribbling things down on a small

pad that he had produced from his suit-jacket pocket.

Mylo the screen was also staring at him intently and every time he spoke, whatever he had said would appear, written on Mylo's screen. There would be no going back on his answers then.

"So that was not long before you came in here?"

Again he nodded. He was not unlike one of those bobble head toys that people put in their cars so they nod at people driving behind them.

He had little or no time to dwell on things as the questions came thick and fast: How did he feel? What did his friends think of Chordona? Was he comfortable around them? Did he trust them? The odd thing was, in Eggo Maniac's mind, there was one blatantly obvious question that he was expecting to be asked.

Whilst Anne had started off so firmly and bluntly with her questions, it was as if she had forgotten the major one. He was once again growing calmer and more at ease with the situation.

He could trust Anne and the camera man and it was evident that they had his best interests at heart. They were also doing a lot for his friends, as they had been informing him in between questions, so all was well on that front too.

"Who was it who came to see you then, to talk of this harmful rainbow?"

"Ah well, that would be Emereldon and the guardians."

Eggo Maniac stopped dead in his words.

Had he been tricked? He wasn't entirely sure, lulled into a sense of security – possibly.

"I knew it," said Anne Weavers. "I just knew the clouds would be involved somehow."

"Would you like me to raise our defences?" said the camera man.

"Yes of course, do it now. I am aware of the power of the guardians and their abilities to cloak themselves from detection. So the clouds have discovered our little rift into their own dimension. Well it matters not anyway. Our plans are underway."

Eggo Maniac was now the audience member as the drama unfolded in front of him. He was front row and centre, the best seats in the house. He would learn more about Anne Weavers from her behaviour in this scenario.

She barked orders at the camera man and Mylo. Both obeyed her every command and whilst Eggo Maniac was not sure what they were doing, it seemed they were doing it with a great degree of urgency.

Eggo Maniac stood up to leave as he could be of no more assistance. This was not allowed however and Anne was quick to inform him.

"Take a seat Eggo Maniac, I'm going to need to extract a bit more information from you."

Chapter 14
True Intentions?

Rod's eyes fluttered then closed. He tried again; they closed once more. Desperate to see where he was and frankly, how he was, he opened them with some degree of effort and sat upright.

He was perched on top of a chest of drawers. This was strange to him as the object he had clung onto for dear life felt like a table.

Perhaps he had moved.

Perhaps he could stop waking up in random rooms and positions. He had lost count of the amount of times he had blacked out through this whole process, but he was certain it was more than three.

Well, he hadn't lost count if he was candid with himself, as that would have made him a terrible mathematician. He wasn't happy about these repeating scenarios that was for sure. Still things were visible now. The room was pitch-black when the bosses had left it, so at least he could finally see its interior décor. That was if this was the same room.

He had obviously been blown away at some point as he could not find the table he had initially grabbed. Thinking about that, where were Yod and the other socks he had rescued? Where was Tod? He rushed around searching every corner and nook and cranny of the room.

The trouble was the room itself was small and hid very little. It had grey, patterned skirting boards and white and gold striped wallpaper that ran up to grey coving. There were four doors, one in the centre of each wall. At present all were shut.

There were no windows and the only source of light was a golden chandelier that drooped down over the middle of the room. Rod debated opening a door, but then it struck him quickly that opening doors and endless mazes was all he had done since attempting to locate the bosses.

He also believed that they had every intention of getting rid of him, so perhaps some thinking outside of the box was required. He moved to the chest of drawers and opened the top one.

Nothing in it.

The second one contained some blankets and the third contained a pile of socks. "More prisoners then," he said to himself.

Rod tugged at the drawer and sure enough it came out in his hands. Emptying the drawer he expected to see the socks come alive with their newly found freedom, but they did not. They just flopped there, like a pile of, well, socks.

The drawer was reasonable in its weight – not too light that it could be thrown, but also not too heavy that he could not brandish it about the place.

Suddenly it dawned on him. This was it. This drawer was his way out. Excitedly he shifted the chest into the centre of the room and leapt on top of it. He then dragged the drawer up from the floor and placed it beside him.

Aware he was probably being watched he addressed the bosses.

"That's it. You have forced me to take matters into my own hands. I'm going to wreck this place until you release me, Tod and all the other sock prisoners you keep in here, even that obnoxious, overgrown stocking."

There was no retort of any sort, not that he anticipated one mind you.

So he began.

First he grabbed the drawer and swung it at the chandelier. It connected with it and made the lights wobble; not bad for a first attempt.

The second was far more effective. It smashed into the base of the chain that held the lights upright, causing the whole thing to crash down onto the floor and erupt into a multitude of little pieces. He had obliterated it.

This felt good and for the first time since Rod had embarked on this journey, he was thoroughly enjoying himself.

It was now that he noticed a small glimmer of blue light, peeking through a tiny crack that had been made when he hit the base of the chandelier off the ceiling.

There was something up there.

He held the drawer tightly, for this was his tool, his weapon of choice that would lead to his freedom, well either that or something interesting. He swung the drawer backwards and then, with all his might, he thrust it forward absolutely battering the area of ceiling where he had found the crack.

Sure enough another layer emerged and this motivated him further. He launched the drawer forward and this time split more of the plaster away. Why this whole place had been decorated using human methods and tools was beyond him.

His plan was working, but he needed to increase the intensity, and he did. If someone was watching Rod he would have been deemed insane. This pink cloud held a look of contempt combined with rage on his face and thrashed around as if his life depended on it, which, incidentally, it probably did.

He was half covered in bits of white plaster and the odd bit of grey paint where he had occasionally struck the coving. Goodness knows how he managed to hit that when it was quite far away from him. This pink cloud was in a frenzy and it seemed that his energy knew no bounds.

Finally he dropped the drawer and dived down to the floor below. A huge chunk had fallen but he had managed to get himself out of the way. As he lay amongst the debris of his handiwork he analysed the drawer, if one could even call it that now.

All that remained were a few bits of wood. The base of the drawer had long fallen out and Rod had basically been beating the ceiling down with a glorified plank of wood. This was irrelevant now as his weapon of choice had served its purpose. The blue light that ran through the hole was huge.

He scurried up the chest of drawers and grabbed onto the edge of the hole in the ceiling and hauled himself up without even bothering to take notice of what was above him.

He now stood on a road built of diamond blocks. The width of the road was fair. It was five diamond blocks wide and Rod had estimated that the side of each square block was roughly a metre in length.

At the side of this was a line of similar sized blocks that were emeralds, and then sitting by this were blocks of grassland that held an oak tree in every other block.

It was bizarre.

It was like walking down a diamond road, with emeralds either side, in a forest. It was amazingly well lit and Rod could not work out what the light source was.

It was possible that the blue light that had burst through the cracks in the ceiling of the room below was all that lit this odd landscape; but surely it could not be that.

He then wondered how he had managed to break through diamonds when it quickly hit him that he hadn't. He looked in every direction and he could not locate the hole he had made. How he had managed to get up here was anyone's guess. Behind him was a drop and in front of him was the rest of this road. Rod only had one choice and it was a simple one – forward.

Eggo Maniac had spilled his guts, not literally of course for that would have been nasty and disgusting. He had told them absolutely everything, ensuring he had missed nothing out. Everything had happened so quickly and if he was blunt with himself, he wasn't quite sure how it had all transpired. Still he was not too keen on his current surroundings. He was now in what Anne had described as isolation.

They were concerned that Emereldon and the guardians may have done something to him to try and attack the citizens of Chordona. He had gone willingly, after all he had no desire to harm anyone. The room he was confined to had a bed, and rather worryingly, bars. It resembled more of a prison cell to him.

Eggo Maniac just hoped he could be of use to Anne. He wanted to help her. It was obvious she cared about him, otherwise she would not have gone to the measures she had.

Anne had set up a meeting with a surgeon who was going to perform some kind of operation/scan, he wasn't sure which. Surely it would be okay though, he did trust Anne.

The sound of footsteps broke his train of thought and Eggo Maniac stood up and moved towards the bars to see who was coming. Perhaps this was the surgeon now.

It wasn't. To be honest it wasn't anything. He could hear the footsteps getting closer but still had no sight of whoever it was.

"Hello Eggo Maniac, I think you and I need to have a quick chat."

He shot around to see a blue figure, complete with a ragged, hooded cloak draped around him, sitting casually on his bed. It was Emereldon.

What could he do? How did he get in? There must have been some sort of alarm system for the building? Frantically, Eggo Maniac examined the walls but could not see any switches.

"Who are you kidding Eggo Maniac? There is no alarm switch in here. This is a prison cell. Why would they give you the option of setting off an alarm?"

Eggo Maniac opened his mouth to shout, but the intruder had predicted this. As he did, the cell filled with smoke, the same smoke that Emereldon had used when he first encountered him. Within seconds the egg stood face to face with the blue, rock like figure, much as he had done previously.

This time though, the conversation would be very different.

Eggo Maniac opted to stay silent. There was nothing he could say. He had an inkling that Emereldon would know everything anyway and lying would just make things even tougher for him. Where was Anne though? She had promised that she would...

"Protect you? That's what she told you is it not?"

"Yes that is what I was told. Are you reading my mind?"

"On this occasion I shall ask the questions."

It was obvious that Emereldon was upset and more worryingly, it was obvious that he wielded great power in order to get himself in and out of the building without being detected.

"You are right Eggo Maniac. I do wield great power, but this is not the point of my visit. I wish to know when you, in your mind, made the decision that I had been lying to you?"

"Excuse me, but I don't understand."

"It's a pretty simple question. I told you when we first met, that regardless of what happened, I would not lie to you, under any circumstance. Is that not correct?

Don't answer that I'll do it for you. It is correct. Therefore at some point, you must have decided to trust Anne Weavers, the camera man and any other joker that aligned themselves with those two maniacs.

You chose her side over mine. You did not believe what I had said to you, hence you can only have assumed that I was not telling the truth. Now you can answer this one - is that correct?"

"I never thought about it like that, but yes I suppose. I am sorry."

Eggo Maniac's voice was timid. He was at the mercy of Emereldon whilst he was stuck in this room, shrouded in smoke.

"You still haven't realised what has happened have you? This is not a room, this is a prison cell. There are bars that are detaining you. It is not possible for you to leave of your own free will. Whether you like it or not Eggo Maniac you are a prisoner of the side you opted to trust."

The blue, rocky figure laughed as he finished his sentence. This was cut short by a swift and astonishing outburst from Eggo Maniac,

"That's not true. I am here because they are worried about me. I am waiting for the surgeon to come and analyse me. Anne cares, she does care."

Silence.

Emereldon's laughter stopped through disbelief and Eggo Maniac had to catch his breath following his rant. He wondered what might happen to him for defending Anne Weavers to the enemy.

Eyeing up Emereldon, he clenched his fist. He was angry now. No one was going to change him, or make him join something he did not believe in. Eggo Maniac knew that Emereldon would outmatch him, of that there was no question. He would go down with a fight though.

The blue figure returned an icy, cold glare. The longer the silence remained, the more heated the situation grew. Finally Emereldon stepped forward and gestured at Eggo Maniac to put his hands down by his side. He was beaming now and this further enraged the egg. He spoke to his potential opponent in a more jolly manner.

"Put them down Eggo Maniac. You do not want to do this. Trust me on that. It seems you do possess loyalty, however misguided that may be, but you are loyal which is impressive in itself. We are not going to clash about this here. I just want to take you on a quick journey and then I'll happily bring you back, unscathed, to this cell or room, whatever it is you wish to call it. Does that sound acceptable?"

"I guess it does. Okay I shall come. I shall trust you."

Eggo Maniac dropped his hands by his sides and walked over to Emereldon. The blue figure reached for his cloak and wrapped it around Eggo Maniac.

There was a brief sound, like a strong gust of wind. Following that, Emereldon swept his cloak aside and Eggo Maniac opened his eyes.

"We're on the rooftop again, like we were before. Why have we come back? I have seen my friends revelling in all they are doing. I assume that we cannot be seen or touched, like last time?"

Emereldon nodded in confirmation. He then proceeded to ask Eggo Maniac, "Why is it, do you think, that you have not succumbed to the rainbow disease yet?"

"Probably because you put some kind of spell on me."

"It was not a spell. I gave you a small dose of my power which blocks the infection. It's astounding to me that you still don't trust me, despite the obvious assistance I gave you in performing that particular act."

Eggo Maniac did not reply to this. He continued to observe everything in front of him. He was not entirely sure what the point of this could be. This was nearly identical to the scene he had been involved in earlier.

Bruce and Howard were settling on the reclining chairs chatting and drinking the odd coffee or sparkling mineral water. The Sheep Brigade had now ordered a swimming pool and were splashing around in that and taking turns on the diving board while the ant was just sunbathing. He accepted that some of the activities had changed but they were still having a jolly good time, something that could not be said for him.

"I am glad that you are starting to look more closely Eggo Maniac. You are right to point out that the activities have altered slightly and that everybody is enjoying themselves, but please watch even more carefully. Scrutinise them and you will see exactly what I am talking about."

Eggo Maniac took this on board and watched carefully. Why couldn't Emereldon just tell him. Why did he have to go through this silly ordeal of games and riddles. It really was all smoke and mirrors with Emereldon, excuse the pun, he thought to himself.

His cynicism was set to continue until he stopped abruptly. He could see what his guide was talking about. They were all now covered from head to toe. The rainbow had purged them of their original colours and taken a grip of them.

According to Anne Weavers this was normal though and Eggo Maniac had seen the camera man and Anne covered in the rainbow. It was merely the method of adapting to Chordona and sadly Eggo Maniac could not do it himself, because this Emereldon had put something inside him which prevented it from happening. He would address this issue now.

"I want you to take out of me, whatever it is you put in, so that I may be able to savour the delights of Chordona and adapt properly."

"Is that what Anne told you the rainbow was then; a means of adapting?"

Eggo Maniac was hasty in his answer.

"Yes of course it was. Take a look down there. They are all

enjoying themselves – it's great."

"Just hold on for a moment then."

Sure enough, just as Emereldon had finished speaking, Anne Weavers and the camera man arrived. Both could have been mistaken for children's television presenters with their rainbow suits. They did not stand out however, merely blending in with everything else around them.

"Okay everyone I would like you to follow me please," said Anne. She wasn't particularly loud in her order and it was quite impressive that each and every member of the group immediately stopped what they were doing and followed her.

The camera man opened the door which led down into the building and all wandered through it without making a sound.

"Would you like to go too?" said Emereldon.

Eggo Maniac ignored this comment and the pair of them walked slowly behind the group.

The camera man moved to slam the door shut and Eggo Maniac shielded his eyes in fear of being hit, but quickly remembered that physical objects offered no real threat to him whilst he was in this state.

One thing he did notice was that the huge ant remained outside. It was attempting to do as it was told, but kept bumping into the door as it was too large to fit inside. After the door had shut it continued to rebound off it.

Emereldon had also noticed this and was quick to share his thoughts.

"That ant is just stupid then is it? It is not capable of learning basic physics with regard to space. Is that the reason it continues to bash its head against the door?"

Eggo Maniac ignored him and made his way into a long room that contained an equally long dining room table and chairs. The group sat down on it, with Anne at the head of the table and the camera man taking the seat on the other end. As soon as all were seated a series of rainbow-coloured waiters entered carrying various pasta based dishes and presented them to all around the table.

Anne called one over and insisted that he take his dish outside to the ant, whose banging on the door was still audible.

"Well I suppose you were wrong then. She is just giving them a healthy meal and she has even given one to the ant outside. I would say this shows how much she cares as she has not forgotten about anyone. I suspect there will probably be a dish of pasta on its way to my cell."

Eggo Maniac's words were smarmy to say the least.

It did not faze Emereldon one bit though. He sniggered and gestured for Eggo Maniac to continue to watch.

Anne addressed the group. "Thank you all for coming. I have had these special pasta dishes prepared specifically for you. I do hope they satisfy your palettes. They will give you the energy required to complete the next stage of my, our plan."

The group replied to her in unison.

"Yes Miss Weavers."

Eggo Maniac could even hear the ant shout it from outside. It was just a coincidence of course. These ants had exceptional hearing.

"What I am asking you to do is, for a group of individuals like yourselves, a simple matter. We are all going to break through the small rift we have found that will lead us back to the Adamantium dimension, to Earth to be precise. It will be a nice homecoming for you all."

The group smiled at her. It was odd, as the smiles were in no way individual. They all possessed the same awkward and fake quality.

Another strange aspect of everything unfolding in front of Eggo Maniac was, that he couldn't believe that one of them had not yet asked Anne a question.

They all seemed happy to go along with everything. This was not the usual behaviour of Howard and Bruce for starters and he had never seen Private Lunatic sit this still for this long, ever.

The camera man cleared his throat; it was his turn to speak.

"Whilst you have been here on Chordona, you must accept that we have treated you well and have shown you a new found way of life that you would all like to continue. We are gradually spreading this throughout the Ignacium dimension and it is now your turn to have the honour of being the first to take it to the Adamantium dimension, more specifically to Earth."

The entire room applauded at precisely the same time, in perfect unison. It was more like robotic clapping. Even the ant from outside managed to keep the soulless rhythm.

The lights dimmed in the room. It was nearly pitch-black and the clapping ceased.

A small, green sphere of light hovered in the centre of the room and then drifted to Anne and lit up her face. She was now emblazoned in green and Eggo Maniac could not get past her uncanny resemblance to that of a fairytale witch.

"She is a witch of sorts, not what you would think of on Earth, but she, now let me get the expression right, wields great power," said Emereldon.

Anne remained in silence whilst everyone stared at her face. This time she spoke with a little more aggression and her voice had altered slightly, it had gone up in pitch.

"Your objective is simple. We have enemies in the Adamantium dimension known as the clouds. We expect you to land on Earth and make yourself seen to the general public. We want you to talk to them, give interviews on television and make yourselves as famous as possible.

This will make the people of Earth revere you. You will be like nothing they have ever seen. I shall control the media to ensure you are portrayed in a good light."

The group nodded together in response to this.

Anne's mood then drastically altered and as it did, one could feel the fervour in her voice. She was livid, yet calculated. It was a frightening combination and merely portrayed the sheer venom and contempt she so clearly held for the clouds.

Her eyes glowed red and it was her incredible control of her anger that frightened Eggo Maniac. Even Emereldon did not appear to be quite so tough now.

Anne had risen to her feet at this point and Eggo Maniac would not have been in the least bit surprised had she started salivating at the prospect of defeating the clouds. She was hissing now.

"This of course will eventually lead to the emergence of the clouds. They are the biggest TV watchers in their universe and will learn of your presence. In order to ensure they are controlling the direction of their programming, they will show themselves and that is when we shall strike – right into their hearts."

She tightly screwed her hand into a fist and slammed it onto the table. The group did not react to this. Only the camera man, who was seated at the opposing end, acknowledged this gesture. However even he harboured some fear of Anne Weavers.

"We will leave in one hour," said. She stood up and left the room, quickly followed by the camera man who scurried behind her like an obedient dog.

The group continued to eat, in silence, which was not like them.

Eggo Maniac felt a hand touch his shoulder, "You see Eggo Maniac, everything I told you is true. I do not need to read your mind to see that you are concerned by the behaviour of your friends. This is not like them is it? They are too quiet, too boring and more importantly, they are too compliant."

Emereldon was right, of that there was no doubt. Eggo Maniac had chosen the wrong team and now would have to rectify that.

He gazed into the stone man's eyes, sighing in disbelief as he spoke. "Anne said they would move in one hour. It is indisputable that they are being controlled, sadly I see that now, when it is potentially too late. I have been a fool."

"There is no time for self-pity and absolutely no time to rue missed opportunities. It is never too late. There is much that can be done, but you must trust me Eggo Maniac, you must trust me and the guardians whom I brought to visit you. We are going to have to stop your friends without hurting them and remove the rainbow disease. That way we can get to Anne Weavers and, I'm afraid to say this, destroy her."

Eggo Maniac nodded. He didn't want to hurt anyone, but he had seen first-hand what Anne's intentions were. She had to be stopped whatever the cost.

"What do we do now then?"

"Now Eggo Maniac, now we leave for the final showdown. Now we leave for Earth."

Chapter 15
Affinities

The diamond road that Rod had taken turned out to be far shorter than he had predicted. Unlike every other element of his journey this one had been oddly straightforward.

He was unsure whether he should be pleased by this or not, although it had reached the point where he no longer cared. He, and quite frankly the entire species of clouds, had been messed around for far too long by folk they could neither see nor meet.

Still he was now in front of a cottage, a very ordinary cottage. It had one floor with a straw thatched roof and had a traditional country feel to it. The walls were white and the windows were round and well lit. A quaint, oak door finished the look and small puffs of smoke exited the cottage chimney. That combined with the bright, yellow light inside insinuated that someone was at home.

Under normal circumstances Rod would have knocked at the door and politely waited for it to be answered and hope that he would be invited inside.

This was not the normal practice of this new, fed-up Rod, who simply pushed at the door and entered. Rod considered that this was fine as it was not locked and therefore whatever was inside was not of great importance. He stopped for a second and questioned his own thought. Would what he just contemplated not be similar to the way the bosses thought of the clouds? Whoever resided here was of no relevance as the door was not locked.

Rod moved back to the front door, closed it gently behind him and knocked.

No reply.

Well now I have good and fair reason thought Rod and he

floated back inside.

Towards the back of the cottage he could hear a fire crackling and chose to follow the sounds. The building was decorated like a traditional British country home, complete with wooden floorboards, portraits of goodness knows who and lengthy mirrors. A few hooks with keys on them, wooden shelves and a couple of display cases containing china figurines adorned the walls.

Rod reached the fireplace quickly as this tiny cottage really was as small as it appeared from its exterior. A round rug of a red and black chequered design was in the centre of the room with a luxurious, red sofa and two matching armchairs completing the scene.

Strangely one armchair faced away from the rug and fire and was pointed towards the corner. The fireplace itself was of the white marble variety which blended in seamlessly with the white walls behind it. On a black mantelpiece above it was a wooden statue of a crocodile and beside this a figurine made of plants.

Rod turned around so that he was opposite the armchair facing the corner of the room. He sniggered at first and then spoke.

"I think it's probably about time we had a chat."

The armchair swivelled round and on it sat a perfectly ordinary human. He wore a navy-blue suit, white shirt and red tie, complete with matching red handkerchief that stuck out of his suit-jacket pocket. His hair was shoulder length and dark. It was a slight contrast to his bright, blue eyes, but suited him nonetheless.

His skin was tanned and gave him a healthy glow. He wore a gold ring on his finger, which bizarrely looked as though it should have held a jewel within it, yet had nothing. The stone must have, at some point, been removed. He sported shoes that were black and shone; they must have had so much polish on them it was unbelievable.

Overall he possessed handsome features and Rod would have assumed that this was what humans would have referred to as a handsome man.

In his hand he held a wine glass that contained an odd black liquid. Sipping from it his expression began to change. Initially he gave off an air of nonchalance about everything, but after he had laid his eyes on Rod, he seemed particularly upset. His lip curled upwards slightly as he addressed his new visitor. "You've got a lot of nerve showing your face around here."

Rod floated backwards slightly, preparing to defend himself if necessary. The pink cloud's retort was swift.

"I don't think you're in any position to say that to me. You've got a lot of nerve putting me through all the trouble and grief to find you."

"How do you know it was me?"

"Just a hunch," said Rod.

The dark haired man drank from his glass once more before retorting to this potentially unwelcome guest. He swilled the remaining liquid around in his glass watching it intently. Without even looking up at his guest he casually enquired.

"Don't you know who I am?"

Rod did not respond. He analysed this rude man sitting comfortably in his chair. At this point Rod decided that truly he had had just about enough of the constant abuse, rudeness, violence and frankly the vulgarity of everything he had endured.

He cackled, in his mind at first, but he soon let it out loud.

Strangely the man in the chair was not affronted by this. He just stared at Rod, taking the occasional swig from his glass, whilst this strange, pink cloud floated in front of him, giggling uncontrollably.

Slowly, the man's face began to change its expression. He tried to remain composed, but was struggling. He averted his gaze from this cloud. He could not hold it in. He simply could not contain himself. He, too, broke out into laughter.

His laugh was far deeper than Rod's and boomed throughout the cottage. It was now a game of who could laugh loudest, as Rod increased the volume.

The man followed suit, as a tear trickled down his cheek. Rod was clutching his sides as if they were going to explode at any moment.

The pair could contain themselves no more, not that they had been doing a good job previously.

The man had put his glass on the floor and was now standing on his feet. He stretched out his arms and Rod did the same. They hugged each other briefly and then returned to their original starting positions; Rod floating in front of the chair and the man sitting back down in it.

As the laughter died down the man inhaled deeply.

"Oh my goodness, I'm amazed we were even able to keep up that pretence for so long. How are you Rod? You look well. It has been a long time since I have seen you."

Rod was calming too and had positioned himself on the sofa by the man, relaxing back with his hands behind his head. He was extremely at ease.

"Yes I'm fine thank you boss. It was quite a journey to get here though, so you're safe as usual. How are things?"

"They are good Rod. Did you like the stocking? He is adamant that he is the head guard of the socks. I thought he would make a nice change for you. I appreciate he was no challenge for someone of your skills, but then who actually is?"

The pair chortled briefly before the boss handed him an empty glass.

Rod left the room and re-appeared with the glass filled. Clearly he had been to the kitchen. He placed himself back down onto the sofa.

"How is Tod then?"

The boss smiled at Rod's question.

Rod chuckled again. "Is the 'oracle' a sock yet?"

"Presumably, I mean he was sucked out of the room for that reason so one can only assume it is the case. They make very few errors down there in the conversion process."

Rod wiped some sweat from his brow; he felt at home now.

"What is happening then with regard to the Ignacium dimension? From my understanding they took Eggo Maniac, Howard, Bruce the spider and that weird Sheep Brigade with them. What is going on there? I dispatched Emereldon and the guardians, well not the door one, but you follow what I mean."

The man stroked his hair back.

"That is going well. I must say Rod that it was a wise move on your part to send that lot. Their loyalty is unwavering and I think they will cope well. They have taken a camera. Once they clash with the group that you and your pal created, our TV ratings are going to go through the roof. That will settle the majority of the clouds. Our rule will continue without opposition."

Rod sipped from his glass once more. He had enjoyed his role thus far in the mission. It was quite out of the norm for him.

The boss was pleased with his decisions and actions, besides which, the impending battle between Emereldon and the guardians would make for some fascinating viewing. He was looking forward to it himself.

Oxford Street was, as usual, full to the brim with people. Shoppers, tourists, city workers and every type of person you could imagine moved swiftly through the street and surrounding areas.

Just outside a music shop, stood the entire Sheep Brigade and the giant ant, on which sat Howard and Bruce. The group had maintained their rainbow-coloured forms.

Sadly, no one had yet noticed them. Well that wasn't entirely true, but people took a quick peek and then moved forward. One person even asked the Sheep Brigade to get out of the way so that he could get into the store.

Before they knew it, two security guards had approached them and asked them to move along as they were making it difficult for customers to get inside.

Anne Weavers then sprang out of nowhere and explained that they were part of a special promotion for London and that she had been granted permission for them to utilise any part of the pavement on Oxford Street that she desired. Peculiarly the guards bought this story and backed down without so much as a question.

Stranger still was that Anne had not retained her rainbow-coloured guise and had returned to her ordinary grey suit.

Anne gained the group's attention and signalled for them to follow her. She marched them up the road and then down a side street until she had reached Soho Square.

In the middle of the square was some nice greenery and a few benches and this was where the ant decided to go. It had little other choice as this was the only place in which it could fit.

The rest just stood on the pavement, save for Howard and Bruce, who were still sitting atop the ant. The huge buildings surrounding the grass towered over them and Anne noticed that there were more bikes than usual chained to the railings on the pavement.

A few people picnicked and had no issue with the ant. Anne cleared her throat and addressed the group.

"Thank you all for coming and supporting our mission. I'm not going to bother spending time on niceties as you all know how I feel about you and your array of talents.

This is Soho Square. It is surrounded by offices and buildings of great importance and thus I believe that this would be a good place for you to start your publicity campaign. Now you may wonder as to why people are not reacting to you.

This is because at present I have put your pictures out to the press as a publicity stunt. You are all set to become major attractions and it will take a little bit of time for that to filter through.

Once it does you will need to carry a pen at all times for autographs. Do not get too used to the fame though. The objective is to draw out those clouds and to defeat them. It is likely there will be a time for combat.

So all you have to do for now, is to stay here, smile, be nice and sign autographs when people show up. I've marketed you as super heroes in case you were wondering."

Anne reached into her pocket and pulled out some black marker pens. She handed them around to the Sheep Brigade and threw two directly into the hands of Howard and Bruce respectively. One more was also chucked at the ant who caught it and examined it.

Anne cleared her throat again.

"I understand that some of you may not know how to use a pen, but if necessary just draw a picture, or make some kind of mark. Anything will do."

The group all nodded in unison. They were a bit zombie like, but then that was the effects of the rainbow. There was little Anne could do about that apart from removing it, but then they wouldn't listen to her and obey her every whim and she couldn't let that happen.

Emereldon clicked his fingers. Within seconds the three guardians joined him, gradually taking shape as if they had been there all the time. Eggo Maniac looked over his shoulder and watched them all closely.

Slimax changed shape and did not stop moving. His red blubber squelched and made other inappropriate sounds as it oozed around.

This time Eator had a bit more body to him than just his head. A neck and chest were beginning to materialise.

This only left Miss Terious for Eggo Maniac to analyse; but once again she did not reveal herself in any way, shape or form. She was the first to speak however.

"Emereldon, I have found them. They are in a place called Soho Square. It is in London and only a few streets from this building."

Eggo Maniac peered over the edge of the tiny wall in front of him. He just did not understand why everyone had to hang around on rooftops. There they were in Central London, Tottenham Court Road no less, gazing down at the general public, who were now the size of ants.

Emereldon did not formally acknowledge her, but instead waved for her to continue.

Miss Terious obliged, "I feel that if we move now, we could be quick to strike and that this 'element of surprise' will affect them all."

"But not Anne Weavers, she knows we are coming and it's what she wants, she even said so herself. I fear we have lost the 'element of surprise'. What we really want is Anne Weavers herself... alone."

Miss Terious was fast to respond. It was evident that she respected Emereldon immensely, but for some reason, she was not happy with his current train of thought. Eggo Maniac was adamant that she felt insulted. Her voice altered from her usual soft and tranquil voice to one that showed a hint of aggression, "But Emereldon, Anne Weavers is never alone, otherwise we would have done this before."

"Oh is that so? I wouldn't speak out of turn if I were you Miss Terious. We shall all move and make ourselves known to them."

The guardians stared oddly at the blue, rocky figure, at least

228

Eggo Maniac assumed that was what they were doing. He could not make out what Miss Terious was up to as he could not see her face, or any other part of her, save for the cloak.

"That would play into her hands. Surely Anne Weavers is watching everything her little team is doing? I mean they stand out. They are rainbow-coloured."

This voice was odd. It was fairly high pitched and sounded out of sorts considering the appearance of the menacing being to whom it belonged.

It was Slimax.

Interestingly enough Emereldon ignored him completely.

The next to speak was Eator. Now Eator possessed an almost growling and savage tone, far more suited to his image mused Eggo Maniac.

"I think you must listen to us Emereldon. If we are to attack them directly, then Anne Weavers will find our whereabouts instantly. There must be another way."

"And this is why we shall approach it this way. I have to say I expected more from you three, you are guardians after all."

The three guardians all took a step back and stood side by side, like three naughty children who had just been told off.

Emereldon continued.

"You see the problem we have is I suspect that Anne Weavers is already knowledgeable of our whereabouts even now. She is not stupid and she will have readied herself accordingly.

It is for this reason that there is no true way of startling her. She wants us to attack her little bunch of brainwashed creatures and so we shall. That way she will be stunned because we have done what she expected, therefore shocking her. Understand?"

The guardians shrugged. They didn't really, nor did Eggo Maniac, in fact the only person who did comprehend the plan was Emereldon and that was only just. The blue figure beamed.

"Off we go then."

He grabbed Eggo Maniac and dragged him over the side of the building.

The guardians followed suit and all landed on Tottenham Court Road. There were fewer people around than normal and considering it was three o'clock in the afternoon there should have been far more members of the general public present.

It was only Eggo Maniac who had noticed this. As he went to mention it, Emereldon hauled him off again.

They now moved like lightning, in and out of cars, through alleyways and side streets and then managed to scale a wall to the top of a building.

Eggo Maniac had shut his eyes and eventually he could feel that he was no longer moving. He knew he was on the rooftop of some other building.

"This is it then, Soho Square and there they are," said Emereldon. He pointed down and all that was in front of him was a sea of people surrounding the rainbow-coloured folk.

The ant was the only one who was remotely fully visible and even then, kids and adults alike were crawling up his back, jumping off him and generally treating him as an adventure playground.

Howard had been mobbed by people and was desperately

wielding a black marker pen, fending off the hordes with autographs.

Bruce was on the floor, on his back, whilst people flicked through his pages.

The Sheep Brigade was probably suffering the most. They were giving people rides around the square, which took a long time as there were too many people realistically to move.

Eggo Maniac observed them carefully. His friends would never have willingly agreed to this. It was clear that this had all been orchestrated by Anne Weavers.

Emereldon was right. They were under her control.

Howard loathed crowds and frankly was frightened by them.

The high pitched tone of Slimax interrupted his train of thought. "This is ridiculous. They are already defeated."

Eator snarled in agreement.

Emereldon was fast to question them both. "They are not. This just means they have mass support from the human general public. It could be more difficult this way because some of those humans could be willing to stand and fight with them."

"Ha ha ha and you think they would stand a chance against us? That will be of no consequence to me. I'll happily consume humans as well as those others."

"And that is why you are a savage Eator. If you eat those humans, who I might add, are being controlled against their will, then what does that make you?"

Emereldon's words were harsh. Eggo Maniac considered that to be the most aggressive he had ever heard him.

Eator backed down immediately.

Emereldon turned around and stood facing the three guardians, "Let me explain something to all of you. We are not here to destroy anyone except Anne Weavers and even then it would be preferable to capture her. We will meet resistance, I am fully aware of that, but I do not wish harm to come to any human. Is that clear?"

All nodded in response to him.

"Now it is evident that Anne Weavers is not present at the moment. We must knock out the group when they attack us, but I do not want any permanent damage to them. Remember that it is not their decision to fight us.

I suspect that once the battle begins Anne Weavers will show herself. At that point all attention is to go towards capturing her; in short – no permanent damage to anyone and get Anne Weavers as quickly as possible."

"And what about the camera man, what if he shows up?"

"You can eat him, by all means Eator."

The guardians laughed.

Eggo Maniac joined them awkwardly, he didn't mind the camera man.

Emereldon raised his fist, "Guardians, Eggo Maniac, we move."

The five figures then leapt off the side of the building and descended onto the square below.

Chapter 16

Whose side?

Rod swilled the dark liquid in his hand and watched as it moved uncontrollably, splashing the sides of the glass. The cottage was fairly warm as the open fire raged and Rod was as comfortable as he had been in a very long time.

The boss was kicking back, too, and had reclined his armchair for more comfort. He adjusted his suit-jacket and was so laid back he could have been asleep.

"Boss, shall we watch the impending confrontation? The cameras must be ready by now."

The boss nodded and fidgeted around in his armchair, obviously searching for something.

Seconds later he held a remote and pointed it above the fireplace. A quick click of the red power button on the blue remote caused the area behind the mantelpiece to open up, revealing a huge television set. It was flat screen and 8K, as all would expect of the clouds.

The ornaments that were standing on the top of the fireplace were now obstructing the view. Rod was about to get up and remove them when the boss gestured for him to stay on the sofa.

The boss pressed his index finger against his forehead and it started to glow blue. This energy then began to wrap itself around the statues and ornaments and anything else that was in front of the television and it quickly shifted them onto the floor.

Rod found it interesting that this blue light surrounding the objects had lifted them and placed them down in such a gentle fashion.

"I learned that trick in this night realm I visited quite a long time ago. It's cool don't you think?"

Rod gave the boss a thumbs up and then took another sip. The television set came on and sure enough in front of them was Soho Square, filled with people approaching the rainbow-coloured group.

The boss was quick to explain.

"We are not quite live at the moment Rod. We are experiencing a lag, but this is on purpose. This show that we are putting together is an extremely risky one as we are not guaranteed to get the outcome we desire. We have our A list going though, in terms of celebrities, endorsements and of course the studio team."

"Is it Zod and Zoddy then? I assume they will be the presenters."

The boss winked at him.

Obviously it was then.

Rod's question was answered seconds later when, sure enough, the most popular presenting team on cloud television appeared on set, live from just above Central London. The set itself was entirely silver, which included the desk they sat behind. On the front of this was a brilliant white logo that read "cloud TV exclusive".

Rod grinned, it was plain, yet elegant. This was going to be an absolute ratings monster. It could well be the biggest show that they had ever put on.

Behind the desk sat two ultramarine clouds. One sported a purple and blue striped tie and white collar whilst the other had a similarly coloured purple and blue bow, which sat gently on the top of her head.

That was the trouble with being a cloud – not having any legs or actual body meant when one did dress up, which was rare, as clothes were largely irrelevant, the choice was very limited.

The collar and tie was about as much as this Zod could muster and similarly the bow was about the range for Zoddy.

Female clouds used to wear necklaces, but then they were often mistaken for chains and therefore some were deemed to be escaped convicts and thrown straight back into prison on the ground, where they would have to serve time. Needless to say that fashion trend ended very quickly.

Zod was the first to speak, "Welcome everyone to this extravaganza. Tonight we have what many believe to be the greatest show in the history of cloud TV."

"Well Zod that's quite a statement but you are right. Tonight we shall have a battle of epic proportions. We have the rainbow-coloured Sheep Brigade, Howard the unstoppable pizza box, Bruce the enigmatic encyclopaedia and the giant, the colossal ant."

Zoddy's commentating style complimented Zod's well. Yes, this was going to make Rod a producing and creative legend of cloud TV.

"My goodness Zoddy. Look at the size of that thing. I've never seen anything quite like it before. It makes the humans look like, well ants."

The pair chuckled at Zod's joke before Zoddy continued.

"That's right Zod, but what we need to take note of now are their opponents."

"And who might they be Zoddy?"

"Well Zod, I'm just flicking through my fight programme, which incidentally you can purchase for the bargain price of fifty cloud dollars, not including postage, packaging or airmail, and I see that tonight it will be…"

She paused for suspense.

Zod pleaded with her, "Come on Zoddy, you gotta reveal it to us. The suspense, the anticipation is too much for me to handle."

"It is tough Zod, but just calm down and I think you will be pleasantly surprised. Tonight they will go up against… a team of mystery opponents."

A monumental "Oooooooooohhhhhhhhh!" filled the speakers of the television set.

Rod was interested by this and had to ask, "Boss did you add a live studio audience?"

"Yes I did Rod. Everything you have done to this point has been perfect. I just wanted to add my own personal touch to it. Keep watching, they should pan in and scan them all now."

Sure enough the boss was correct. The cameras rotated to a seated audience of about five hundred clouds, all impeccably dressed, wearing either traditional ties, bow ties or bows.

"They're a well turned out bunch," said Rod.

"Yes well, seeing as this is going to be our biggest television triumph of all time, I put a dress code on the tickets. That way it all comes together to add to the spectacle."

Rod liked that; it gave the event a touch of class.

"Is it pay-per-view?"

"Well Rod, what we have done is quite clever. What you are currently watching is not. This is what I like to call a teaser. It's like the pre-game show. The audience are all watching this part free of charge, but after five minutes of the action beginning then wham! We hit them where it hurts and take their money.

I believe that despite this being pay-per-view, it is the event of the century and for that reason we will easily get the highest rating in the history of cloud TV. I mean what else are they going to watch?

We control the networks and all they are offering at the moment are repeats of old programmes that they have all seen hundreds of times. This should be quite brilliant."

Rod was elated at the news. He was going to make a lot of money from this, easily enough on which to retire with more remaining.

He had met his part of the bargain by organising and manipulating everyone into this showdown and the boss had certainly sorted out the financial side of things and the more intricate elements of broadcasting. Yes things were going swimmingly. All he had to do now was sit back and watch the action unfold.

Emereldon tore through the air towards the ant. As he descended, the general public, quite wisely, moved out of the way and ran for cover.

This one movement had worked an absolute treat as it had forced so many of the humans to leave Soho Square. The ant was attempting to get to his feet as Emereldon landed on him, smashing him back down to the ground. He stood on the ant's back and at this point Howard and Bruce showed up and crept towards him.

The rocky figure considered the unique position he was in, watching three warriors about to engage in combat whilst standing on the back of an ant.

However seconds later a large crash caused both Howard and Bruce to fall off into a crumpled heap on the pavement below.

Eggo Maniac had made his entrance and the murky-green egg had clumsily fallen onto the ant and somersaulted into Howard and Bruce. It was like a bowling ball crashing into a set of skittles.

This was not Eggo Maniac's intention. To the passer-by it must have been impressive and deliberate, but it was not.

Upon standing the egg began to gloat as he attempted to cover up the fact that this manouvre was purely accidental.

Emereldon laughed before turning his attention to one of the corners of Soho Square. Here, the Sheep Brigade was in full combat mode against the three guardians.

Private Lunatic had managed to roll directly into Slimax, splitting him into two separate parts. This would not hurt Slimax of course, as he managed to reconnect himself together and continue the battle.

Commander Winters was firing some eggs at Eator and whilst this sounded like a harmless food fight, it was not. These eggs, upon making contact with anything, cracked open and out poured a green acidic liquid. This was melting everything it touched including tarmac, stone and metal lamp posts.

Eator was extremely nimble as he ducked and dodged and made his way closer to his opponent.

It was here that Private Ostrich charged into the mix, head still tucked inside his wool of course, brandishing what can only be described as a wooden, meat cleaver. How this would do any damage was beyond Emereldon, but, like the eggs, there was more than met the eye regarding the strange instrument of war.

The cleaver cut things down and seemed to have incredible power. It sliced through the concrete with ease and Eator was very quick to get out of the way.

This left only Miss Terious, who was the furthest away from the ant. She stood in the shadows of a building and was not doing anything. Her natural aura seemed to frighten everyone away regardless.

In front of her were the two remaining members of the Sheep Brigade, Lieutenant Figs and Private Cannon. Figs was tightening his red bandana around his head in a nervous fashion and Private Cannon, well as you can probably guess, Private Cannon was holding a weapon that can only be described as, well, a cannon.

This thing was enormous and it was larger than the sheep itself. It was an incredible feat that he could even carry the weapon let alone use it. It was black and had a green and red button on the back facing Private Cannon as opposed to a trigger. The barrel was directed at Miss Terious and could have quite easily shot out car tyres; such was the diameter of the weapon.

This did not even cause Miss Terious to flinch. It was a stand-off. Lieutenant Figs and Private Cannon were nervous. This cloaked figure was not bothered by their presence in any way.

Emereldon continued to observe with great interest. The tension rose and rose and despite the furious combat and panicking humans running in all directions, this particular area was quiet.

Nobody wanted to make a move.

There was sweat on the faces of the two sheep and they glanced at each other before Lieutentant Figs nodded.

"Let's do this," said Private Cannon. The pressure had got to him as he opened fire.

Enormous, pink, cannon balls belted out of his gun at the target.

Miss Terious vanished and re-appeared to the left of the blast impact. More came her way and they all seemed to have minds of their own.

Emereldon quickly saw that this was because they actually did. These were pink, sentient cannon balls. Upon closer inspection it was possible to see tiny faces grinning insanely as they chased their target.

Miss Terious was fast though and dashed around the square still pursued by these pink, homing balls. There was little time for Emereldon to continue watching the scene as the ant had begun to move and jostle around, evidently quite upset about the presence of two unwanted visitors on his back. Eggo Maniac clung on for dear life, whilst Emereldon knelt down, clutching the bristles on the ant's legs.

"Remain still Eggo Maniac. You must show some sort of balance," said Emereldon.

Despite the best moves of the ant, he managed to keep calm and more importantly showed about as much movement as a statue.

The same could not be said for Eggo Maniac however. He was being hurled from one area of the creature to another and soon the inevitable came.

Launched up into the air, he descended and who would have believed it, landed smack bang onto Howard and Bruce. It seemed that whatever he did he could get one over on that pair.

The ant suddenly stopped and awkwardly stretched its head around to check that there was nothing on him anymore. He was satisfied and glared at Eator, who was the closest of his opponents.

He lashed out, but as he did, he stopped in mid thrust of his front leg. His eyes closed and he sank to the floor unconscious. On top of his neck knelt Emereldon who had pinched him.

"What did you do?" said Eggo Maniac.

"Just a handy little trick I learnt a long time ago. Do not fear for the ant, he is merely asleep and will be for a few more hours. It's all about finding different pressure points you see. Now we must deal with those two."

Eggo Maniac turned around to see Bruce and Howard making their way towards him in a menacing fashion. They had clearly recovered from his earlier cannonball roll and his crash-landing which had flattened them.

The expressions on their faces were aggressive and perhaps, despite the mind control that held them, they could still feel emotions.

Eggo Maniac reached out his hand, "Come on chaps. Shall we put this all behind us then? I mean we are all friends are we not? Just don't listen to that Anne Weavers. She is controlling you. Let's be allies again."

Not a single word affected their mood and the pair continued on like a couple of brainwashed zombies. They didn't even speak.

Emereldon leapt in front of Eggo Maniac. "Get back. I shall have to deal with this. They cannot hear you and at present they have no idea what they are doing. If we get them out of this trance, they will have no recollection of this event, so please, allow me."

"They won't remember anything?" said Eggo Maniac.

"Yes, that's right. What's your point?"

"Well there's only one thing to do then. Howard, I am smarter than you and Bruce; I think you'll find that I have a far greater knowledge than even your encyclopaedia can deliver. I am the leader of this group and…"

Eggo Maniac flew back and rolled across the pavement. Whilst he was gloating, Bruce had managed to get a quick strike at him and had connected.

Oddly Emereldon had allowed this to happen.

Eggo Maniac got back to his feet; he was not in the best mood now. "What did you do that for?"

"You deserved it, what with all that arrogance."

The blue figure chuckled as he finished speaking and then rolled out of the way as Howard kicked out at him. He held out his hand directly in front of him and it began to glow a bright, blue colour.

This captivated Howard and Bruce who now stepped up the pace and marched directly to him. Of course this was a trap and as they got to within a metre of Emereldon the blue light shot out and wrapped around them both.

It did not stop there though.

The light continued to move and wrap, move and wrap, until the two warriors were in the process of being mummified. There was no escape for them, none whatsoever.

Eggo Maniac raced over and by now it was not possible to see what was underneath the light. This process continued until they were now in the middle of a great ball of yarn.

At this point Eggo Maniac heard Emereldon speak to himself, "That will do."

The light stopped moving and then made a flash.

When Eggo Maniac opened his eyes he could now see his two friends were still. They were trapped inside a large, blue boulder. It was transparent, hence his ability to see them, but they were not moving, not even an inch. This boulder was the same shade of blue as Emereldon, except of course it was transparent.

The egg stared at Emereldon who was quick to answer the obvious question that was coming his way.

"No they are fine Eggo Maniac. Did you not listen to what I said earlier? The aim of this mission is not to harm anyone save for Anne Weavers, who worryingly has not revealed herself yet. Still we can go and have some fun with the Sheep Brigade now."

The pair ran over to assist Eator first. He had his hands full and Eggo Maniac could see that he had now grown his full upper body complete with two arms of considerable length.

He still floated though, but this added advantage of having his two arms meant that he was able to strike out at his opponents rather than just relying on his traditional eating method.

There was a multitude of potholes around Eator now, clearly from where the acidic eggs had landed. He also sported a hole in the back of his cloak, which must have meant that at some point he had been hit by one.

His red skin and spiky fur were on show for all to see now, but this intimidating appearance did not affect the Sheep Brigade at all.

Perhaps this was down to the mind control used by Anne Weavers. Yes that must be it, pondered Eggo Maniac.

Emereldon grabbed out at Private Ostrich, yet the sheep evaded his grasp and the blue figure nearly received a sliced arm for his troubles. He ducked as an acidic egg landed close by him and decided to focus his attention on Commander Winters.

This was a wise move as the weapon the sheep carried was large and cumbersome thus lessening his agility. Emereldon swept his long leg across the ground, connecting with Commander Winter's hoof and flooring him instantly.

Before the sheep could even dream of getting back to his feet, he had been leapt upon and Emereldon had grabbed his shoulder and utilised yet another of his famous pinches.

Winters slept like a lamb.

All that remained now were Private Ostrich, who was possibly the most lethal of the bunch, Lieutenant Figs, Private Cannon and Private Lunatic.

Miss Terious still sprinted around the sides of the buildings as yet more of Private Cannon's tracking bombs chased her.

"She must be preparing for something big," said Emereldon to himself. Surely a guardian as tough as Miss Terious could deal with a couple of sheep.

Lieutenant Figs was the next to fall.

Emereldon had managed to get to him quite easily, yet Private Ostrich was still the main problem. He was frenetic in the manner in which he wielded his wooden cleaver and no one could touch him. From afar it looked as if Eator and he were performing an intricate dance of some description.

Emereldon decided he would deal with the other two sheep first.

Private Cannon did not notice his approach, as he was far too busy firing yet more of these pink balls at Miss Terious, or at least this is what Emereldon thought. As the rocky man edged closer, the sheep turned, weapon and all, and unleashed a barrage of ammunition directly at him.

Emereldon dropped to the floor, so hard and so fast, that his impact made an indentation in the tarmac below. He was close enough though and dived forward with his rock like fist connecting with Private Cannon's weapon.

It shattered into pieces on the ground and as Private Cannon reached into his woollen stomach to grab another tool to use against his opponent, he dropped on the floor asleep.

Miss Terious stopped and stood still. The destruction of Private Cannon's weapon meant that the pink balls dropped to the floor and vanished.

Slimax moved to the side of Emereldon and said, "The sheep that kept rolling into me, it's run away."

"Impossible. It is under the influence of Anne Weaver's rainbow mind control. It cannot have escaped. Everything we have ever seen that has been subjected to that is obedient to the extreme. I have seen one warrior stand up in front of an army in an attempt to fight them. Such is the power of its hold."

Slimax shrugged, he could only inform Emereldon of what he had witnessed.

"Slimax stay alert, there is no way that Private Lunatic has fled the battlefield. He must be gearing up for some sort of counter or hidden attack. Maintain your wits about you."

Emereldon's orders were firm and for the first time since they had entered the battle, he had seemed concerned. A thud broke his train of thought and he saw that Private Ostrich had finally fallen.

Miss Terious had dealt with him then.

He wandered over to her, smiling, "How did you do it? He was quite the character."

"I just told him to stop, and he did."

"Well done Miss Terious. Now the only remaining opponent we have is this Private Lunatic. Where do you think he could be? He cannot have left as the power of the rainbow…"

"Emereldon he has left."

Miss Terious was extremely confident in her answer.

"That is not possible. You would be aware as well as anyone about the powers of the rainbow. It cannot be as simple as that. He is under mind control."

Eggo Maniac trotted over to see what all the commotion was about. It was quite unnerving to him that Emereldon was so upset by this. Even when he betrayed him, the blue figure took it with acceptance and even a hint of amusement. This was different though, Eggo Maniac was certain that he had seen a drop of sweat on Emereldon's brow. He didn't know that rocks were capable of perspiration.

Quickly the rock giant waved at Slimax and Eator. They disappeared quickly out of sight and only he and Miss Terious, plus a bunch of sleeping outcasts, remained.

This saddened Eggo Maniac. He had never truly reflected on the group and who they were, yet he had just summed it up aptly in his mind. They were outcasts, both from society and everyone else that they had encountered.

Oddly he noticed Miss Terious signal as if she was communicating with someone else, someone who was watching but not there. It must be the clouds gauged Eggo Maniac.

Emereldon nodded at her.

"They are no longer filming. This has been a ratings success and now they want live shows in the cloud realm. That is fine, but we cannot escape the urgent matter that this Private Lunatic has escaped. In no way is this acceptable. We must track him down. Why has the rainbow power failed?"

Eggo Maniac could not help but to listen, then it hit him.

Numb, he felt numb. He knew exactly what was coming.

Miss Terious removed her hood. As she did, her cloak fell to the ground.

A very familiar grey suited woman stood in front of him.

It was Anne Weavers.

Chapter 17
Wanted Superstar

"What a night and what a match. Ladies and gentleman that was an extravaganza of combat, the likes of which I have never witnessed before as a broadcast journalist. Your thoughts Yoddy?"

"It was a tremendous, tremendous match. Emereldon and the guardians came to fight and boy did they deliver. This will have to go down as one of, if not the greatest piece of combat in cloud TV's illustrious history. Back to you Yod."

"Well it started with the rainbow stained warriors making quite the entrance and I think we could all have predicted that they were going to deliver. There was no question about that.

Their opponents arrived in magnificent style, crashing into the scene from high atop the buildings of Soho Square and then the battle erupted.

These warriors, gladiators, gave their all to the very end. I have to say though that Emereldon would have to be my man of the match. He was immense in the way he carried himself and delivered knock out blow after knock out blow. A real competitor here on cloud TV. What did you think Yoddy?"

"Well I..."

The boss muted the television screen.

Rod laughed, "Don't you think they're overdoing it a bit boss? I mean it was good viewing, but Emereldon was putting them to sleep, not smashing them into oblivion."

"That's why the pair of them are the number one commentary team of cloud TV. They can make lots of things sound far more fabulous than they actually are.

We should get a ratings update through shortly which will

inform us of how well we did and how much money we made."

The boss grinned at this point and adjusted his tie and suit-jacket. He was ever so pleased.

Rod chuckled to himself once more.

This time the boss questioned him. "Just what is so amusing Rod? I assume it's the fact that you have helped to create the largest and hopefully most profitable fight in cloud TV history."

"No boss, although I am thrilled about that. It's just this commentary team, they verge on the ridiculous in their descriptions. Just listening to the way he painted Emereldon as some sort of champion is amusing."

This comment did not sit well with the boss. He placed his hand on his chin, evidently contemplating something. There was clearly an issue that Rod had brought to his attention with his latest remark.

The pink cloud nervously took a sip from his glass and attempted to stare subtly at and read the thoughts of the boss. It did not work at all of course.

The boss was unreadable.

This was probably one of the reasons that he was indeed, the boss.

After a couple of minutes he finally spoke, "I think you have a good point there Rod. This is something that could have escaped my attention, but I am grateful to you for bringing it up."

Rod nodded and smiled at him, pretending to demonstrate that he knew what the boss was talking about. In reality he did not have a clue and waited for the boss to continue, which he did.

"Emereldon spoiled that. He did not let the fight go on for a sufficient of time. That could have easily been drawn out for an hour long main event style show, yet he ended it after about twenty minutes.

That is not good enough.

There was hardly any focus on finding Anne Weavers once the fighting commenced and these were all points that were made clear to him by our storyline writers.

My goodness, he nearly gave away the identity of Miss Terious and that is not supposed to be revealed for a few weeks, let alone today. If any of the audience have caught wind of that plot twist then I am going to be livid to say the least."

Phew thought Rod. He had begun to harbour concerns that the boss was upset with him but fortunately it was with Emereldon. At least he could rest easy now.

A few whirring sounds interrupted Rod's thoughts and he quickly stared at the screen. Underneath it a piece of paper was emerging and he soon realised that those sounds were that of the printer.

The paper emerged slowly and Rod was sure that this must have been the ratings information. If this was good then the boss would be pleased and everything could go ahead as planned. If they were bad or not up to the expected standard, well, that did not bear thinking about.

The boss gestured at Rod and the cloud immediately floated over to the television, which still showed Yod and Yoddy discussing something in an animated fashion, albeit on mute.

He tore the piece of paper out from underneath the screen. He could not bear to look at it and shielded his eyes whilst he passed it over to the outstretched hand of the boss.

"Can't you cope with the tension Rod?" said the boss.

Rod shook himself to indicate that this was indeed the case.

The boss nodded and cackled, then went immediately silent.

Rod closed his eyes. Surely silence was not a good thing? They had been preparing for this moment for a long time now and he just hoped it had delivered sufficiently. By all means it should have. They had predicted numbers only recently.

As the event had started they were both confident that it would be a success, but this was the real telling point. This was where they would discover if they had delivered.

"Open your eyes Rod. Do it now."

Rod obliged. He squinted at the sheet of paper which the boss now held firmly in front of him.

"Over five hundred million views. That's basically the entire population."

A smile that ran from one side of Rod's face to the other emerged.

The boss shared one of a similar size.

They had done it. Rod was made. There was only one thing to do now.

The boss smirked, "You are quite right Rod. The next viable step is a live televised event featuring these new stars that we have created."

This was going to be great. Finally they could bring the unrivalled and thrilling action of combat live to the masses. Rod was bouncing up and down with excitement. He was not aware that he was doing this, but nevertheless he was.

The boss rose up from his chair and stood by the pink cloud. He put his arm around Rod.

"Well done. This is it Rod. After today's success I'm taking you to the big time. You are going to have the ride of your life. Now go and message those commentators whilst they are still on air and have them announce that there will be a live event featuring everyone today and that tickets will be limited.

Don't forget to add that if a cloud is not able to get to the event, then it can still be purchased at home on pay-per-view."

The boss laughed as he finished. Rod joined him. Things were great.

Eggo Maniac was lying on a bed in a cell. It wasn't too dissimilar to the one that he had been held in on Chordona, save for the difference in colour of course.

He was in a navy-blue room that did not even have a window. Inside was a bed with blue sheets, one blue pillow and there was a toilet in the corner which oddly was red.

The floor was metal, but still maintained the same blue colour as the walls and in front of him were some red bars that kept him where he was.

The ceiling above him slowly flashed a gentle red and then a burgundy colour which lit the area well. Eggo Maniac reckoned that he had been in this cell for at least three hours now.

He had not had a visit from anyone, nor had he had any communication. His only recollection was asking what on Earth was going on regarding Anne Weavers and the only reply he had received was a sly grin; well, that and Emereldon sneaking up behind him and performing his sleeping pinch manouvre that he dished out.

After that he had woken in this room. Strangely he had picked up a bad habit of doing that – waking up in random places and they were not good ones. That was the way he had entered this world; waking up in an alleyway.

He wondered what would become of him, after all he had fought on Emereldon's side against Anne Weavers only to discover that Anne Weavers was actually with them and on Emereldon's team all along.

Well that was how he had perceived it. There was probably a bit more to it than that. The trouble with having so much time on your own is that you over think things, not to mention dwelling on the most irrelevant of thoughts.

What had happened to the camera man? What about the others who were now infected with this rainbow power thingy. Where were they? Why did Emereldon and Anne Weavers seem so distraught that Private Lunatic had escaped? Why did it matter? He was just a rainbow-coloured sheep.

It was not…

Then it struck him.

Private Lunatic was not a lunatic at all, or if he was, he was a highly intelligent one. His natural colours when he met the Sheep Brigade were that of a rainbow anyway. He must have either abstained from all the luxuries that were on offer on Chordona or he must have found a way not to get infected.

He had snuck off towards the end of the battle when few were watching and despite Anne Weavers attempting to control and command him, he had left. What was his plan then?

Maybe he would deliver some sort of daring rescue mission and save Eggo Maniac? No that was unlikely. In truth Eggo Maniac had spoken with very few of the Sheep Brigade except for Commander Winters and Lieutenant Figs and that was due to their rank.

He had not given Private Lunatic the time of day, so there would be no reason for the sheep to come and bail him out of prison. He would have to plot his own escape.

Emereldon and Anne Weavers huddled around a screen in a large room that was full of buttons, levers, flashing lights and controls of all different kinds. There were multiple screens sticking out, yet they concentrated on one.

On it was Eggo Maniac in his prison cell and towards the bottom of the screen were some subtitles. They were his thoughts.

"Still he has shown no concern whatsoever for the ceiling and the flashing. You were correct Anne. It was my assumption that he would have scrutinised everything in the room. Alas the brain reading continues."

Anne stroked her hair back and once again adjusted her jacket. She continued to concentrate on the words that appeared in front of her.

Emereldon finally took a step back.

"This is getting us nowhere. I don't think he has any idea where that crazy sheep has gone. They have no sort of allegiance to one another. He has admitted this himself. He doesn't even think that Private Lunatic will attempt a rescue."

Anne swivelled her head around to answer. "You may be right, but at least then we are cognizant that Eggo Maniac is loyal. He genuinely has not attempted to contact anyone. He is lost and on his own. We can work him onto our side."

"But he will not trust us now. We have been recording his every thought and whim. We are both capable of reading minds, but not to the extent of this machine.

This is absolutely invasive. I cannot remember the last occasion that we conducted a mind reading that was this thorough. Intrusive is not the word."

Anne gestured in agreement. "He doesn't know, so it doesn't matter. Now do you wish to carry on with the machine or shall we leave him to it?"

"Yes just keep it going. You never can tell. We may find out something of interest that can assist us. We do need to go and pay him a visit soon though. After all he will start to get lonely."

As Emereldon finished he began to laugh. It must have been contagious as Anne, too, joined him.

The people of London seemed to have gone back to their usual lives and their own business. Private Lunatic had managed to escape and make his way down to Trafalgar Square.

Amazingly he was able to trot through the crowds of people with little notice. There was an art exhibition on at the National Gallery which featured a great deal of sculpture, so people assumed he was advertising for that.

This was quite the odd thing about London. There was always so much going on, that anything out of the ordinary did not seem that way. Clearly this was how the group had been able to walk the streets with such ease.

Growing in confidence now Private Lunatic crossed the road heading for Westminster. "Look it's Private Lunatic," said a passer-by. "Sheep Brigade," said another.

Private Lunatic had forgotten about his fame that had been developed by Anne Weavers.

He dashed into the nearest alleyway and sprinted to the end, hopping over a fence and finding himself in a tight space with two large wheelie bins on either side of him. This was not what he had expected.

He clambered onto one and then jumped to the other. He could now see over the fence and noticed that nobody had followed him. Letting out a sigh of relief he gathered some composure and surveyed the area around him.

There was a back door directly in front of him and judging by the stench of food waste pouring out of the bins, he considered this must be a restaurant.

That probably wasn't the ideal place for a sheep, but nonetheless he jumped down and poked his head through the door. He was right, it was a kitchen.

Two chefs prepared meals and worryingly he could smell lamb.

Well now he had two choices, face the crowds where he would inevitably be spotted by that blue, rocky man or try and get through this kitchen and attempt to find a way out of London. Then he could disappear into the countryside where he could live peacefully.

There was of course a third choice and it was one that he really should take. He could rescue the Sheep Brigade and the other members of the group.

Mindful of what was the right thing to do, he carefully leapt onto the ground and crept down the alleyway. The hordes of people were still there, but he was just off Trafalgar Square so this was to be expected.

This would be easy.

He had to draw attention to himself in order to draw out those guardians with the hope of finding his friends. He also required the presence of Anne Weavers to rid them of that rainbow power, but he knew all about her.

Private Lunatic held his head high and marched out onto the pavement. His pride led the way whilst people naturally avoided him and cars stopped as he crossed over to Nelson's Column. He climbed over the lion and then up to the point where Nelson himself stood.

From this vantage point he could see all over London, therefore nobody could take him by surprise. Inside Private Lunatic was giggling hysterically. Everything was in place and absolutely everything was going to plan, just as he knew it would.

Anne leant over Eggo Maniac and prodded him. Still no movement, not even an inch. The egg was still, eyes closed and expressionless.

Emereldon moved forward and prodded him. Still there was no

movement, not even a flinch. Ducking down, the rocky warrior leaned towards Eggo Maniac's mouth to listen.

"I cannot hear any breathing, but then I must confess, I do not know whether eggs breathe or not."

"Do you think he's..." Anne did not finish her sentence, although from her tone of voice it was fairly obvious to what she was referring.

Emereldon shook his head, "I don't think so. He's alive but this is not sleep. Perhaps he is toying with us."

Grabbing Eggo Maniac, he raised him up into the air.

Anne Weavers stepped back and looked slightly uneasy about this.

"No stop, put him down. We cannot be sure he is bluffing."

"Why should I do that? I'm not going to be made a fool of by an egg that changes sides more than the wind. It is time... Aaaaarrrrrgggghhhhhhh."

Eggo Maniac crashed to the floor. Emereldon waved his hands frantically and charged around the room. "It burns, it burns."

In desperation the rocky warrior plunged his hands into the toilet where there was at least water to cool them down. Shaking them dry he walked to the centre of the room and joined Anne who was examining the fallen egg.

Eggo Maniac's body was different now. It had changed colour and Anne was adamant that his arms and legs had shortened slightly, whilst the actual circumference of his egg shaped body had expanded.

No that can't be right, she mused to herself. The one change, that was not up for debate was the fact that Eggo Maniac had changed colour.

The unattractive, murky-green had vanished and had been replaced by a bright shade of crimson. Anne moved her index finger out and slowly pushed it towards the body.

Emereldon grabbed her hand and drew it back. "Don't even think about that Anne."

"Get off me. You have just had your hands in a toilet. That is disgusting."

Ignoring her outburst Emereldon continued, "His body, it is red-hot. It will burn you and potentially scar you."

Anne shook her hands in a futile attempt to clean them and suddenly stopped. The penny had dropped. She moved over and stood by Emereldon staring down at this completely crimson body.

Eggo Maniac had his eyes closed, and as before, he was completely motionless. There was not even a hint of movement.

For once the pair were stuck. Possessing the high intellects that they did made this a difficult scenario for them. They were not used to not being able to know what to do.

A shiver ran down Anne's spine.

Emereldon had now managed to locate a pole in the corridor and was prodding away at the possibly lifeless body of Eggo Maniac.

"Well he cannot be dead. He's changed colour and is emitting some serious body heat."

Anne nodded in agreement before responding.

"Do we inform the clouds? Rod will probably want to know as will the boss."

"I would imagine they already know by now. The issue we have is that he was the comedy element of the show. He knocked down a couple of those warriors through sheer fortune and foolishness. The crowd and the folk at home will want to see him, not to mention the missing one."

"Well I suggest we shift our attention to the missing sheep. Let's lock this cell back up and if he comes around then so be it, he still cannot escape. If he doesn't, then we will have to throw him to the…"

"Mistress Anne, Mistress Anne."

Anne and Emereldon swivelled around to see the camera man sprinting down the corridor. His voice was full of panic.

Anne waved at him, urging him to carry on with what he was saying.

"It's Private Lunatic. We have found him."

The pair smiled.

So things would go their way after all, thought Anne to herself.

"Finish your words camera man and be clear and concise." Emereldon's tone with the camera man was far harsher than Anne's.

He stopped and wiped a drip of sweat from his brow. "Private Lunatic has scaled the full height of Nelson's Column in Trafalgar Square. He's currently perched at the top sitting by Nelson's head. He wants you to come and confront him."

"Who does he want? Emereldon or me, or both? Does he want the guardians too?"

"He said that he wants absolutely all representatives of the clouds to come to him at once."

Emereldon laughed at this suggestion, "He must be insane. He will be destroyed by one of us, let alone all. Come Anne, shall we give him what he wants?"

Anne began to walk past the camera man before she took a quick step back. She gently held his tie and looked closely at it.

"This tie, where did you get it? I'm not sure that red matches with your blue shirt. Perhaps yellow would have been a more sensible choice, and where is your jacket?"

The large, blue figure behind her sighed. He had witnessed Anne do this so many times to the camera man that it had become monotonous.

The camera man stuttered. "W-w-w-e-ell i-i-i-i-it was a bit hot and…"

"That's no excuse for not being able to dress properly. You are fully aware of the standards I expect. Upon my return I expect to see you wearing a white shirt, red tie and a jacket."

She smiled at him, in a gentle way.

The camera man breathed a little more easily. This was false hope on his part.

Anne, who was still holding him by the tie, threw him into the cell with such accuracy that his head landed directly into the toilet bowl. She walked over slowly and flushed the lavatory twice.

She then pushed his head further down into it, to ensure that he was getting a good soaking.

"Thank you for your information camera man. You may now want to thank me for cleaning up your hair and setting you on the way to becoming a cleaner and smarter worker."

Between desperately attempting to inhale air and fixing his appearance the camera man did indeed reply.

"Thank you mistress Anne."

She nodded in approval of her thanks and pulled him up once again by the tie, and hurled him back out of the cell and into the corridor wall.

She left the cell and Emereldon flashed his hand at a control panel on the wall and the bars rose up to seal off Eggo Maniac once more.

The camera man hastily got to his feet and scuttled off back down the corridor, probably to take a much needed shower.

Eggo Maniac was alone once more in the cell. As the footsteps faded, a wide grin flickered on his face but only for a split second. His eyes remained closed and his face reverted back to the same emotionless expression he had held before.

Chapter 18
One Sheep Army

Hundreds of clouds moved back and forth against a purple canvas. They were all of a variety of shapes, colours and sizes and were working hard. This was an organised regime to say the least.

Every single cloud there knew what it was doing and where it was supposed to be. There was very little communication between any of them, save for the odd passing of a tool or placing of a ladder.

Some busily constructed seating, others were painting the cloud TV logo and those who were tasked with the most important job of all were building the ring.

This was going to be the arena in which the warriors from London would do battle against the guardians, in front of a live crowd on pay-per-view. A certain element of excitement had captured the workers and all were looking over everything extremely carefully to ensure perfection.

Overseeing all of this and ensuring a general sense of perfection, via a television screen in his cottage, was the boss and his guest, Rod.

The boss was once again sitting back down in his armchair, whilst Rod had returned to the sofa.

"You see Rod, the key to a successful operation is to ensure that everything is constructed and built to perfection. We are an entertainment brand and it's important that we behave as such. I don't just want a ring, I want an arena with music, lights, sound effects, gimmicks and I want to hype this live match as much as possible.

We could potentially create some superstars from this. I like the Sheep Brigade as a stable of warriors, but we must have them all, which leads me to my next issue.

The construction and running of the show is done. It is wonderful and it's ready. There's no question about that. I need to know what we are doing about this unfortunate mishap."

Rod gulped.

The vanishing of Private Lunatic was a serious issue and one to which he did not really have an answer; well he did, but not one that the boss would want to hear. The boss fiddled with his tie once more before continuing.

"This sheep has escaped our clutches, just because it is rainbow-coloured. Would I be correct in surmising that?"

"Well I suppose that would be correct."

"I thought so. Therefore who would you say is responsible for this, shall we say, miscarriage of duty? To elaborate on that, I find it incredulous that someone as intelligent as Anne Weavers can infect a whole group, yet nothing happens to the egg, so we have to send in Emereldon to persuade him.

Also an assumption is made that Private Lunatic is infected, but in actuality he is not, because he has rainbow-coloured wool anyway and no one thinks to perform any test."

The boss inhaled deeply. His rant over, he calmly sat back and regained his composure. He took a swig from his glass, finishing off the contents.

Handing it to Rod, he ushered the pink cloud out of the room towards the kitchen to top him up.

Whilst Rod was completing this task, the boss continued to pontificate and Rod listened closely.

"I would have thought that the fact that Private Lunatic had rainbow-coloured wool would have been reason enough for Anne or that camera man to pay more attention to him. Tests should have been carried out and then we would not be in this mess.

The Eggo Maniac situation is not so bad as he is easily manipulated, or so we think. Perhaps there is more to him than meets the eye.

The bottom line is I demand that these two fighters make it onto my network, otherwise there will be serious repercussions for Anne, the camera man, anyone else involved and certainly for you Rod."

A thin finger pointed straight at Rod and the cloud quickly sipped at his drink pretending that he had not noticed.

This further aggravated the boss.

"Do not hide away Rod. That sheep is in Trafalgar Square and I want it caught, brainwashed and brought back here in time to fight. I have a good mind to put his name down on the card to add some much needed pressure.

Failure to deliver him will result in you becoming a sock, something your old friend Tod is about to have happening to him."

"How long will it be?"

"For what? Don't waste my time."

Rod elaborated on his question. For some reason he had forgotten his feeling of fear, "How long will it be before Tod is transformed into a sock?"

"I don't know precisely - a few days is the norm. Why do you ask?"

The boss was interested in Rod's new take on the situation. The sudden lack of fear in the cloud and his concern for his friend had obviously driven him to show some bravery. Perhaps this could be manipulated.

He smiled now and waved at Rod, urging him to speak his thoughts. The boss had a new plan, a new tact to utilise. As opposed to threats, he would bargain with Rod.

This unnerved the cloud slightly so the boss offered him some light words of encouragement. "I think I may have been too harsh there. Please do tell me of your concerns."

"I would like to negotiate for Tod's release please. I am more than aware that I am not in a position to bargain, but please hear me out."

The boss grinned oddly as a sign that he was listening.

Rod cleared his throat, "I can guarantee you the capture of Private Lunatic and a regular live, weekly fighting show on two conditions."

"This is intriguing. Go on."

"I need the release of Tod. Please do not turn him into a sock. Between him and myself we can create an entire roster of superstars that will make the need for Private Lunatic seem pathetic. We can write storylines, create feuds between them and genuinely create a product that will have a colossal, high volume weekly audience."

"What about pay-per-view? I like pay-per-view."

"Well that's just it. That fits in perfectly. If we have a weekly show containing fights with a few of our middle of the road warriors plus a couple of big stars, we can create a championship that they all compete for and those matches can be exclusive to pay-per-view.

It's brilliant. We hook them in with storylines on the weekly TV show and then if they want to see the outcomes and the endings, we broadcast those live on pay-per-view. We will make an unbelievable amount of money from it."

Rod was excited as he finished his inpromptu pitch. He stared at the boss, desperate to see if he was on board with any of his ideas.

The trouble was the boss was difficult to read at the best of times, let alone when he was mulling something over. His hand was on his chin, whilst the other swilled the liquid around the wine glass.

Rod had witnessed him do this before and the sense of anticipation that had built up in the cloud seemed to make time slow down as he waited, quite literally on the edge of his seat, for an answer.

The boss stood up and paced across the room, back and forth, still clutching his chin and was evidently close to a decision.

Rod continued to concentrate until finally he stopped.

The boss' mouth opened and Rod was hanging on his every word.

"It is without doubt an interesting proposition. The idea of a regular, weekly show which essentially builds up to matches that we can sell, featuring stars that we have created, is a different concept."

He sipped from his glass and finally removed his hand from his chin.

"In short Rod, it's brilliant."

The cloud beamed. Elation filled his body and although he tried to hide his jubilation he could not.

"Can we do it then boss? Can we? It will be the greatest show ever to hit cloud TV, I can assure you of that. The best thing is we can make the stars too. We shall have complete creative control."

Rod was now bouncing around the room, like a balloon that had been blown up and released. He was all over the place with glee.

The boss grabbed him and put his arm around Rod's shoulder.

"There is one condition of course Rod. Find the sheep and it will happen. I'll put your friend Tod's punishment of being turned into a sock on hold, but only for the moment. Go and get Private Lunatic and everything you desire will be yours."

Private Lunatic scurried past Nelson's feet and placed his front hooves into his woollen coat. He produced a pair of binoculars and observed the surrounding area.

It could not be long now before his foes arrived. He just had to stall them and keep them busy for a while. That was his plan.

He looked around him. Next to Nelson he had constructed what was essentially a trench, except he hadn't done any digging, but he had built up a barricade and had placed various pieces of weaponry on each corner of the base of the statue.

According to his calculations, which were never incorrect, he could hit a target from any angle. The trouble was there was only one sheep and four cannons to operate. Lunatic also had no desire to injure any of the general public below.

This was an almost impossible task as he was in Trafalgar Square, one of the hottest tourist destinations in the world. He was relying on people scattering when they saw that a battle was occurring as had happened previously in Soho Square.

Lunatic placed down the binoculars and did some final checks on each weapon, ensuring that they were fully loaded, safety catches off and generally ready to go.

A large crashing noise caused him to abandon this and rush to the side that looked over the square below.

They were here then.

Emereldon must have had the same agenda as himself, hence why his entrance was so dramatic. Having a blue, rocky giant of an entity land straight in the middle of Trafalgar Square had the desired effect.

People sprinted in all directions and this allowed Private Lunatic to open fire more quickly than he had thought he would be able to.

Acidic eggs rained down on the blue figure, but he placed his cloak over his face and vanished, re-appearing a few yards back and out of range of the eggs.

Lunatic looked down and could see Slimax and Eator beginning to scale the column. Slimax did it with ease, sticking to the structure and smoothly ascending it. He was like a slug, but super fast.

Eator on the other hand had a bit more difficulty. He had grown to his full form and was gripping on with his claws and teeth, performing a slightly slower climb, but nevertheless he would make it.

Private Lunatic was concerned by the appearance of Eator. It was rare for this creature to get to his full form, as he would usually eat his body to quell his insatiable appetite, hence why most saw him as just a floating head.

If he had managed to stop himself from consuming his own body, it could only mean that he was saving himself for a serious meal.

More than likely he had set his intentions on Private Lunatic.

Still there was little time to dwell on such things and Lunatic grabbed his wooden meat cleaver and hurled it down at the two attackers.

Eator leapt out of the way and found himself back on the ground below, close to the two lions, who despite being statues, were becoming more and more appetising to him by the minute.

Slimax did not have the sense to shift or had no desire to make the effort. Regardless, the cleaver sliced through him from top to bottom, splitting him in half.

Private Lunatic looked down and waited for the results.

Oddly Slimax did not make a sound. Both parts of him were still, but then they quickly shook.

Lunatic knew what would happen next.

The two parts of the monster combined and jiggled around, whilst making a squelching sound and that was it. Slimax was as good as new.

Private Lunatic would have to act faster. He began to shoot down at his target with yet more acidic eggs. These worked better and managed to dislodge Slimax from the column.

He collapsed on top of Eator, but there was still not time for Private Lunatic to revel in his small piece of glory.

Quickly approaching him from the sky was Anne Weavers. She was leaping and rebounding off the side of buildings and was poised to make her jump onto Nelson. Private Lunatic ripped one of the cannons from its mount and unleashed some pink spheres that tracked Anne Weavers and followed her around the square.

Forced to alter her course, she hopped and skipped trying to lose these homing missile balls.

One hit a lamp post and another the pavement itself. Two brief explosions showed Anne why it was wise to get out of the way of these projectiles.

One continued to follow her and Private Lunatic shot out three more for good measure and quite frankly, to keep her busy.

The sheep inhaled a deep breath, not because he was tired, more for relief. A hand reached out for him and he ducked, evading the attacker. He rolled himself into a ball and hurtled towards the large figure. He connected with the left shin of Emereldon.

It did not even dent him.

Lunatic collapsed on the floor in a heap. He was used to smashing through walls with this technique, but up against the rock solid figure of Emereldon was another story. He was no match for the giant.

Opening his eyes he could see a great, blue hand reaching out towards him. There was only one possible outcome of this. Lunatic did not even bother to resist. He stayed where he was and closed his eyes.

He had done his part, completed his mission. After all he was only trying to buy some time. He had done it. The cold hand gently gripped his shoulder and Private Lunatic happily fell fast asleep.

"We have got him boss. We have got back Private Lunatic. He put up quite the fight it has to be said, but we have got him."

The boss smiled at Rod.

This new concept of compromising and making deals with

other beings might just have some merit to it. This cloud was far more motivated by reward than fear. Anyhow the boss now had to keep his end of the bargain.

He took out a small metal square from his inside suit-jacket. It was silver and had a red button placed firmly in the centre of it. He pressed and held down the button and spoke into it.

"Sock department, sock department, do you read me?"

After a short whirring sound a crackly voice replied, "Yes boss we are present. What do you desire?"

"You have a cloud down there who is scheduled for transformation. Please release him."

This time there was a pause before the reply came through.

Nervously the being on the other end of the line stated.

"We have many clouds who are awaiting that procedure boss. Is there a specifically named one?"

The boss grunted, whoever he was speaking to should be able to work out who it was he wanted to save. He sighed.

"I guess it's times like these that really emphasise why I am the boss. Rod, what is the name of your friend again? Was it Bod?"

Rod shook his head fiercely.

"No boss, his name was Tod and he is a purple cloud."

The boss waved in confirmation. "Sock department, his name is Tod and he is purple. It's the cloud I asked you to keep on hold."

The buzzing and crackling continued and Rod was certain that he could hear various pieces of machinery combined with a mixture of screams through the interference.

"Rodger that boss, we have located him. Where would you like him extracted?"

"Well not here. He's not actually supposed to be privy to this place. How about you just place him back in his home. Oh and let him know that Rod will be contacting him soon for some very serious planning. He should get some rest before this so that he is fresh to work."

"No problem boss, will do."

The connection cut out as the boss released his grip on the button.

Rod floated over from the sofa and bowed his head, "Thank you boss. You will not regret this. Shall I commence work?"

"You had better. I am expecting big things from you and I cannot wait to witness the results - mass pay-per-view figures and even higher regular weekly numbers. I am excited about this Rod and it is you who has created and harboured this feeling. Do not let me down.

Now go and see your friend and begin. I shall ask for progress updates sporadically."

Rod had just one more question, "Oh and boss, would it be okay if you were to transport me back?"

The boss waved him away in a gesture that obviously meant no.

Rod floated out of the house. It was worth a try, not that it bothered him anyway. He was feeling extraordinarily smug about everything now. It was all going his way.

Eggo Maniac remained on the floor in the cell. He was still red and motionless. There was a particular ebullience about him though and despite his lack of movement and expression, something was happening, something good.

He looked healthy.

A team of Anne's scientists had deduced that he was in a state of perpetual hibernation, whatever that meant.

Do eggs hibernate?

Mind you, do eggs walk and talk and clash with pizza boxes and encyclopaedias in combat situations.

There was a slight difference to the scene now. Eggo Maniac had been joined by an equally unconscious Private Lunatic.

Emereldon had shown the decency to place the sheep on the bed and had steered well clear of the boiling hot egg in the middle of the cell.

Anne Weavers stood outside waiting for Emereldon to leave now that he had tucked Private Lunatic up in bed.

"Do you not think that's going too far?" she said.

"Apologies Anne, I just got carried away. According to Rod he is supposed to join our roster, so I figured that showing a few niceties wouldn't go amiss. I mean he is going to be working with us in time."

Emereldon glided over Eggo Maniac.

Anne noticed how careful he was when he was close to the egg. "Was he truly that hot?"

Emereldon nodded, "Unbelievably, I've never felt anything like it and I have touched molten lava before."

"That does not make any sense though. If he was that high, temperature-wise, would he not melt the floor?"

This was a salient point and one that Emereldon could not answer, so he didn't. He just shrugged instead.

Anne ensured the cell was locked and both walked slowly down the corridor. Everything had now been settled aside from the issue with Eggo Maniac, but he was locked up and therefore could not escape. All they could do now was wait.

The trouble was, this was not something that either Anne Weavers or Emereldon were used to doing. They lived for action and sitting around wondering why a captured egg had become red-hot, yet did not melt the floor, was hardly their idea of a good time.

Back in their control room Emereldon put his feet up on the back of a chair, Anne Weaver's chair to be precise.

Anne knocked them off, yet they returned instantly.

She clipped them off, but Emereldon would not stop.

"Do you have to be this annoying when there is no task at hand?" she said.

"What can I say, I am bored. The construction of the live event set does not require our assistance so what more can we do?"

"Maybe I'll take a holiday. I might go back to Chordona and…"

"Surely you aren't referring to that planet in that dimension that believes you are going to lead a rebellion against the clouds? I mean they assume you work for them if I'm not mistaken?"

Anne growled at his words. "Whatever you say Emereldon. I can do what I like there and no one will be any the wiser. Why do you not take leave to your own home world, oh, wait a minute, you don't have one."

This struck a nerve with Emereldon who stood up. "I didn't say I had no home world, I just don't have any idea which one it is. I have to have been born somewhere."

"Do you? You might have been created for the amusement of the clouds. That's what happened to that egg like creature in the cell."

Anne was now standing opposite Emereldon. Both held aggressive poses and both gritted their teeth. They had never fought before, but then that was due to their solid focus on achieving their mission objectives.

Now that they had none, but to sit, wait and observe, they had the time to think about each other.

A screen whirred into life and Rod appeared on it. He observed the pair briefly. "That's enough. You two obviously need a break and I am ordering you to go on holiday together."

"But sir, that cannot be right. He's not right in this.."

"That's enough Anne. It is a direct order. You are to go on holiday, somewhere of your choosing, but you are to go together."

"Yes sir," both warriors answered simultaneously.

"Off you go then, you have a week, then you must come back for our first live show," said Rod.

The cloud watched through the screen as both left the room. In all honesty he had only just thought about the idea of sending them on holiday together. Their ill-feeling towards each other would surely grow if they were forced to spend time with one another.

When it reached its peak, Rod could use their anger and resentment to deliver quite a feud and quite a series of matches between the two. Now that was good for business.

Chapter 19
Beat the Machine

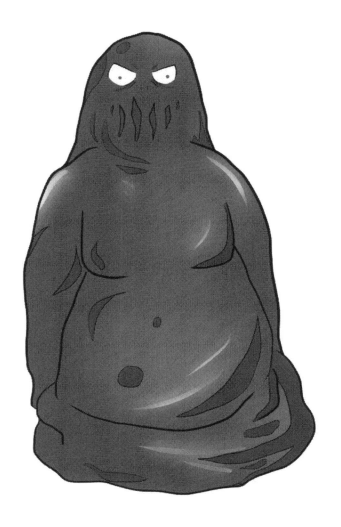

Private Lunatic awoke in a haze. His last memory was that of Emereldon putting him to sleep by pinching his shoulder. He had allowed the rocky figure to do this, so he had no complaints. At least he was on a bed and a reasonably comfortable one at that. It was better than sleeping on the streets, that was for sure.

He stared down at Eggo Maniac. He was bright crimson and motionless. Climbing down from the bed he waved his hoof over the body of Eggo Maniac.

He could feel the heat that was emanating from the body. It was ferocious. Can't be long now, Lunatic thought to himself.

There was little to do in the cell. It was high tech and therefore was pretty much impenetrable, well, it was for now. Private Lunatic knew that he would be escaping shortly and there was nothing anyone could do about it.

The sound of footsteps echoed down the corridor and the sheep had been expecting them.

The camera man appeared, wearing a white shirt, red tie and suit-jacket. Obviously he had taken the advice of Anne Weavers. He stood in front of the cell, peering in and checking that both prisoners were there.

"Couldn't you have done that from your control room? I assume you have multiple cameras zooming in on us," said Private Lunatic.

"You're the one in the cell. I hardly think you're in a position to use sarcasm."

"We shall see. We shall see. What is it you want anyway? Where are the two that captured me? They could at least have the decency to come and interrogate me themselves."

The camera man laughed. Between giggles he managed to utter a reply, "Do you think that they would bother with a prisoner like you?"

He coughed slightly and then continued, "They have gone on holiday. You're not important enough for them to spend their time worrying about you."

"So you are the lowly rank that must deal with me then?"

This comment from Private Lunatic stopped the camera man's laughter instantly. It was as if he had flicked a switch.

Grimly the camera man now pointed at this upstart, "Don't you speak to me in that manner. I am in charge around here and I am free to deal with you as I see fit, so you had better start showing me some respect."

Private Lunatic turned his back on the camera man and walked over to the bed, lying down on it and stretching out whilst yawning.

The camera man bellowed some insults at him, but he ignored them. This caused the camera man to storm off down the corridor.

Things were now going well. If the person in charge is irritated, then he will not think of, nor make sensible decisions. Emereldon and Anne Weavers were not even in the vicinity. This is going to make things far, far easier chuckled Lunatic to himself. He peered over at Eggo Maniac again. Far, far more straightforward he mused.

Strangely enough San Francisco had been the chosen place for the holiday. Anne Weavers had chosen it and Emereldon had merely gone along with the idea.

He didn't mind where they travelled, but did consider Earth to be an odd choice. For starters he looked nothing like an earthling, although Anne could pull it off, and secondly they were such irrational creatures.

They would jump and run away from you in fear without any idea regarding who you were. San Francisco though did have the air of a more accepting place than most.

Emereldon kept the hood from his cloak up at all times as they entered Union Square. It was surrounded by huge shops, departmental stores and hundreds of people. There was an art exhibition currently taking place here and that intrigued Emereldon.

"This is fabulous. Did you choose the place for my benefit?"

Anne nodded before responding, "Yes, I chose the planet and the city, but I selected it because I felt that there were many things that both of us would take an interest in."

The rocky figure waved in affirmation. "How did you know I held an interest for art?"

"Come on now Emereldon. It was obvious. Why have so many of our missions or confrontations taken place in Central London and Trafalgar Square of all places recently? That was down to a sheep however.

You can't get enough of taking in any form of art when you have the opportunities. Trafalgar Square itself hosts two galleries; not to mention numerous theatres around the corner.

Don't tell me you did not have a quick, now what was that word you used, perouse, whilst you were there?"

Emereldon blushed, which was very odd for a rocky, blue giant.

"I must apologise for my action leading up to this point then Anne Weavers. I have behaved like an…"

"Don't say it. I have not exactly been pleasant and must apologise for my behaviour too. It was almost as if we were set up to fight and yet I have no idea why?"

"What you say bears some truth and I, too, cannot think of a possible reason that this is the case. Someone or something is trying to disturb us."

The pair stopped walking and looked around Union Square. They could not sense anything, yet were fully aware that they were being watched and worse still, manipulated.

That feeling disappeared instantly.

"Whoever or whatever was watching us has withdrawn," said Anne.

"And they did it because they knew that we had detected them. Something is amiss here. Perhaps we should investigate further."

"Why bother Emereldon, between the two of us I am confident we can deal with most foes. I think we have frightened whatever it was away. I would not want to take on beings with the reputation that you and I have.

Let's enjoy the gallery. I believe it's showcasing some impressionist art."

Emereldon smiled and pulled down his hood.

Surprisingly the people around did not take any notice of his blue, rocky head.

Anne grabbed his arm and began to lead him towards the paintings, "They probably think you're part of the exhibit."

The couple chuckled as they approached the paintings.

"No. You have made them aware of our presence."

Rod slammed his fist into a series of colourful buttons that were on the wall beside him.

The camera man cowered in fear in the other corner of the control room.

The pink cloud was livid. After his first point of manipulation he had managed to get Emereldon and Anne Weavers at each others' throats and now this camera man had ruined everything by letting them know they were being watched.

Fortunately Rod had pulled the plug before they could detect just who it was that was observing them.

Rod picked up the camera man by the tie and pulled him closer to his face, "Tell me, what would you have done if I had not been here? Would you have carried on knowing that they would have eventually discovered it was you watching them?"

The camera man nervously shook his head.

Rod lifted him from the ground, still by the tie, and launched him across the room onto the other side. He crashed into a few screens and then slumped on the floor.

"It's a good job I decided to come down here and check on the prisoners myself, otherwise goodness knows what could have happened."

Rod then produced a key that materialised in his hand. He moved back to the wall and waved it over a thin, rectangular screen. The screen then broke into multiple pieces and re-assembled itself forming a keyhole. Rod placed the key directly into it and turned it clockwise.

A loud, clicking sound filled the room, before all the walls flipped around, revealing plain, purple walls. The controls vanished; the plethora of panels, controls and screens were gone. The walls were blank now.

The camera man stood up and walked to the centre of the room, equally shocked and disorientated by what was occurring.

"I wouldn't do that if I were you," said Rod.

The camera man took heed of Rod's words and instantly darted to the opposite side of the room.

In the centre of the room the floor opened and underneath it a screen revealed itself. The purple walls then moved further and further away until they were out of sight.

It was as if the room was so enormous that one could not see the walls. It just went on forever. The camera man was now sweating profusely, which caused Rod to giggle. As he did so he reassured the camera man.

"Relax, this is the way it is on my own planet. I just want to be more at home. You will understand what I mean in due course. Do not worry, when it is time to leave I shall put the walls back to normal and the control room will stand as it once did."

The camera man calmed himself now and moved towards the circular monitor that had appeared in the floor.

"Yes do join me and I shall talk you through what is happening. This screen will allow us to watch absolutely everything we, or should I say I, want.

You will notice that it is currently monitoring Eggo Maniac and Private Lunatic in the prison cell. I wish to discover more information regarding his red-hot appearance. However I have one more pressing matter to attend to first."

Rod raised his hand. On the wall behind him, a tiny, black dot materialised. Immediately it grew into a large, oval shape. The camera man and Rod observed the hole intently.

It was pitch-black and neither could see anything in it at all.

A purple hand pushed its way through the darkness and then another. The camera man noticed the smile on Rod's face grow and grow until he was absolutely beaming.

Out of the darkness emerged a familiar, purple cloud. He looked slightly dazed and not entirely coherent, but nevertheless he was back - somehow.

"Tod," said Rod with as much enthusiasm in the cloud's voice as any being had ever heard!

"Rod?" said the purple cloud in a confused state.

Rod bounced towards his friend, as did Tod.

As soon as they met an instant high five and continuous bounding around the room was the order of the day.

The camera man stood and watched as the two clouds became hysterical, giggling and dancing their way around the room. So Rod did have a heart then considered the camera man, who had only seen the harsher side of the cloud.

Eventually the commotion subsided and Tod brushed himself down.

"Did you rescue me Rod? One minute I was in a queue on a

conveyor belt to be transformed into a sock and then I was suddenly grabbed by a hand, pulled off and thrust through this gateway which led me here."

"Yes I did, sort of, but I think there are a few things you need to understand about me Tod.

Firstly to answer your question; yes it was I who freed you, but it was at a price. Fortunately my guardians were able to capture Private Lunatic.

Secondly I am not an apprentice Tod.

I am the leader of the clouds and second only to the boss.

My ruse as an apprentice was initially an experiment so that I could monitor cloud activity from, excuse the pun, ground level. It just so happened that I quite enjoyed your company so I stuck around longer than I should have.

Thirdly I do not have time to go into all the ins and outs, but I was essentially controlling our journey to meet the bosses, who were merely hologram projections created by Miss Terious, who in turn is actually Anne Weavers.

Lastly, you are now to work with me and create the grandest fighting spectacle our civilization has ever seen and it's going to be on a weekly basis. Everything clear?"

Tod instantly switched back to the bewildered expression he had worn when he entered the purple control room.

Rod grinned at him once more, "Don't you worry about it Tod. Just know that I am in charge and you are here to assist me. Got it?"

"I-I think so."

"Good. Now let's get back to watching Private Lunatic and

Eggo maniac. I think we might need to run some tests on the egg. I would like the mind reading tool activated now camera man and I want Private Lunatic and Eggo Maniac monitored by it. You have to use the split screen option to achieve this. Is that fine?"

The camera man paused briefly, before speaking.

"Apologies Rod for mentioning this, but since you converted this room to make you feel more at home, the control panel for the mind reading device has gone. Would you like me to…"

"Then go to the prison corridor and do it manually. There is a switch just outside the front of the cell that they currently occupy. If you are quiet and dare I say, subtle, then you will be able to achieve this easily. Off you go."

The camera man bowed and turned around.

He stopped once more.

Rod had seen this coming.

"I know the door has gone. I shall open a small portal for you."

A black hole opened close to the screen in the floor, much like the hole that Tod had entered. The camera man walked straight through it.

Private Lunatic was lying on his back, eyes closed, seemingly asleep. To the passing eye and the cameras in the cell, he was just that - fast asleep.

In reality he was wide awake, waiting for his chance. Lunatic had caught wind of some of the plans and was mindful that the clouds would probably try to infect him with that rainbow controlling disease that they had used on the other members of the group.

He had learned that the clouds focussed on violence and television ratings so had made a pretty, simple prediction that they would make his friends fight something dangerous, or worse still, each other.

His train of thought was swiftly interrupted by a shuffling and then a clicking sound. Looking upwards, he could see that the colour of the ceiling was gradually altering to a reddish colour. He knew precisely what this was.

The clouds were trying to read his thoughts.

This was an easily rectifiable situation he mused.

Jumping up from the bed, Private Lunatic began to scream, then shout, then squawk – like a bird. He tucked his head and legs into his wool and proceeded to roll around the room at great speed, still squawking of course and ensuring that he did not once come into contact with Eggo Maniac's body.

He bounced and cannonballed off various walls, the lights and even the ceiling. The commotion he was making was quite startling. So much so that the camera man sprinted to the front of the cell to check on what was happening.

Even though he was obviously protected from the raucous Private Lunatic, he still deemed it necessary to take a couple of steps backwards so that he was not struck by the sheep.

"Stop it, stop it at once," he said.

Private Lunatic ignored this and, if anything, upped the ante and was even louder faster and more dangerous. Despite this, he still did not make contact with Eggo Maniac.

The camera man now further away pleaded once more.

"Stop it or I'll, I'll…"

"What will you do?" said Private Lunatic, who now sounded like a dog as he let out the howls and growls whilst he rushed around the room.

Suddenly a loud speaker sounded out.

"Camera man you are to return to the control room at once. We will deal with this from there."

The announcement gave the camera man a sense of relief and he ran towards a portal at the end of the corridor. Noting the fact that the camera man had abandoned him, Private Lunatic maintained his insane demeanour.

"Nothing is working. He's beating the machine. We cannot pick up any of his or Eggo Maniac's thoughts."

Upon Tod finishing his sentence Rod slammed his fist into his other hand, then quickly shook it as he had clearly hurt himself.

"How does he know how to beat it? He's acting like a maniac. I mean he is Private Lunatic, but this is ridiculous. Not only can we not discover what he is thinking, but his behaviour is equally irritating."

Rod was now floating from one side of the room to the other. He was evidently comtemplating the situation, whilst Tod observed him.

The purple cloud could still not believe that his apprentice was the leader of the clouds, well second in command to the boss, and that he had saved them. In all honesty Tod was concerned about some of the things that he had said to Rod, belittling him along the way.

If Rod was ever angry with him, he had a whole back catalogue of insults directed at him from Tod that he could call upon. This could easily result in a charge of treason for Tod.

All those times he had mocked Rod or his choices, and this was one of the most powerful clouds around. Had he known he would have approached everything differently. He would have to make up for it and that must start now, confirmed Tod to himself.

What could they do about this crazy animal? Tod scrutinised the movement of the sheep. Despite the random nature of its movement and its bizarre noises, it never touched Eggo Maniac. It would not get close to him.

"That's it," said Tod in what sounded like a eureka moment.

"What, what is it?" said Rod, desperately hoping his friend might have stumbled across the answer.

"Whatever the sheep is doing, it is calculated. It is on purpose. That's why he won't touch Eggo Maniac, he knows that will hurt him. This whole façade is to beat the mind reading device is it not. If he is rushing around insanely as he is now, then he does not have time to think, hence there is nothing to read - correct?"

"Well that is the current method he is using to beat the machine," said Rod.

"Then let's just let him tire himself and be done with him. Why do we need his thoughts? It's probably more dangerous to leave him in captivity. Let's stick him in your new show in the ring, but we won't brainwash him with the rainbow. We will let him be himself."

Rod was gleaming now. Excitement had taken over and this idea of using Private Lunatic was absolute genius; it really was. The audience would be able to relate to a repressed character like Private Lunatic because they were all, well, repressed too, by the cloud regime.

This could be a ratings winner.

Rod finally spoke. "I like this idea Tod. I am pleased with you. We will put Private Lunatic into the show, straight into the main event."

Chapter 20
Rebirth

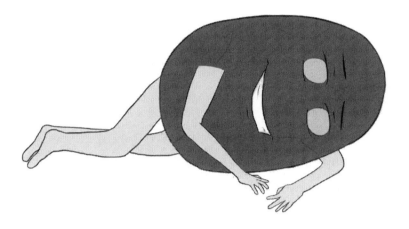

The arena was magnificent. It truly was a glorious sight that had been constructed with the greatest of care and attention.

The boss sat in the upper echelons of the arena on a grand throne built out of white gold and embellished with emeralds, diamonds and rubies. It sparkled so much that the room itself did not require any lighting.

He wore the same flashy, navy suit, white shirt and red tie and was once again sipping at a dark liquid from a wine glass.

Beside him stood Rod and by his side, Tod. The pink and purple clouds had dressed for the occasion and wore white with pink and purple ties respectively, for in a few moments the gates would open and the first set of paying customers would enter the arena for their premier, live, arena-based fight show on cloud TV.

At present the stadium was an empty place. It would hold at least 150,000 fans seated and was the largest of its kind. Rod had taken the idea for its design from the various sports stadiums on Earth.

The humans packed into these grand theatres to watch people kicking and throwing around circular and egg shaped balls.

He was starting to sweat now. Whilst he had been assured of ticket sales and that the event was sold out, Rod was yet to see it himself.

Sensing his concern, Tod leaned over to him, "Do not worry Rod. The sheer cost of these tickets will ensure that the public show up. They won't have shelled out all that money not to come. Have a little faith in yourself."

Rod thanked his friend.

Tod was right.

He should just sit back and enjoy the show.

He gazed out over the stadium that he had built. It was oval in shape and erected from solid silver, hence giving it, a well... obvious silver colour. At each end there were enormous, blue and red statues of muscular, cloud warriors, that looked as if they were going to clash. They leant over the doorways to the floor of the arena and above them were mammoth sized television screens so that the audience members in the upper tiers could see.

In fairness these were not required, as clouds possessed exceptional eyesight, so that whichever seat they had was almost like being in the front row.

Rod noticed that the confectionery sellers were all in place, floating up and down the aisles selling programmes, food and drink.

Everything was ready; everything was fit for purpose. In the box below them, Rod could even hear the cloud TV presenters bellowing about what a great event it was going to be and how exciting everything was.

Rod pulled out his planned script of fights, or the card for the evening as the humans would call it, and examined it closely. He had noticed from the corner of his eye, that the boss was doing the same thing, therefore he considered he ought to double-check it, just to be sure everything was in order. Anyway if it wasn't okay there was little he could do about it now. Everything had been printed and delivered to the sellers.

"Rod," said the boss.

"Yes boss, how can I help you?"

Rod was quite impressed with how confident he had sounded

in his retort.

"Rod, I have just one small enquiry about all of this."

"Yes boss, please go ahead, please feel free to ask me anything you wish."

"I have the right to do that whether you like it or not."

Rod nodded nervously now, perhaps he had overstepped the mark slightly there.

"I have been looking at the card for tonight, as you call it, and I would like to know who is in the main event? On this list of matches, it has Howard and a question mark. I want to know who it is."

The boss sounded half serious and half jovial, Rod could not decipher which. This was pretty normal for the boss as he loved to maintain ambiguity and, or total secrecy. Hence why they were located in the secret corporate box in the stadium which no one else, not even the building clouds, knew anything about.

Rod and Tod had had to construct this area of the stadium themselves, under cover of night.

Rod opted to choose the latter, hoping that the boss was in a good mood and excited by the event.

"Well boss, if I told you that then it would ruin the suspense."

The boss swilled his drink around in his glass and took a swig.

The mood lottery continued.

Finally he smiled.

Rod breathed a sigh of relief.

"I like it Rod. Surprises are always great fun, providing they are good surprises of course."

The boss continued to chuckle away to himself.

Rod moved to the wall to his left and pressed a button that sat by a small speaker. He spoke into the speaker demanding that the gates and turnstiles open and the audience be let in to their seats.

A confirmative grunt was all he was met with and slowly the various privileged clouds, who had managed to obtain a ticket to this once in a lifetime debut show, trickled in.

Rod was nervous once more, but was soon reassured by Tod that all were taking their time so that they could buy souvenirs, food and programmes; also the general public would want to take a look at the stadium, as they were the first to use it.

Tod was absolutely correct.

Within ten minutes the place was packed to the rafters and the atmosphere was electric. Now all Rod hoped was that the matches were just as good.

Rod again moved back to the side of the wall, held the button down and spoke. "As soon as the last cloud has made its way to a seat, let the show commence. I want this done within five minutes, we have to keep in time with the TV schedule and advertising. If necessary get security to usher in those who are late."

Another grunt of a reply and that was that.

The lights in the stadium cut out leaving everything in darkness. The crowd 'whooped' in approval before being plunged back into light and seeing the most famous musical band in cloud music; 'The Polka Clouds'.

The yellow and black polka dotted cloud began banging on the drums, followed by the pink and black bass player, red and black guitarist and the lead singer of the group, the blue and black polka dotted cloud.

They were all known by their colours as opposed to their real names which gave them a certain sense of anonymity and the gallons of make-up they wore made it impossible to tell who was male and who was female. Not even the singer, blue dot's voice was enough to decipher the gender.

The crowd went wild and Rod even noticed the boss humming along, he had not put him down as a fan of 'The Polka Clouds'.

Anne Weavers sat backstage in the female locker room. She and Emereldon had only arrived back that morning and both were far from pleased that they would see some action in the ring tonight.

She could not remember the last time she had had a holiday and now that she finally felt rested she was going to be thrust back into battle with Lieutenant Figs of the Sheep Brigade.

Clasping the card for tonight's matches she ran her finger down the list, stopping at each bout. In truth she had memorised the fights so she did not really need to do this.

Emereldon was scheduled to enter the ring directly after her match in order to clash with Commander Winters. That would not be an easy match, but it is one she was confident that the blue warrior would win.

She stopped for a moment. Why should she care how Emereldon performed, whether he prevailed or not. She could not put her finger on it; but regardless she still wanted him to be victorious and preferably not to get injured.

That sheep carried a lot of weapons so anything could occur in theory. It was only a standard four sided ring with three sets of ropes around it so the sheep could take more or less anything into the arena.

That was not good.

She had been forced to hand over the mind control elements of the rainbow disease to Rod so that she could not fix her or anyone else's match. That was a pain seeing as she had taken the time to capture them. She didn't resent Rod of course, that would be foolish, but neither did she entirely respect his methods.

The camera man continued to sit and stare at the circular screen in the centre of the purple control room floor. He had been told that everything would have returned to normal and had assumed that Rod had forgotten to do this when he left for the live event.

He did not dare point this out to the pink cloud though, so he was left stuck in the purple room with nothing there other than the screen in the floor that focussed on Eggo Maniac and Eggo Maniac alone.

Fortunately Rod had at least allowed him the decency of leaving a door, well black hole, that led to the corridor so he could go to the toilet, get food etc...

He was bored, absolutely bored out of his mind now. He was a camera man who was not able to operate a camera because he could not comprehend how this strange cloud system used by Rod and Tod, worked.

Anne should never have become involved with the clouds he thought to himself.

He observed Eggo Maniac. He couldn't say why he bothered.

He was crimson, still and just lying there – doing nothing. This was not unlike what the camera man was doing, absolutely nothing.

He would not even get to see the big, weekly fighting show debut. What was it they had called it, ah yes, 'Monday Madness'. Perhaps it would be a failure and that would be the end of Rod.

It wouldn't be though and the camera man was acutely aware that he was just clasping at straws. The clouds could not get enough of fighting and this event would surely quench their thirst.

An odd vibrating sound quickly began to emanate from the screen in the floor. Perhaps there was an issue with its positioning and it was rumbling against some steel girders or something equally sturdy.

Upon closer inspection the camera man's eyes widened. There was no vibration; this was a noise that was coming directly from Eggo Maniac's cell.

Rushing through the black oval and down the corridor containing the prison, the camera man stopped.

Eggo Maniac was rumbling. He wasn't moving at all, but there was definitely noise coming out of his body. It sounded as if his stomach was growling and he was ravenous for food.

The camera man wasted no time and sprinted down to the control room. He entered and searched for a phone or an intercom; anything that he could use to contact Rod.

There was nothing of course, but had Rod bothered to turn the control room back to its original state then there would have been multiple methods he could have used to contact the cloud.

However he hadn't.

Sweat rolled down the camera man's cheeks. If Rod did not get this information then he would be in big trouble. He might even get turned into a sock or whatever else the clouds did to punish their servants for failure.

The screen in the floor flickered and the camera man rushed to check what was going on. Of course there was nothing he could do. He could not operate it.

The image of Eggo Maniac dropped from the screen.

It was blank now – nothing on it.

A scream was all the camera man could muster and tears joined the drips of sweat that dripped down his cheeks.

This was a nightmare.

Everything that could possibly go wrong was happening and he had no method of telling anyone about his plight.

The screen crackled this time and a rough outline of Rod flickered intermittently. Through the interference it spoke.

"Camera man, camera man are you there? Well I presume you are there for there is nowhere else you should be. I have an issue with the reception as I am at Monday Madness, which is quite far away and high up; I'm sure you can appreciate this. Anyhow, I'm getting an odd reading from Eggo Maniac's cell. Any idea what is going on in there?"

The camera man breathed heavily and then scrambled over to the screen, ensuring he was in direct view of Rod. In reality he was lying down on top of it. That was the sign of just how desperate he was to be seen.

"Sir, sir I have been down to check the cell and there is an odd rumbling coming from Eggo Maniac's stomach. It sounds like he is hungry. He is not moving at all, he's just a bit noisy."

The screen crackled a bit more and after what seemed an eternity Rod replied, "Probably nothing to worry about then. If he's not moving then I am not concerned. Just keep an eye on him, okay. Should anything else happen then I wish to be contacted immediately. Is that clear?"

"But how do I…"

Before the camera man could finish his question the screen went black and then switched back to Eggo Maniac's cell. The rumbling sound continued. This noise was going to get very irritating, very quickly.

Emereldon made his way down a large, silver ramp and entered the ring. The lights had all changed to a variety of shades of blue for his entrance and some human, classical music played in the background.

Commander Winters was already in the ring waiting for him, still rainbow-coloured and looking exceedingly tired. The glazed expression that ran across his face, as it did with all the other rainbow infected entities, was evidence of that.

Emereldon removed the hood of his cloak, but kept it on. Usually He didn't take it off in public or when fighting, so this would be no different.

The ring itself was square and had a white surface with black sides. There were three ropes that ran around the ring and these, too, were all black. The corner posts were relatively high up and Emereldon could envisage that were someone to fall from one, then they would probably injure themselves quite badly.

In fairness the blue giant was still shocked by the sheer amount of hype that had preceded the fight. The entrances were spectacular, regardless of who entered the ring and the huge screens played weird videos, showing lots of different pictures and videos of the fighters as they entered.

Emereldon had watched Anne's fight eagerly and she had made short work of Lieutenant Figs. She had put him to sleep very quickly and the crowd had really lapped it up.

He had wanted Anne to win and was very pleased that she had. He didn't know why he felt this way as only a week and a half ago, he couldn't stand her mere presence.

His focus was taken back to the ring.

The crowd roared.

They had been excited all night and Emereldon had noticed that some clouds were holding up signs and placards with his name on it. One was even drinking from an Emereldon cup.

He hoped he was going to be paid some royalties for all this merchandise.

Commander Winters rushed at him instantly, hooves out clutching a couple of beaten up swords. He swiped and slashed at him, but Emereldon was far too fast and leapt up onto the top turnbuckle of the ring.

He jumped down and aimed his rock-hard fist at Commander Winters.

The sheep was far more agile than he had expected and dived out of the way poking a sword at him. He blocked it with his forearm and Commander Winters tossed the swords out of the ring, quickly realising that they would not be strong enough to pierce Emereldon's rocky exterior.

The pair circled each other close to the ropes, each warrior seeking out a weak point to exploit.

Emereldon could sense the tension from the crowd, eager to see who would win.

Then something bizarre occurred.

Commander Winters fell flat on his face. Out of nowhere he collapsed.

Emereldon did not wait to see why this had happened, but took it for the opportunity that it was. He reached out, grabbed the sheep's shoulder and put it to sleep.

That was it.

Match over.

Commander Winters was fast asleep, snoring, too, for good measure.

Emereldon raised both his arms in glory and the crowd reacted wildly. It wasn't quite as positive as the reception he had received upon his entrance. It now sounded like a mixture of cheers and boos.

Looking over his shoulder he could see why.

Standing in the corner, just by the ring apron was Anne Weavers. It was evidently she who had tripped Commander Winters, thus propelling Emereldon to victory.

He had been assisted by Anne.

He had cheated.

He didn't care though, he had won.

He waved at Anne and gestured for her to come into the ring.

She obliged, straightened the lapels on her suit-jacket and flicked out her hair. She wanted to look her best.

Emereldon grabbed her arm and both stood in the centre of the ring with their arms in the air, soaking up the reaction of the audience, both boos and cheers, they didn't mind.

They had both won and inadvertently become interesting to the crowd. They were stars, they didn't know if they were heroes or villains, but they were stars nonetheless.

Eggo Maniac's body continued to rumble and the camera man was sure that it was getting louder. It could of course have been due to the fact that he had been subjected to the noise for over an hour now and perhaps it was grating on him so much that he thought it was louder than it actually was.

Whatever the reasoning he could take it no more. Simply put he had to have a break. Even clouds took breaks he pondered as he walked out through the hole in the purple wall.

Just five minutes, five minutes and then I'll be back and refreshed and more able to concentrate he told himself. The camera man's justification continued as he put things into perspective. The egg hadn't done anything for hours so there was no reason why anything should happen in the five minutes whilst he was away.

He walked down the corridor past the cell, taking one last look at the egg before making his way down some stairs and into a kitchen/lounge where he could finally get a break.

He was only a two minute run away from Eggo Maniac's cell so if anything serious happened he could be back in a flash. Opening the fridge he grabbed a cool bottle of water and sat down onto a somewhat attractive and expensive leather couch. He rested his head back onto the cushions and checked his watch.

He was only going to be five minutes at most.

The grumbling noise inside Eggo Maniac had indeed grown louder, in fact it was causing his body to vibrate on the floor. It was very noticeable, so much so, that had anyone been watching they would have certainly taken an interest in it.

The once vacant and glum expression on the egg's face slowly altered. His mouth widened, yet his eyes remained firmly closed. Eggo Maniac was smiling, almost grinning. Everything was finally going his way, going to plan.

Nobody was watching him and he was well aware of that.

The timing could not have been more perfect if he had tried.

"Are they allowed to do that Rod? Is it permitted within the rules?"

"Erm, I don't actually know boss. You see we haven't assembled a rule book. The only thing we have informed the competitors of is that if their opponent is unconscious then they have won."

The boss rested his head on his fist for a moment, his hair brushing down over it. His blue suit was immaculate, as it always was and he had to be the smartest and best dressed person in the audience.

Whilst the boss mulled this over, as he usually did, Rod observed Tod in the corner.

The purple cloud held a tablet that had a direct link to the camera in Eggo Maniac's cell and had been ordered by Rod to inform him if anything unusual was occurring.

Rod noticed that he was twitching and was desperate to ask what was going on. Of course he could not do this whilst he conversed, or rather waited, for the boss to respond.

"I think I quite enjoyed the spectacle of the pair of them defeating the sheep. Keep it the same then. Do carry on, I wouldn't want the event to be spoiled by you speaking with me."

Rod bowed and rushed over to Tod.

The pair had to whisper so that they did not give away anything. Tod answered Rod's question before his friend had even asked it.

"I have lost the connection to Eggo Maniac's cell. All I can see is blank, well nothing."

Rod snatched the tablet away and fiddled with it, pressing a series of areas on the screen.

Still nothing happened.

He turned it off and then on again.

Once again nothing occurred. Rod held it tightly now and shook it. At first gently but this quickly became more vicious as it was clear that the problem was not going to be fixed.

Rod smashed the tablet onto the ground, shattering it into pieces.

This brought about the attention of the boss, who was giggling away to himself, not in a jovial manner though, but a sinister one.

"Is there a problem Rod? Surely there cannot be. I was just about to commend you on how everything was running so smoothly."

"No, nothing boss, just a few nerves about the main event. I merely dropped the tablet and it broke. I'm just going to check something outside."

The boss nodded and reverted his attention to the window and watched out over the arena. It was nearly time for the main event.

Rod rushed out of the room and found himself his nearest communications link screen. He immediately dialled in the code that would put him through to the camera man in the control room.

As the screen revealed the purple walled room it became increasingly clear that the camera man was not there. He was not at his post.

Rod clenched his fist and slammed it into the wall. "Camera man when I get hold of you, you will pay for deserting your post."

Eggo Maniac had now turned to a dark shade of purple. The grin was still on his face, but it somehow seemed to be lifeless. There was no energy behind it. His body jiggled slightly and then went still.

The top of Eggo Maniac's head made a thumping sound. It was light at first, but then it gradually grew louder and more fearsome.

A tiny crack appeared. It was not there for long however, as it started to split.

A silver hand broke through the top. It tore away the top layer of shell and as it did the rest of the egg part of Eggo Maniac's body split. It fell apart either side and all that laid on the ground were the broken pieces of shell from Eggo Maniac's body.

Standing in the centre of the mess was a tall and slim, silver figure. Long, wavy, blue hair cascaded down its body to the level of its waist.

It held out its arms and these were defined and toned to perfection. The fingers at the end of its hands were long and artistic and it posed with such grace that had anyone seen it, they would have been in awe.

Its eyes were purple and shone beautifully and its lips were perfectly formed and smiled in a welcoming manner. The whole figure glistened except for a sleek, sleeveless, loose, red dress that stopped just above its knee. Its feet were petite and it did not wear any shoes.

Stroking back its hair, it spoke, "Well this is it then. I am here. I am born. I think I'll switch the television cameras back on now. In fact I think I shall have every single camera from cloud TV on me."

Its voice was soft and calm with more than a hint of arrogance in it. It waved at the camera in the cell before addressing what it knew was an almost universe-wide audience.

"Hello everyone. I am much obliged to meet you. My name is Felicity. I am precisely what Eggo Maniac intended and what Private Lunatic helped to protect. Speaking of which, I'll be coming to free him just about now."

Chapter 21
Parity Check

In the centre of the ring floated a white cloud sporting a black bow tie.

It was the legendary announcer Buod.

In his hand he held a microphone whilst he watched the crowd cheer. The atmosphere was electric and he was soaking up the energy and enjoying himself.

He raised his hand and silence enveloped the stadium. Anyone could have heard a penny drop.

Clearing his throat Buod began.

"Ladies and gentleman it is now time for the main event of the evening. Are you ready?"

The crowd roared once more and Buod had to wait until the hysteria had calmed.

"Then for the thousands in attendance and the millions watching around the universe and on cloud TV…"

The crowd waited on the edge of their seats.

Buod was a master at controlling audiences and at present he was demonstrating this perfectly. He placed the microphone by his lips and as he did so, he could feel more and more clouds setting their eyes directly upon him; which was what he desired of course.

"Then let's do thisssssssss…"

His words were slightly drowned out by the raucous reaction of the crowd.

A live cloud orchestra suddenly appeared at ringside and played a slow piece of human classical music. The tempo of this quickly sped up and Buod commenced his announcing.

"Introducing first, the being that will face the mystery

opponent. He is from Soho, London, England, Earth and has found his way here through much peril and adventure."

At this point Howard emerged on the ramp and strutted down towards the ring. He seemed confident, even cocky and genuinely looked as if this was all he had ever wanted to do.

Buod continued, "He weighs in at two hundred and sixty one pounds and is the most versatile man in the sport today. Making his debut live, right here on Monday Madness, this is Howard."

The noise was deafening. Howard was drawing in the most over the top reaction from the crowd so far. Stepping through the ropes he moved and stood on the top turnbuckle, raising his arms up high, as if he had already won.

The music stopped and he quickly jumped back down into the ring below.

After a brief pause some heavy rock music bellowed out and Private Lunatic appeared at the top of the ramp.

"Currently making his way to the ring, he is from the mean, backstreets of London, he weighs in at one hundred and twenty pounds. He learned his trade in the asylums and is the master of insanity… Ladies and gentleman I present to you, the terrifying, the mad, Private Lunatic."

More eruptions from the crowd ensued, however the one entity that was not pleased by the whole thing was Private Lunatic, who made his way to the ring in a very timid and non-motivated manner.

The music cut out as soon as he stepped through the ropes.

He had brought a few weapons with him, tucked inside his woollen coat of course.

Private Lunatic observed Howard, who was still putting on this arrogant façade. Clearly that was being controlled by someone or something else as this simply was not in his character. The bell rang and it was time to brawl.

Tod raced out of the corporate box to speak with Rod. He had just witnessed this Felicity creature taking over the network, albeit briefly, and announcing that she was going to come and assist Private Lunatic.

As he rushed through the door he collided with another being who seemed to be equally desperate to get to its destination. As Tod picked himself up from the floor he noticed the other being was indeed Rod.

"D-d-d-d-d-i-i-i-d you see it?"

"Of course I did Tod. I was coming to find you so that we could sort this mess out together."

"But I don't have a clue what to do Rod? If she's so powerful that she can take over an entire TV station and broadcast herself without so much as pressing a button then goodness only knows what she will be capable of in the arena."

Tod looked longingly at Rod. He was desperate for an answer of some sort and hoped dearly that his friend had it.

This time Rod was slow to respond. Evidently he was dwelling on something and whatever Tod had just said to him had quelled his manic behaviour.

Rod had an idea.

He smiled and patted Tod on the back, "Tod my friend, I think you may just have solved the problem."

"I have?"

"Yes you have. Don't sound so shocked. We shall let her enter the arena and indeed we shall let her help her friend. It will be a good surprise and will surely boost interest in the show, not to mention ratings.

Perhaps we can take some pictures of her as she came out of Eggo Maniac in the cell. If we stick those on T-shirts and other memorabilia then we could make even more cash.

The best thing is the boss probably thinks it is all part of the show and that it is a truly clever idea. In fact it's brilliant marketing."

Tod listened to his friend ominously. It sounded okay and it sounded like an interesting idea. The only problem was that it was highly unlikely this Felicity person was going to comply.

She had just broken out of a cell, so she probably wouldn't view the clouds in the best light. She could do anything like destroy the arena, or worse still attack himself and Rod.

"Stop worrying Tod. Everything will work out and everything will be fine. I understand your reservations and we don't completely know what she will do but that's the fun."

"Rod did you just read my thoughts again?"

"A little bit yes. Look, just relax, come with me back to the box and you can kick back and be entertained by Monday Madness. This little twist could be the groundbreaking moment we needed."

Tod sighed and floated back to the room with Rod. His friend was right of course. There was nothing they could do about it. They might as well just watch, and anyway the corporate box that they were in was hidden so they should be fine, hopefully.

Howard had been remarkably hard hitting and Private Lunatic had spent most of his time tucked up in a ball, rolling here, there and everywhere to evade a clobbering.

He had discovered that whilst Howard was strong, he was not particularly agile and this was an advantage. The only trouble was that he did not want to hurt his friend.

His plan was to outlast Howard and tire him, hopefully then providing him with an opening. The crowd was slowly losing interest in the bout as there were no blows landed thus far. Certain sections had begun to jeer, but this did not bother Private Lunatic in the slightest. It wasn't as if he wanted to compete anyway.

Leaping over yet another mistimed fist, the sheep found himself on the top rope. He positioned himself to jump and to strike Howard's knee, hopefully bringing him down to the canvas.

The stadium went black, jet-black.

Nobody could see anything and Private Lunatic jumped down from the top turnbuckle onto the ground below. He didn't know whether Howard was going to continue his fight or stop; therefore being outside the ring was the safest option.

Everything was quiet, although Private Lunatic could hear some of the security staff whispering to each other asking whether or not this was part of the show.

The screens at either side of the ring sprang to life and on them it read, "She's coming…F"

Private Lunatic smiled. He knew what was about to happen.

Hundreds of silver fireworks shot up into the sky, exploding and lighting up the stadium. Some loud and aggressive music with a slow tempo played out to the crowd.

As the fireworks flickered away, the lights in the stadium returned and standing at the top of the ramp with her back to the audience was Felicity.

Her body sparkled and her blue hair waved around her waist. She still wore her loose, red dress and the crowd erupted. It was clear that she was a master of manipulation and this audience was eating from the palm of her hands.

Every camera in the arena zoomed in on her, ensuring they recorded her from every conceivable angle. She smiled at them and winked before jumping backwards up into the sky and landing softly in the ring just in front of Howard.

The pizza box, headed figure lashed out at her, but she merely raised her arm and the blow was blocked. Still smiling, she clicked her fingers and the abrasive music stopped.

The crowd was electric and she fed off their energy.

She grabbed Howard's shoulder and flipped herself over him, grabbing him by the waist and tossing him into the corner.

He landed with a thud and quickly sprang back to his feet, ready to meet this new opponent head on.

Felicity blew him a kiss and this enraged her opponent. In actuality it was the first occasion that he had shown any real emotion since becoming infected by the rainbow. He sprinted at her and thrust out his arm in an attempt to strike out at her neck area.

She vanished and appeared behind him.

Howard, however, could not halt his momentum and continued on into the ring post.

He hit it hard, with his pizza box head slamming into the top turnbuckle. In a daze he stepped backwards.

He had little time to regain any sort of composure however, as Felicity now held him by the waist.

She had wrapped her arms around him and even Howard knew that this was not a good situation. She dropped backwards to the floor and as she did so she kept hold of Howard, pulling him above her head and extending her arms, thrusting his pizza box head into the canvas.

Surely this was it now. He wasn't going to get up from that. Private Lunatic watched on in awe, what a fighter this Felicity was. He had struggled with Howard, but she was making short work of him.

Howard clutched the bottom rope and started to drag himself to his feet. He was leaning into the ropes and his arms now loosely held onto the top rope. He was hunched over and could barely stand.

Private Lunatic ran around to the side where Howard was propped up, "Just give up Howard. This isn't you who is fighting. You are being controlled. For your own safety you have to quit."

His words fell on deaf ears.

Howard let go of the ropes and stumbled forward swinging his apple crumble arms left and right with no real aim nor target. Felicity waved to the crowd, "It's time to finish the job."

The crowd roared with approval. All were excited now, of that there was no doubt.

Felicity backed herself into one of the corners of the ring and sprang forward outstretching her leg and delivering an enormous kick to Howard's face.

He dropped to his knees and collapsed on his back. He was unconscious - knocked out.

The announcer, Buod, scurried into the ring, straightened his bow tie and put his microphone to his lips, "Ladies and gentlemen, the winner of the match and the main event of the evening, Felicity."

As the crowd cheered, Felicity clicked her fingers and her theme music, that she had played earlier on her way to the ring, kicked into gear. She jumped onto the top rope and whilst maintaining impeccable balance, waltzed around the ring, lapping up the applause.

Just as the hysteria reached its peak, Felicity clicked her fingers once more and the lights and the music in the stadium cut out.

A split second later the light had returned, yet neither Felicity nor Private Lunatic were at ringside.

They had vanished.

All that remained were the cloud announcer and the unconscious body of Howard, flat out in the ring.

A couple of dark, blue clouds made their way down the ramp with a stretcher to collect Howard. The announcer spoke into his microphone once more.

"Thank you very much for coming out tonight ladies and gentleman, we hope you enjoyed the show and please don't forget to stop by our various kiosks and merchandising stalls to grab yourself a few souvenirs. Thank you for watching and don't forget that tickets go on sale for our live event next Monday, tomorrow morning, eight o'clock sharp."

Chapter 22
Who's Bad Now?

Applause had taken over the secret corporate box, well, the boss, Tod and Rod were clapping anyway.

The evening had been a major triumph and early ratings had suggested that Rod may just have broken his old record of the fight in Soho Square with this spectacle.

More importantly, for his own health and safety, the boss had enjoyed himself and that, in Rod's eyes, was one of the main objectives.

"Well Rod I have to say that you have done well. Your friend Tod, too, I'm almost glad that we didn't end up converting him into a sock now."

The two clouds laughed nervously.

The boss stood up and moved towards the clouds. He grabbed them both and looked each one in the eye. The smile from his face had gone and Rod feared that this could be the…

"END? No, no, no dear Rod. You two are now my cloud TV team. We, well you, are going to continue to revolutionise cloud TV. Does that sound good?"

The two clouds nodded in agreement and as they did so, the boss pulled them close to him and gave them a hug. They were pressed hard up against his navy suit and clearly the boss had no idea of how strong he was because the hug had become painful now.

He was crushing them.

Fortunately he finally let go and made his way to the door of the box, "Thank you for a wonderful evening and I look forward to seeing that Felicity character again next week. She was a wonderful surprise. Now I believe a feast is waiting for me in the dining room. I shall take my leave now."

The door opened and the boss marched outside. Rod breathed in heavily as did Tod; in fact they did it pretty much in unison. Neither had any time to rest as Rod rushed over to the button on the wall next to the small speaker.

Frantically he pushed it, pressing down so hard it seemed like his entire life depended on it.

The response was quick, "How can I help you Rod?"

The tone could only have been that of Anne Weavers. She was cheerful now as both she and Emereldon had been victorious in their matches.

Rod's tone was not quite so casual, it was more of a frenzied response.

"I need to know what is going on in the locker room. Where is Private Lunatic and more importantly where is this Felicity person?"

The usual buzzing and crackling noises ensued whilst Anne was obviously chatting to someone about the whereabouts of this Felicity.

Rod tapped the wall with his fingers, quickly and sharply. The anxiety was exhausting.

Finally Anne's clear and calm voice could be heard again.

"Apparently, according to Emereldon, she's just sitting back here in the locker room with Private Lunatic. She hasn't budged an inch. She just came back, sat down and is now talking away with the crazy sheep."

"What do you mean hasn't budged an inch?"

"I mean Rod, that either she is so powerful that she can escape at any time of her choosing, or she is so stupid that she doesn't realise that by sticking around she will be captured. The fact that we are now aware that Private Lunatic is far more intelligent than we gave him credit for would suggest it was the first one."

The line crackled, but this time it was the fault of Rod. He was mulling something over.

Tod observed him, attempting to read his mind, but was cut off.

Tod reminisced about how he used to enter Rod's mind on a regular basis. Little did he know just how powerful his apprentice was. Of course he had probably never read Rod's mind on reflection, only what Rod would allow him to discover.

Rod pressed down the button, this time more softly, "What do you mean she's too powerful?"

"I mean exactly what I said. If she is this relaxed and made such short work of Howard, then I believe she must be so confident of escape that she really is that powerful. Whatever she wishes, she can probably achieve."

"That's what I thought you meant. Do not let her leave. We are coming down to the locker room this instant."

"Understood Rod."

The line cut off.

Rod waved at Tod and the purple cloud followed him.

This was not a good situation by any stretch of the imagination, but at least she was still present.

At least she could be spoken to - persuaded perhaps.

In truth this whole affair made the issues surrounding Eggo Maniac seem like nothing at all.

That was probably a good thing for the well-being of the

camera man.

Felicity kicked back on the bench. Her silver skin glistened brightly underneath the lights of the locker room. On the opposing bench sat Private Lunatic. He, too, was equally calm and they were very comfortable with the silence which they had created.

The rest of the competitors had scarpered very quickly upon their arrival and this was fine, as it gave them far more room in which to settle.

The locker room was long and narrow with plain, white walls and wooden benches that ran down the full length of each wall. At the top end there were around twenty silver lockers that took up the space on that wall. The only other decoration of note, if one could even call it that, were some rows of pegs that ran above the benches. All in all it was hardly an inspiring place, but it served its purpose.

Lunatic had now closed his eyes and was about to take his first decent nap in ages when Felicity gently informed him, "They are coming down here you know and at quite some speed. I think they could be nervous."

Lunatic opened his eyes and grinned.

"Yes well this is all part of the master plan isn't it? I wouldn't imagine they will find what they seek with us. This is our chance to turn the tide in our favour, the favour of the Ignacium."

Felicity and Private Lunatic chuckled together before the blue-haired woman replied, "This is true. I sense they are extremely concerned by our presence, so much so that they are actively panicking and are about to enter the room..."

As she spoke the handle shook in a frenzied manner and the door burst open.

"Now," Felicity's purple eyes flared up slightly as if she was congratulating herself for being so clever and precise.

Standing in front of them were the pink and purple clouds, Rod and Tod, panting as they were clearly out of breath from their run.

"I had no idea that the size of this stadium was so large," said Tod, still gasping for air.

Rod attempted to hide his lack of fitness by adjusting his tie and portraying himself as a business man. He floated over to Felicity, not too close of course. He ensured he was out of striking distance and addressed both her and Mr. Private Lunatic. "Miss Felicity and Mr. Private Lunatic, I wish to make you an offer."

"You haven't even said hello yet," said Private Lunatic.

Rod ignored this and carried on.

"My business partner Tod over here and I have put together something that we feel will please you. We have created two very specific, highly paid contracts for you to join our Monday Madness events, pay-per-views and any other fighting shows we may choose to put on in the future.

You will both be billed as main event fighters and for that reason the pay in your contract will reflect that. We will give you a large share of any profit from merchandise and other television appearances you make and those that are associated with you and your brand. In short, we would like to make you superstars."

Rod backed away once he had finished speaking and signalled for Tod to leave the room.

The purple cloud nodded and left.

Rod stared at both of them. He wanted to read their minds and under normal circumstances he could have easily penetrated Private Lunatic's mind, but something was protecting him, shielding the sheep.

He presumed it must have been Felicity as when he had tried to enter her mind he was blocked out immediately. This was tricky now as he could not read their thoughts nor gauge any kind of emotion from the expressions on their faces.

He would simply have to wait and this was difficult for him. He was a 'doer', patience was for those that were left behind.

Private Lunatic rose up from the bench and jumped down onto his hooves, "I think I've heard enough of this. Only hours ago I was locked up in a cell and now you wish to negotiate. I find this astonishing. We do not want anything to do with you. You are Adamantium and we, Ignaci…"

"Just stop right there Private Lunatic."

Everyone's attention was taken by Felicity, who was now sitting in an upright manner, looking as if she, excuse the pun, meant business.

"I don't think we need to reveal all just yet."

"What more is there to reveal? He has basically just told us of your allegiance," said Rod. It was clear that this latest piece of information had angered him.

Felicity stood up and moved closer to both Rod and Private Lunatic who were now close to the door of the locker room. Felicity's voice sounded sly and cunning, "He only speaks for himself dear cloud. He has no authority to say anything on my behalf."

"Felicity what are you talking about? You are not following the plan as ordered and…"

"Quiet Lunatic. I will sort out my own dealings."

Felicity stood opposite Rod now and the two gazed into each other's eyes.

It was a stare down.

Neither intended to lose and the intensity within the room rose tenfold.

Rod was used to glaring at other beings. He used the technique to put across his authority when required. He had learnt this from the boss who had, of course, done the same to him. This Felicity person was good though. She did not even move an inch. Her eyes simply did not blink.

Suddenly the door burst open.

Rod turned around, but Felicity continued to test him with her stare. It was Tod clutching two brown clipboards with some paperwork attached to them and a couple of pens.

Inevitably these were the contracts. Rod was pleased to see him, for if he had been any later, he would have surely been defeated in the showdown.

Felicity averted her gaze from Rod and now placed it firmly on the purple cloud, "Is that for me?"

Tod nodded and handed her a clipboard.

She took it and signalled to Private Lunatic that he should do the same.

Reluctantly he grabbed one and both sat back down onto the benches to study them. They were only two pages long and Felicity smiled as she reached the end.

"This is a lot of money. Combine that with the merchandise sales and we could be onto a winner here."

Rod and Tod were beaming now. This could be it. This could be the signing and therefore the deal of the century. She seemed genuinely interested too.

Private Lunatic on the other hand was far from content, "Felicity we cannot put our names to these. It is against everything that we have done. It is treason."

"For you maybe, but not for me. I'm in this for one reason only and that's to get ahead."

She swivelled around and faced the clouds. "I accept these conditions."

Before she could sign the papers, Private Lunatic had launched himself at her and whipped the pen out of her hand. He stood, almost snarling to the side of her.

"You have forgotten our mission. We are from the Ignacium and are here to destroy the Adamantium, not to join its game show. I shall not allow you to do this. There is no way this is going to happen. It will be over my body."

Felicity casually stood and yawned, whilst stretching out her arms.

"Do you want this one signed to a contract or is he dispensible?"

The two clouds grinned and nodded together whilst answering in unison, "He's dispensible, definitely dispensible."

Felicity grabbed Private Lunatic with such speed that he simply did not see it coming. She gripped his shoulder and pinched it gently, the sheep fell to the floor.

He was asleep.

"That's one of Emereldon's moves," said Tod.

Felicity tapped the purple cloud on the back, "Actually there are a few others who know how to use it, me being one of course. Now what are you going to do with him? I would suggest you infect him with the rainbow disease and have him become your slave. That way he can still participate in the show."

"An excellent idea Felicity and one which we shall utilise. Here, take this." As Rod finished speaking he handed Felicity another pen.

She signed her contract, returned it to him and shook the pink cloud's hand.

The deal was done.

Felicity had signed with Rod and Tod for cloud TV and would be their main star.

Rod could not help but feel a great sense of satisfaction. He had overcome many odds. His plan had worked and even better was the fact that he had a new star who worked for him.

The rain pelted on the streets of Central London. It was another typical day in the capital. The general public used umbrellas, hoods, hats and some even resorted to holding newspapers above their heads in order to avoid a soaking.

The skyline was grey and little had been reported of the fight in Soho Square. Most people had written it off as a simple, freak accident or special effect from a movie that had gone wrong. In all honesty no one could remember it. It was as if it had not happened, and it hadn't, as far as the general public were aware.

Of course in reality it had and was most definitely real, but Anne Weavers had seen to it personally that it was covered up oh so well. That's what being a prevalent person within the media can do for you, well that and having mind erasing powers.

High above the streets stood three figures on a rooftop. It was one of the larger buildings in the city, but not the tallest. They didn't want to be too obvious of course.

They all wore dark, grey cloaks, not tattered ones though. These were pristine, as if it was the first occasion they had been worn. The material waved in the wind, yet the figures stood perfectly still. Their features could not be made out, just white outlines for their eyes.

The odd thing was that their feet could not be seen. Where they should have been was just a shadowy outline. It didn't make any sense at all, but then it did not matter, no one could see them, not even the clouds. They had made sure of that.

The being in the centre of the three was the largest and towered over the others. To the right of him stood what could only be described as the most elegant and the third was fairly inconspicuous.

The sleek, slender one stepped forward, "Isn't it funny how we find ourselves back here, just where we started."

The larger one was the first to respond. "I can't say I'm that surprised, although what I do find odd is the way in which we have come together. That is the astonishing part for me."

The third remained silent.

The larger one questioned this, "Have you nothing to add? No thoughts on this? Surely this would be the time to…"

"I shall tell you when it is time. Lest you forget that Emereldon."

The bigger figure took a step back in acknowledgement of his mistake. Clearly he had agitated this third member. He tugged at his hood and as it fell, Emereldon was revealed in all his glory, feet and all.

The slim figure was the next to reveal itself and sure enough, the familiar sight of Anne Weavers materialised, although this time she was wearing a navy-blue suit as opposed to her grey one.

The third figure remained hidden beneath his robe. He was obviously not to be questioned as the other two said nothing and were clearly waiting on his words.

They did not have to wait long.

"Felicity is out there now. She has joined the Adamantium for money, nothing more. It has to be said that Private Lunatic has surrounded himself in honour by not defecting. We shall strike sooner rather than later."

Anne and Emereldon nodded in agreement. The third figure watched this.

"Good, I'm glad you agree. There is a long way to go now and we must ensure our victory. Having been on the inside with you Anne, it leads me to believe that these clouds are as incompetent as they are careless. I doubt that this Rod character will have even noticed my exit."

"I doubt he will have my lord," came Anne's reply.

The mystery figure was amused by this and giggled slightly to himself.

Both Anne and Emereldon were unnerved by this and did not join him. It was evident that these two were in awe of whoever this mystery person was. Well, it was either awe or fear, but there was certainly a healthy respect for him.

He waved at them, urging them to stand.

They obliged immediately.

The third figure slowly disrobed and revealed an all too familiar pale complexion, his immaculately styled, dark hair being the give away.

It was the camera man.

This, however, was a very different camera man to the one that all around had known. He oozed confidence and power and possessed a commanding presence.

He was completely different, in almost every conceivable way. Even his appearance seemed slicker. He wore a navy-blue suit, white shirt with a red and white striped tie. Strangely he was now wearing a pair of white gloves too.

He turned and faced both Anne Weavers and Emereldon once more. Both bowed before him instantly.

"Yes I have found it somewhat odd playing the part of a subordinate. It's not my style, but it has given me the information that I require to fell this cloud empire."

The pair rose and spoke in unison, "For the Ignacium Lord Anarchis."

As they finished both Anne and Emereldon shuffled around behind this 'Lord Anarchis'.

He raised one hand and some flames of fire ignited within his palm. Oddly it did not burn or even blacken the white gloves which he wore. He cackled slightly and then spoke in a dry, yet confident manner.

"I never really did care for those camera things. Now it is time, now it is time, now it is my time for me to fulfill my destiny. This is my time."

www.nocternabooks.com

Principal Events in 1

C000172633

	National and International	*Regional*
January	Eisenhower assumes duties of C-in-C Allied Expeditionary Force. Battle for Cassino begins. Allied landing at Salerno. Russians advance over 1939 Polish frontier.	NUAW Norfolk County Committee reports 2,000 members recruited in a year. Suffolk farmers protest at inadequate farm prices.
February	National Health Service White Paper. German offensives against Anzio beachhead. Mutual Aid Agreement with French Committee of National Liberation.	Worst raids on Clacton and Colchester cause extensive damage. Bury St Edmunds by-election. Norwich conference to discuss juvenile delinquency. "Big Week" raids from East Anglian bases.
March	Commons votes for equal pay for teachers. Miners' strike begins. Travel to Eire suspended. Russians advance in Ukraine and enter Romania.	Serious drought—many wells run dry. Fire damages Samson and Hercules House in Norwich. Many die when two US bombers collide and crash in Henham Park. Theatre Royal, Norwich, licensed to give Sunday forces concerts.
April	Home Office bans all overseas travel. Russians recapture Odessa and advance to Czech frontier. Italian King announces intention to abdicate. Allies capture more Pacific islands. White loaf reappears in shops.	Coastal belt from Wash southward forbidden to public "for operational reasons". Airfield construction programme for USAAF completed. Invasion vessels begin to assemble at Harwich.
May	White Paper on post-war employment policy. Conference of Empire prime ministers. Allies capture Cassino and launch offensive from Anzio beachhead. Russians reoccupy Sebastopol.	East Anglian assault troops marshalled for D-Day invasion. False rumours of enemy parachutists in Suffolk. Fire at Little Chesterford ammunition dump.

9-50

LB KNX

EAST ANGLIA 1944

EAST ANGLIA 1944

by

R. DOUGLAS BROWN

TERENCE DALTON LIMITED
LAVENHAM . SUFFOLK
1992

Published by
TERENCE DALTON LIMITED

ISBN 0 86138 076 2

Text photoset in 10/12pt Times

Printed in Great Britain at
The Lavenham Press Limited, Lavenham, Suffolk

Contents

Index of Illustrations vii

Introduction and Acknowledgements viii

Chapter One   Waiting for the Action 1

Chapter Two   Death from the Skies 15

Chapter Three   Distant Guns 31

Chapter Four   Domestic Disturbance 42

Chapter Five   Operation Overload 53

Chapter Six   The Day They Went Ashore 67

Chapter Seven   From the Killing to the Kissing 79

Chapter Eight   Germany's Last Throw 95

Chapter Nine   Problems on the Farms 109

Chapter Ten   To the Frontier 122

Chapter Eleven   The Lights Go on Again 137

Chapter Twelve   Post-war Prospects 150

Notes on Sources 166

Selected Bibliography 171

Index 172

Publishers' Note

The publishers regret that the reproduction of certain illustrations is below the quality that they would normally demand. The *East Anglian Daily Times* and the *Eastern Daily Press*, who kindly permitted us the use of their files, were unfortunately unable to provide original photographs and, consequently, the pictures shown are reproductions from the printed newspapers. The same applies to those photographs from the *Cambridge Evening News* that were so kindly provided by the Cambridge Collection of the Cambridgeshire Libraries. Where applicable, it was considered preferable to show illustrations, even if below our usual standard, rather than no pictures at all. This volume is the sixth of a series which will fully document the events in East Anglia, year by year, and we would welcome any photographs that apply to 1945. These would be forwarded to the author for his use and duly returned.

Index of Illustrations

B-17s en route to Europe ... Frontispiece
Salvaging rags from local residents ... x
Glenn Miller and his orchestra perform-
ing 3
"Save Fuel for Battle" 5
"Rail Transport is Half the Battle" ... 6
Top brass on the saluting base 9
Officers' Club at Ridgewell 11
Boys training at Suffolk Gliding School ... 13
Money collected during "Salute the Sol-
dier" week 14
B-17 crashes on railway track 16
Diploma awarded after 25 missions ... 17
Child escapes bombed house in Boxted ... 19
Stirling bombers 21
P51 Mustang at Leiston 23
95th Bomb Group at Horsham 25
Mr Richard Stokes 27
Air raids at Colchester 29
The Burma Campaign 32
British mortar team in the jungle ... 35
Essex Regiment near Cassino 39
Allies Club in Trinity Street, Colchester 43
British Welcome Club at Lavenham ... 44
American Red Cross dances 45
The Ridgewell Base Band 46
Visiting an Ipswich church 48
Vandalism during the war 51
General Montgomery talking to the
Mayor 54
General Eisenhower at Newmarket ... 56
Demonstration of motor boats 57
Naval vessels ready to leave the Solent ... 58
Wooden warships under construction ... 60
Site of Blomfield's ironmongery shop ... 62
Inspection of an American Marauder ... 65
Aerial view of the Normandy beaches ... 68
1st Royal Norfolks wading ashore ... 72
The scene on the beach after the landing 73
Invasion of Normandy 75
Troops landing on a "Sword" beach ... 77

Headlines mislead the Germans 78
Royal Naval destroyer sunk in the
English Channel 81
The Normandy Campaign 83
Casualty clearing station in Normandy ... 85
Bren carriers in the wrecked village of
Bijude 86
Censorship in action 90
German V.1 flying bomb 96
Flying bombs hit houses at Ardleigh ... 97/98
ATS girls outside their Nissen hut ... 99
Gunners racing to man guns at
Southwold 100
Jeep rides for evacuees from London ... 108
Land girls from a Suffolk WLA 112
"Spend your holiday at a farm camp" ... 113
Levington Drawing Match 115
Harvest time at Ridgewell 118
Mr Edwin Gooch 120
Stradishall RAF station 123
B-24 Liberators dropping supplies ... 126
Advance on Germany 127
"Allies fighting on German soil" 129
The three drums being played at Haecht 130
1st Suffolk infantrymen rest at Geijsteren 131
Preparing bombs at Knettishall 133
Addressing the gathering on Minden Day 138
Celebrations for the Home Guard stand-
down 139
HM King George VI inspecting the
Home Guard 141
Cambridge Gas Company checking the
lamps 144
Demolition of concrete pill-boxes ... 146
Government supplement homes with
"Portals" 152
Water being collected in buckets from
wells 159
American servicemen entertain local
youngsters 163
Operation "Manns" 165

Introduction and Acknowledgements

THIS IS the sixth and penultimate volume in a series that presents the events of the war of 1939–45 as experienced by the people of East Anglia. Earlier volumes have told of life in the region during years when there was stalemate in western Europe and a battered Britain was struggling to renew its strength after serious military reverses, and a later period when the alliance with the United States and Russia was forged and plans were laid to overcome the enemy. The build-up of forces in 1943 was brought to a climax early in 1944, and at high summer the tide of war was turned.

One military historian, Mr H. P. Willmott, has suggested that June 1944 saw the turn of the tide not only in the war, but in the history of the United Kingdom: "Normandy proved a British swansong, after which her ability to shape events and influence stronger allies declined . . . This month marked the decline of Europe and its subjugation to the will of powers that were not European."[1] This proposition gives added piquancy to a study of the mentality, behaviour and aspirations of ordinary folk living in a region of England where wartime activity was ubiquitous and intense.

From the summer of 1944, when the war entered a new phase, men of several East Anglian regiments found themselves fighting in critical campaigns in many parts of the world: Burma, Italy, France and the Low Countries, and Greece. Many were in the assault brigades which landed on the Normandy beaches. This narrative account of 1944 is consequently much concerned with military operations on the various fronts and the experience of the men of the eastern counties who were involved; but it remains a social history rather than a military history and so it gives equal attention to the consequences for those who remained at home.

I have made good use of the official histories of the regiments associated with the eastern counties: *The Royal Norfolk Regiment*, by Lieutenant-Commander P. K. Kemp; *The Essex Regiment*, by Colonel T. A. Martin; and *The Suffolk Regiment*, by Colonel W. N. Nicholson. I wish to record my indebtedness to these authors and to express my thanks for permission to quote from them. Almost equally important as a source for information about the Normandy invasion is Norman Scarfe's *Assault Division—A History of the 3rd Division*, while Carlo d'Este's *Decision in Normandy* and H. P. Willmott's *June 1944* are not only informative but also thought-provoking accounts that help to place the exploits of the East Anglian troops in proper perspective.

For detail of events in the eastern counties the regional daily newspapers have been a principal source and I acknowledge with thanks my indebtedness to their publishers, the Eastern Counties Newspapers Group Ltd and Cambridge Newspapers Ltd. The late Mr Hervey Benham's *Essex at War* preserved much

viii

information which could not be published during hostilities, and Mr Michael Bowyer's two definitive works, *Action Stations* and *Air Raid!*, are models of research; I have used all three as basic sources.

For an insight into the private thoughts and attitudes of East Anglians who spent these war days on the home front, the personal diaries preserved in the Mass Observation archive at Sussex University are of paramount importance and, as in earlier volumes, I have quoted extensively from them. I wish to express my thanks to the custodians of the archive and to Ms Dorothy Sheridan, BA, the archivist, and her staff for their guidance and assistance.

Another important diary—the most complete and detailed account of life on a United States air base in the region during the war—has been published as a book, the Reverend James Good Brown's *The Mighty Men of the 381st: Heroes All*. I have taken a number of vivid extracts from this work, and I am appreciative of the author's readiness to permit reproduction.

I have consulted primary sources at the Public Record Office at Kew and various documents held at the Local Studies Department of the Norfolk County Library at Norwich, the Cambridgeshire Local History Collection at Cambridge Central Library, and the Suffolk Record Office at Bury St Edmunds and Ipswich. I wish to thank the staff at each of these institutions.

My thanks are also offered to all who have helped with photographs to illustrate the text, particularly to Mr Ian Hawkins, Mr Dave Osborne and Mr Jock Whitehouse, and to the staff of the Department of Photographs at the Imperial War Museum in London.

R. DOUGLAS BROWN

Stoke-by-Clare, Suffolk.
June 1991.

WVS worker Mrs Ringrose, head of the area Central Salvage Depot in Tostock, Suffolk, collecting rags from a local resident, Mrs Copping. *Imperial War Museum*

CHAPTER ONE

Waiting for the Action

THE TIME had come. As a New Year opened, the world was waiting on an event which must change the course of history. No one could yet mark the calendar with the day on which it would occur, but three all-powerful war leaders—Roosevelt, Stalin and Churchill—had lunched together in the Soviet Embassy in Teheran in November and had then agreed a season for action. With a due sense of the solemnity of their decision Winston Churchill had noted:

> Together we controlled a large preponderance of the naval and three-quarters of all the air forces in the world, and could direct armies of nearly twenty millions of men, engaged in the most terrible of wars that had yet occurred in human history.[1]

These forces were about to be redeployed in the greatest combined operation ever planned.

Throughout the early months of 1944 there was intense public anticipation of the day when a great Allied army would go forth from Britain's shores to invade the European mainland. Hopes and dreams were shaped around that event. People had endured over four years of war: near-siege and privation, danger and discomfort, family separation and loss of personal freedom. They were impatient for the victory in war that would bring them the hoped-for rewards of peace. Meanwhile there were the pains of a pregnancy to endure as the invasion force took shape, gained strength and prepared to enter the fray.

The *Eastern Daily Press* began its editorial comment on the first day of the year:

> There is one universal hope today. It is that the year upon which we are entering may see the end of the war . . . Though it is now 1944 and things have changed very greatly since 1940, the responsibilities laid on the individual will call for just the same kind of courage and for even firmer resolution and more fevered energy.

The "fevered energy" was much in evidence. Troops swarmed over the East Anglian countryside, marching, firing with live ammunition, manoeuvring their armoured vehicles; they were billeted in countless homes and commandeered public buildings. Off duty, they packed the pubs and cinemas. The skies over the eastern counties throbbed and echoed as the great bombing offensive on German targets continued at an ever-increasing tempo. The east coast ports and estuaries were full of shipping involved in keeping open the sea lanes, and the beaches were the scene of elaborate invasion rehearsals.

The towns and villages of East Anglia offered a very limited range of

1

amusements and diversions to these tens of thousands of servicemen and women during their leisure hours. In their run-down wartime condition they could seem deeply depressing to strangers far from their own homes. A Mass Observation report described conditions in Bury St Edmunds in February 1944:

> On Sunday the town square is dreary and dull, very cold and bleak. Outside both cinemas there are long queues waiting for 5 o'clock, when the programme starts. Groups of American and English soldiers are leaning against shop-fronts in a bored and apathetic way. The one small, cheap cafe, "The Victory Cafe", is full to over-crowding, with Americans seated at the marble-topped tables or waiting in the gangway to take their turn at the seats. Later a Salvation Army band gathers and starts up. There is a stir of interest among the onlookers. Some more soldiers come into the Market Square and take their places among the others leaning on shop-fronts, and stare listlessly at the worshippers. Any woman passing is stared at and comments made on her appearance . . .[2]

Strenuous efforts were made to cater for the needs of the troops. The services made their own arrangements; Entertainments National Service Association (ENSA) concerts were given from time to time, and some of Britain's best-known stage and screen stars performed. The Americans provided glamour by bringing over Hollywood super-stars. Bing Crosby, for example, toured USAAF bases, beginning at Ridgewell, Essex, where he sang such favourites from his repertoire as "White Christmas", "Blue of the Night" and "Buddy Can You Spare a Dime" to an audience of four thousand, including many locals who were smuggled into the hangar.

Civilian authorities tried hard to provide suitable facilities. In Norwich the Theatre Royal—with the backing of the Lord Mayor's Anglo-American Relations Committee—was granted a licence in March for Sunday performances, provided only members of the forces in uniform were admitted and no admission charge was made. Unfortunately this almost coincided with the temporary closure of one of the forces' favourite Norwich haunts, the Samson and Hercules House in Tombland, which was badly damaged by a fire during the early hours of 17th March. The main dance hall suffered only from the water pumped into the blaze, but the unique portico supported by two large wooden effigies—one holding a club and the other the jawbone of an ass—fared badly. There was some consolation when a few weeks later a big department store, Buntings Ltd, which had been damaged in air raids two years before, opened as a "Super-NAAFI", its whole interior transformed to give it the look of a residential hotel (NAAFI: abbreviation for Navy, Army and Air Force Institutes).

For those still in their own homes the hardships of everyday life were undiminished: rationing of food, clothing and fuel, the inconvenience of the blackout, long hours of overtime work or compulsory service in Civil Defence and the Home Guard. The air raid sirens still wailed regularly. The British diet at this time was adequate to maintain health, but it lacked excitement. The *Eastern Daily Press* published a leading article during January which began with the words: "Probably a good many mouths watered liberally one day this week when we were

Glenn Miller and his orchestra played at the USAAF air base at Thorpe Abbots on 1st September 1944.
Photo courtesy of Ian Hawkins

promised at least a lemon apiece some time in the not too far distant future."

There was nothing facetious about this; at about the same time William Stock, in Chelmsford, wrote in his diary:

> I brought my landlady a lemon—one of about twenty which my father had sent him from my cousin in the RAF in North Africa. Lemons are a fabulous fruit now, and, oh, to see (and eat) a banana again![3]

There was no increase in the number of clothing coupons during 1944 (four per month), but when some restrictions were removed on 1st March to permit men's suits to be double-breasted and to have turn-ups, buttons on the sleeves and four waistcoat pockets—all of which had been banned during the previous two years—the *Eastern Daily Press* thought it worth another leading article, this one expressing confidence that "quite a number of male hearts will beat with renewed vigour at the news of the end of utility clothing".

The government juggled with the rations and restrictions. In March it announced an increased supply of canned meat and fish, an increase in the weekly milk allowance from two to two-and-a-half pints and a temporary doubling of the jam ration. The cheese ration, on the other hand, was cut from three ounces to two

3

ounces per head per week. At about the same time an almost pure wheat loaf returned to the shops. Oats, barley and rye had formed ten per cent of wartime flour, but now the use of oats and barley was stopped and British flour and bread consisted of 97½ per cent wheat and 2½ per cent rye. A government spokesman boasted that only the UK, among all the countries of Europe, was enjoying unrationed flour and bread. During the summer there was "a bonus issue" of bacon: six ounces instead of four for a few weeks.

As the summer approached beer was in short supply. Production was restricted, there was a large temporary population in the region, and some supplies were directed to the armed forces abroad. As a result at harvest time little or no beer was available for the workers in the fields, and when they—and others working overtime—laid down their tools in the evenings and made for the pubs they found them closed.

The chairman of the Licensed Victuallers' Association told Thingoe Licensing Justices at Bury St Edmunds on 9th August that there was no public house in the eastern counties that could open for an hour during the day and two hours at night and go on pulling beer. Publicans were urged to stagger their hours. At Bury and Ixworth the licensing justices told them to open for an hour or ninety minutes at lunchtime and then from 8 pm to 10 pm. In Cambridge they experimented with 8 pm to 9.30 pm opening during the week, promising to open at the weekend from 12.30 to 1 pm if they had enough beer left. William Stock, in Chelmsford, noted on 7th August that "all the pubs round here were shut this evening, having sold out".

The Ministry of Fuel and Power announced on 1st January that "the coal supply position in the Eastern Region is extremely acute, on account of transport difficulties". Because coal was being stocked for military operations, and because some of the stocks in merchants' yards were reserved for emergencies in case supplies were further interrupted, domestic supplies were to be severely restricted. In Cambridgeshire, Huntingdonshire, Norfolk, Suffolk and Essex no domestic premises were permitted more than four hundredweight during the month of January, and no family was permitted to have more than five hundredweight in its coal-shed. There was a general warning that most consumers would have to manage on even smaller quantities.

Many cottages were heated by paraffin stoves, but the great majority of homes depended upon open coal fires. Advertisements appeared in the press recommending peat as an alternative.

There was a general shortage of consumer goods in the shops and second-hand items were briskly traded. William Stock reported on the Chelmsford shops:

> The shortage of crockery and good cooking utensils is becoming acutely felt. The thick plain crockery and the shoddy tin pots and pans which are all that are now obtainable in most places are so unattractive and highly priced that a good many people would rather go without.[4]

The public was kept under constant pressure to consume less. These advertisements were published in the *East Anglian Daily Times* during the first few months of 1944.   *East Anglian Daily Times*

The fear of an enemy invasion of Britain had not been entirely removed from people's minds. There were two scares in Suffolk during May. The first suggested that parachutists, probably hostile, had landed in the Mildenhall area, and for nearly two hours RAF station defences at Newmarket were held in a state of readiness. The second came three days later, when parachutists were said to be active in the Stradishall area[5]. A party of US airmen, completing a cross-country walk at Hempstead, Essex, and waiting for a truck to pick them up, was challenged by a six-year-old boy who cautiously stuck his head through a partially opened door: "Are you Germans?" On being reassured, the youngster made an immediate response: "Have you any gum, chum?" Further evidence of a certain jitteriness is provided by William Stock's diary entry when the invasion of France took place: "The main topic arising in conversation was the expectation of a German counter attack."

Great efforts were made to sustain civilian morale. Typical of the newspapers' role was "a New Year stock-taking" by a columnist in the *East Anglian Daily Times*:

5

RAIL TRANSPORT is "Half the Battle"

WAGONS loaded with WAR FREIGHTS run 10 MILLION MILES every day

BRITISH RAILWAYS
GWR · LMS   LNER · SR
CARRY THE WAR LOAD

Rail Transport is Half the Battle says the *East Anglian Daily Times* on 17th February 1944.
East Anglian Daily Times

It is transparent that the whole ambitious Axis strategic plan has collapsed like the proverbial house of cards . . . The Axis has shed the Italian partner. Germany, with a few coerced and conscripted satellites, who hourly grow more restive under the yoke, stands alone in Europe, menaced by a steadily constricting stranglehold . . . In Italy, Allied armies are pressing Hitler's army of occupation back towards Rome . . . Those piratical pests, the U-boats, have been out-fought and out-manoeuvred. Supplies and troops from America are steadily pouring into Britain. Meanwhile, the *blitzkrieg* has come home to roost in Germany . . .

This picture of an enemy facing defeat was reinforced by the display of captured German equipment. Three captured German planes—a Junkers Ju.88, a Messerschmitt Bf.109 and a Focke Wulf Fw.190—were repainted in RAF markings and camouflage and RAF pilots took this "Enemy Aircraft Flight" on tours of UK bases. In one of their earliest displays they flew over four Essex air bases—Rivenhall, Great Dunmow, Andrews Field and Earl's Colne.[6]

There were some for whom these propaganda methods were insufficient, and who wanted nothing less than an assurance that God was advancing alongside the

Allied armed forces. An Ipswich clergyman put into circulation a story that a "vision" of Christ on the Cross had appeared in the sky over Ipswich during an air raid in April. He did not claim to have seen it himself, but he told his congregation that he had investigated the matter and he was completely satisfied about the authenticity of the vision. It was much debated in the correspondence columns of some local newspapers, and there were some to whom it offered comfort. When the Mass Observation organization invited its correspondents to express their views, however, they gave short shrift to the story. ". . . like seeing castles in a fire", declared Winifred Last of Bury St Edmunds. "A hallucination finding credence among the emotional and credulous wish-thinkers", said a fifty-year-old retired science mistress living in East Bergholt. "Complete nonsense", said a Bishops Stortford correspondent. Only a college lecturer in Norwich entertained the possibility: "I believe that these visions *could* be given by God, but I don't think they were. Mass suggestion is amazingly strong."[7]

Calculations about the effect upon public morale (as well as the obvious security considerations) led to concealment of the fact that Winston Churchill had been unwell when he flew to the Teheran conference with Stalin and Roosevelt. Soon afterwards, when he flew on to North Africa, he was (in his own words) "completely at the end of my tether"[8]. He went to Marrakesh to recover from pneumonia, but nothing was disclosed to the public until mid-January, when he was again quite well and on the point of returning to London.

Women were in the forefront of the war effort and performed a major part of the civilian activity, much of it in the form of voluntary service. Mr Ernest Bevin stated in March that seven million women were in war work or in the forces, including 2,500,000 married women, yet there remained a desperate shortage of labour. Royston and District Hospital closed down at the beginning of the year, refusing to admit any cases, because it was without a single domestic employee. When the matter was raised in the Commons the Ministry of Labour produced the necessary staff within a week. A Cambridge general practitioner warned that surgeries might have to be cancelled because doctors could not find domestic staff.

Many women volunteers undertook work involving dull routine, like making camouflage nets. This was a task to which members of the Cambridge Women's Voluntary Service devoted themselves for three years, until there were enough nets and the operation was suspended early in 1944. Women whose pre-war tasks had been in kitchens or fields now found themselves doing skilled factory and office work; contrariwise, many women with academic qualifications cheerfully tackled menial tasks if they were considered to be the priority of the day.

There was, of course, another kind of woman: those who felt that social position had imbued them with natural powers of leadership. There was a good supply of these in East Anglia. Miss Winifred Last, a local government employee whose work brought her into contact with many of them, gave this caustic description in her diary:

7

Mrs S—— is a strong-willed, one-time handsome but now aged, witty woman of varying moods, a dominating type who can be very gracious and kindly, and also very hard. She is definitely a "Poor Law type", who knows how to put the lower classes in their places and to freeze any attempt at equality or familiarity. As with most of these people, in their opinion the working classes are there merely to do as they are told.[9]

Many intelligent women found it less easy to lose themselves in these high-profile activities. In February 1944 Mass Observation invited some of them to indulge in a little introspection, and this, from an East Bergholt woman, was a typical response:

I feel that the continued war, with all its destruction and suffering, is having a most depressing effect on my mind. I am more and more conscious of the appalling chaos it is causing and the enormous problem with which we shall be faced when hostilities cease . . . War conditions have given me less time for mental occupation and reading. It has also limited my radius of action, so that I am conscious of the narrowness of my life and its uselessness, as far as the war is concerned, beyond the usual village war activities and the giving of hospitality to one or two American airmen.[10]

For the majority of people in East Anglia pre-war life had been frugal, and they endured the additional hardships of wartime with quiet fortitude. An American visitor, the Reverend James Good Brown, chaplain at the USAAF base at Ridgewell, visited dozens of homes and lectured to women's organizations and church and community gatherings in sixteen towns and villages during the year. He noted these impressions in his diary:

The English people whom I have met are, on the whole, satisfied with little rather than with much. Their outlook is not the same as that of an American. The two countries are entirely different. The American always wants more, more, more. But in England there is a greater degree of contentment with what one has and less hunger for something else . . .[11]

Such generalizations are, of course, dangerous. Mr Brown went on to observe that "the Englishman knows that certain means of transportation are faster than others, but he is apt to say 'Why go faster?' Or 'Why change the stove when this one heats?' Or 'Why put in electric lights when the oil lamps furnish light?' . . ."[12]

He had scarcely written these words when a joint statement by the RAF and the USAAF revealed that aircraft were about to be revolutionized as the result largely of the efforts of men nurtured in East Anglia. The *East Anglian Daily Times* provided the information that there had been built "a jet-propelled fighter aircraft which flies propellerless at extreme speed at great altitudes". Soon this remarkable jet-propelled plane would be in production, and an air correspondent writing in the *Cambridge Daily News* promised that it would have "the sound of a giant whistling kettle on the boil".

With regional pride, the papers related the part that had been played in the development of jet propulsion by a thirty-six-year-old group captain in the RAF,

Frank Whittle, who had been an experimental test pilot on float seaplanes at Felixstowe during 1931–32 and had then spent three years at Cambridge University obtaining first-class honours in the mechanical science tripos in 1936, followed by a year's post-graduate work. In Cambridge in 1933 he had initiated the work that was to produce the first successful jet-propulsion aircraft engine. The first successful jet flight had been made in May 1941 by Flight Lieutenant Philip Edward Gerald Sayer, an old boy of Colchester Grammar School, who had joined the RAF in June 1924, becoming a test pilot at Martlesham Heath before going to the Gloster Aircraft Company as chief test pilot in 1935. He was killed on 22nd October 1942, when he was thirty-seven.

Although the "jet" plane was thus a British design, its development over several years had become a united Anglo-American effort, and the first experimental flight of a combat plane designed to have two jet engines had been made in the USA in October 1942.

Cambridge University was involved in the war effort in many ways, and the

At Brightlingsea a local private joined the "top brass" on the saluting base. He is seated beside the Sector Commander, Brig.-Gen. H. G. Seth-Smith. Speaking is Captain J. P. Landon, RN, Naval Officer in Command. *Photo courtesy of Mrs Hervey Benham*

9

Honours Lists during 1944 recognized individual contributions. Whittle was made a CBE. (He was to be knighted in 1948.) Three Cambridge professors received knighthoods in the New Year Honours List: Professor Ernest Barker, Emeritus Professor of Political Science; Professor Frank L. Engledow, Professor of Agriculture; and Air Vice-Marshal Norman D. Kerr MacEwen, who was chairman of the Soldiers', Sailors' and Airmen's Families Association. A fourth appeared in the Birthday Honours List in June: Professor G. I. Taylor, Yarrow Research Professor. Mr E. G. Gooch, the Norfolk man who was president of the National Union of Agricultural Workers, was awarded the CBE.

Another name in the Birthday Honours List was that of Mr A. J. Munnings, who had just been elected president of the Royal Academy and who now became a knight. A native of Mendham, Suffolk, he had studied in Norwich, had returned to Mendham when he was twenty, and six years later had moved to Swainsthorpe, near Norwich. After a period in Cornwall he had made his home at Dedham.

Cambridge University gave as generously as it received. At a special ceremony in May it awarded honorary doctorates of law to two Commonwealth Prime Ministers: Mr John Curtin of Australia and Mr Peter Fraser of New Zealand. The Chancellor of the University and former Prime Minister, Lord Baldwin, conferred the degrees. This was made an occasion for full peacetime pageantry. In this, and other similar ways, every effort was made to emphasize the world-wide partnership in the Allied cause. In February, at a ceremony in the United States Embassy in London, the deeds of ownership of the site of the home of Abraham Lincoln's ancestors, at Swanton Morley, Norfolk, were passed to the National Trust.

Amid much extraordinary wartime activity some aspects of society remained unchanged. Men reached their peak and collected fame and honour; others ran their course and passed away. Sir Gurney Benham, High Steward of Colchester and three times its mayor, proprietor of the *Essex County Standard*, died in May at the age of eighty-five. Most newspaper obituary notices, however, told of lives cut short. One of Suffolk's best-known families was twice striken in 1944. In June Lieutenant-Colonel John Murray Cobbold of the Scots Guards, who was chairman of Cobbold and Co., the Ipswich brewers, and had been Sheriff of Suffolk in 1934, was killed in London by enemy action at the age of forty-seven. Only a short time before, his cousin, Major Robert Neville Cobbold of the Welsh Guards, had been killed in action.

The deaths of many others, less well known, were recorded only in the telegrams delivered to their families. One exceptional occasion was the Culford School speech day in July, when the head, Dr J. W. Skinner, reported that sixteen old boys had been killed on active service in the previous year.

The contrasts inherent in the circumstances of the time were never more stark than in the week of the Normandy invasion. While men were wading through surf and explosives to win a foothold on foreign soil, the Cambridge University Madrigal Society sang madrigals and part-songs on the river under King's College

Edward G. Robinson visits the Officers' Club of the 381st Bomb Group of the USAAF at Ridgewell, Essex, 5th July 1944.   *Photo courtesy of Dave Osborne*

Bridge to a large and appreciative crowd. "The mood of the crowd was reflected in the quiet, lazy lapping of the river", the *Cambridge Daily News* reported.

Some in Newmarket, too, seemed extraordinarily insulated from the stresses of wartime. The town had achieved unique status as Britain's wartime racing centre. A remarkable number of people still managed to attend its meetings. When the first two of the classic races, the 1,000 Guineas and the 2,000 Guineas, were run in May, trains from London were packed; race-goers queued at Liverpool Street Station from 6.45 am to be sure of getting tickets, and trains with seats for seven hundred departed with twelve hundred on board and others left behind on the platform. There were frequent prosecutions of car-owners who used rationed petrol to get to the course.

The Jockey Club in Newmarket claimed an almost mystical status. When its premises broke the blackout regulations, showing bright lights from six ground-floor windows in the middle of the night, the behaviour of the custodian was astonishing. A policeman went into the club and switched off the lights, but twenty-

11

five minutes later they were on again. When challenged, the man in charge replied: "I don't care. I'm independent of the police or anybody else in Newmarket." When summonsed, he failed to appear in court or to send a letter, yet the magistrates contented themselves with the observation that it was "a bad case" and imposed a fine of three pounds.

Relations between the resident Newmarket establishment and service units temporarily posted to the area were not always cordial. During January a senior officer had to intervene on behalf of a soldier who was put on a charge because the tank he was driving along the High Street was alleged to have frightened a racehorse.

Some other sections of the population who seemed to have lost sight of the national purpose were fiercely castigated, particularly the miners, shipyard apprentices, London bus crews and Manchester gas workers whose deep discontent led to strikes in the early part of 1944. The Bishop of Chelmsford, Dr Henry Wilson, wrote in his April diocesan letter:

> The constant strikes and trade disputes of various kinds are indications of the beginning of that easy-going point of view which will do more than anything else to prolong the war indefinitely. When we carry our minds back four years and contrast the spirit which inspired the nation in those dark days with that which is beginning to infect us now, we see a notable lack of concentration upon the supreme issues. In 1940 when we stood alone we saw a wonderful vision. That vision has been lost by many today.

Men and women in the forces could not protest or strike, but a strong feeling developed in the country that they and their families were bearing unfair burdens. Army pay had been fixed in 1942, since when the great mass of workers had received substantial increases and the soldiers had been left out. An effort by some Members of Parliament to secure them increases was defeated after a Commons debate in March by sixty-three votes to forty, but only after Mr Anthony Eden had intervened to screen the Minister of War, Sir James Grigg, from the strength of feeling in the House.

Eight weeks after the Commons vote the government published a White Paper announcing some limited increases but insisting "The government are satisfied that no general increase in pay is required." Privates who were "proficient" should progress more rapidly to the five shillings a week maximum rate of pay. The allowance for the children of ratings and other ranks was to be at a flat rate of 12s 6d (instead of a scale descending from 9s 6d*. This White Paper was well received. In May it was announced that service pay back-dated to 1st January would be paid to Civil Defence workers and the National Fire Service (NFS).

Expenditure on the war—so far as it could be measured in cash terms—was running at a little over £13,250,000 a day, according to the Chancellor of the Exchequer, Sir John Anderson, in a statement to the Commons in January. He

---

*In the currency of the time there were twenty shillings to the pound and twelve pence to the shilling.

Boys training at Suffolk Gliding School.   *East Anglian Daily Times*

estimated that the cost during 1944 would total five thousand million pounds. UK annual revenues had just exceeded three thousand million pounds for the first time ever; to cover ordinary expenditure as well as war, a deficit of £2,750 million would have to be met by borrowing.

No wonder the government worked so hard to take money out of circulation by organizing special National Savings campaigns. After the "Spitfire Fund" of 1940, the "War Weapons Week" of 1941, the "Warships Week" of 1942 and the "Wings for Victory Week" of 1943, the theme chosen for 1944 was "Salute the Soldier". Special week-long efforts were made in every town and village during the summer, and, as in all previous campaigns, most districts exceeded their targets spectacularly. There were the usual over-simplified suggestions that the amount saved in a particular community would meet a specific war purpose—the people of Norwich were told that a million pounds was "the cost of adopting the Royal Norfolk Regiment" (whatever that was supposed to mean) and the people of Colchester were assured that the £350,000 they set out to collect would equip and maintain a battalion of the Essex Regiment for twelve months.

The public response everywhere exceeded the targets set. Norwich aimed for

At each centre the total collected day by day during "Salute the Soldier" weeks was prominently announced. This display was at Colchester. The Borough Treasurer, Mr L. J. Barrell, who acted as honorary secretary of the local Savings Committee, is seen on the left.

Photo courtesy of Mrs Hervey Benham

£1,500,000 and raised £1,603,725; Cambridge set its target at a million pounds and raised £1,231,212; Ipswich raised more than a million pounds, Colchester £574,212, Great Yarmouth £365,000 and Bury St Edmunds £287,000. The Suffolk villages of Raydon and Holton, near Hadleigh, collected £28,302, which represented nearly fifty-seven pounds from each of their 497 inhabitants.

Books and newspapers were collected almost as energetically as paper currency, and scrap metal with the same diligence as coinage, as the government maintained its campaign to salvage and re-cycle such materials. During 1943 a Ministry of Works team had worked its way around East Suffolk and Norfolk, searching for old machinery, railings and gates for the war effort. In January 1944 it arrived in Bury St Edmunds, the last of the larger eastern region towns to be visited, setting itself a target of between three hundred and five hundred tons. Later it turned to the West Suffolk countryside, warning that a "mobile sweep team of women locators" would search every village in the area for scrap metal. Afterwards the team moved into Cambridgeshire.

In truth, though, there was not much more to be done in preparation for the great military operation ahead. Virtually everybody had been mobilized. Practically everything had been commandeered, diverted or rationed. The momentum had to be maintained, the exhortations were increased, the training intensified. For how much longer? That was the question in everyone's mind.

CHAPTER TWO

Death from the Skies

THE PEOPLE of East Anglia had no chance to ignore the grim realities of war. Bombers flew over their heads almost continuously, day and night. As the war now neared its climax, these were nearly all "friendly" bombers, but they provided frequent evidence of the lethal cargoes they carried. So many Allied war machines were in action, from bases tightly packed into a small area, that there were inevitably accidents. No quiet village or crowded town could feel entirely safe. Scarcely a week passed without a mishap and scarcely a month without a major disaster. In July the Regional Commissioner reported to the Home Office that emergency services had attended 177 plane crash fires in the eastern counties during the first six months of 1944[1].

January set the pattern. On the fourth day of the year a Flying Fortress due to join a raid on Kiel caught fire on take-off from Ridgewell, Essex, and dumped its bombs in a field near a farmhouse. Houses for miles around were shaken. The pilot tried desperately to land the plane safely but in the darkness it hit a narrow strip of woods three miles from the base, crumpled and burned to a charred mass. All ten of the crew were killed. It was the pilot's twenty-fifth and final mission before he was due to return to the USA. Disasters like this shocked the fighting men as much as the civilians. The base chaplain, the Reverend James Good Brown, who buried the men "in the very first row of the newly opened American Cemetery" in Cambridge, afterwards unburdened himself to his diary:

> At the military funeral, there was no feeling of glory, I assure you. One need only hear the words of the men who gather around me in the cemetery after the funeral, and hear them talk to me as we ride home together in the truck back to Ridgewell Aerodrome . . . —One flier, an innocent boy, said to me when the funeral was over, "Sometimes I wonder about all this." I could only respond, "Believe me, I do a lot of wondering, too."[2]

Three days later the pilot of a damaged US Fortress bomber returning from Ludwigshafen dropped out of formation and sought the first airfield he could find as soon as he came over England. When, at only two hundred feet, all the engines went dead and the plane was headed straight for Stradbroke, he deliberately stalled the plane and brought it down heavily in a field at Wilby. Four members of the crew were killed and others injured. On 24th January another B17 bomber was in difficulties over Diss, but the pilot crashed it in a ploughed field near the Norfolk village of Shelfanger. It tore the roof off a barn but narrowly missed cottages. The plane burst into flames and one of the crew died. The others, though dazed, proceeded immediately to make the bomb load harmless.

February provided an example of the kind of mishap that counted as only a minor irritant. A low-flying plane struck a power line. The plane flew on undamaged, but many towns in Suffolk and Norfolk—including Ipswich, Stowmarket and Framlingham—lost their electricity supply. At the Ipswich Hippodrome the music-hall star Nellie Wallace was just beginning her act; in darkness she kept her audience amused for twenty minutes until the lights went on again.

Many pilots gave their lives in their efforts to avoid crashing on East Anglian homes. There were two such incidents during March. An American Mustang pilot on a practice flight saved Nayland but plunged to his death, his plane scraping the rooftops. He kept its nose up long enough to clear the main street, then it hit a tree and burst into flames. The tail of another plane broke away over Colchester and the pilot lost his life trying to crash-land on a car park near the football ground, narrowly avoiding homes in Layer Road. At Upper Hellesdon near Norwich a

The scene at Yeldham, Essex, after a B-17 of the 381st Bomb Group at Ridgewell has crashed on a railway track near the base on 13th July 1944. *Photo courtesy of Dave Osborne*

16

pilot's efforts were less successful and his bomber crashed on a bungalow; it was burnt out, injuring a woman and her three children.

At mid-morning on 29th March the dull drone of a force of Liberator bombers flying over East Suffolk on their way to German targets was shattered by a shearing sound, the whine of revving engines and a succession of great explosions. Two planes had collided in mid-air. They crashed in Henham Park, on the Earl of Stradbroke's estate. Gordon Reynolds, a gardener there, afterwards related:

> There was a terrible roar. The whole countryside shuddered. Planes and debris hurtled into nearby woods. Black oily smoke and orange flames shot skywards. For a time there was eerie silence. Even the birds had stopped singing. Then there was the biggest explosion I had ever heard. The ground beneath me seemed to tremble and lift. Wreckage flew in all directions. Beside me a large jagged lump of shrapnel cut into the ground. I grabbed at it. It was red hot. All about me other razor-sharp pieces were slicing through the air. I was very frightened.

This "diploma" was issued to flyers of the 390th Bomb Group after they had survived 25 missions. This one was issued to R. G. (Bob) Schneider, who had flown all four missions during "Black Week" in mid-October 1943, when the 8th Air Force lost 153 B-17s in four raids—on Bremen, Marienburg, Münster and Schweinfurt.   *Courtesy of Ian Hawkins*

Diploma
390 th.
BOMB GROUP

This is to Certify that R. G. SCHNEIDER a member of
WITTAN'S WALLOPER BOMBING COLLEGE HAS SUCCESSFULLY COMPLETED
HIS TWENTY FIVE MISSIONS AGAINST HITLER'S HOT SHOTS AND IS
NOW ELIGIBLE TO RETURN TO GOD'S COUNTRY (THE LUCKY BASTARD)

Missions Completed

1. Meulan-Paris-Fr.
2. Kerlin-Bastard, Fr.
3. Stuttgart, Gr.
4. Watten, Fr.
5. Beaumont-Sur-Oise, Fr.
6. Bordeaux-Merignac, Fr.
7. Emden, Gr.
8. Emden, Gr.
9. Hanau, Gr.
10. Bremen, Gr.
11. Marienburg, Gr.
12. Munster, Gr.
13. Schweinfurt, Gr.
14. Duren, Gr.
15. Wilhelmshaven, Gr.
16. Gelsenkirchen, Gr.
17. Duren, Gr.
18. Munster, Gr.
19. Bremen, Gr.
20. Rjukan, Nor.
21. Gelsenkirchen, Gr.
22. Emden, Gr.
23. Kiel, Gr.
24. Bremen, Gr.
25. Bremen, Gr.

PROFESSOR OF BOMBING

DEAN OF FORMATION

17

Sixteen of the flyers died, as did about a score of those who had rushed to the scene to try to drag the crews from the wreckage and to fight the flames. The biggest explosion came fifty minutes after the planes came down, destroying two ambulances and almost wiping out a team of US Air Force fire-fighting engineers.

The last few days of March saw two more crashes of planes from the Ridgewell base. In the first a Flying Fortress returned from a raid on Rheims, in France, with its tail held on only by a few pieces of metal and holes in the fuselage so big that watchers from the field could look straight through it. Three of the crew had been killed by flak. The plane circled Ridgewell at six thousand feet and five survivors parachuted down in turn. Hundreds of the men on the base gathered to watch. The pilot and co-pilot then took the bomber back to the coast and baled out when it was over the sea. Spitfires were sent to shoot it down, but it splashed into the water before they could do so[3]. Before Ridgewell had had time to get over this incident, there was another three days later. This was on a day when no mission was flown, but a plane went for a short flight and crashed just off the end of the runway when returning. It caught fire and was completely destroyed. All six men on board lost their lives[4].

A Suffolk flyer was awarded the Victoria Cross for an exploit on 30th March. Twenty-three-year-old Pilot Officer Cyril Joe Barton, who was born at Elveden, was captain and pilot of a Halifax bomber taking part in a raid on Nuremberg. It was attacked by German fighters while seventy miles short of its target and the damage done to it made it impossible for Barton to communicate with his team. The navigator, bomb-aimer and radio operator baled out, but Barton flew on and released the bombs himself, then struggled back to England and crash-landed on one engine as the fuel ran out. He was killed, but the six other members of his crew survived.

A B-24 bomber from Bungay which belly-landed on 27th April among a flock of sheep at Flixton near Diss and caught fire narrowly missed a village church and skirted the roofs of a farmhouse. Two land girls and several labourers helped the four crew out of the wreckage, succoured others trapped inside until help arrived, and threw earth on the burning plane, which had a load of incendiaries and ammunition on board. Several of the crew were killed.

An American bomber crash-landed in a field just outside Bury St Edmunds and exploded on 24th May, after some of its crew had baled out. Two Bury NFS men and a Bury Air Raid Precautions (ARP) Rescue worker were seriously injured. During the same month a bomber from Little Walden crashed and exploded near Ashdon in Essex and a local woman was killed.

In July a Flying Fortress crashed with its bomb load on the railway at Great Yeldham. Four bombs exploded, killing seven of the crew, seriously injuring two others and blowing out fifty yards of track. Air-base cranes removed the wreckage and railway engineers had the track restored and trains running in less than four hours—"the slickest railway track-laying and repair job I've ever seen", said a US officer in charge at the scene[5].

When a bomb blew out the side of this house in Boxted during February a bed in which a child was asleep was left hanging over the edge of the floor. The child was rescued unhurt.

Photo courtesy of Mrs Hervey Benham

Early in September when an RAF bomber crashed and exploded at Pampisford, Cambridgeshire, its wreckage was strewn for half a mile around. Four of the crew were killed, as well as a Cambridge cowman and four American soldiers who rushed to the scene in a jeep. Pampisford Hall suffered some damage.

At the end of December a Flying Fortress struggling to get airborne from Framlingham on an icy morning careered into the centre of the village of Parham. All the crew were killed in a mighty explosion and every house was damaged, but the inhabitants suffered only minor injuries.

Bombs sometimes exploded accidentally before they were brought near aircraft. On 30th May fire occurred in an ammunition dump in woods in Little Chesterford Park near Saffron Walden. After a first big explosion the whole district was evacuated and all approaches picketed by the military. The NFS moved, without casualties, a hundred patients from the nearby Jewish Hospital for Incurables, which was severely damaged. Three major explosions, and many lesser ones, caused widespread blast damage and fires in several nearby villages. The military authorities undertook aerial reconnaissance, firemen in treetops kept track of the smaller fires, and it was late in the afternoon before the firemen, after a

19

desperate eight-hour battle, brought the situation under control so that people could return to their homes[6]. Most of the heaviest ammunition was saved, but watch had to be maintained on the dump for weeks afterwards. No information about this disaster was released until nearly five months later, when it was announced that Chief Regional Fire Officer H. J. Benton and Assistant Fire Force Commander R. C. Welch had been awarded the OBE and MBE respectively and Section Leader L. C. Crickmore had been awarded the BEM.

Only three days after this disaster the first of fifty wagons of an ammunition train passing through the station at Soham in Cambridgeshire caught fire. As it was immediately behind the locomotive, the fireman was able to jump down and uncouple the rest of the train. He ran back to the footplate and the driver opened up the regulator, but they had gone only 130 yards when the wagon blew up. It was 1.45 am. The whole town rocked, and people sleeping as far away as Bury St Edmunds were wakened. A gasometer burst into flames, the station was completely destroyed, and 550 shops and houses were damaged. Rest centres were opened and a thousand emergency meals served to the homeless. The locomotive ended up in a huge crater. The fireman, twenty-one-year-old William Nightall of Littleport, and a signalman, Frank Bridges of Soham, whose box was blasted, were killed. The driver, forty-one-year-old Benjamin Gimbert of March, was among thirty-five people injured. US army bulldozers demolished the remains of the station-master's house, then with the track repaired, trains ran again the same evening; but it was nearly a week before Soham had its gas supply restored. Gimbert and Nightall were both awarded the George Cross, the citation asserting that their outstanding courage and resource had "saved the town"[7].

A few weeks later the bomb dump at the US air base at Metfield exploded.

The main weight of bombs, however, was delivered by the RAF and the United States Air Force to targets in Germany and the German-occupied territories in Europe. Day after day the people of East Anglia were able to monitor the progress of this relentless bombing campaign.

During the early weeks of the year the bombing programme, both British and American, was in great difficulties. During 1943 the RAF had concentrated on bombing the Ruhr and Hamburg until, in November, it had turned its main attention to Berlin. After that things began to go badly wrong. In a raid on Leipzig on 19th/20th February it lost forty-four Lancasters and thirty-four Halifaxes —nearly one in ten of the planes despatched. On the last night of March it suffered its worst-ever loss when ninety-four of 795 bombers sent to attack Nuremberg failed to return and forty-eight others came back badly damaged.

In five months Bomber Command lost 1,047 planes, the majority shot down by German night fighters. That was more than the RAF's front-line strength on any

Stirling bombers.   *Photo courtesy of Jock Whitehouse.*

one day during the period[8], and this phase was later described as Bomber Command's "greatest test and defeat of the war"[9]. It was no longer in a position to sustain a major night offensive against German cities, and a fundamental re-examination of tactics was called for[10].

Between mid-November 1943 and the end of January 1944 first the Stirling bombers and then the earlier versions of the Halifax bombers were withdrawn from attacks on Germany. For a time Sir Arthur Harris, the Bomber Command chief, found himself with a force reduced by about thirty per cent and its bomb-carrying capacity by about twenty per cent[11]. British factories worked frantically to turn

out Lancaster bombers; retraining of pilots was organized; a new bomber support group took over a clutch of airfields in north Norfolk, of which Little Snoring was one, and trained crews to operate the radar with which Mosquitoes were being equipped; a new Pathfinder school was established at Alconbury and Pathfinder forces moved into Downham Market; and bomber streams were reorganized so that a force of eight hundred planes could arrive over a target and drop its bombs within twenty minutes.

The Eighth USAAF, conducting its daylight bombing raids from East Anglia, had also taken a severe battering during 1943. Its daylight raids on Germany had been virtually abandoned after that on Schweinfurt in October, when it lost sixty of the 291 Fortresses it sent out. Thereafter it recognized that long-range fighter protection was essential on deep penetration raids. This first became available with the delivery of P-51B Mustangs fitted with long-range fuel tanks, which could reach Berlin. From January 1944 these planes were flying from Boxted, Leiston, Raydon and Rivenhall.

During January and much of February America's "Mighty Eighth" was almost inoperative. Then it mounted a programme of concentrated bomber attacks which became known as "the Big Week". The bombers penetrated ever deeper into Germany, to Brunswick and Frankfurt, to Wilhelmshaven and Ludwigshaven, to Schweinfurt and—the biggest raid of the war to date—to Leipzig and Oschersleben. On seven February days the Eighth Air Force flew 3,300 bomber sorties, hitting railway marshalling yards and supply trains, submarine pens, bridges, oil refineries and aircraft factories. It dropped six thousand tons of bombs, and RAF night attacks during the same week added a further 13,177 tons. At the same time the new long-range fighters tried to wipe out the Luftwaffe in the air.

The Americans then turned to Berlin. The 95th Bomb Group at Horham was the first to bomb the German capital in daylight, on 4th March, but this raid did not develop because other formations were forced back by bad weather. In the first full-scale attack, two days later, the USAAF lost sixty-nine bombers—9.8 per cent of the force deployed—despite accompanying Mustangs. The Berlin raids continued, and those living near the Thorpe Abbots, Attlebridge, Rattlesden and other bases watched the bombers come and go during March and April.

By the spring of 1944 the RAF had largely overcome its problems and the USAAF had established daylight air superiority over Germany. Allied strategic bombers were then required for the forthcoming invasion of Normandy, and were brought under the control of the Supreme Allied Commander. The weight of attack was switched to enemy railway communications in France, Belgium and western Germany, though, between the invasion priorities, both RAF and USAAF continued to attack more distant targets.

There was one unique raid in which a Suffolk pilot took a leading role—and lost his life. Group Captain Percy Charles Pickard, an old boy of Framlingham College, Woodbridge, led a force of eighteen Mosquito fighter-bombers to bomb

A P51 Mustang—"the fighter with a bomber's range"—photographed over Suffolk in August 1944. This plane, "Dragon Lady", was with the 357th Fighter Group at Leiston, Suffolk.

Photo courtesy of Ian Hawkins

A 95th Bomb Group air crew at Horsham after returning from the first daylight raid on Berlin on 4th March 1944. *Photo courtesy of Ian Hawkins*

23

the prison at Amiens. He was commanding officer at Sculthorpe in Norfolk, and had already made his reputation as the first RAF officer to win the DSO three times in one war. He had developed close contacts with the French Resistance. Now his planes were ordered to breach the walls of the prison with almost surgical precision, so that about a hundred political prisoners held there could make their escape. One of them was an important Resistance leader facing execution. The Mosquitoes began their mission from Hunsdon in Hertfordshire on a bleak February day amid snow showers. They successfully demolished parts of the prison walls, but as many prisoners were killed as escaped and Group Captain Pickard was shot down by German fighters.

The bombers were not the only aerial spectacle for East Anglians during 1944. Those living near Bircham Newton watched Air–Sea Rescue planes come and go on their missions to find airmen who had "ditched" in the North Sea. Residents near Langham observed planes which concentrated their attacks on enemy shipping and U-boats. Those whose homes were around the fighter stations near the coast, such as Coltishall, saw a great variety of planes in action including Beaufighters, Spitfires, Typhoons, Mustangs and Defiants.

The sight and sound of aircraft had become so closely woven into the pattern of daily existence that for most of the time it was scarcely noticed. What set people talking was not so much the spectacle of the bombing forces leaving East Anglia as the later reports of the destruction they had caused. There were three distinct attitudes towards the Allied bombing campaign. The official view, conveyed in communiqués and government statements and generally accepted, was that the air forces were inflicting immense damage in almost non-stop, highly successful raids that would hasten the end of the war. Another view, not widely known but forcibly held by many of the men who were flying the planes and dropping the bombs, was that the bombing strategy was being bungled at the highest level. A third view, expressed by a small minority of people including a well-known Ipswich Member of Parliament, was that the nature of the raids was morally indefensible.

The crippling scale of the losses of Allied bombers in the first three months of the year has been indicated above. No hint of this reached the public. Newspapers and radio maintained a steady stream of success stories and concentrated with satisfaction on the raids on Berlin. Thus on 3rd January the *Cambridge Daily News* front-page headline was:

BLAZING BERLIN HIT AGAIN

and an *East Anglian Daily Times* front-page lead on 1st February reported:

> The Battle of Berlin is rapidly approaching a decisive stage. The RAF's big raid on Sunday night brought the tonnage of bombs dropped on the capital in the last three attacks, launched in four nights, to well over 5,000, and probably a total not far short of 25,000 tons since November 18th. The city's industrial life has been substantially crippled by these colossal blows.

The crew of the Pathfinder B.17F of 813 Squadron, 482 B.G., who flew to Berlin on 4th March, 1944. The flight crew are standing behind, starting second from left, left to right. Others are ground crew.

Photo courtesy of Ian Hawkins

And again on 17th February:

BERLIN LAST NIGHT A CITY OF RAGING FIRES

60,000 Men launched mightiest air blow of war

Early in "The Big Week" Mr Winston Churchill reviewed the war situation in the Commons, and his statement on 21st February and the daily communiqués painted a picture that was entirely reassuring. This encouraged newspaper assessments such as that in the *Cambridge Daily News*: "By day and night, from the west and the south, Germany's capacity for making war is being hit hard and often by the air strength of the United Nations."

On some of the air bases a different view was expressed. At Ridgewell the padre, the Reverend James Good Brown, attended a briefing before a raid in which his bomb group lost six planes and fifty-six men, and afterwards he wrote:

25

When the curtain is drawn back in the front of the briefing room and the ribbon runs from Ridgewell to Berlin there is always a dead silence in the room. No one wishes to speak. Men glance at each other with a look of anxiety mixed with fear. The very thought of Berlin does not offer any sense of comfort.[12]

After the Leipzig raid during "The Big Week" the flyers who had taken part were awarded a presidential citation for battle honours and became entitled to wear a blue ribbon. Newspaper editorials praised their bravery and argued that the losses on the raid were compensated for by the gains. James Good Brown's diary struck a very different note. The plan, he noted, had been to send eight hundred bombers on this raid, with several hundred Allied fighters as escort—more than a thousand planes altogether. When the force was thirty minutes in over the Continent, however, it had been recalled. Most of the Eighth Air Force returned to England, including the fighter planes, but three combat wings went on to the target area. One of these was the 381st Bomb Group at Ridgewell. Brown, its padre, described their feelings:

We never got the message to cancel the mission. Instead of 700 bombers going to the target, only about 180 ships went through. And what is worse, these had no fighter escort. The Allied fighters never took off from England. For a few Flying Fortresses to go deep into Germany without fighter protection was suicide. And that is what it turned out to be. They were met by hundreds of German fighters. Our Group did not have a ghost of a chance. Our men were helpless against the onslaught. Thus the loss of over 50 bombers was not from the 700 to 800 that were scheduled to go to Oschersleben, but from the few that went to the target.

It is common knowledge on the base, especially with the fliers, that the whole raid was messed up; that someone higher up made some mistake . . . Oschersleben knocked us out. It was like a sledgehammer blow or a hit below the belt, and did not help the morale of the Group, especially because the truth was revealed that the Eighth Air Force had fouled this one up. Ten days passed before the 381st was able to fly another mission, this one to St Adrien, France . . . Another eight days passed after the St Adrien raid before we were able to regain our strength . . .[13]

The raids went on and were developed. In March there was a first attack on Vienna. In April over 1,100 planes went out during a single night and Cologne had its worst battering. And by 28th April:

FURY OF ALLIED AIR OFFENSIVE STILL MOUNTING

Assault reaches new peak with 5,000 planes over Europe in 24 hours

The switch in attention from Germany to France as D-Day approached and the build-up of Allied fighter strength reduced the risks, but day after day Brown noted in his diary something of the cost to just one of the bomb groups taking part: 3rd March, one plane lost; 6th March, one plane lost; 6th March, Berlin, three planes lost; 8th March, one plane lost; 20th March, one plane lost; 24th March, three planes lost. With each plane lost, ten men were posted dead or missing—until mid-April when a new policy put only nine men on board. On the first anniversary of the arrival of the US 381st Bomb Group at Ridgewell, Brown noted that only two of the original flyers were still there. "After six months from our first bombing raid almost the entire original Group had gone down in combat", he noted[14].

Replenishments of men and machines flowed across the Atlantic. Between October 1943 and June 1944 the Eighth Air Force doubled its size. Three bomb groups arrived in East Anglia in January, taking over the bases at Matching and Glatton—which had been built by the Americans during 1943—and Horsham St Faith, a well-established airfield which had just been provided with three new runways. In February two more bomb groups brought their Flying Fortresses to Deopham Green and Eye, and in March another two—flying Liberators—occupied newly completed Boreham and Stansted. In April three new bomb groups arrived at Mendlesham, Lavenham and Debach.

Eventually a point was reached, during 1944, when the needs of the US air chiefs had been fully met and airfield construction in East Anglia was brought to a halt. New bases at Bentwaters and Beccles, built for the USAAF, were taken over by the RAF. Bentwaters was under care and maintenance for six months until six Mustang squadrons moved in in October, and Beccles was taken over by Coastal Command from August.

The third view of bombing policy involved a moral challenge. Its most articulate advocate was the Ipswich Member of Parliament, Richard Stokes. Although he was a successful businessman, Stokes was a Labour MP and no left-wing wimp. He was a Catholic, had been educated at the Royal Military Academy

Mr Richard Stokes, Ipswich Member of Parliament.

at Woolwich and at Trinity College, Cambridge, and had then served in France in 1916–18, becoming a major and winning the Croix de Guerre. The views he expressed in 1944 were distinctly unpopular. "Flattening all these towns in Germany by indiscriminate bombing is going to stand as a lasting disgrace", he declared. "I protest against the awful stories we read of these mass bombardments, children on fire, hundreds of people roasting in shelters, and all the rest of it . . .". And he was critical of the government's "unconditional surrender" policy.

The *East Anglian Daily Times* took Stokes to task in a leading article: "It should go forth that Mr Stokes' statement should not be considered to express public sentiment in the town which he represents in Parliament." The Mass Observation organization, however, collected diaries from several East Anglian residents in which they expressed grave misgivings about the bombing, although in most cases they accepted that it might be necessary to win the war. There was also a widespread anxiety that the scale of the raids might lead to renewed Luftwaffe attacks on Britain.

German bombing continued from time to time to disturb the lives of the people of the eastern counties. Luftwaffe raids were resumed in February after a lull, but they were small in scale compared with earlier attacks and the bombers were usually aiming for London. But they kept the warning sirens wailing over a large area, and this and the noise of anti-aircraft guns and RAF night fighters disturbed the sleep of thousands of people. The Regional Commissioner's report on the first three months of the year noted that fifteen people were killed and seventy seriously injured in raids on twenty nights. There was a renewed popular demand for the "Morrison" steel table shelters—well over six thousand were distributed in the non-metropolitan areas of the eastern region during the first half of the year[15].

During January bombs were dropped near Newmarket, March, Braintree and Dunmow. During the night of 13th/14th February a large number fell along the Suffolk and Essex coasts: twenty-four high explosives fell on Frinton and Walton and several on Brightlingsea, and an estimated six hundred incendiaries, many of which fell into the sea, were released over the Dovercourt Holiday Camp. That night Clacton had its worst raid, with a mass of fire bombs on the town centre. Marks and Spencer and a furnishing shop were completely gutted; two hotels, a draper's store and a large bakery were extensively damaged; and a number of other shops were hit. Pier Avenue and Station Road were littered with incendiaries. When three of them came through the roof of the crowded Odeon Cinema—which was showing a war film at the time—soldiers in the audience threw their greatcoats over them and remarkably no one was injured[16]. The raiders were greeted by a particularly heavy barrage along the coast and two were brought down, one near the pier.

The most devastating attack was in the early hours of Tuesday, 23rd February, when Colchester was the target. Soon after midnight a single bomber spread at least six hundred incendiaries and several phosphorous oil bombs over an area of seventy-five acres, and almost a third of the town was threatened with destruction by flames. There were 130 separate fires at St Botolph's shopping centre, five of them involving important buildings. Two clothing factories were burnt out, machinery crashing from top floors to the ground. A big furniture depository and a furniture shop were set ablaze, and an ironmonger's and other shops were destroyed. Fires were started at the Plough Hotel. Seven bombs crashed through the roof of the Empire Cinema but it still stood. Altogether fourteen properties were totally destroyed and about a hundred badly damaged. Several families lost their homes at Blackheath, but there was only one casualty—a seventy-year-old woman living in Vineyard Street was seriously burned when an incendiary fell on to her bed[17].

Colchester firemen had gained experience of the big raids on London and the Thames estuary, but this was the first time they had to fight fires in their own town. The military, including American troops, Civil Defence personnel and Fire Guards, gave them assistance (four soldiers were subsequently fined for loot-

Colchester suffered severely in air raids during February 1944. This photograph shows some of the damage in Stanwell Street, with the skeleton of Hollington's factory in the background.
Photo courtesy of Mrs Hervey Benham

ing—the only case of its kind that occurred in Colchester). One of the most remarkable achievements was that of two schoolboys who joined Fire Guards in a hazardous climb up an iron ladder to the roof of St Botolph's Church, carrying buckets of water and stirrup pumps. Three incendiary bombs had started a fire there; they extinguished it and saved the church[18]. The conflagration spread and surrounding towns sent seventy pumps and five hundred men to help. Over three million gallons of water were used during the night before eventually the fire was contained.

The following night, when a formation of German bombers attacked London Docks, one of them was caught in an anti-aircraft "box barrage" and the crew, apparently under the impression that their plane had been hit, baled out. The plane was, in fact, intact. It flew on pilotless and reached Cambridge, slowly losing height until it belly-landed on allotments close to St George's Church in Chesterton. Despite its bomb load, it did not explode. Residents in nearby houses raised money for war charities by charging those who wanted a close view of a Dornier 217[19].

The Chelmsford, Dunmow, Halstead and Saffron Walden areas were bombed in March, and there were incendiaries on Southwold, but no great damage was done. In April the Luftwaffe turned its attention to East Anglian airfields. Sometimes their planes tagged on to a returning RAF or USAAF formation and thus arrived undetected. On 12th April, for example, twelve German night fighters followed a force of B-24s and fired upon one of them as it was landing at Framlingham. A week later Luftwaffe planes sneaked in among returning bombers and put Little Snoring out of action by distributing anti-personnel bombs on the runway. A few days after that six Messerschmitts suddenly appeared amid a force of 125 bombers landing at a number of Norfolk and Suffolk bases and destroyed ten B-24s. They shot down eight of them and destroyed two on the ground. Anti-aircraft guns accidentally brought down another near Norwich. Thirty-eight American airmen were killed and twenty-four injured. This was the Germans' most successful raid of its kind, but it proved to be a last desperate effort. One of the German planes was shot down at Ashby St Mary.

The last bombs dropped by German planes on East Anglia were high explosives on Bungay, Seething and between Ipswich and the coast on the night of 27th/28th June. By that time they could be treated as a minor irritant, for there were major developments afoot. The newspapers of Wednesday, 7th June appeared with the headline that everyone had been waiting for:

LANDINGS ON BROAD FRONT ARE 'THOROUGHLY SATISFACTORY'
—The Premier

With understandable hyperbole, the *East Anglian Daily Times* opened its leading article that day with the words:

From this day to the ending of the world, June 6th, 1944, will be remembered . . .

CHAPTER THREE

Distant Guns

A S THE New Year opened the guns were being fired far from Britain. Though thoughts at home were concentrated on the coming cross-Channel invasion of the Continent, bitter fighting was going on in the south of Italy, on the Eastern Front in Russia and in the Far East.

Early in 1944 the *Suffolk Regimental Gazette* reported that Admiral Lord Louis Mountbatten, Supreme Commander, South East Asia Command, had visited a battalion of the regiment in Burma. He had arrived in a jungle clearing only a mile from the Japanese positions. He had spoken to as many men as could be relieved from the front line, telling them of the progress of the war to date and assuring them that the Germans would be beaten in 1944.

American forces advancing along the chain of Pacific islands towards Japan were bearing the brunt of the Far East fighting at this time, the Combined Chiefs of Staff having decided at a conference in Cairo in November 1943 that the main effort against Japan should be made in that area. Plans that had been discussed earlier for the recapture of Burma had been frustrated; resources that would be essential for such a major campaign had had to be withdrawn as part of the preparation for the invasion of Europe.

Climate had a great influence on events. The Burmese terrain consisted largely of tropical rain-forest and tree-clad or scrub-covered hills, rising to eleven thousand feet in places, and the climate was such that campaigning was almost impossible except between November and May. The Japanese thought, therefore, that the Allies were likely to launch an offensive during the dry season of 1943–44 against their front east of the Chindwin River, and so they decided on a forestalling operation.

Accordingly in February 1944 a Japanese division opened a diversionary attack in Arakan, and in March three divisions launched a main attack along the Chindwin front. The objective was the Allied base at Imphal, which was forty miles over the frontier, inside India. Its loss would have cut a main British supply line, and the whole future of the campaign in Burma, the continuance of the air-lift to China, even the fate of China itself, would have been threatened. Mountbatten, anticipating these moves, issued orders to the British 11th Army Group on 14th January to put pressure on the Japanese in the Chindwin River area and to advance on the Arakan front, with Akyab as the ultimate objective.

Before this, however, the 2nd Battalion of the Suffolk Regiment—part of the 123rd Indian Infantry Brigade of the 5th Indian Division—was already engaged in

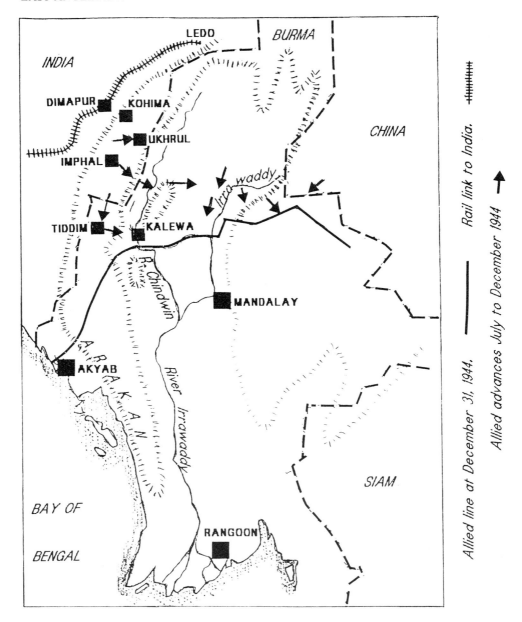

The Burma Campaign. During the Japanese offensive of March to July 1944 the British were contained in a pocket around and south of Imphal and had troops in three forward areas to the south and south east. From these bases they began their advance in July 1944.

difficult jungle warfare in the Arakan; as 1944 began it had just been ordered to capture a series of hill features in the Mayu range. Its first objective was a small hill matted with dense bamboo and undergrowth, identified as "Bamboo". A daring guerrilla platoon led by a young officer of the Royal Norfolk Regiment, Lieutenant D. Lee Hunter, made a reconnaissance. Several weeks' work went into preparing a way into the jungle, usually by finding animal tracks and hacking through to enlarge them. Then mules could be taken forward, followed by jeeps, and finally sappers, bulldozers and locally hired labourers to complete some sort of road. The advance was limited to the speed at which these approach tracks could be cut.

When the Suffolks were ready to make the assault on "Bamboo" hill, on 24th January, it took them three days of hard fighting to reach the summit. It proved to be a strong bunker position, and they were soon driven off again by enemy fire. An officer described the situation as he arrived on the scene:

> Dust some four inches deep rises in a stifling fog and makes the men look like cobweb-covered ghosts. The battalion occupies a wide front with company localities on dominating hill features. The hills are very steep with knife-like crests. Positions are hollowed out of the hillsides and platforms built up. Except in a few clearings, ground visibility is restricted to a few yards. Everywhere there is dense scrub, growing to a height of 10 to 12 feet, mostly of elephant grass or bamboo . . . Malaria is taking a rather heavy toll.
>
> The fighting has died down, the opposing forces being at extreme small arms range and seeing very little of each other. The enemy fires a few shells, patrols go out, mortars and machine guns open whenever the enemy shows himself . . . The area is stiff with small bears, deer and other game which can be mistaken for enemy patrols. Elephants have been in the area, but have cleared off.[1]

The Suffolks won two Military Medals during this engagement, but two of their company commanders were killed. Then, when the Japanese facing them were withdrawn because of shortage of food and ammunition, they followed up and occupied "Bamboo" and other hills without difficulty.

The Japanese called off their campaign in the Arakan on 24th February, and General Slim was able to transfer the 5th Indian Division from the area by air when a main Japanese offensive, aimed at Imphal from north and south, developed in March. The situation at this time was that about 155,000 men and eleven thousand animals were concentrated within the Imphal perimeter, with enough food and ammunition to hold out for five weeks, and all roads and tracks to the Imphal Plain were securely guarded. This was initially a defensive deployment, but it also represented the assembly of the largest possible reserve for a counter-attack. Other vital positions were held with minimum forces, notably a garrison at Kohima, north of Imphal on the supply route from India.

Three Japanese divisions—a hundred thousand of their most highly trained troops—crossed the Chindwin River on 17th March. Five days later they stood on the Burma–India border, and on 29th March they cut the main supply route from Bengal. The threat to Imphal was acute. The attack was not broken until 22nd

June, and the last Japanese was not driven out of India until 25th August. East Anglian regiments played a decisive role in this campaign.

The 2nd Suffolks had by this time spent four months in continuous contact with the Japanese and were considered veteran jungle fighters. On Sunday, 18th March they were airlifted in Dakotas two hundred miles over impenetrable jungle from the Arakan area to Imphal. For most of the men it was their first experience of flying, and the rapid movement of a whole regiment with its guns, mules and jeeps in such a short time was considered a logistical triumph. In the days that followed, the whole of the remainder of the 5th Indian Division was similarly transferred.

Among reinforcements brought from India were the 2nd Battalion of the Royal Norfolk Regiment and the 1st Battalion of the Essex Regiment. The Norfolks, flying in Dakotas, concentrated on 9th and 10th April at Dimapur, which was on the main Bengal–Imphal road, and the Essex men arrived after a long train journey at Bokkajan, ten miles north of Dimapur.

During the fighting that followed, the Suffolks took up several defensive positions on the approaches to Imphal and were most of the time in an area about ten miles from the town. There were nightly engagements, but the Japanese failed to penetrate the Suffolks' defences. The Norfolks, on their arrival in Dimapur, at once set out southward to help to relieve the garrison at Kohima. After one serious clash with the Japanese they reached Kohima in time to help to bring out the wounded when the siege was raised on 18th April. The Essex battalion, which had had special training in jungle penetration warfare, was directed to prevent any Japanese getting through the Naga Hills to cut the main road and rail links southward to Kohima and Imphal.

By this time the Japanese were on the defensive, their supply lines stretched, but they still occupied strong bunker positions on the hills overlooking Kohima and strong positions on the approaches to Imphal from south and south-east. The Norfolks joined the efforts to drive them out. An operation which began on 25th April typified the problems of warfare in this jungle country.

The Norfolks, leading a brigade group of nearly six hundred men, set out at last light to capture a dominant spur of land. A direct frontal assault was impossible and it was necessary to make a wide flanking movement, which involved a march of eighteen miles through dense jungle. Not far away another force was seeking to capture an adjoining height. For four nights and three days the Norfolks made an uncomfortable and perilous way through the undergrowth, only to have the whole operation cancelled on the 29th because of the failure of the complementary operation on the other hill.

A new operation was substituted, aiming to occupy a ridge. It involved a difficult trek through almost impenetrable jungle where often it was possible to see only five yards ahead and where there was a continuous downpour of rain. The group overran many Japanese positions and in the final stages came under heavy fire and suffered many casualties.

A British mortar team in action in the jungle during the Battle of Imphal-Kohima, which lasted from March to July 1944.
Imperial War Museum

The main objective was occupied, but there remained one Japanese bunker keeping up a vicious machine-gun fire. Captain John N. Randle, a twenty-six-year-old whose home was in Radlett, Hertfordshire, charged the bunker single-handed with a rifle and bayonet. Although he was hit frequently by bursts of fire and mortally wounded, he got close enough to throw a grenade through the gun-slit. As he died, he flung his body across the slit to seal it off. For this he was awarded a posthumous Victoria Cross—the fourth for the Royal Norfolk Regiment in this war. His action opened a track to a road along which the wounded could be evacuated, and some days later the whole of the hill was captured.

At the same time another nearby hill was taken, leaving only one other position overlooking Kohima in Japanese hands. The Norfolks were assigned a role in dealing with this final threat to the town, but the battalion was now so weakened—reduced to fourteen officers and 366 other ranks, many of them suffering from dysentery—that their effort failed and they had to be withdrawn to rest. This was their last operation in the fighting around Kohima, in which they lost in total seven officers and 790 other ranks killed, and thirteen officers and more than 150 other ranks wounded.

In May the Allies went on to the offensive. The Suffolks, who had also been resting, now launched their biggest operation of the whole campaign. They were ordered to attack a dominating feature in the high ridges on the eastern side of the road from Kohima to Imphal. This was given the code name "Isaac". The action began on 3rd June and was successfully completed after three days' fighting. By 7th June the Japanese were in full retreat from the area, and the Norfolks had sufficiently recovered to lead the chase down the Kohima–Imphal road for a time, riding in lorries behind a troop of Sherman tanks. There was one big and costly engagement on the way, but on 21st June the road was finally opened and supply convoys were able to get through to Imphal again.

Meanwhile the Essex battalion had been fighting its way southward through almost impenetrable jungle. Very few white men had ever moved into the Naga Hills before them; only a few small parties of any kind, with local porters, had attempted to cross this territory. The battalion began by recruiting Naga interpreters and Indian porters, but even so each soldier had to carry 63½ pounds of equipment and arms. The theory was that they could be independent for a period of five days and would be kept supplied by air drops. In practice these did not always arrive.

So the Essex Regiment men set off into the jungle. Not only was there dense undergrowth and creeper so thick that it could take a whole day to cut through one mile of it, but the hills were very steep. Animal tracks sometimes helped—there were wild elephants in the area. There were also mosquitoes, and it was soon obvious that the country was highly malarious. The Japanese were there too, dug into strong bunkers on hillsides, behind natural camouflage which concealed their presence until the Essex men were almost upon them.

The battalion struggled forward and reached the flank of the Kohima battle on 10th May. It did not join in the set-piece battle for the town, and on 4th June it was ordered to make its way to Advance Brigade HQ at Phakekedzumi, continuing its special role of long-range penetration. This "march" took the Essex battalion seven days, and immediately they arrived they were ordered to keep moving—to the area of Ukhrul, further south, to try to cut off the Japanese retreat. Ukhral was a mountain-top fortress village about thirty-five miles north-east of Imphal. This horrific trek took twenty-six days. One of the officers who took part, Captain P. P. S. Brownless, declared afterwards, "The extreme misery of the march is impossible to describe"; but he made this effort:

> The monsoon was at its height: the sky a lifeless white and the rain pouring in steady torrents, day after day, hour after hour. The weary column of men and mules plodded down and then up the slippery mountain tracks, waded through torrents, trudged for miles through thick mud . . .

The column was marching over corpses, corpses sunk in the mud, with a helmet or a piece of equipment or a limb showing, and past an almost continuous line of dead pack animals . . . This continuous line of dead stretched for twenty to thirty miles.

The men staggered through the mud and up the slopes, borne down by the weight of their great packs. All were tortured with exhaustion because all were sick. We were so upset that few could eat the already short rations. Many were marching with temperatures and tick typhus had begun to break out. We had been sodden for weeks, were covered with mud, and we stank. Hollow-eyed, wasted, hungry, and yet incapable of eating more than a minute meal . . .[2]

During this journey, during which the Japanese were just one day's movement ahead of them, they had to build or rebuild jungle bridges across countless torrents and ravines, and at the end of it they had to establish ambushes on the main road out of Ukhrul.

Afterwards they went on to Imphal, then back to Dimapur, and finally—by an eight-day train journey—to Bangalore, where they remained for two months "for rest and rehabilitation". By that time most of them were hospital cases[3] and it was found that there were only about thirty to forty Essex regulars left among them[4].

The Suffolks suffered almost as badly. There were sixty to seventy hospital admissions every week, and at one time the battalion had just six fighting officers and only two rifle companies of eighty men each, instead of four of 130 men each. At the end of August they were withdrawn to rest at Imphal, and the battalion saw no more fighting.

The Japanese-planned invasion of India had collapsed, and they estimated their dead at sixty-five thousand. But there remained three Japanese divisions still to be driven back to and beyond the River Chindwin.

In Europe the principal Allied objective as 1944 began was Rome. The Italians had formally surrendered in the previous August after the Allied invasion of Sicily, but the Germans had then moved many more divisions into Italy. In September Allied forces had invaded the "toe" and the "heel" of mainland Italy, followed a week later by much bigger Anglo-American forces landing in the Gulf of Salerno. They had formed into two groups, British and American divisions in the US Fifth Army on the western side of the country and British divisions in the British Eighth Army to the east. The Fifth Army entered Naples on 1st October, by which time the Eighth Army had taken Foggia, almost opposite on the Adriatic coast. At the turn of the year the German Field-Marshal Kesselring held a strongly defended line across the country; this included a monastery-turned-fortress at Monte Cassino, south of Rome. The Allies' route northward was overlooked by mountains on both sides and therefore vulnerable.

The expectations of newspaper readers were raised by reports such as that in the *Cambridge Daily News* on 8th January that "British and American troops have stormed the outer ring of the Cassino defences". There followed a regular stream of encouraging front-page headlines:

[17th January] **RING ROUND CASSINO TIGHTENED**

[3rd February] **FALL OF CASSINO IMMINENT**

[10th February] **TREMENDOUS HUN LOSSES AT CASSINO**; and

[16th February] **CASSINO MONASTERY DESTROYED**.

But what was really happening? On 22nd and 23rd January about fifty thousand Allied troops landed at Anzio, sixty miles behind Kesselring's front and thirty-five miles from Rome. On 27th January the *East Anglian Daily Times* front-paged their view that:

REAL BATTLE OF ROME OPENS.

Efforts were made in January and February to assault the Cassino strongpoint. The monks in the monastery on the summit of Monte Cassino, above the town, were advised to leave and the Allies then subjected the whole area to heavy bombardment. These attacks were beaten off and the Allied offensive petered out in face of strong German resistance.

Troops of the Eighth Army were switched from the Adriatic front to lend support, among them the 1st/4th Battalion of the Essex Regiment. As soon as they arrived, the Essex men were moved forward to within sight of Monte Cassino and ordered to prepare to join an assault on Monastery Hill; but other infantry which launched a first attack fared so badly that the whole operation was cancelled. The troops waited while senior officers spent a few weeks exploring various alternative plans, and for the Essex men this was a bad period—the weather was appalling and uninterrupted shelling caused casualties and seriously restricted movement.

The over-optimistic reports from the front dried up for a while, but then American correspondents began to file despatches of a different kind and the Prime Minister was questioned in the Commons on 22nd February. Mr Churchill told the House:

> I sent a telegram asking for a stricter censorship on alarmist reports about the position in the bridgehead, not by correspondents there but by persons in Naples and Algiers. Such words as "desperate" ought not to be used in a battle of this kind when they are false—and still less are they to be used if they were true.

This rather ambiguous comment raised laughter in the House.

On 3rd March the Essex battalion was briefed for what was to be a third battle for Cassino and was given the task, with a squadron of New Zealand tanks, of capturing the monastery at the summit. The attack was launched on the 15th, preceded by such a tremendous air and artillery bombardment that, in the words of General Alexander afterwards, "It seemed inconceivable that any troops should be left alive after eight hours of such terrific hammering"[5]. The German paratroops who garrisoned Cassino, in fact, put up a fierce resistance and held on to Monastery Hill.

On the first day of a five-day battle, New Zealand infantry occupied the greater part of the bomb-shattered town of Cassino. The 4th Indian Division (of which the Essex battalion was part) then attempted to move up the first foothill behind the town, on the way to the monastery on the summit. After ferocious fighting during the night they had made some progress and occupied an area in and around an old castle, which was alive with German snipers. Through that day and three more they fought on against German resistance and counter attack, but at 4.30 pm on the 19th the effort to capture the monastery had to be abandoned.

By 6 am the next morning the remnants of the Essex battalion were back where they had started five days before, counting their losses, which were so heavy that it took many months to recover. Altogether 2,400 of the troops engaged in the battle were casualties. The Essex battalion left the Cassino area (and the Fifth Army) on 2nd April and took over a section of the front on the Adriatic coast. There, for three months, it alternated between service in the front line and in reserve.

Men of the 1st/4th Essex Regiment, in a ravine near Cassino, February 1944.

Imperial War Museum

Reports of the Cassino battle had by that time taken a different tone. A Reuter report on 20th March, with the news that the Germans were still holding a "toe-hold", went on to assert that "Cassino will live in history as the bloodiest square mile in the Italian campaign". On 29th March an Allied communiqué admitted that Allied troops had been withdrawn from the eastern slope of Monastery Hill in a "strategic retreat". The Essex battalion's ordeal at Cassino was not mentioned until an army press release on 14th April which reviewed the battalion's service since arriving in Italy. This document suggested that it had scored a chain of successes: it had been among the troops taking part in the battle for Cassino, it had helped to capture an important peak on 17th March, and during the next four days it had assisted in smashing repeated enemy counter-attacks.

By that time, however, there was other evidence from the Italian battlefield. On 3rd March a hospital train arrived at Barnwell Station, Cambridge, bringing several hundred wounded men from Italy. These included men who had been brought straight from the Anzio area, many of them stretcher cases. Civil Defence first-aid personnel transferred these latter to a long queue of ambulances and the walking wounded made their way to double-decker buses. All were taken to various hospitals in East Anglia.

It was nearly two months before the Allies were ready to take the offensive again, but on 18th May Polish troops under British control cleared the remains of Cassino town and reached the monastery on the summit. The northward advance then resumed and on 5th June readers of the *East Anglian Daily Times* read the news of the previous day's culminating triumph:

FIFTH ARMY TROOPS ENTER ROME
Hitler orders German evacuation

Later in the year the newspaper published a list of seventeen officers and other ranks from East Anglia who had been awarded decorations "for gallant and distinguished services in Italy". There was a separate announcement of the award of the Victoria Cross to a Suffolk man serving as a company sergeant-major in the Coldstream Guards. This related to an earlier phase of the Italian campaign, more than a year before, during fighting at Salerno. Peter Harold Wright, who was twenty-eight, was a member of a large family farming at Wenhaston—one brother was in the Navy and another a prisoner of the Japanese. In September 1943 during an attack on a steep wooden hill near Salerno in which all the officers in his company had become casualties, Wright had taken over, silenced three German posts and "with complete disregard of heavy shellfire and machine gun fire" reorganized what was left of his company. "It is due to this warrant-officer's superb disregard of the enemy's fire, his magnificent leadership and his outstanding heroism throughout the action that his battalion succeeded in capturing and maintaining its hold on this very important objective", the citation read. Immediately after this action Wright had been awarded the DCM—the highest award that a GOC in the field could bestow on his own initiative. When the citation had been forwarded to the War Office, it recommended a VC, which the King approved; such substitution, it was stated, was unprecedented. Wright collected his VC at Buckingham Palace in November.

From the Eastern Front—where, in 1944, over sixty per cent of the German Army was stationed[6]—the Red Army provided encouraging headlines week after week. On 4th January the front-page lead story in the *Cambrige Daily News* was headlined:

RUSSIANS BACK IN POLAND

On 29th January the lead story was headlined:

LENINGRAD BLOCKADE SMASHED:
RED ARMY 40 MILES FROM BALTIC

23rd February was the twenty-sixth birthday of the Red Army and that day the red flag of the USSR flew above the borough coat of arms over the main entrance to the council offices in Cambridge at the express wish of the Mayor, Mr W. L. Briggs. He saw it as a tribute from the people of Cambridge. The Union Jack and the Stars and Stripes flew on either side. Later in the year the Mayor handed over to a representative of the Soviet Red Cross at a ceremony on Market Hill an ambulance paid for by subscriptions raised during 1943 by the people of Cambridge Town and University under the auspices of Cambridge Anglo-Soviet Friendship Committee. It went as a gift to the people of Leningrad.

On 19th March 1944 the Germans occupied Hungary and imposed a Quisling regime, but ten days later the headlines were:

BERLIN SAYS RUSSIANS THRUSTING
INTO RUMANIA

And by 10th May:

SEBASTOPOL FALLS AND ALL CRIMEA
IS LIBERATED

*

CHAPTER FOUR

Domestic Disturbance

HUSBANDS and boy friends had been away from home for years. A new generation of girls had reached puberty in completely artificial circumstances in which the neighbourhood supply of boy friends had disappeared into the Services. On the other hand, the region had been flooded with tens of thousands of young men who had been removed from their own homes and womenfolk. The loneliness, the frustration, the disturbance of normal standards were incalculable.

Most people managed to cope with these problems in socially acceptable ways, but their intensity and scope was shown in many instances. There was no disapproval of the action of seventy girls who responded when the clerk to the Chesterton Rural District Council publicized an appeal for "nice young ladies" to write to men on the submarine *Universal*. But what deductions were to be made when the Mayor of Saffron Walden announced that he had received a letter from a sailor seeking girl pen-friends "with a view to matrimony" and 1,700 responded?

A great deal of effort went into opening and running "Welcome" Clubs for servicemen and women stationed in East Anglia, particularly those from overseas. When one was opened in Ipswich in April, in the former Poole's Picture Palace in Tower Street and staffed by the Women's Voluntary Service, the Mayor, Mr C. W. English, spoke about the temptations for young people. He said:

> For members of the Forces wanting to spend an hour or so with the opposite sex, almost the only social roof hitherto has been the public house, but, although there has been ready enough cooperation by licensees, there has been some trouble.

He had tried to get more teashops open in the evenings, but staffing problems arose. "Now, in this club, we want members of the Forces, British, Dominion, United States and other Allied nations, to share their leisure hours with the people in the town."

A similar "Allies' Club" was opened in Colchester under the auspices of the WVS in July. Initially it confined its membership to four hundred service members and a hundred civilian girls, but the numbers quickly increased to over two thousand. Substantial financial support was given by the British War Relief of California and by the Treasury[1].

There were just too many men with time on their hands, and just too many lonely women and girls. Most towns in the region were encircled by air bases and military camps, and when hundreds of off-duty airmen and soldiers invaded them in search of relaxation and—if possible—female companionship, the local population

Clubs and canteens were opened in many places to cater for the needs of Allied service men and women. This was the Allies' Club in Trinity Street, Colchester. *Photo courtesy of Mrs Hervey Benham*

came under pressure. One young man noted at the time his "feeling of incredulity upon hearing that my mother had been 'chatted up' by some G. I's during a cycle ride into Braintree. Was nothing sacred! She was then at the ripe old age of 45."[2]

Acute social problems had arisen during 1943, and there had been much argument about how seriously they should be regarded[3]. At a conference on the subject one parish representative declared, "There is a lot of loose living at the moment"; while another asserted, "a lot of this so-called immorality is rather exaggerated". While the Mayor of Bury St Edmunds, Alderman E. L. D. Lake, thought he saw "definite signs of an improvement in moral conditions during the previous year", others at the meeting reported "greatly increased" demands on the Diocesan Moral Welfare Association, with its home for unmarried mothers and babies full to over-flowing.

During February 1944 the Mass Observation organization questioned its correspondents in East Anglia about their attitudes. Two of them—both well-educated women school-teachers in their fifties—responded as follows[4]:

LAVENHAM: A group outside the historic Guildhall following the opening, on Monday, of the British Welcome Club, to be run by the W.V.S. Left to right: Lieut.-Col. S. E. L. Baddeley, Miss Mary Gray Major Russell Fisher (Oxford, Idaho), Mrs. Weller Poley, Mr. R. P. Winfrey, Lord Belstead, Mrs. Widdicombe, Lady Belstead, Mrs. Prior Palmer, and Major Adelbert D. Cross (Springfield, Mass.). The equipment for the Club has been provided, thanks to a generous gift of money from the British War Relief of North Carolina. (Photo by Eastern Press Agency.)

British Welcome Club opened at Lavenham Guildhall.   *East Anglian Daily Times*

I think the modern frankness on the subject is a very good thing. This frankness causes many cases to come to our ears which in earlier days would have been hushed up. I doubt if sexual immorality is so much greater than in earlier days . . . With several million Americans over here, waiting and idling, one must expect a lot of bad hats—even a small percentage would mean a large number. Many only want friendly contact with decent girls. I *know* about this: the students of this college are really doing unofficially a good war job in being friendly with these men, and the men very greatly appreciate it.

I think the development of sexual morality in recent years has been along rational, sensible, more biological lines than previously . . . One of the worst aspects of the present time is the precocious sophistication of the ignorant ill-educated adolescents being turned out of our schools at the pathetic age of 14 with film stars as their heroes . . . The gradual change from Victorian prudery and hypocrisy to the present more rational and realistic attitude has made most people less harsh to those who have fallen below the still usually accepted code of "not forestalling the marriage vows", as the Church of England Mothers' Union so genteely expresses it.

About one problem there was no argument. The influx of young people into public houses caused concern at the various licensing sessions held in the region during February. Police superintendents at Bury St Edmunds, Woodbridge, Hadleigh and Dunmow reported that more young people, and especially young girls, were visiting public houses and creating difficulties for licensees. The trouble, it was remarked at Woodbridge, was that "young people, by a little artificial aid, make themselves look older than they really are".

Apart from the pubs, there were the dance halls, where drink was freely available. Local authorities and church committees were very concerned about under-age drinking. In Parliament, the Norwich MP, Sir Geoffrey Shakespeare, suggested to the Home Secretary that there should be a "no treating" order and that young people should have to produce identity cards marked with their dates of birth, but the Minister turned down these ideas. He did promise that the situation

British WLA girls and 8th USAAF men at a dance organized by the American Red Cross. RAF, WAAF and ATS were also invited to these events. Return dances were held at a WLA camp in Suffolk.
Imperial War Museum

The Ridgewell base band, "The Rockets", played at many local gigs.
USAAF photo, courtesy of Dave Osborne

in Norwich would be kept under close observation. Hartismere Rural District Council, which administered an area of Suffolk with fifty parishes, called a conference of parish representatives and asked them to devise practical solutions to the problems. Should girls under sixteen be banned from village hall dances? The conference concluded that such a ban would be difficult, if not impossible, but agreed that the age rule should be strictly enforced in pubs.

The probation officer for Ipswich, Miss W. E. Grant, stated in her report for 1944 that more girls were beyond control and had come before the courts. She referred to girls going out with Americans to the country for dancing; not all girls who went out by transport returned the same night. The West Suffolk County Medical Officer of Health told a Sudbury audience:

> Unbelievable things are happening in some of our villages and people say they can do nothing about it. There are not enough strong people in them to say not only that these things are wrong, but that they must not be.

At another meeting—in Newmarket—the Recorder for Ipswich, Mr Grafton D. Pryor, said: "I am not going to condemn the youth of the country wholesale, but I do say there is a very lax moral note prevailing among some of our young people."

Doubtless they had in mind such cases as that at the Juvenile Court at Eye when two girls aged fourteen and fifteen were sent to approved schools for three and four years "for consorting with coloured American soldiers". Another charge, used at Norwich, was "having carnal knowledge" of girls under fourteen. In some towns—particularly Cambridge, Norwich and Great Yarmouth—and even in some villages, women were prosecuted for using their homes as brothels, most of which were stated in court to be patronized by Americans. One case in Cambridge involved a mother and her two daughters; another two sisters at Girton. The usual penalty was three to six months' imprisonment. A number of women were prosecuted for giving false names—they were living with Americans, posing as their wives and adopting the men's names. Some servicemen were sent to prison for bigamous marriages, at Newmarket, Stowmarket and Ipswich; and at Norfolk and Suffolk Assizes there were many undefended divorce cases.

There was little doubt, then, that the ordinary constraints had broken down in the exceptional circumstances of the time. What could be done to bring the situation under control? Many, including local authority councillors, believed that the Church should be left to deal with these problems. The Diocesan Moral Welfare Associations in Suffolk and Norfolk made great efforts, concerned with young girls of fourteen to eighteen, young unmarried mothers and young wives whose husbands were abroad. Arrangements were made for local hospitals to report all illegitimate births to these associations so that they could arrange follow-up. In Suffolk the association encouraged, as an experiment, voluntary women's patrols in the streets of several towns to keep an eye on young people.

Many voices in the Church doubted, however, that its efforts in prayer and social service would be adequate to deal with the problems. Much prayer was offered, as when Cambridge churches united to stage an ambitious "Christian Campaign Week" opened by the Bishop of Chelmsford, Dr Henry Wilson, at the Guildhall. He called on Christians to form their own "home guard" to protect the Christian ideal of home and family.

The Archbishop of Canterbury, Dr William Temple, had earlier declared that women police were needed to deal with homeless and destitute women and children, with those who had been victims of sexual offences, with the care of girls aged fourteen to seventeen, and with watching at places like public houses, dance halls and at camp entrances, "where many foolish girls were inclined to hang around". The main obstacle to the appointment of women police, in Dr Temple's view, was "sheer, downright, stark prejudice".

The idea that women police should be employed had been canvassed for a long time. Most East Anglian authorities had debated the matter throughout 1943 and had shown themselves to be strongly opposed to the idea. When the Essex Standing Joint Committee tried to shelve the question for two years, the MP for Maldon, Mr Tom Driberg, raised the matter in Parliament. The Home Secretary, Mr Herbert Morrison, made it clear that the government wished to encourage the appointment

Many East Anglian girls established friendships with American servicemen and helped them to explore the towns and villages. This group were visiting an Ipswich church in July 1944. Bill Donze, on the left, married Beryl Farrow, standing beside him, and settled in Suffolk.

Photo courtesy of Mrs Donze

of women police, particularly in districts with large numbers of troops. In March nearly two hundred organizations sent representatives to a London conference which demanded that women be recruited.

Mr Morrison's Ministry called upon police authorities to consider the appointment of policewomen as a matter of urgency. The Mayor of Bury St Edmunds, Alderman Lake, observed that the Home Secretary had practically told them they had got to appoint women police and declared: "It is not much good kicking against it." When the King's Lynn Watch Committee resolved in May to appoint two policewomen and a woman member of the committee congratulated it on changing its mind, there were indignant cries of "We were forced to." The Essex committee met again and resolved that, as a temporary arrangement, it would recruit an inspector, sergeant and twenty-three constables; within a few weeks a woman officer had been transferred from the Metropolitan Police and had recruited two young women just demobbed from the services. There was still stiff opposition to the idea that there was any permanent place for women in the force, and only a few recruits had been signed up by the end of the year.

Some standing joint committees found a delaying tactic. Since 1941 there had been a Women's Auxiliary Police Corps, members of which had civilian status, did clerical or telephone switchboard work and never went on street patrol. Instead of appointing women to fill vacancies in the establishment of the regular force, committees considered appointments to this auxiliary corps. The wage for these jobs was only £2 17s a week, and when the West Suffolk committee considered the matter, one member, Lady Briscoe, doubted they would ever get suitable recruits at this figure; they would have less pocket-money, she said, than domestic servants or land girls. Pay for regular policewomen was £3 16s a week, and Lady Briscoe proposed that regular policewomen should be appointed.

The West Suffolk committee resolved to appoint seven auxiliaries, two in Bury, two in Newmarket, two in Sudbury and one at headquarters. When it met again two months later only two women auxiliaries were at work—and they had been allocated to the force by the Central Selection Committee, which dealt with WAAF volunteers for police service. The Chief Constable, Major C. D. Robertson, insisted that he had made every possible effort but that applicants in response to his advertisements had been unsuitable. He was pessimistic about the chances of finding anyone else. The committee told him to keep trying and decided to tell the Home Office that £2 17s was inadequate pay to attract women to the force.

Three more months passed. The Standing Joint Committee met again and still the Chief Constable had only two auxiliary policewomen on duty, although a third was on a course of instruction. Lady Briscoe noted that there were two vacancies in the regular force and proposed that they should be filled by women, suggesting that women with experience in the ATS and WAAF police might be attracted to take up the work as a career. The Chief Constable stoutly resisted this idea, arguing that it was not an appropriate time to make such appointments and that the choice was too restricted to appoint women who might be with them for twenty-five years. Sir Charles Rowley, Bart, moved that the question be deferred until the war ended, and this was agreed by twenty-one to eight. The Marquis of Bristol made no bones about it: he would not have women police either at that time or in the future.

The Standing Joint Committee in East Suffolk was equally resistant to the idea of women police. The Chairman, Lord Cranworth, like the Mayor of Bury, thought it had no option but to obey what was felt to be an instruction by the Home Secretary. It was decided to appoint, "if possible", two women police sergeants—one at headquarters and one at Lowestoft—and nine constables: two to cover Stowmarket, Needham Market and Eye; two for Woodbridge, Saxmundham, Felixstowe, Aldeburgh and Leiston; two for Beccles, Bungay, Halesworth and Southwold; and three at Lowestoft. When the year ended, there was no sign of any of them.

Lord Cranworth admitted that the problem of the moral welfare of young people had "created some feeling in the county" and there had been pressure to employ women police, but he insisted that they were unable to recruit any. As an alternative, and after discussion with the Bishop of the diocese, the Finance Committee of the County Council would be asked to vote three hundred pounds a year to help the diocesan authorities. That was how matters were left.

Norfolk County Council received a report from its standing joint committee on 1st July that "as the result of representations by the Home Office" it had reviewed an earlier decision to appoint two women constables, and had now authorized the recruitment of one woman sergeant and ten women constables, and also the purchase of additional police cars for use by the women officers. The Isle of Ely decided in June, without much argument, to appoint six Women's Auxiliary Police Corps, for Ely, March and Wisbech.

There were two other committees in each county which concerned themselves with social problems, the probation committees, responsible for dealing with young offenders; and the public assistance committees, which had to cope with many of the victims.

There were now large numbers of black Americans in East Anglia. Although they fathered some of the illegitimate children born during 1943 and 1944, the people of the eastern counties were generally relaxed about their presence and, especially in the rural areas, displayed a generally friendly attitude towards them. Despite this attitude, however, a few remarkable solecisms occurred, such as a show presented by boys of Littleton House School at Girton, and the report of it published in the *Cambridge Daily News*, reading, in part:

> Being a nigger show, it was appropriately named "Blackout Minstrels". The negro songs were of an exceptionally high standard and the scenes were colourful . . .

So were some of the reactions, although only one letter of protest found its way into print. "I think that, without searching far afield, material could easily have been found for children at an impressionable age without caricaturing in such incredibly bad taste the members of another race", a correspondent admonished. "The absurdity of the show is more clearly seen if one could imagine African school-children rendering English folk songs with chalked faces and thinned lips for increased effect."

Fraternization between English women and Italian prisoners-of-war remained illegal during the early months of 1944, and led a few women to be brought before the courts. Thingoe magistrates at Bury St Edmunds dismissed a case brought against two Barrow women who declared they had merely replied when two Italians had asked them the time. The charge had it that their behaviour was "likely to prejudice the discipline of the prisoners", and the chairman of the bench issued a general warning to people not to speak to or fraternize with prisoners-of-war. Ely magistrates fined a twenty-two-year-old married woman five pounds because a policeman and an army officer had found her in a farmhouse at Wilburton with three Italians "sitting round a table covered with books"; she had told them that she was teaching them English. Soon afterwards, as we shall see in a later chapter, the rules were relaxed.

Cambridge University students were in trouble when they revived the pre-war Guy Fawkes Night Rag. The local newspaper reported that it was "attended by violent and senseless features". A bonfire had been lit on Market Hill. No one minded that, but afterwards four cars had been overturned, two buses so damaged as to be put out of service and considerable damage done to traffic signs and notice boards. Proctors and police on the scene had been unable to stop it. Subsequently two students appeared in court, the episode was given much critical attention in the national press and the Mayor of Cambridge announced that he had been "bombarded" with letters and phone calls from all over the country. A lively correspondence in the *Cambridge Daily News* produced some who thought the virulence of the attack on the students was out of proportion; many local civilians and visiting Americans had joined in the fracas, they argued.

Ipswich and Norwich had earlier suffered outbreaks of vandalism. The Ipswich Corporation transport authority advertised in the *East Anglian Daily Times* on 12th February:

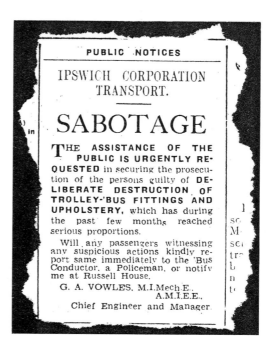

Although there was no spectacular increase in criminal activity during the war, vandalism occurred, as this advertisement in the *East Anglian Daily Times* in February 1944 indicates.

East Anglian Daily Times

51

This led the General Manager of the Eastern Counties Omnibus Company to write to the paper from Norwich: "Leather and moquette seats have been cut, rubber from seats removed, electric light bulbs and fittings broken or stolen, and even chromium-headed screws removed."

Serious crime was rare, however, though there were two murders by American servicemen. In January two black American soldiers were court-martialled and found guilty of murdering a crippled Colchester taxi-driver. One was sentenced to be hanged, the other sent to hard labour for life. On 3rd December two American GIs, after a heavy drinking session, broke into a camp armoury, stole carbines and ammunition, and went poaching in a wood at Honingham Hall, near Norwich. Sir Eric Teichman, diplomat, traveller and prominent Norfolk landowner, who lived at the hall, had just finished lunch when he heard shots from his wood and went to investigate. He found the two GIs and when he challenged them, one shot him dead. The men were eventually arrested and one of them, a twenty-seven year-old from Pittsburgh, was court-martialled at Attlebridge and sentenced to death.

There was no abnormal increase in the ordinary range of criminal activity during 1944, but the courts were kept busy with minor offences. One of the most frequent causes of prosecution was misuse of petrol, which was tightly rationed. At Thetford Police Court in May a labourer was sent to prison for a month for kissing an eighteen-year-old land girl whom he had approached while she was working alone in a field. The annual report of the Ipswich and district probation officer stated that juvenile crime in his district was not so terrible as in some other parts of the country: evacuees had been well behaved; country people had been most sympathetic as foster-parents; most of the trouble that had occurred had been due to kindly treatment by the Americans—youngsters had taken advantage of it. In Norfolk more than thirty local organizations were represented at a Norwich conference called to discuss juvenile delinquency, but the Chief Constable declared that the problem was less serious in Norwich than in other big cities. The Mayor (Mr W. J. Finch) thought there was decreased parental control, and the conference set up a panel to investigate and make proposals. In Cambridgeshire the Chief Constable reported in December a decrease in adult crime but an increase in juvenile crime.

*

CHAPTER FIVE

Operation "Overlord"

A N OUTLINE plan for "a full-scale assault" against the coast of France had been drafted in London during the summer of 1943 and accepted at an Anglo-American conference in Quebec in August. The Russians, who had been locked in a deadly struggle with the Germans in eastern Europe since June 1941, had grown impatient in their demands that the invasion plan should be implemented. When the heads of government of Britain, the USA and Russia met at Teheran in November 1943, Stalin urged that "Overlord" (as it was code-named) should be launched not later than the end of May; thereafter May or June became an agreed target date.

This was not public knowledge, but there had been enough clues during the later months of 1943 to indicate to any intelligent observer that the invasion would not be long delayed. During January it was announced that "Britain's invasion team" had been chosen, that General Dwight Eisenhower (who had been named the Supreme Commander of the invasion forces at the year end) had taken up his post in Britain, that General Bernard Montgomery was to take command of all Allied ground forces for the invasion, and that final preparations were in hand.

Almost immediately Montgomery embarked on a programme of visits to troops who would take part in the invasion. His itinerary included East Anglia. At Bury St Edmunds Miss Winifred Last joined an admiring crowd and afterwards wrote in her diary:

> General Montgomery called to see the Mayor at the Borough Offices today and some of us waited on Angel Hill to see him. I was more thrilled than I've ever been at Coronation or any such event. It was quite informal. A little bit of cheering when his car came along. He looked nice, more vigorous than I'd expected, unassuming, carefree, and as though he enjoyed his popularity . . .[1]

He visited the 3rd Division at its training camps in Scotland; the 1st Suffolks and the 1st Royal Norfolks were two of the battalions from eleven different regiments that made up the division at this time. It was the division Montgomery had commanded in 1940 and that the enemy had pushed back into the Channel, and now he told them that the Germans would soon have good cause to be aware of the 3rd Division again. He added: "This war began a long while ago. I am getting fed up with the thing. I think it is nearly time we finished it."

The responsible officers had known for more than six months that it was to be an assault division, and training had proceeded accordingly. It had been tough and varied, covering not only mock landings on defended beaches in co-operation with

General Montgomery chatting to the Mayor and the Chief Constable during a visit to Bury St Edmunds Town Hall.   *Imperial War Museum*

the Navy and exercises in close liaison with tanks of an armoured division, but also the kind of house-to-house fighting expected to follow—when men might have to take a flying leap, head-first and fully armed, through a window into a room held by the enemy, and then to fight from room to room with grenades and tommy guns. The 1st Royal Norfolks did street fighting training of this kind in Aberdeen during March. In one exercise East Anglian regiments found themselves as nominal "enemies" when the 2nd Battalion of the Essex Regiment was called upon to represent the German forces that would be faced on D-Day.

The 1st Suffolks, stationed at Nairn, spent many wild dark nights and many bitterly cold days on the beaches during these final months of training. The scenes at night were often like a film set, illuminated by arc lights set on the low cliff and the roving lamps of bulldozers that moved in and out of the sea collecting shingle to build beach obstacles and a breakwater.

There were also exercises at sea. Troops were taken out in infantry ships ten miles from the shore, where they were loaded into the smaller assault craft swinging at the davits. These boats were then lowered into the water and run in to land. On one of these exercises there was near disaster when the assault craft were lowered in a rough sea in the middle of the night while the infantry ship was rolling heavily. They swung wildly and crashed against the side of the parent ship, and then one of them was dropped on top of another which was already in the water. Several of the assault craft sank and the exercise was aborted, but no lives were lost.

The Commanding Officer of the Suffolk Regiment, Colonel W. N. Nicholson, visited the 1st Suffolks at Nairn in the course of these exercises. Afterwards he noted their readiness for action in these words:

> I had never seen a fitter battalion. You could recognise this outstanding quality even when they were standing still on parade and before they gave some training demonstrations. There was a bitter north-east wind, the snow came in skurries, it was freezing hard; the men were not wearing coats and obviously didn't need them; the sea off the coast was grey black with lines of white breakers—they had been in it up to their armpits on a landing exercise a few days previous and they were none the worse. The least observant of soldiers could not have failed to be greatly impressed by their radiant health and strength . . ."[2]

By this stage of the war the East Anglian regiments had lost some of their original members to other arms—paratroops and commandos—or for overseas service, and they had been considerably diluted by men drafted from other parts of the country. But the regional pride survived. In the case of the 1st Suffolks, for example, natives of the county still made up half its strength and the CO declared that with this "solid core of Suffolk soldiers . . . the battalion always belonged unmistakeably to the Suffolk Regiment"[3].

General Eisenhower meanwhile toured US fighter and bomber stations with Lieutenant-General Carl Spaatz, Commander of the US Strategic Air Force, and Lieutenant-General James Doolittle, US Bomber Chief. The US Ninth Air Force transferred its fighter units to airfields near the south coast during April, in order to provide better fighter cover for the invasion fleet. But most of the bases from which both American and RAF bombers flew were still in the eastern counties and from them a great bombing offensive was maintained for months before D-Day. Attention was increasingly given to targets in northern France, where, in a three months' campaign, only four of eighty designated rail targets escaped serious damage. In order to keep the Germans in the dark as to Allied strategy, however, twice as many bombs were dropped on targets in the Pas de Calais area during this same period[4].

Eisenhower gave the men on the US bases in East Anglia a challenging message: a time was coming when they would be flying from dawn to dusk and he would drive them so hard that they would have no sleep or food for weeks—but they would still "knock them [the enemy] out of the sky".

Churchill joined in the rhetoric, in characteristic style. In a fifty-minute radio talk on Sunday, 26th March he said:

General Eisenhower about to board his private train at Newmarket during a visit to Eastern Command to inspect airfields in April 1944.   *Imperial War Museum*

The hour of our greatest effort and action is approaching . . . When the signal is given, the whole circle of avenging nations will hurl themselves upon the foe and batter out the life of the cruellest tyranny which has ever sought to bar the progress of mankind.

By the end of March 1944 planning was sufficiently advanced to brief the corps commanders of the invasion troops with the aid of maps, aerial photographs and large-scale models of the landing beaches, but with all place-names coded. During April and May 1944 the top war strategists and commanders, British and American, met at St Paul's School in London to put the finishing touches to the "Overlord" plans. Churchill and Eisenhower attended these meetings and King George VI spoke briefly at one of them, on 15th May. The discussion covered every aspect of the first phase of the campaign—to D+90. As the gathering broke up Eisenhower observed that Hitler had "missed his one and only chance of destroying with a single well-aimed bomb the entire high command of the Allied forces".

Three British and two American divisions were to make the initial landings on the coast of Normandy, on beaches between the Rivers Orne and Vitre. They were to be preceded by three divisions of airborne troops, dropped by parachute or towed across the Channel in gliders. British and Canadian forces were to land on three beaches (code-named "Sword", "Gold" and "Juno") and push south and south-east to establish an eastern (left) flank based on Caen. On the western (right) flank US forces were to land on "Omaha" and "Utah" beaches, some racing north-westwards to capture Cherbourg and others pushing southward. The hope was that the individual beachheads would be consolidated into one and given a depth of at least eight miles, if not on the day of the landings then over the next day or so. The eight divisions landed on D-Day were to be increased to thirteen on D+1, to seventeen on D+3 and to twenty-one on D+12. The aim was to establish a St Malo–Rennes–Laval–Alençon–Argentan–Lisieux–Deauville line by D+25 and to reach the Seine by D+90[5]. At that stage the entire Allied force would have swung round in an arc and realigned itself for the advance on Germany.

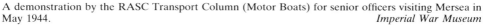

A demonstration by the RASC Transport Column (Motor Boats) for senior officers visiting Mersea in May 1944.   *Imperial War Museum*

In this invasion plan the East Anglian regiments featured strongly. On "Queen" beach (part of "Sword", at the extreme eastern end of the front) three regiments forming the 8th Brigade were to make the initial assault—the South Lancs and the East Yorks to be first ashore, with the 1st Suffolks close behind them. The 185th Brigade, comprising the 1st Royal Norfolks and battalions of the King's Shropshire Light Infantry and the Warwicks, with Staffs Yeomanry tanks, was to follow up, landing two hours later. The reserve was to be the 9th Infantry Brigade—battalions of the Lincolns, the King's Own Scottish Borderers, the East Yorks Yeomanry and the Ulster Rifles. The landings on "Sword" beach would be supported by two battleships and a monitor, one heavy and four light cruisers and thirteen destroyers[6].

At the other, western, end of the British front, the 2nd Essex battalion would be among the forces following three to four hours behind the first assault brigades of 50th Division on to "Juno" beach.

In one of the later reinforcing divisions—the 59th Infantry Division—another battalion of the Royal Norfolks, the 7th, would be included. As we shall see, it arrived in time to play a full part in the assault on Caen.

The American invasion troops embarked at West Country ports and British troops mostly at Southampton and Portsmouth, though ports right round to Tilbury and Felixstowe in the east were used. They assembled in an area just south of the Isle of Wight, which became known as "Piccadilly Circus", and then followed minesweepers down five marked channels.

The enemy-occupied coast was, of course, heavily fortified. The beaches and the sea approaches were mined, and the Germans had constructed multiple lines of underwater obstacles offshore and steel-girder and wire fences, concrete walls and anti-tank ditches on or near the beaches. Powerful guns emplaced along the coast could sweep the beaches and the exits from them. There was a defended zone

A composite photograph giving a panorama of invasion craft and accompanying naval vessels ready to leave the Solent.   *Imperial War Museum*

extending back four to six miles from the foreshore, with strongpoints at intervals of a thousand or so yards or so along its forward edge.

This was a formidable barrier to overcome. Immediately before the landings Allied air and naval bombardment would blow holes in it so that the armoured bulldozers, mine-clearance tanks and bridging vehicles could get ashore to deal with the remaining obstructions. In so far as the Allied bombers had not already destroyed roads and railways, French Resistance fighters could be depended upon to disrupt German communications and delay reinforcements.

Before the invasion troops landed, British and American bombers made sustained attacks. In two waves the RAF dropped five thousand tons of bombs on German coastal batteries, shortly before midnight and then between 3.15 and 5 am. As the airborne divisions landed, American bombers took to the air to drop some 4,200 tons of bombs on roads and bridges in and around Caen and on shore batteries and beach obstacles. Altogether 3,440 heavy bombers, 930 medium and light bombers, and 4,190 fighters and fighter-bombers took part.

At sea, by the end of May an invasion fleet of nearly seven thousand craft was assembled. For the destruction of the German defences and support of the ground forces there were more than 1,213 combatant naval vessels; there were 4,126 landing ships and landing craft; and for support operations there were 1,590 reconnaissance and maritime co-operation aircraft[7].

Enormous quantities of supplies had to be concentrated at suitable dumps ready for rapid transport to the Continent as soon as facilities were available for landing them. After the invasion, until a first-class port could be captured for the landing of supplies, all five assault beaches were to be provided with breakwaters behind which merchantmen could shelter and unload, but on "Gold" and "Omaha" beaches artificial harbours, christened "Mulberries", were to be installed. They were composed of large ferro-concrete caissons supplemented by blockships and floating piers, which had to be towed across the Channel and positioned off the Normandy coast. These harbours were designed to take seven ocean merchantmen, twenty coasters and up to four hundred tugs and a thousand lighters, so that each one could handle seven thousand tons of stores daily.

Wivenhoe Shipyard in Essex made a significant contribution to the construction of these unique harbours. This yard had fallen derelict before the war, but had been restarted at the outbreak with a labour force of fifty; by 1944 it was employing 350 men. They constructed two tank landing "buffers" (known during their construction by the code name "Whale"): steel structures, each measuring about eighty feet by sixty feet and weighing about 550 tons, with concave decks at both ends, to accommodate the bows of the tank landing craft. These buffers or linkspans were designed to hinge on to the ends of tank landing piers and to rise and fall with the tides, regulated by compressed air, so that all cargo unloaded on the piers could pass rapidly ashore. They were successfully towed across to Arromanches before D-Day[8].

Yards at Brightlingsea, Wivenhoe and Rowhedge built wooden warships. A motor minesweeper is seen under construction in the lower picture and on trials in the picture above. A vessel of this type required 250 elm and oak trees.
Photo courtesy of Mrs Hervey Benham

    As the invasion plans took shape, there was a carefully calculated effort to mislead the enemy. Bombing patterns in France were designed to deceive and a complete picture was created to suggest a principal assault on the Pas de Calais in mid-July. Sixty per cent of the air raids on northern France were directed against the Pas de Calais, but before D-Day all German airfields within 130 miles of Normandy had been neutralized. Between 1st April and 6th June 144,800 bomber missions were flown by the RAF and the USAAF in these operations, with losses of 1,616 bombers and nearly twelve thousand men killed and missing (compared with ten thousand dead, wounded and missing on the ground on D-Day itself)[9].

The German Luftwaffe, on the other hand, managed only about 120 reconnaissance missions over Britain in the two months before invasion, but opportunities were carefully provided for German intelligence to gather a certain amount of information. Elaborate efforts were made to suggest a great concentration of troops in Suffolk and Essex, in the area between Great Yarmouth and Southend. An impression was created that this force was being increased by one and a half divisions every day, until it became a phantom army group of fifty divisions. New permanent buildings were constructed in camps, roads were built or widened, tank parks created and coastal hards resurfaced and artfully illuminated. Hundreds of "landing craft" appeared in all the harbours and river mouths. They had come not from shipyards but from the scenery workshops of the Shepperton Film Studios, which worked overtime to produce these "props" of canvas, wood and tubular steel. Wireless activity was designed to suggest that the main invasion force was being concentrated in the region. This ambitious exercise in deception had been put in hand in December 1943, with orders that it should be completed by 15th April 1944[10]. It was maintained up to and beyond D-Day and was remarkably effective.

Meanwhile, in workshops and shipyards a furious pace was maintained. There were comparatively few factories in East Anglia, but they made a significant contribution. For example, Paxman diesel engines made in Colchester powered many of the D-Day tank landing craft. At the outbreak of war Paxman's Britannia Works had been a sad sight, in general disrepair. The Ministry of Supply had taken it over and had repaired, reconditioned and extended it. The Paxman management remained, a mainly female work force was recruited and trained, and it became an assembly and testing works for the production of the Paxman Ricardo diesel engines for tanks and tank landing craft (TLCs). Components were brought there from 550 sub-contracting firms all over Britain.

In February 1944, at a time when it was at its highest production in preparation for the invasion, it suffered a serious set-back when a German air raid on the St Botolph's area of Colchester started a fire which destroyed two-thirds of the Britannia Works*. Engine assembly was concentrated in the surviving part and testing switched to the Standard Works nearby. The bombed area was cleared and the factory was rebuilt on a much enlarged scale, to become one of the most up-to-date factories in Britain[11].

The east coast was a hive of activity. Royal Observer Corps volunteers were called for to man ships of the invasion fleet and came forward in considerable

Site of Messrs Blomfield's ironmongery shop at St Botolph's Corner, Colchester, taken 23rd February 1944.

numbers—thirty-nine from Colchester, for example. Those selected underwent intensive training. St Osyth became a training ground for combined operations under the style of HMS *Helder*. Training in small boat seamanship for the coxswains and crews of landing craft occupied a considerable fleet of motor yachts and launches. Amphibious tanks appeared at Mersea. In the estuary of the Colne there were minesweepers, minelayers and motor torpedo boats, armed patrol yachts and landing craft of various kinds. West Mersea was a patrol yacht base and later headquarters of the Royal Army Service Corps Motor Boat Company, known as the "Army's Navy"[12].

At Harwich preparations for D-Day became obvious in mid-April when the first invasion ships began to assemble there. The minesweeping fleet covered a thousand miles a week keeping the channels clear, and on D-Day over seventy vessels of various kinds sailed from the estuary of the Orwell.

The Thames, too, was packed with shipping. A. P. Herbert noted the remarkable sight there:

There have never been so many ships in London River before . . . There were not enough berths in the River for all the ships. They anchored them, in long lines down the middle of the lower reaches . . . One saw an endless forest of ships—transports, hospital ships, landing ships, tankers and barges . . . By degrees the ships were worked down river towards the mouth—to the domain of Southend Pier.[13]

With all this activity, the coastal area was no place to let inquisitive people roam freely; from 1st April a wide belt extending from the Wash round the east and south coasts to Land's End was declared a "protected area" and forbidden to the public "for operational reasons". Earlier there had been restrictions on holiday visitors, but now there was a complete prohibition on the presence of non-residents. It affected all the coastal towns—King's Lynn, Cromer, Sheringham, Great Yarmouth, Lowestoft, Southwold, Aldeburgh, Woodbridge, Felixstowe, Harwich, Clacton, Frinton and Walton, Brightlingsea, Wivenhoe, Maldon, Burnham-on-Crouch, West Mersea and Southend—together with Canvey Island, many adjoining rural districts and also towns a little way from the sea, including Ipswich, Beccles, Stowmarket, Saxmundham, Halesworth, Colchester, Chelmsford and Brentwood.

At Easter police checking identity cards were much in evidence in the one-time holiday resorts; they ordered unauthorized visitors to leave immediately. These checks caught out some of the residents; at Clacton and Harwich some were brought before the magistrates and fined for not carrying their identity cards. A man who had used binoculars (banned under another regulation in effect from 8th April) was also fined.

In this closed coastal belt preparations began for the embarkation of the invasion troops, mostly, as outlined above, along the south coast. "Assembly areas" were organized in three zones. At a depth of seven to ten miles inland there were "Concentration Areas" with hutted camps and other semi-permanent buildings. Next came "Marshalling Transit Areas" which provided accommodation for up to forty-eight hours. Then, along the coast itself, were "Embarkation Areas" where no accommodation was provided.

The movement of troops into the coastal Assembly Areas began in May. The 1st Royal Norfolks moved to a camp at Haywards Heath and the 1st Suffolks to Horndean near Portsmouth. The 2nd Essex were a little to the west at Beaulieu. All took part in a final large-scale exercise involving a landing in the Littlehampton area, which was designed to practise movement control and test the machinery for marshalling and embarkation. General Montgomery and the Secretary of State for War, Sir James Grigg, spent thirty minutes with the Suffolk battalion.

Men were counselled to write their wills and to put any spare cash into official savings schemes. The Suffolks organized its own welfare scheme; each man provided details of his next-of-kin and this information was sent to officers' wives or mothers so that they could keep in touch with the men's families and help to circulate any information that became available[14].

The battalion CO, Lieutenant-Colonel R. E. (Dick) Goodwin, decided that the time had come to tell his company commanders more about the invasion plans.

Late one afternoon they drove out to a lonely spot on the Downs, and there he produced a diagram and explained what would be the battalion's allotted task and how each company would play its part. The coastal area for the landing was still not identified, nor were any place-names mentioned. Some officers asked a few questions, and then the diagram was burnt and the ashes trampled into the grass. In the gathering dusk the party returned to camp[15]. A week later the Suffolk and Norfolk battalions (with the rest of the division) paraded for an inspection by King George VI; he spoke to several men of the Suffolks. The camps were then sealed, money was changed—for francs—and each man received a small guidebook giving phonetic renderings of useful sentences in French.

Towards the end of May the company commanders were given their first glimpse of the model of the beach sector, on which all place-names remained coded, and two days later the battalion CO briefed all officers and NCOs down to platoon sergeant. This lasted seven hours. The model was again displayed together with a large-scale map, many photographs showing beach obstacles, defences and landmarks, and a series of wave-top views of the run in to the beach. Representatives of the Royal Navy and RAF attended to explain the support and protection they would provide, and officers of the Royal Artillery, Royal Engineers and Royal Armoured Corps detailed their tasks in support of the battalion. During the three following days the companies were briefed and the troops were given a chance to ask all the questions they wished.

Marshalling for embarkation began at last on 30th May. While this was going on there were ENSA concerts, cinemas and games, and much last-minute cleaning of weapons and ammunition.

Although the troops who were going were now well aware of the imminence of the task ahead, every effort was made to prevent information getting to others. For weeks previously there had been much public speculation. William Stock, in Chelmsford, made these entries in his diary during April[16]:

All military leave is now cancelled, as I have heard from several sources . . .

The word invasion is on everybody's lips now. It crops up in every conversation.

In Bury St Edmunds, Miss Winifred Last noted on 23rd May: "Ten trains from Bury were cancelled today. Lots of soldiers on train. They looked excited and were loaded with kit . . . Planes are buzzing over."[17]

But even on the bomber bases most men still had only their hunches. After US bombers at Ridgewell, Essex, had repeatedly hit French targets during the first few days of June, James Good Brown noted in his diary:

These missions reveal something to all of us, though it is only a surmise . . . Something is up. We are smashing the coast of France. It feels to us in the briefing room that something is brewing. But we dare not say a word or give a hint. We were, in fact, told nothing.[18]

On 5th June there was an obvious clue, with the first of two days of hectic

64

Air Chief Marshal Sir Strafford Leigh-Mallory, Air C-in-C, chatting to an armourer during the inspection of an American Marauder Wing at Andrews Field, Essex, in May 1944.

Imperial War Museum

effort, painting aircraft with alternate black and white stripes on wings and fuselages. This was to ease the problems of aircraft identification for the Allied gunners who would be manning the defences of the invasion fleet. While this went on extra precautions were taken on every airfield in Britain; hundreds of civilians were detained until the last plane landed on the Monday evening.

Many people living in East Anglia were well aware by this time that events were unfolding dramatically. In the Colchester area, for example:

> Residents were roused from sleep, aware that something exceptional was literally "in the air". Fleets of fighters swept low over roof-tops, and glider trains could be clearly seen in the night sky. For those living by main roads the roar of passing convoys was added. Many stayed up all night, and turned anxiously to their wireless sets for confirmation that the awaited day had at last dawned. [19]

For some the war came too close for comfort—as when, soon after midnight, an Army Bren-gun carrier caught fire while travelling in convoy along Ipswich

Road, Colchester. The crew of the vehicle leapt out but one soldier was killed when ammunition began to explode. Civilians in the houses nearby ran to surrounding fields and dived into ditches. Two houses were wrecked and many others damaged.

At about 10 pm on 5th June at Rivenhall, a US base in Essex, a major stuck his head into a hut where a couple of dozen crewmen were assembled and called out: "Better hit the sack early, you guys. I've a hunch there's going to be an early briefing tomorrow." One of those crewmen recalled later:

> It was the earliest briefing I ever had. We were roused at 2 a.m. and after a hurried breakfast of powdered egg and toast we gathered in the briefing room in front of some top brass. Col Coiner [Colonel Richard T. Coiner, jun., commanding officer of the Bomb Group] was standing alongside a map of Western Europe and introduced General Sam Anderson, the 9th Air Force Bomber Command leader, to the assembled company. Coiner—a man with a flair for the dramatic—went on: "Gentlemen, this is it—we are going to spearhead the invasion."[20]

The weather outside was dreadful, but the briefing officer made it plain that this was a day like no other and that regardless of the elements Allied planes would fill the sky that morning. And fill the sky they did, taking off before dawn.

There had been high drama at Allied headquarters. There were only three days in early June upon which the operation could begin: when there would be the moonlight required by the three airborne divisions that were to go in by parachute and by glider during the night to secure the vital flanks, and when the low tides required for the landings and the demolition of the underwater obstacles in the forty minutes after first light would be present together. These three days were from 5th to 7th June. After that it would be a fortnight before the tides were suitable again. D-Day had, therefore, been planned for 5th June.

Early on the 4th Eisenhower received unfavourable weather forecasts and decided he must postpone the landings for twenty-four hours. Part of the assault force had already embarked. A naval squadron had sailed from the Clyde three days before to reach appointed stations off Normandy beaches at the correct time. It had to be held back for twelve hours, and while it was carrying out time-wasting manoeuvres it ran into a convoy in a fog. Fortunately there were no mishaps.

Later the forecast was for improving weather, and at 4.30 am on 5th June Eisenhower took the irrevocable decision. Operation "Overlord", the Allied invasion of Europe, went ahead on Tuesday 6th June, 1944.

*

CHAPTER SIX

The Day They Went Ashore

THE BRITISH public was told in a mid-day radio announcement on 6th June that the invasion had begun, and next day, with understandable hyperbole, the *East Anglian Daily Times* opened its leading article with the words: "From this day to the ending of the world, June 6th, 1944 will be remembered."

The invasion took place on a fifty mile stretch of Normandy coast on five main beaches, code-named "Sword" (at the eastern end, just north of Caen), "Juno", "Gold", "Omaha" and "Utah" (at the western end, in the Cotentin Peninsula, at the northern tip of which lay the port of Cherbourg). The immediate British aim was to drive inland from the three easternmost beaches to capture Caen and Bayeux. The objectives of the Americans, going ashore on the two western beaches, were to seize Cherbourg and to drive south-eastwards to link with the British army. The British and American armies would then advance towards Paris and the German frontier.

Before dawn on D-Day thousands of vessels were strung along the English Channel for as far as could be seen in any direction, and aircraft—with their newly painted black and white identification stripes—filled the skies. In the British landing sector over a thousand RAF bombers attacked the German coastal defences between 3 am and 5 am while other specially equipped aircraft jammed the German radar to mask the approach of the invasion fleet. As soon as the RAF had completed its task, the naval bombarding force of 140 warships moved into position between 5 am and 5.15 am and fired their guns to destroy the coastal fortifications, each ship concentrating on one particular shore battery. Similar attacks were made in the US sector further west.

Virtually every air base in East Anglia flew missions to the invasion area during the day. The 95th Bomb Group of the USAAF at Horham was typical: "All the Group's planes would go out, bomb their assigned targets in France, return, load up, get refuelled and take off immediately. And so it went on. The sky was never still."[1]

Even before the invasion had been publicly announced on 6th June, most people in the eastern counties guessed what was afoot. In Chelmsford, for example, William Stock noted:

> Even before I got up I thought something big was happening because of the number of aircraft going over . . . [At the hospital where he worked] Sister L. came in and said "Thank goodness it's started. It was the suspense that got you down . . ." One of the first things my boss said was "We can expect a few air raids now." [Earlier, there had been a

general tendency to see any German raids on Britain as a response to Allied raids on Berlin.] A nurse came in and said "I wish it didn't have to happen. Still, it'll soon be over now it's started—in a couple of weeks, do you think?" "A couple of months, perhaps," I said. "Probably six months or more."[2]

Altogether British and American planes flew more than fourteen thousand sorties during the day, while the Germans managed only 250 sorties[3]. Action was not confined to the Normandy beaches; aircraft and naval craft simulated the approach of a large force to the Pas de Calais, hoping to divert the enemy's attention.

The landings by 3rd Division troops—including the Suffolk and Royal Norfolk battalions—were on a seven-mile front near Ouistreham, a pre-war resort with a population of fewer than 2,800. Behind what had once been a magnificent holiday beach there were shady paths beside a pleasant canal which linked Caen with the sea. The beach and two important bridges over the canal and its companion river Orne were the first objectives of the British troops. After that they had to seize Caen and establish a bridgehead south of the Orne.

The 2nd Battalion of the Essex Regiment was part of the 56th Independent Infantry Brigade of the 50th British Division, which was assigned "Gold" beach near Arromanches. There the Essex men were to go ashore three to four hours after the first assault and make a dash six miles southward to capture Bayeux and occupy the high ground to its south.

Between these two British divisions the 3rd Canadian Division was assigned "Juno" beach and part of "Sword" and was to help to take Caen and the important high ground west of the city.

The 1st Suffolks embarked at Portsmouth, the Royal Norfolks at Newhaven and the 2nd Essex at Lymington. For them the operations began in the early hours of 3rd June. During the three following days the experiences of all the men were similar, and they are well illustrated by the Suffolk story. The Suffolk battalion marched from Victoria Barracks to the Portsmouth Harbour Station through deserted streets, with no one to watch except a group of Wrens who waved from the windows of their sea-front billets. In the dock area the men paused and munched chocolate and biscuits and drank tea, while "ship-sheets" were checked and parties of about thirty arranged. Then they marched down to the quay and were ferried in a paddle steamer to the vessels in which they were to cross the Channel.

These vessels were of two types. The more fortunate found themselves on board eleven-thousand-ton LSIs (landing ships, infantry). Two hundred of the men were put on a much smaller LCA (landing craft, assault). The LSIs were manned by the Merchant Navy, the LCAs by Marines. This made a difference; for their last

An aerial view of the Normandy beaches as Allied forces pushed inland on D-Day.
Photo courtesy of Ian Hawkins

breakfast before facing the enemy the Merchant Navy provided the assault battalions with "egg and bacon, coffee, white bread, marmalade, and all the sugar and butter one could wish for to make a good foundation for the forthcoming frolic"[4]. On the LCIs troops were packed like sardines and had to be content with tins of self-heating cocoa or kidney soup.

Then came the twenty-four hour postponement. Those who were on the larger infantry ships stayed there; those on the smaller craft were brought ashore for a few hours to use the canteens; those who had not embarked were marched back to barracks and returned the following morning. During the Suffolks' shore wait "several of the troops found some amusement in having their hair cut; the fashion spread round the ship of having the head practically shaved and then cutting out a large 'V' sign!"[5]

Eventually at 8.45 pm on 4th June the vessels carrying the 8th Brigade, including the Suffolks, weighed anchor and moved down the Solent with an escort of five destroyers. The vessels carrying the 185th Brigade, including the Royal Norfolks, sailed at 10 o'clock the next morning, and the LCIs with the Essex men on board sailed at 5 pm that afternoon. On the Suffolks' vessels nearly all the troops were on deck, quiet and serious. A padre said prayers over the loudspeakers. The Essex men "gambled or grumbled awhile, or even quietly read a paper-back thriller, and then tried to get a few hours sleep before the strains and excitements of the coming day"[6]. The sea was choppy. Practically everyone was sick.

After the vessels had slipped their moorings and were well out into the Channel, the troops were given a final briefing. Sealed packages were broken open. "Poland" on the maps and the model they had been shown earlier was then seen to be Caen, and "Queen White" part of the long beach near the mouth of the River Orne. There was the unwelcome news that "beach obstacles have been considerably increased during the last few days and the 21st Panzer Division has moved nearer to the beach area".

One can only guess at the private thoughts of the men after that. Their minds must have ranged forward to the flying metal over the beaches ahead of them, and backward to the families they had left behind. It is unlikely that many of them pondered battle plans and campaign objectives; much more likely thoughts were of the discomforts of wading ashore through waist-high water and of being assured of rations when they were hungry.

Their training had prepared them—to a degree. "Usually socks can be changed about three hours after landing; by this time boots become fairly dry, and, luckily, salt water is never so wet or so cold as fresh."[7] They knew, too, from their training experience that boots must not be removed whilst they were in the fighting line: they became quite soggy with perspiration and if the opportunity to remove them for a while was taken, feet quickly swelled up so that it was difficult to get them on again. As for sustenance, each man carried rations for forty-eight hours after landing, in two separate twenty-four-hour waterproof packages:

Each ration contained biscuits, oatmeal blocks, tea, sugar and milk blocks, dehydrated meat blocks, chocolate, sweets, chewing gum, meat extract cubes, salt. In addition a "Tommy" cooker with stand and two tins of fuel, a waterproof tin of 20 Players [cigarettes], with a rough edge for striking matches, and four vomit bags very stoutly constructed![8]

After the first forty-eight hours, much would depend upon the quartermaster, the cooks and their equipment coming safely ashore.

Having crossed the Channel the invasion fleet anchored about seven miles offshore. On each of the infantry ships there were eighteen assault craft swinging at davits and at about 6 am troops on the first vessels to arrive climbed the steep ladders to the top decks and clambered into these smaller craft, thirty-five men in each. As the boats were lowered into the water, to cries of "Good luck" from the ship's crew, it was just getting light.

When it was the turn of the Suffolk battalion to go ashore, they circled the bigger vessel until the assault fleet had formed into four columns and then, at 7 am, they made for the shore. The run in to the beach, between a double row of lighted buoys marking the swept channel, took a hundred minutes. The men could not discern the coast ahead but they heard much ominous rumbling from that direction. Bombers streamed overhead, warships sailed alongside the columns and pumped shells ashore, and soon fighters could be seen patrolling the beaches. Amidst all this noise and excitement the troops were given cocoa and sandwiches. Then the beach was ahead of them and, on a signal from the flotilla leader the craft fanned out into line abreast. Major Charles Boycott described the minutes that followed:

We seemed to rush at the beach, the details coming into ever sharper relief . . . a mass of twisting, jerking wrecked craft, through which it seemed impossible to pick a path. There was a grating of the keel and we were aground. "Down doors" and out I leapt. I cannot remember how deep the water was, but we must have splashed through it for about 20 yards or so. As I got out of the craft I just missed falling over a corpse rocking face up in the surf. This made me think about enemy fire; for the first time I noticed the waterspouts being kicked up by the bursting bombs and shells. I increased my pace sharply. We were on the beach: a background of shattered, smoking seaside houses with naked slats in their roofs; the narrow stretch of sand covered with tanks and men; a pungent, burning and explosive sort of stink . . .[9]

There were some mishaps, the most serious of which was the loss of the boat carrying the regimental quartermaster sergeant and the stores. The men were rescued and eventually rejoined, but for a time there were supply difficulties.

The Suffolks arrived on the scene an hour after the assault battalions of the South Lancs and the East Yorks, which had been spearheaded by twenty-four amphibious tanks, accompanied by flails, bulldozers and armoured vehicles and followed by the divisional artillery. Their designated tasks were on or adjacent to the beach, and it had been hoped that by the time the Suffolks landed the beach would be reasonably clear, at any rate of aimed small-arms fire[10]. In the event the two assault battalions suffered so heavily that some units were unable to advance,

Men of the 1st Royal Norfolk Battalion wading ashore in Normandy on D-Day.

Imperial War Museum

and only about half the tanks, flails, bulldozers and armoured vehicles survived the first few minutes. The Suffolks arrived to find tanks and carriers burning and others moving about helplessly. The Germans were shelling and mortaring the beach quite hard and the scene looked a shambles:

> The men waded through about 30 yards of water up to their waists, and the next 15 minutes was "like a nightmare", with the troops crouched down behind any cover they could find, wrecked vehicles, etc. and hoping for the best. Although the whole of the battalion was on that narrow beach—about 30 yards—and everyone close together, there were probably not more than a dozen casualties.[11]

The Norfolks landed ninety minutes later and had a dry landing, the steepness of the beach and the state of the tide enabling the landing craft to get in close enough for ramps to reach the shore. The beach was by this time becoming congested but the Norfolks suffered no casualties there and reached their concentration area in good order. They moved forward by noon to their first objective.

The scene on the beach after the landing.   *Imperial War Museum*

In front of the Suffolks where they went ashore were two parallel coast roads with a row of seaside villas between them; beyond that was low ground with small cultivated fields separated by big ditches, a number of small orchards and one or two woods. The Suffolks began by capturing some of the houses near the beach, in which German snipers were hiding; it proved difficult to locate and eliminate them and the Suffolks lost two officers killed and twelve men killed and wounded.

By 9.30 am the battalion had assembled near Hermanville-sur-Mer, a village about one-and-a-half miles inland. Each company was allotted a specific task. They were to advance behind a barrage laid down by the guns of a cruiser, HMS *Dragon*, and a destroyer, HMS *Kelvin*[12]. One company moved south-east through orchards and occupied Colleville without opposition. Another had the task of eliminating a nearby German fortress code-named "Morris", where there was a battery of 105-mm guns. Naval and artillery fire was directed on it, but before the Suffolks moved to attack, a white flag was raised and a smartly dressed German officer, a colonel and sector commander, appeared and gave himself up. After talking with a Suffolk officer he went back to the strongpoint and came out with his whole garrison[13].

After this the Suffolks' orders were to capture a German headquarters codenamed "Hillman" and then to consolidate on high ground about three thousand yards from the coast, near Perriers-sur-le-Dan, to form a firm base for further forward movement. The battalion of Royal Norfolks that had followed them ashore was then intending to pass through the Suffolks and to continue the advance.

By the time the Suffolks had moved to attack "Hillman", however, the position on the beach was getting out of hand. At high tide there should have been a width of thirty yards in which vehicles could manoeuvre laterally along the beach, but bad weather had built up the tide so that the width was barely thirty *feet*. There was soon serious congestion. It was five hours before some of the first artillery ashore could move off the beach to a gun position inland. Fifty guns went into action while still on the beach, some actually standing in several feet of surf, and landing craft deposited men and vehicles among them as they fired.

The three infantry battalions of the follow-up 185th Brigade struggled ashore by 11 am and assembled at headquarters at Hermanville. Their plan was for the King's Shropshire Light Infantry to mount tanks of the Staffordshire Yeomanry and ride them in an advance along the main axis to secure Caen as quickly as possible, with the Royal Norfolks and the Warwicks following behind to mop up and secure objectives captured by the mobile column. The tanks, however, were caught in the congestion on the beach and so the KSLI were ordered to advance on foot.

Meanwhile the Suffolks found the assault on the fortress "Hillman" a more difficult task than they had been led to expect. It was the local German coastal headquarters and it had a maze of deep concrete bunkers and pillboxes, all connected by trenches. Its outer defences of wire, anti-personnel and anti-tank mines covered nearly three-quarters of a square mile. Because much of it was underground and well camouflaged, intelligence reports had failed to assess it correctly. An additional problem was that the preliminary naval bombardment from a cruiser offshore had failed to materialize because a key liaison officer had been killed.

Artillery, mortars and tanks began a bombardment of the fortress at 1.10 pm and then, under cover of a smoke screen, a single infantry company, augmented by a breaching platoon and three mine clearance teams, crawled forward through the corn. They blew a gap in the first wire, cleared a lane through the minefield and marked it by white tape, and then breached the inner wire. But as the first assault platoon passed through this gap they were greeted by a murderous hail of machine-gun fire. A second assault platoon moved forward, and both then found themselves pinned to the ground and unable to move. The company commander, Captain

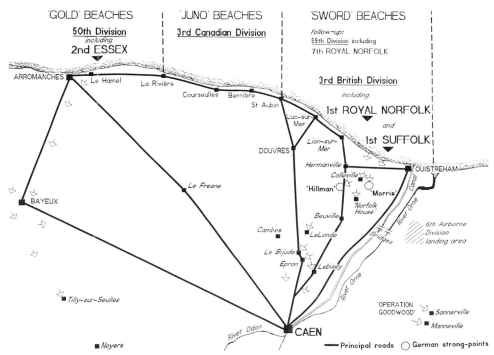

East Anglian battalions taking part in the 2nd British Army invasion of Normandy. They had embarked at Portsmouth, Newhaven and Lymington. Some of the follow-up divisions embarked at Felixstowe and Tilbury.

Ryley, was killed. Casualties began to mount. Flails were used to enable a tank to go in, but its armour-piercing shells had no effect on the steel cupola from which the machine-guns were raking the Suffolks.

There was stalemate for several hours until more tanks were brought up. The infantry followed them in and tackled each concrete emplacement in turn. Many of the defenders fought until they were blown out with heavy explosive charges. The German regimental commander was among those killed. The Suffolks mopped up, and the resistance ended at 8.15 pm[14].

As D-Day ended the Suffolks were digging in their guns and mortars, and they began night patrolling at 11.30 pm. Their losses for the day had been two officers and five other ranks killed and about twenty-five other ranks wounded. All objectives had been taken, with 270 German prisoners.

This prolonged battle at "Hillman" had serious consequences. When it became obvious that it would take some time to subdue the fortress, the Norfolks—who were to pass through the Suffolks at this point—moved over to the left and began to by-pass the position. This proved hazardous and during the afternoon they found themselves pinned down for two-and-a-half hours by enemy machine-guns at "Hillman". To make matters worse, they came under fire from their own tanks as well, the crews mistaking them for Germans. They suffered nearly 150 casualties, including one officer and thirteen other ranks killed[15]. By 7 pm they reached a wooden area on top of a gentle rise between Beuville and the Orne bridge, where there was a solitary house, which was thereafter known as "Norfolk House".

About two hours later, on a warm and sunny evening, the spirits of both the Suffolks at "Hillman" and the Royal Norfolks at "Norfolk House" were somewhat revived by the sight of gliders bringing airborne reinforcements:

> The sky seemed to be completely obscured by an enormous swarm of Dakota aircraft towing gliders. They came in perfect formation right over our heads and released their gliders, which turned through 180 degrees and came in to land away on our left. Following them up a few minutes later came a large number of Stirlings which dropped the containers of equipment.[16]

The delay at "Hillman" tied up two squadrons of those tanks which it had been intended should carry the KSLI along the main axis to Caen, and by the end of D-Day Caen had not been captured. Two infantry companies got within a mile of the northern suburbs of the town, but finding themselves exposed and without support they had to withdraw. The historian of the 3rd Division, Norman Scarfe, afterwards admitted: "We felt pretty disappointed and frustrated NOT to have got into Caen as planned on D-Day"[17].

The 2nd Battalion of the Essex Regiment fared better. Its intended landing place on "Gold" beach, near the village of Le Hamel, was being fiercely defended by the Germans when the Essex men arrived, so they went ashore instead 1,500 yards further east. Despite coming under artillery and mortar fire they reached their assembly point without casualties. By mid-afternoon they were complete except for three vehicles which had been "drowned". At about 4 pm they set off for Bayeux, led by a platoon mounted on Bren carriers, with two other platoons following on bicycles (which they had brought with them). They were aware that fighting was continuing behind them, but with some tank support they "brushed aside any opposition"[18] and by 9.30 pm were digging in about a mile-and-a-half from Bayeux. Their flanks were secure because the 2nd Glosters and the 2nd South Wales Borderers on either side had progressed equally well. At the end of the day the only Essex losses were four men wounded by sniper fire.

Despite the set-backs the British D-Day operations were pronounced a success. Exits had been forced by the 3rd Division from "Sword" beach and by the 50th Divison from "Gold" within the first hour, and after two-and-a-half hours the British Second Army had landed over thirty thousand men, three hundred guns and

Opposite: These two pictures show troops of the British 3rd Division—which included many men from Norfolk and Suffolk—landing on a "Sword" beach on D-Day.

seven hundred armoured vehicles. By the end of the day 156,000 men had waded ashore and the assault divisions in the British sector were consolidating their beachhead.

In the American sector the troops who went ashore on "Utah" beach moved inland rapidly to seize their objectives, but on "Omaha" beach there were difficulties getting ashore and fierce resistance by strong German forces. Over two thousand men were killed, wounded or posted missing.

The Germans were slow to react on D-Day. Field-Marshal Rommel, who commanded the army group occupying northern France and the Low Countries, had gone home to Germany to visit his wife on her birthday, convinced that the weather was too bad for an invasion. Throughout 5th June the Germans remained unaware that the invasion fleet was at sea, and even when it was realized that a large-scale invasion was in progress, both Rommel's headquarters and the Paris headquarters of the German Supreme Command in the West thought it a diversionary operation prior to a main assault in the Pas de Calais. The elaborate exercise in deception that had been carried out in East Anglia over the previous six months had been remarkably successful.

CHAPTER SEVEN

From the Killing to the Kissing

THE SITUATION on the morning after D-Day was not all that the military planners had hoped for. Over 130,000 Allied ground troops and over 23,000 airborne troops had landed in France, but apart from the assault on the beaches and the advance on Bayeux almost nothing had gone according to plan. There had been slower than anticipated progress by the lead infantry and there had been delays in landing armoured units.

Montgomery's master plan required the early capture of Caen, the bridges over the River Orne, and the high ground south-east between Caen and Falaise, as this was the gateway to a broad, long, flat plain which extended south-eastwards towards Paris. That was where Montgomery intended to make his main effort, in good tank country. His immediate problem after D-Day was to anchor the eastern flank securely, blocking any attempt by the Germans to roll him up and defeat the invasion or to interfere with the American force making for Cherbourg.

The first success was the capture of Bayeux, and this achievement fell to the 2nd Battalion of the Essex Regiment. On the morning after their arrival in France they advanced on the town, expecting to meet strong resistance and supported by tanks of the Sherwood Rangers, but as they entered, the Germans withdrew from its southern limits. The inhabitants reacted cautiously, but eventually the tricolour flags were produced and "many a bottle of wine and fiery Calvados"[1].

By the morning of 7th June the front was stabilized on the Caen–Bayeux highway, and there it remained for several weeks. Caen was only four miles from Bayeux but it was not to be captured until 9th July. The armour needed to assault Caen was not available.

> The campaign in Normandy rapidly turned into a series of vicious, smaller unit actions, a classic confrontation at close quarters, with no holds barred. As it is in most wars, the dirty business of winning battles fell to the infantryman. Despite the vast array of sophisticated and deadly weapons of war available to both sides, success or failure in Normandy ultimately became the ability of the foot soldier to take or hold ground.[2]

Back on the beaches the build-up of armoured divisions and supplies was behind schedule, and so it continued throughout June. A shortage of artillery

Opposite: The front page headlines in the *Cambridge Daily News* on 7th June show how the Germans were misled into thinking that the Normandy invasion was secondary to a main attack on the Pas de Calais.

ammunition soon began to limit operations[3]. The strong cruiser/destroyer striking forces that blocked both ends of the English Channel and the innumerable Royal Navy escort vessels guarding the endless convoys carrying supplies were effective against enemy action—there was remarkably little interference by the Luftwaffe. This was particularly important for the transports that sailed ceaselessly from Parkeston Quay with military supplies, for they faced a longer voyage than most.

The bad weather was less easily coped with. In the third week of the invasion there were three or four days of gales which not only delayed landings but badly damaged the synthetic harbours, assembly of which was still incomplete. One of them, in the American sector, was destroyed by a gale on 21st June.

The enemy inflicted a few blows on the Navy. A solitary Junkers Ju.88 made a surprise early morning torpedo attack on 12th June on the destroyer HMS *Boadicea*, which sank in two to three minutes. Only twelve of her crew of 188 survived. Among the victims was her commander, Lieutenant-Commander Frederick William Hawkins, a native of Freston, Suffolk, and an old boy of Harwich County High School. For his family, living in Ipswich, this was a second grievous loss; his brother, Ron Hawkins, a distinguished wartime pilot, had been killed in October 1943 in a raid on a petroleum refinery near Ghent*.

Despite the difficulties a million men had been landed in France by the end of June, yet "by early July the British were in serious trouble as a result of a rapidly growing shortage of trained infantry reinforcements"[4]. There was increasing congestion in the bridgehead because not enough territory had been captured to permit armoured forces to move freely. Nor were there the forward airstrips that had been planned, so that all but a fragment of the air force continued to operate from bases in Britain.

Because of these problems progress was slow, but the war chiefs maintained an unworried demeanour. When Churchill visited the British beachhead a week after D-Day he noted:

> Montgomery, smiling and confident, met me at the beach as we scrambled out of our landing-craft. His army had already penetrated seven or eight miles inland. There was very little firing or activity. The weather was brilliant. We drove through our limited but fertile domain in Normandy. It was pleasant to see the prosperity of the countryside. The fields were full of lovely red and white cows basking or parading in the sunshine. The inhabitants seemed quite buoyant and well nourished and waved enthusiastically.
>
> Montgomery's headquarters, about five miles inland, were in a chateau with lawns and lakes around it. We lunched in a tent looking towards the enemy. The General was in the highest spirits . . .[5]

There were many men from the eastern counties for whom things did not look quite so satisfactory. The Royal Norfolks had been stuck for a week at "Norfolk House", most of them in slit-trenches. They had lost two officers and eight other ranks killed and thirty to forty wounded on 7th June when the 185th Brigade was

*See *East Anglia 1943*, Chapter Two, page 28.

Three Ipswich men lost their lives when the Royal Navy destroyer HMS *Boadicea* was sunk in the English Channel on 13th June 1944 by a German glider bomb. There were only 12 survivors.

Photo courtesy of Ian Hawkins

ordered to advance towards Caen and take the village of Lebisey. A battalion of the 2nd Warwicks began the attack but met strong opposition and was soon pinned down. The Royal Norfolks went up to try to retrieve the situation, came under heavy fire and, with no artillery support available, had to pull back at dusk with what was left of the Warwicks. After that the battalion remained at "Norfolk House" for the rest of June, doing a great deal of patrolling but nothing more. The weather became appallingly bad and they rigged up tarpaulins over their trenches. British newspapers came with the mail each day, and morale was not helped by the fact that neither the BBC nor the press made any mention of the part that the 3rd Division had played in the seizure of the bridgehead[6].

The experience of the 1st Battalion of the Suffolk Regiment was similar. On D-Day+3 it moved out to attack but could make little progress, and the commander, Lieutenant-Colonel R. E. Goodwin, was severely wounded and had to be evacuated by air to the United Kingdom. (He was not fit to return to the battalion until the end of the year.) On D-Day+4 the Suffolks moved into Le Mesnil Wood, and there they had to stay until the 24th.

The 2nd Essex battalion meanwhile tried to follow up its capture of Bayeux with an advance to the south-west of the town. For a day or two things were quiet; they captured three German soldiers riding a motor-cycle combination and an over-diligent German press correspondent who unwittingly wandered into the Essex lines in his search for "copy". But when on 11th June they were ordered to capture woods near the hamlet of Verrières, their luck changed. The enemy had tanks concealed there, and when at 6 pm the Essex men attacked across 1,500 yards of flat open country they suffered heavy casualties and were soon in a critical situation. Two platoons were taken prisoner; soon after midnight the Germans launched a vicious counter-attack with infantry and flame-throwers and made a serious penetration, but British tanks and anti-tank guns were brought forward and by daybreak Verrières Wood was firmly in Essex hands.

The various Allied bridgeheads were joined into one continuous forty-two-mile front on the morning of 11th June, and the army commanders evolved an alternative to a frontal assault on Caen. They planned to encircle it from east and west. An armoured brigade began to develop the "right hook" on 12th–13th June and captured the important crossroads town of Villers-Bocage virtually unopposed, with welcoming crowds thronging the pavements. At much the same time as they occupied it, however, two companies of a German SS Panzer Corps reached the area and one of its units did spectacular damage to the British force, effectively crushing the advance in that sector. In the ensuing fighting the town was left in ruins. This was the end of the "right hook" effort and Montgomery was forced to abandon the plan to envelop Caen, at least for the time being. Villers-Bocage remained in German hands until August.

By 17th June (D+11) the whole front before Caen had congealed. The 3rd Division faced the flower of the SS Panzer formations, and on many parts of the front the Germans were only 250 yards distant. Over to the west, however, troops of the 50th British Division were still punching at the German defences, and the 2nd Essex battalion, which was part of it, saw fourteen days of practically unbroken action with very little sleep. On the 17th they were ordered to capture the village of Tilly-sur-Seulles, six miles south of Bayeux. It had been occupied by Allied troops a week earlier but they had been driven out and repeated efforts had failed to retake it. After thirty-six hours the Essex men succeeded, but at a heavy cost. Afterwards, when the battalion had lost over a third of all who had landed on D-Day—killed, wounded or missing—there were cases of battle exhaustion in the ranks and it was withdrawn from the line for rest.

In Britain newspapers, radio and cinema newsreels presented a heroic picture of these early days after the invasion, but the more perceptive of the public sensed that there were problems. Thus William Stock in Chelmsford wrote in his diary on 15th June:

> The news from France tonight seemed a little evasive, as though things were not going quite as well as they should. However, the battle is only just beginning and it is too soon to be either optimistic or pessimistic . . .[7]

A day or two later he saw a newsreel which concentrated on the entry into Rome but included some pictures from Normandy, which he "did not think very exciting".

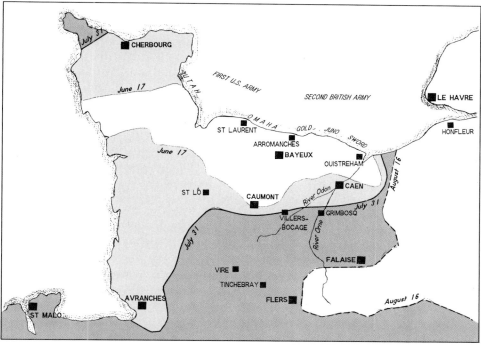

The Normandy Campaign. Besides principal towns, this map shows places of special significance in the operations in which the East Anglian battalions took part.

A new effort to outflank Caen on the west began on 26th June with an attack between Villers-Bocage and Caen to try to force crossings of the River Odon. After vicious hand-fighting and slow progress the British crossed the river on a bridge captured intact, but they soon had to be pulled back. On 30th June the whole operation was terminated, after the attackers had suffered 4,020 casualties. This five-day campaign was a dismal failure.

At about the same time the 8th Infantry Brigade was ordered to capture a group of villages just north of Caen: La Londe, with the nearby Château de la Londe, La Bijude and Epron. The 1st Suffolks' special responsibility was to take Epron. The advance began at 4 pm on 27th June. Very quickly it was realized that the Germans had prepared a much more elaborate defence system at the Château de la Londe than had been supposed; the garrison comprised three companies of tanks, a company of infantry, a platoon of sappers and the headquarters company of a Panzer regiment. The British attack was beaten off.

A new plan had to be hurriedly devised. The Suffolks' company commanders gathered around two hurricane lamps in a barn late that night and Lieutenant-

Colonel J. G. M. B. Gough, who had taken over command, explained it to them. Two hours later the infantry moved to a "forming-up line" behind a hedgerow, and only then were they given their first food for nearly twenty-four hours—biscuits and one small tin of stew between each five men. It was the best the quartermaster could offer because of the loss of all cooking utensils and food containers when one of the landing craft had been sunk.

While it was still fairly dark, a heavy barrage was laid down on the enemy positions for eight minutes. It was lifted at a rate of a hundred yards every three minutes and behind this screen of fire the 1st Suffolk infantry, their equipment and clothing saturated by heavy dew, moved forward at first light over flat open cornfields, with the wheat little more than knee-high. They were on the left flank of the attack, with the 2nd East Yorks on the right. They met heavy artillery and mortar fire and of nearly one hundred men in the three Suffolk platoons only twenty-four reached their objective. These survivors dug in in slit-trenches in an orchard but soon faced six German tanks bearing straight down on them, plus thirty German infantry attacking from the rear. One of the company commanders, Major D. W. McCaffrey, described what happened next:

> Things became rather bad for us in our incompleted slit trenches. When the Boche shouted "Kamerade Tommy" I saw the chaps nearest the tanks surrender, then others following suit. When I saw that I had lost control, I took a header into a large thorn bush . . . The Germans searched the area, but we were not located. I then had the mortification of seeing some very brave men being marched off as prisoners.[8]

Though one officer, Lieutenant Woodward, won the Military Cross for his part in this attack, it was a sad day: the Suffolks' total casualties were seven officers and 154 other ranks killed, wounded or missing. A private who was sent into the Suffolks' trenches as one of the replacements noted afterwards that they were under constant shellfire and so plagued by mosquitoes that sleep was impossible.

> One man in my dugout lost his nerve and wept and shook for hours until we could stand it no longer. I at last offered to take him to the Regimental Aid Post, which I did, and there were plenty of shells flying about. There were huge bomb craters, which made walking difficult. However, I got him to the R.A.P, where I saw a room full of men who were shaking and crying for fear . . .[9]

At this heavy price the château was captured in the end, and the Suffolks remained in the area until 16th July. They held a memorial service in a garden pockmarked by shell-holes. It was conducted by the battalion chaplain, the Reverend Hugh G. Woodall, a man who had already spent a large part of his time in Normandy helping with the burial of those who had died—friend and foe alike.

By the end of June the 3rd Division objectives targeted for capture on the first day or shortly thereafter were no closer to being attained, and criticism began to be heard of the conduct of the campaign on this eastern sector. Elsewhere things were going well. Cherbourg had fallen to the Americans on 26th June, a week was then spent mopping up and the Americans, after a brief respite to refit, were ready to

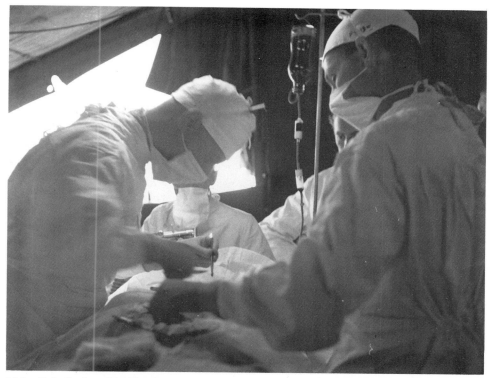

Major C. J. Gordon, RAMC, of Ipswich, performing an operation in a tent at a casualty clearing station in Normandy, 24th June 1944. The patient had suffered bullet wounds in the abdomen.

Imperial War Museum

begin a new offensive. The port was such a tangled mess that it was a month before it began to function.

An all-out siege against Caen had become unavoidable. The 59th Infantry Division, which had arrived in Normandy after delays in crossing the Channel because of gales, now took the centre position, with the 3rd British Division on its left and the 3rd Canadian Division on its right. A new battalion of East Anglian troops thus joined the battle, for the 59th Division included the 7th Royal Norfolks.

The attack was made in three phases. La Bijude and Lebisey Wood were to be taken in the first phase, and the newly arrived 7th Norfolk battalion was then to move between them in the second phase to capture Epron. Each battalion involved had one squadron of tanks as close support. When on the night of 7th/8th July the Norfolks marched to their forming-up position, eight hundred yards from the Château de la Londe, they had had no news of the fortunes of those conducting phase 1 (it had, in fact, been unsuccessful at La Bijude).

Bren carriers in the wrecked village of Bijude after its capture, July 1944.   *Imperial War Museum*

At 7 am the Norfolk infantrymen moved forward for their first encounter with the enemy. There had been an aerial and artillery bombardment, which raised so much dust and smoke that visibility was reduced to three hundred yards, seriously handicapping the tanks leading the attack. As the leading infantry companies came into the open, through the cornfields in front of the Château de la Londe—still occupied by the 1st Suffolks—they met heavy fire from German artillery and machine-guns and mortar bombardment. They suffered heavy casualties—in one of the two advance companies every officer and the sergeant-major. The wireless was out of action, there was a complete lack of information and general confusion reigned. Soon the attackers had to withdraw to the château area and the second phase of the assault was pronounced a failure.

A new effort began almost immediately. The remnants of three companies of the Norfolks were reorganized into one composite company of about fifty, to be held in reserve. The fourth company, with tank support, moved forward at 2 pm behind a heavy artillery barrage to make another effort to take La Bijude. They met heavy small arms and mortar fire but after an hour of stiff fighting they occupied the village. Then, linking up with the 7th South Staffs, they attacked Epron and cleared it of the enemy by 10 pm. By last light the whole battalion of Norfolks was reorganized in Epron. During the day three officers and thirty-one other ranks had been killed and seven officers and 111 other ranks wounded. After thirty-six hours in Epron, clearing up the battlefield and holding a memorial service, the battalion moved back to the coast to rest and re-equip.

On the same day that the 7th Battalion of the Royal Norfolks captured La Bijude and Epron, not far away the 1st Battalion captured Lebisey Wood and nearby high ground dominating Caen. The preliminary artillery bombardment was supported by the guns of HMS *Warspite* offshore. Behind this barrage the British troops went forward against stiff opposition, and by 10 am the Norfolks had cleared Lebisey Wood and dug themselves in. Although they had lost twenty-five men killed and seven officers and eighty-four other ranks wounded, this operation was rated a great success.

After two days of hard fighting of this kind the northern half of the Caen, as far as the bank of the River Orne where it passes through the town, was occupied by British and Canadian troops. German resistance was savage and casualties were described as "staggering". Before the war Caen had been a flourishing commercial and university town of fifty-five thousand people. By the time it was captured on Sunday, 9th July the summer sunshine illuminated a scene of devastation.

With the fall of Caen Norfolk and Suffolk battalions were brought out of the line for their first rest for five weeks and the almost-forgotten luxury of baths and clean clothes. In the village of Blainville the local folk made up a team to play football with the Norfolk lads, while the Suffolks went back to the seaside to play darts in the divisional club at Luc-sur-Mer. There they received a bread ration—half a slice each; until this time they been fed only biscuits.

After the capture of Caen the Allied commanders decided the time had come to make a powerful armoured strike across the River Orne and into the good tank country towards Falaise. They had available a massive force of 2,250 medium and four hundred light tanks. The 1st Royal Norfolks and 1st Suffolks were among the infantry battalions of the 3rd Infantry Division assigned an important role in this operation, code-named "Goodwood". It began at 5.30 am on 18th July with the RAF and the USAAF making "one of the most awesome air attacks ever launched against ground troops", and with artillery and naval bombardment then delivering nearly a quarter of a million rounds on to the battlefield[10].

The ground attack was launched at 7.30 am. The British encountered more resistance than had been expected and a major tank battle developed. It became a day of intense heat, the air laden with dust and mosquitoes, and by the time the fighting ended the countryside was cratered like a moon landscape and littered with wreckage. The overall breakthrough that had been hoped for was not achieved, four hundred tanks were lost, there were 5,537 infantry casualties and the offensive was terminated on the day it began.

The 1st Norfolks' turn to advance came at 2 pm, by which time the masses of transport ahead had raised enormous clouds of dust. At 7.30 pm the battalion was ordered to join a brigade attack on the village of Manneville, but at last light they were still two hundred yards short of the Manneville Wood, near the village. When they moved in at dawn the following morning they found the Germans had left during the night. The brigade settled there for nine very uncomfortable days, subject to periodic shelling and mortar-bombing. A deluge of rain flooded the trenches and they were constantly under fire. The orchard around them was reduced to a collection of broken stumps. The Norfolks suffered a steady flow of casualties and noted their first serious case of nervous exhaustion.

The Suffolks' specific task was to take the nearby village of Sannerville. As the battalion went forward it passed groups of demoralized German prisoners and walking British wounded in ones and twos, but it found no sign of the enemy in or about Sannerville. The Suffolks then had a similar experience to the Norfolks: eleven days sitting in dug-outs and being shelled.

The Norfolks were relieved and moved back for rest on 25th July and the Suffolks on 31st July. The Norfolks played a number of cricket matches and were entertained by an ENSA party. The Suffolks, in the neighbourhood of Beuville, found some solace in the celebration of Minden Day. One of the men went round the village asking for roses, and the local nuns collected a large armful. Three bunches were laid on Suffolk graves at Hermanville. The troops pinned the others to their hats, turned out in best battle dress and relaxed as best they could, going to the cinema or simply resting quietly. "If the small supply of beer which had been collected could have gone further, it would have been an old-time Minden Day."[11]

The only consolation after the failure of "Goodwood" was that the whole of Caen was at last in Allied hands and that two important river crossings—of the Oden and the Orne—had been made. It was almost two months since D-Day. The Allied armies had behind them the remarkable achievement of landing a mighty armed forced, establishing a substantial bridgehead and beating off fierce enemy counter-attacks; but there had been unanticipated delays, big disappointments, serious local defeats and heavy casualties.

Back home in East Anglia little of this was reflected in the newspapers read by the men's families. The local press depended for news of their regiments upon information provided by the army. The first story about the Suffolks appeared in the *East Anglian Daily Times* on 3rd August. It was brief, reporting that the regiment had been represented on the beaches on D-Day, had been in action against a Panzer division, had faced "stiff resistance" and been engaged in "fierce fighting", and that its "skirmishing" in the Caen sector had helped to pin down

German forces while the Americans pushed on to Cherbourg. The first story about the Royal Norfolks followed on 12th August and was even less informative. The regiment, it said, was among those that had assaulted Caen; it had "advanced through minefields against determined German resistance", and it had been switched to the Odon sector, where the division of which it was part had shown "gallant aggressiveness".

These sanitized stories gave no indication of how the men were faring or of how many casualties they had suffered, and so families found no clue to the chances that their menfolk would come through—which was all that most wives wanted to know. The casualties could not, of course, be concealed; many families had by now received the fateful telegram telling them that a man had been killed or posted missing. Hospitals in the eastern region were taking a share of the wounded from the front. The first casualties arrived in Cambridge within a week of the D-Day landings and were treated for their wounds in the Leys Annexe. Reporters from the local press were permitted to interview them. Soon after, the Reverend James Good Brown noted in his diary:

> Our general hospitals are now crowded with the patients from France . . . I have seen more than 700 new cases come to one hospital, arriving on two trains, all coming from the front lines in Europe. This is but one hospital near us. War is terrible! To look at those rows and rows of men, 30 men in one ward and some wards with 60 men and it being only one of many hospitals in England—this is to see the result of war.[12]

Many of these casualties were brought back in vessels of the Harwich fleet operated before the war on North Sea crossings by the London and North Eastern Railway Company. They had been converted to hospital ships. One of them, the *Amsterdam*, hit a mine off the French coast on 7th August and there was heavy loss of life among patients and crew, almost all of whom were Harwich, Parkeston or Dovercourt men[13].

At about this time Mass Observation asked its regional correspondents what they thought about the reports from the battlefield. Two of its East Anglian contacts replied as follows:

> The news we are getting now seems to be severely censored and we do not get the "hot" news of the Americans. The facilities given to our war correspondents seem to be too restricted by War Office officialdom. I believe it is accurate as far as it goes, but it doesn't go far enough.

> I don't think we get told lies, either by radio or press, but there are omissions, I'm sure. Many of them must be for security reasons. I sense a falsifying of the perspective in our favour . . . On the whole, I think we get a fair deal about news, having regard to public safety.[14]

While Operation "Goodwood" ran its disastrous course in Normandy, on the central front—between the 3rd Division troops around Caen and the Americans away to the west—every infantry battalion of the 30th Corps was used throughout July to maintain relentless pressure on the German forces, until their resistance at

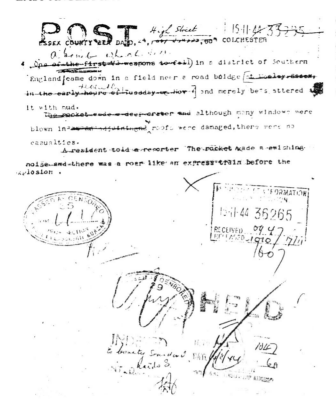

Censorship in action. The text of a story for the *Essex County Standard* was "held" for a week by the Ministry of Information censors and then released for publication with all place-names and actual dates deleted.

Photo courtesy of Mrs Hervey Benham

last began to crumble. The 2nd Essex rejoined the action after their brief respite, and they rounded off this phase with what the battalion officers afterwards called "a copybook battle". On the last day of July they were ordered to capture high ground known as Launay Ridge. The battle was preceded by an RAF bombardment, and the Essex Infantry advanced behind an artillery barrage. One officer wrote:

> The attack was an incredible sight. We walked slowly twenty yards behind the barrage. Not a man even ducked or took cover for a second. Bullets and shrapnel all over the place, but we had wonderful luck and few casualties. Major Holme and Major Browne walked calmly in front of the troops as if on a picnic.[15]

The battalion captured much German equipment and some prisoners. Then, on 2nd August, it was withdrawn to rest.

The 7th Norfolks also joined in this big southward thrust in the *bocage* country south-west of Caen—small fields ringed by earthen banks three or four feet high and overgrown with dense shrubbery. From 14th to 26th July they fought around Noyers, and as the month ended they were moved into reserve.

By 25th July the American forces in the west had regained their breath and were ready to attack. American planes from East Anglian bases assisted with saturation bombing before the advance began; within two days German opposition began to crumble; and on the 30th American armour drove unopposed into Avranches, which was the gateway to Brittany and southern Normandy. It was the first time an Allied attack had made a real break in the German defences.

The US First Army, which had landed on the beaches on D-Day, was now joined by General George S. Patton's Third US Army, which officially became operational on 1st August and immediately began a spectacular advance. German resistance proved less than anticipated; it seemed that nothing could stop Patton's army, and soon it was racing westward towards Paris. There then seemed a chance of catching large numbers of German troops in a "pocket" between these Americans to the south and British, Canadian and US forces to the north.

The Germans, apprehending this danger of encirclement, made a desperate attempt to break out of the trap. They launched a counter-attack, aiming to drive back to the coast at Avranches and so cut the link between the two American armies. This attempt was defeated, and the 7th Battalion of the Royal Norfolks played a notable role in the battle. It was ordered on 6th August to relieve a battalion of the Monmouths in the front line near a scattered hamlet called Sourdevalle. When they arrived there at 5 pm they came under very heavy artillery bombardment which was made worse when Thunderbolts of the Tactical Air Force mistook the battalion headquarters for an enemy strongpoint and strafed it. After that came a major counter attack by the 10th SS Panzer Division, with tanks and infantry, which began just as the Norfolks were relieving the 3rd Monmouths. The two battalions formed a composite force to beat it off, and the situation was saved by the arrival of twenty Sherman tanks of the Fife and Forfar Yeomanry.

In this engagement a Royal Norfolks corporal won the Victoria Cross. Though serving with the regiment, twenty-four-year-old Sidney ("Basher") Bates was not a Norfolk man but from Camberwell. In a charge against the enemy his Bren-gunner—who was his great pal—was killed. Bates seized the light machine-gun and advanced on the Germans, firing from the hip and shouting, "Take that, you bastards, and that, and that."

The Germans poured a hail of machine-gun fire on him as he ran towards them. He was almost immediately wounded and fell to the ground, but he got up and ran forward again, spraying bullets before him as he went. His actions had a clear effect on the enemy riflemen and machine-gunners, but mortar bombs continued to fall around him and he was hit a second time. Again he staggered to his feet and rushed towards the Germans. They appeared nonplussed at their inability to check him and started to withdraw. He was hit a third time by mortar-bomb splinters and sustained a wound that was to prove fatal. He fell to the ground but continued to fire his weapon until his strength failed. By that time the Germans had withdrawn and the situation had been restored[16]. He died two days later.

In this day's fighting at Soudevalle the Norfolks lost thirty-two killed and 144 wounded. The battalion then held on to its positions, in the face of severe shelling and mortar bombardment, for three more days until relieved during the night of 9th/10th August. It withdrew to Le Reculey, where it regrouped into two companies.

Meanwhile a little to the north-east the Canadian First Army fought its way towards Falaise, hoping to link with Patton's men. The American First Army and the British Second Army, in the Caumont area, did their utmost to squeeze the sides of the pocket. Ahead of them lay the challenge of forcing a crossing of the River Orne where it flowed south of Caen. The 7th Royal Norfolk was one of two battalions that led an initial advance. Riding on Churchill tanks of a Royal Armoured Corps regiment, they went forward rapidly with virtually no opposition until on 4th August they neared the river and ran into mortar and shell fire. By last light they had cleared the enemy from the west bank.

Two days were spent in reconnoitring good crossing points. The enemy were in strength on the far bank; later it was found that they were one of the crack divisions of the German army: the 12th SS (Hitler Jugend) Panzer Division. Speed and surprise were essential. The attempt began under cover of darkness on the evening of 6th August. Two battalions of the North Staffordshire Regiment crossed first and then, at 1 am, the Royal Norfolks. They passed through the two other battalions and took up positions on the south side of the village of Grimbosq, at the front of the bridgehead and nearest the enemy.

There was some confused fighting, but the surprise was effective and the Norfolk companies reached their objectives—except one company, which found itself too far to the right. There it came under heavy attack and soon ran out of ammunition and called for assistance, but the other companies could not determine its precise position and so found it impossible to help until daylight should reveal the situation. During the night the lone company beat off three German attacks though it had been unable to dig in, but it suffered heavy losses and, in a fourth attack at 8.15 am, with all its ammunition gone, it was overwhelmed. By that time sixteen had been killed and three-quarters of the remainder wounded. The survivors were taken prisoner.

Later that day (7th August) tanks and guns were brought over into the bridgehead under constant German fire, and at 6.30 pm the enemy launched a fierce counter-attack. The Norfolks took the brunt of heavy fighting, but they knocked out the first three German tanks and eventually the attack was beaten off. The next day saw a bitter day-long struggle in the bridgehead, the Germans counter-attacking seven times in great force; only one Churchill tank survived and the situation of the British troops became precarious, for they were near exhaustion. At 5 pm, however, British reinforcements crossed the river and as daylight faded the Germans withdrew. The Norfolks were relieved that night.

That the bridgehead was held until the reinforcements arrived was attributed largely to the courage of one man, Captain David Jamieson, a six-foot-five-inch twenty-three-year-old bachelor whose home was at Thornham, King's Lynn. He was awarded the Victoria Cross. Jamieson had left Eton in the summer of 1939 intending to go to Cambridge, but had joined up on the outbreak of war. On 7th August he was in command of one of the companies which established the Grimbosq bridgehead, the one which accounted for three German tanks. On the morning of 8th August, when the enemy attacked with a fresh battle group, it penetrated the defences around Jamieson's company and destroyed two of the three tanks giving it support. Jamieson left his trench under close-range fire from enemy arms of all kinds and went over to direct the fire of the remaining tank. He was unable to get in touch with the tank commander by telephone so he climbed up on to it in full view of the enemy. He was wounded in the right eye and left forearm but refused to be evacuated, and when all the other officers had become casualties he reorganized his company, walking among his men in full view of the Germans, for there was no cover. After several hours of confused and bitter fighting the last Germans were driven from the company position.

The enemy counter-attacked three more times that day with infantry and tanks. Jamieson went into the open on each occasion to encourage his men and called up artillery support over his radio. When the Germans withdrew in the evening, they left a ring of dead men and burnt-out tanks around his position.

The operation ended successfully, and after this dramatic episode there was little more action for the 7th Norfolks. For a few days they mopped up and marched north-east of Falaise, where they enjoyed the welcome provided by the French in the area. But on 21st August the battalion CO broke the news that because of its heavy casualties since D-Day it now required major reorganization. 59 Division, being the junior division of 21 Army Group, was to be broken up and its battalions dispersed to provide reinforcements elsewhere. The division concentrated for dispersal on the west bank of the River Orne and there, on 26th August, the 7th Norfolk battalion was officially disbanded. Its A company became part of the 2nd Monmouth, B company went to the 1st Suffolk, C company to the 1st Oxford and Bucks, and D company to the 1st Royal Norfolks.

While the 7th Norfolks were engaged in the bloody battle for a bridgehead across the Orne, the 2nd Essex battalion arrived on the west bank of the river on 8th/9th August, opposite the Forêt de Grimbosq, and joined in hard fighting in difficult terrain. The battle decided, they enjoyed a few quiet days around the middle of the month and swimming parties were able to appreciate the beauties of the lovely River Orne. The Essex men then moved to a village near Falaise, in reserve, and were not involved in the final stages of the destruction of the Germans in the Falaise pocket.

Meanwhile the 1st Norfolks and the 1st Suffolks had been brought westwards with the rest of the 3rd Division to this sector where the German forces were being kept under pressure within a pocket that was being steadily tightened. The Suffolks were ordered to move on the evening of Minden Day, so it was with roses in their head-dress that they set off westwards. They did not arrive until 10th August, by which time the gap between Falaise and the US Third Army had almost been closed. But a German parachute regiment was fighting desperately to cover the retreat of their army, and a new large-scale Allied attack, designed to finish off the enemy forces in the Falaise pocket, commenced on 11th August.

The 1st Suffolk battalion was in bitter, close fighting with the Germans for two days and nights; among its wounded was its commanding officer, Lieutenant-General Gough; and afterwards "for the second time in two months, B company had taken its objective at the price of its own annihilation"[17]. This objective was Flers, a town of around thirteen thousand people about thirty-five miles south of Caen. A Suffolk patrol entered soon after noon on 16th August and contacted the French Resistance forces, and soon the whole town was en fête and the Suffolk men were showered with flowers and kisses[18].

Quite close at hand, on the right of the 1st Suffolks, the 1st Norfolks were in hot pursuit of the Germans near Vire. By 17th August they reached a village called Tinchebray, half way between Vire and Fleurs, which they found relatively undamaged. There they stayed to rest, re-form and train. Reinforcements, including one complete company from the disbanded 7th Battalion of the Royal Norfolks, arrived after a few days and soon the battalion was up to full war establishment again. It remained in Tinchebray for sixteen days.

The Canadians meanwhile entered Falaise on 16th August. It was a small town of about five thousand people which, until this campaign, had been best known as the birthplace of William the Conqueror. The fifteen-mile gap between them and Patton's forces was sealed three days later, by which time some ten thousand German soldiers had perished in the "Falaise pocket". An estimated fifty thousand were taken prisoner. This was judged to be "one of the most crushing and decisive victories ever attained by the Allies during the entire war . . . France was left wide open and undefended all the way to the west wall of the German Reich."[19]

*

CHAPTER EIGHT

Germany's Last Throw

TEN DAYS after the men folk crossed the Channel to confront the Germans face to face, many of their families back in East Anglia experienced a new manifestation of war, the rocket bomb. At Peasenhall and Woolverstone in Suffolk and at Bradwell Bay in Essex on 16th June people heard a loud buzzing sound that was entirely unfamiliar to them, felt a new sensation that the air was throbbing about them, and then saw a strange sight as a dark cigar-shaped object with a tail of pink flame flew overhead. At Peasenhall the first of these rockets exploded in the air over Lodge Farm and blasted a number of houses. What usually happened, however, was that the engine cut out, the noise and the glow ceased, and the rocket glided down to earth, exploding on impact.

By the end of June seventeen of these rockets had reached East Anglia. Most of them fell in Essex, including one near the river in Chelmsford, close to the swimming bath; one at Baker's Hall Farm, Bures; one near Kelvedon; and one at Salcot. Only two caused significant damage: eleven houses were damaged at Crow's Green, Great Saling, on 25th June, and a cottage was set on fire near Braintree on the 30th[1]. Norwich had sight of one of on 26th June, but it passed harmlessly over the city and crashed in open countryside to the north. The same thing happened at Ipswich three weeks later.

The British authorities had known for about two years of the development of these new weapons and had dropped heavy bomb-loads on the sites that were specially prepared for their launch. Sixty-nine of these had been identified by early December 1943 and 140 by the end of May, and RAF and USAAF planes had plastered thousands of tons of explosive on them. East Anglian residents had watched the bombers fly off on these missions (without understanding their special significance) and some on the Essex coast had had the windows of their homes rattled by the reverberations as the bombs fell in the Pas de Calais.

The first rockets exploded in the early hours of 13th June at Gravesend, and during that night twenty-seven arrived, in three waves. The first to reach London hit Stepney on the 16th—the same day that three arrived in East Anglia. London was the main target of the new weapons, and it did not take Londoners long to devise an appropriate name for them; at first they were simply "flying bombs", then "buzz-bombs" because of the noise they made, and finally "doodle-bugs". Later, when they were complemented by a large missile, the two variants were known as V.1s and V.2s. Very little news was released for publication, and nothing concerning the areas in which they fell; references were only to arrivals "in southern England". Local newspapers were forbidden to publish obituary notices of those who were killed. For a few hours the public speculated wildly; some thought the unfamiliar "bangs in the night" indicated an attempt by the Germans to invade Britain. It did not take long, however, for a fairly accurate assessment to be made, despite the censorship. William Stock reported public discussion in Chelmsford:

> One man said he thought perhaps the Germans had been firing rocket-guns. Another man, who had been firewatching all night, mentioned radio-controlled bombs. Somebody else mentioned radio-controlled planes. I had taken my portable radio to work and at 12 o'clock we heard the news of the pilotless planes . . . At lunchtime there was much talk about the new weapon . . . Opinion was more or less unanimous that the Germans would not be able to do much with them, because of the apparent impossibility of using them with any precision. "Just a clever gadget" was one remark.[2]

The Regional Commissioner, Sir Patrick Spens, reported to the Home Office in July:

> During the latter part of the quarter the main subject of conversation has been the flying bomb. Most people did not believe in this weapon, but after the initial surprise the population . . . have on the whole taken the new form of attack philosophically . . . Highly coloured stories are current of the vast damage in London, the large number of people who are evacuating themselves, and the effects upon morale generally. Unfortunately, these stories are spread and encouraged by people who have come from

A German V.1 flying bomb photographed immediately after launching.   *Imperial War Museum*

London. There are at present upward of 80,000, and probably more nearly 100,000, refugees in the region.[3]

For several weeks the government withheld information about the scale of the flying-bomb attack. Churchill decided that the public should be encouraged to sleep in the safest available places at night, and by day to carry on with their normal tasks. "They must have sleep, and they will either wake up well rested or in a better land", he observed[4]. The *East Anglian Daily Times* was among newspapers that published criticism of this policy:

> To the great majority of our people the flying bomb remains something in the nature of a mystery, more or less weird and more or less fearsome merely because of this secrecy. It is within our nature not to be frightened of things we understand . . .

In response to criticism of the censorship the Prime Minister made a statement to the Commons on 6th July. He reported that the Germans had discharged 2,750 flying bombs but that "a very large proportion" had failed to cross the Channel or had been shot down. Most of those that had arrived had fallen on London. The distribution of Morrison steel shelters was stepped up, and about four thousand more were issued in the eastern counties in July, August and September[5].

By mid-July the firing rate settled to an average of well over a hundred per day. In just over a month these weapons killed 3,600 civilians, seriously injured ten

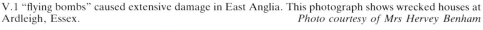

V.1 "flying bombs" caused extensive damage in East Anglia. This photograph shows wrecked houses at Ardleigh, Essex. *Photo courtesy of Mrs Hervey Benham*

Another wrecked house at Ardleigh, Essex, caused by the V.1 "flying bombs".
Photo courtesy of Mrs Hervey Benham

thousand and destroyed thirteen thousand homes. Eighteen V.1s reached East Anglia during July and thirteen during August. When at the end of August the Allied advance in northern France overran the launching bases there, the Germans established new ones in Belgium and Holland and also launched rockets carried pick-a-back on low-flying Heinkels over the North Sea. This put East Anglia in the front line of the attack. On the first day this technique was employed—5th September—four of the nine air-launched missiles landed in East Anglia. Later in the month one damaged the sea-wall at Bradwell and another caused minor damage at the isolation hospital in Saffron Walden. Rockets from the new launching sites in the Netherlands and from the Heinkels, between them, came over the Suffolk and Essex coasts in a continual stream in October and November, by day and night.

The RAF concentrated on shooting down the V.1s, with considerable success—night-fighting Mosquito squadrons from Swannington claimed that they shot down seventy during July and August, and Spitfires and Tempests from Bradwell Bay also did well. Thousands of AA gunners and searchlight troops were moved from the south coast to a belt extending from Great Yarmouth to the Thames. Many of them were girls of the ATS. Not only did they fulfil their duties well, but to Americans at nearby bases "the influx was most beneficial to the Wednesday night dances at the Red Cross Club."[6]

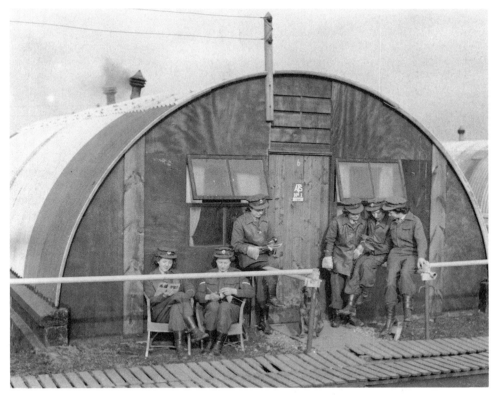

ATS girls of an AA Command Mixed Heavy Battery outside their Nissen hut near Orford.
Imperial War Museum

At first they were housed under canvas with few amenities, usually miles from any village. The weather was bitterly cold and wet, and a great construction project was rushed through at a cost of two million pounds to improve conditions. More than two hundred tippers were constantly employed on the movement of rubble as fifty miles of roads were laid and foundations put down for 3,500 Nissen huts. By Christmas everyone had been provided with hut accommodation, four hostels had been opened and the troops were enjoying films and ENSA visits.

The new defences became operational on 28/29th October and soon produced spectacular results. Houses for miles inland were shaken by the mighty barrage sent up by more than 1,100 3.7-inch ack-ack guns of this defence force. James Good Brown noted in his diary that at night the airmen on the Ridgewell base could see the "fireworks" in the sky and hear the guns very clearly from twenty miles' distance[7]. Night fighters also joined in the defence.

The attacks continued night after night, and the defenders steadily improved their score. Soon more than half the V.1s approaching the coast were being shot down into the sea. The night of 10/11th November provided an example. Twenty-six rockets came in a first wave towards the coast between Southwold and Felixstowe, and all but one were shot down; that one was destroyed by a fighter plane near Chelmsford. Later during the night twelve more V.1s were launched. Six were shot down by the guns between Aldeburgh and Clacton, one was shot down by a fighter near Southwold and an eighth fell victim to a fighter at Dagenham[(8)].

But many of the bombs got through. On 18th October four people were killed and eight seriously injured when a V.1 crashed on a housing estate in Ipswich, destroying fourteen houses and badly damaging four hundred others. Civil defence workers toiled all night in the rubble, with searchlights concentrated on the scene. On the 22nd a farmer's wife and her four children had a remarkable escape when a

AA Command switched batteries from the south to the east coast to combat V.1 rockets. This picture shows gunners of the HAA battery, 127 Regiment, racing to man guns at Southwold during a morning alert. *Imperial War Museum*

V.1 which had been hit by gunfire cut through three large elm trees and exploded in the middle of Blacklands Farm, in Sudbourne, Suffolk. It was 1.30 am and the children were trapped in their beds, but they emerged unscratched. The farmer and his brother-in-law were injured and taken to hospital; cattle in the farm buildings were killed. On the last night of October:

> thousands of families in East Anglia left their breakfast tables to take shelter as the massed A.A. guns on the coast sent up a wall of bursting shells. Watchers saw several bombs blow up in mid-air after having been hit.

The V.1 attacks continued during November. The *East Anglian Daily Times* reported that on the night of 10th November:

> watchers saw the whole sky glow like a sunset as bombs blew up in mid-air and disintegrated with deafening explosions . . . Spectators cheered as the guns or fighters shot down fly-bombs as they came over. Searchlights were busy directing fighters and guns.

There was a great deal of feeling in the Essex rural districts because they had no sirens to warn them of the approach of flying bombs, and only if the wind was in the right direction might the wail of a siren in a nearby town be heard.

On 8th November the German radio broadcast:

> The British government has so far concealed from its people that a more effective, more telling, and therefore more dangerous long-range weapon [the V.2] has been in action, in addition to the so-called flying-bomb . . .

Again, however, the news had quickly spread widely among the public, despite official censorship. William Stock had noted in his diary in mid-September that there was rumour and talk of V.2s in Chelmsford[(9)]. Churchill confirmed the facts on 10th November in a statement to the Commons. The V.2 rockets, he said, had been coming "for the last few weeks". They flew faster than the speed of sound and they had landed at widely scattered points in Britain. The *East Anglian Daily Times* led its front page:

V.2 ROCKET LIKE 'FLYING TELEGRAPH POLE'

Eye-witness stories: Hospitals, churches & schools hit

The first V.2 had landed at Chiswick in west London on 8th September, and a second one landed at Epping almost immediately afterwards. In the first phase they were aimed at London, but many fell short in Essex. One of the first of these hit Weeley in north Essex in November, in the middle of one night. It crashed alongside the bridge near the station and damaged many roofs and broke many windows, but caused no casualties. Later, many exploded in the sea and in mid-air. Others landed in Clacton and between Fingringhoe and Rowhedge (the nearest to Colchester), and one burst immediately over Brightlingsea; windows suffered extensively but there were no serious casualties.

The first V.2 in Suffolk was at Hoxne on 25th September, and the first in

Norfolk was at Ranworth, near Norwich, the following day. Between 25th September and 12th October many appeared to be aimed deliberately at East Anglia, and thirty landed there. There were three in Norfolk on 27th September—at Horsford, Whitlingham and Beighton; and three on the 29th—at Hemsby, Coltishall and Thorpe. That at Hemsby landed in a minefield on the shore and the resultant blast damaged sixty-six homes and a couple of shops. The one at Thorpe landed in a field of sugar beet and twenty-five nearby houses were slightly damaged. Others caused slight damage to the parish churches at Heeton St Lawrence and Spixworth. A few farmhouses in different places suffered badly, and in total several hundred homes were shattered. On 3rd October five V.2s arrived in one day, including one at Hellesdon which damaged four hundred houses over a two-mile radius and another at Hopton which blasted twenty-eight houses. The following day eight people were injured when one exploded at Rockland St Mary.

From 12th October the bombardment was again concentrated on London and also on Antwerp, which was by then in Allied hands. Many rockets still crossed the East Anglian coast, however; one strayed as far as Mundesley, on the north Norfolk coast; another landed close to Mildenhall; and a third at Fulbourn. One, on 18th December, hit the cliff-face five hundred yards south-west of Clacton Pier. The one which did most damage exploded in Chelmsford at 1.30 am on 19th December, killing thirty-nine people, injuring 152 and doing a great deal of damage at the Hoffman and Marconi factories. Sixty other properties were seriously damaged and 340 slightly.

The Air Ministry released more detailed information about the V.2 during December:

> It weighs about 12 tons, has a warhead of 2,000 lbs of explosives, travels at 3,000 mph, and its present range is about 200 miles. It takes about five minutes to reach England from the launching—presumably in Holland—to the moment of impact. It is 46 feet long, 5½ feet in diameter, streamlined, with a sharply pointed nose, and carries four large external stabilising fins at right angles to each other at the rear. The rumbling sound, like thunder, after the explosion, is the noise of the passage of the rocket through the air. It is not heard until after the explosion as the rocket is travelling so much faster than sound.

From some parts of the east coast it was possible to watch V.2s being launched in Holland. Just before dawn on 10th December observers at Cromer watched several thin red streaks shooting up into the sky and disappearing into the stratosphere.

There was no possibility of shooting down this new generation of German missiles, so efforts were concentrated on finding and attacking their firing pads. Many East Anglian airfields joined in this task. Matlask sent Spitfires; and Mendlesham, Rattlesden and Wethersfield were among the American bases which participated.

The coming of the rockets produced other problems for those living in East Anglia. Back in September 1943 the government had made contingency plans for evacuation of children and their mothers from London. Schedules had been drawn up, trains arranged, a billeting scheme sketched out, and lodging allowances of three shillings a week for a child evacuee and five shillings a week for an adult fixed. In theory it needed only a Whitehall voice to order "Go ahead" when the bombs began to arrive.

In the event it did not work out like that. The trains ran to schedule, the billeting officers in the reception areas were ready, but most of the householders who were expected to open their doors to the refugees did not do so. One explanation of their attitude was that the billeting allowances did not cover the cost of food; but a more potent reason was that they had taken in evacuees before and the experience had poisoned the wells of compassion[10].

The first big wave of evacuees arrived in the eastern counties during the week that ended on Friday, 14th July. A retired school-mistress living in Peasenhall described some of the events of that day:

> One day we were a "prohibited area" and the next we were receiving evacuees! That was on July 14th. I had been informed by the Billeting Officer that I had to put one up. I asked for a boy, if possible. The evacuees were to arrive at 3 p.m. At the last moment I heard that they were delayed. We expected fifty. They were to be received in a small room adjoining the village chapel. At the entrance to the chapel the prospective hostesses were gathered in groups discussing the new inmates to their homes. There was a universal desire to choose "suitable" ones! At 7 p.m. the buses came in sight. When all the children got out we found that only about thirty had come.
>
> They were in charge of one of their regular schoolmistresses who seemed to know them all very well. The children had been travelling all day and were obviously very tired. They nearly all carried paper parcels as well as small cases, and also paper bags containing the remains of the lunch, etc., supplied to them by the authorities. Intense sympathy was felt by all for these pathetic, tired-looking youngsters.
>
> The proportion of girls was high. There were only eight boys, the eldest being fourteen, the rest were much younger. There was not one "single" child. All were in couples, threes, fours and fives, and none of the families wanted to be separated! This made rather a problem as most of the homes they were going to were only small houses and cottages. But people rose nobly to the occasion . . .[11]

This school-mistress took one little girl into her home and later recorded:

> I was very impressed at the way they had been fitted out with new nighties, vests, stockings by their local Women's Institute, and everything was clean and tidy . . . I had to stay with her until she fell asleep. She was full of fears, the result of their flying bomb experiences, as well as a very nervous and highly-strung disposition . . .

After some weeks' experience she added that "on the whole" local people were very kind to the evacuees, but found many of them terribly restless, easily bored and not well disciplined. She reported that those who remained in the country looked much better than when they arrived.

These children who went to Peasenhall were part of a surge of 146,000 people out of London during a nine-day period. In some places the first arrivals had appeared three or four weeks earlier, an unofficial exodus of those who had friends or relatives willing to accommodate them. The Evacuation and Billeting Committee in Cambridge was told that ten thousand had arrived in the town by 10th July. Rather more than a thousand of these, including about a hundred unaccompanied children, had arrived under the official government scheme.

To find homes for these, billeting officers had had to issue compulsory orders. Some of these orders had been defied and the Cambridge committee authorized prosecutions. The Mayor, warning that more official parties must be expected almost daily, appealed to residents:

> Many have not only accepted, but welcomed, persons brought by the billeting officers. Thanks must be given to the officers for their tact and patience in a difficult and far from pleasant duty. Efforts are made to spread the burden fairly, irrespective of persons or position . . . I appeal to the public to welcome evacuees brought by the billeting officer. A welcome is better than compulsion for both sides. Official parties are not composed entirely of "nice little girls of nine", but this is a duty we are compelled to carry out during the present circumstances.

Cambridge Town Council discussed the problem, and one councillor complained that big houses in the town had escaped their obligations. The Mayor, defending the billeting officers, replied that many of the evacuees had as strong an antipathy to the folk who lived in big houses as *they* had to the Londoners. "These people say 'We won't go in there—we want to go in an ordinary house'", the Mayor declared.

Similar difficulties arose virtually everywhere. The *East Anglian Daily Times* reported on 14th July that thousands of emergency ration cards had been issued to the stream of evacuees who had arrived in Bury St Edmunds and the surrounding district, but finding billets in the town had become an acute problem. The chief billeting officer, Miss Lees, and her staff worked "at top pressure and under considerable difficulties", but some evacuees were left without billets. Rest centres were opened in schools and halls as a temporary measure, while a street-by-street census was taken of housing space and numbers of occupants. Many householders replied that they had a full house because they had taken in relatives and friends who had evacuated themselves from other areas.

One Bury St Edmunds resident, Miss Winifred Last, noted in her diary at this time:

> Billeting is causing much trouble in West Suffolk. People have had evacuees once and some say they would prefer to go to prison rather than do it again. Most of them cannot afford the wear and tear on furniture, linen, crockery, saucepans, etc., as they have barely enough for themselves. And they haven't the surplus energy to look after additional children, or the desire to have their privacy invaded by persons with whom they have probably nothing in common. Usually, too, it means over-crowding . . .[12]

From all over East Anglia came similar reports. When the Clare Rural District Council met on Friday, 14th July the clerk, Mr R. F. Buckley, described a nightmarish week. On the Monday he had been told to prepare to receive about a hundred mothers and children from London, and he had asked the WVS ladies to work with parish billeting officers to find the necessary accommodation. When the evacuees arrived on the Thursday there had been only four voluntary offers of accommodation—out of three thousand homes, spread over twenty-five parishes. The clerk told his council that the evacuees had been clean, respectable and well cared for. "It was almost an insult to subject such people to a medical examination", he declared. "They were all free from complaint."

He went on to describe the search for accommodation. One worker had visited every big house in her area and had got no response, while the attitude of many cottagers had been "When they are in the big houses, we'll take ours." By 9 pm, the clerk said, most of the evacuees had been accommodated, but some mothers and children had had to remain in rest centres all night.

Some members of the Clare council adopted a defensive attitude. The chairman, Mr Frank Sainsbury—a man who divided his time between public service and a developing grocery business—thought it was not fully appreciated how many people were already in the district. The clerk would allow no such evasion; the population was below that pre-war, he pointed out. A councillor who was a parish priest made much of the water shortage in the area. Another clergyman admitted that he had three vacant bedrooms, but said he already had two evacuees and if he accepted more it would mean that he would be unable to leave his rectory; he thought there were empty farmhouses that could taken over. When someone remarked that these had no water supply—unless it was carried some distance—a third clergyman joined in: "Well, if they can't put up with it, let them go back to London. I think it would be the best thing for them."

Not every member shared these attitudes. The representative of Stanstead, Mr F. Clary, said bluntly: "Why should people whose lives are personally safe not be compelled to accommodate less fortunate people? In eight houses I know there are seventeen bedrooms not used, and they will not be used until there is compulsion."

The councillors must have been shamed into action, for they left the meeting to see what they could do in their various parishes and later in the day the clerk told the *East Anglian Daily Times* that the response had been "magnificent". Many residents had gone to the local rest centre and taken families to their homes, and eight out of every ten of the evacuees had been taken into homes in Clare itself.

Other places either had a better response to the initial appeals or managed to draw a veil over their difficulties. At Beccles the Mayor and Mayoress, Alderman and Mrs Allden Owles, welcomed the arrivals; they were taken in cars and lorries to five centres where the WVS served them light refreshments, after which they went to their new homes. At Bungay part of the same train-load was similarly welcomed and billeted. At Thetford too the Mayor, Mr A. S. Law, and Mayoress met the special train and the WVS took the arrivals in private cars to the Guildhall and provided them with tea, after which girls from Thetford Grammar School helped them with their luggage.

On Monday, 17th July the *East Anglian Daily Times* published a leading article:

> We know something of the difficulties of this sudden billeting—the upsets it may occasion to settled home life. But we refuse to condone selfishness where it refuses to offer succour of this kind to people blasted from their homes or forced to leave them through imminent danger. What can be said of anyone able to do so who turns away, it may be, the wife or children of a soldier or sailor who is offering his all in order to save the life and the homes of these curmudgeon folk? There is only one answer to that. It is that such a person's skin is not worth the saving . . .

Others used stronger language. On the day after this editorial comment was printed, the clerk to Depwade RDC, Mr G. S. Scarlett, asserted: "Anyone refusing to take evacuees when they have room is committing a crime. If they refuse and the evacuees go back and are killed they are guilty of murder." It was no wonder that he had strong feelings, for he had just spent a whole week trying to get twenty-five familes billeted in Diss. According to his colleague, the chairman of the Depwade Evacuation Committee, Mr F. H. Easton, some of the councillors were themselves among the "back-sliders", and there were many large houses in the villages occupied only by man and wife, who had not volunteered to help. Another councillor, the Reverend J. F. Spink, expressed sympathy with those who, he said, had received evacuees into their homes in the past but would not volunteer again while there were dozens of people with many spare rooms who had never taken any, and who told falsehoods time after time to excuse themselves.

The other side to the argument was put publicly by the assistant billeting officer of Witnesham. During the first big evacuation, he wrote, two hundred evacuees had been accommodated in his village. This time:

> . . . where five billets were freely offered on the first occasion, it was difficult to find one. Why? I make no accusation or assertions, but let those in authority who consider the reception areas cruel come and hear some of the true reports of conduct during the first evacuation. Then, if the hosts are to blame, punish them and publish it. If not, publish the facts and let the remainder of England know the cause of the present trouble.

This was rather cryptic but other correspondents were quick to elaborate. A farmer who had made a furnished cottage and a job available to a London evacuee family during the 1939–40 evacuation reported that they had left when it suited them, taking every stick of furniture that had been lent them. And another assistant billeting officer who had a twenty-one-year-old woman billeted in his own home recalled that she "never attempted to lift a cup and saucer because 'the government paid for her keep' and it was the duty of the householder to wait on her".

That there were such people and such behaviour was undeniable; but it was equally true that there were others who displayed heroic qualities. A Ministry of Health welfare officer who visited Cambridge and was told of doors shut against the evacuees described her work in the areas where the V.1s were landing. She told a meeting:

The attitude of the average person is simply amazing. It is amazing how they are standing up to it . . . It goes on day and night. It is so different from the blitz of 1940–41, when you were certain of respite in the daytime. This goes on all the time. And one gets exhausted.

She thought that if only she could get her message across to the general public, even the most hard-hearted would open their doors. "Old people and children need help. They need rest. They will be grateful for a floor to sleep on."

More evacuees arrived, and the problems did not go away. At Newmarket during July the clerk, Mr J. Crabb, reported that letters had been sent to 150 householders, and the "next morning infuriated householders called at the Council Offices and objected violently for one reason or another to evacuees being billeted on them". Miss Winifred Last, who knew Newmarket well, offered an explanation in her diary:

> Horse-racing is in full swing. Stablemen never earn enough to keep families, and so wives are compelled to take in racing men, who are lavish with money and food. One offered my brother thirty shillings the other evening for the privilege of spending a night in one of his armchairs. I daresay many are paying 20 shillings for bed and breakfast. If the owners of the little bath-less boxes called houses in Newmarket can get 20 shillings for a very temporary inconvenience, they will hardly take the bread from their children's mouths because the government have not made fairer and more adequate provision for evacuees.[13]

Newmarket was among many places in East Anglia where householders were prosecuted when they refused to comply with compulsory billeting orders.

On the whole there were fewer problems in Norfolk than in the other eastern counties, at least in the early phase of evacuation. During July over three thousand arrived by train in Norwich, Diss, King's Lynn, Thetford and Lowestoft and many were distributed to the villages. At the end of the month the *Eastern Daily Press* declared that things had gone fairly smoothly, though it added: "It is difficult to escape the impression of a lack of grasp in London of the difficulties at the receiving end of so large an exodus."

As more and more evacuees flooded in, however, the same problems developed as elsewhere. It was alleged that the big houses were not taking their share; in the St Faith's and Aylsham rural district, where there were twenty-nine parsonages—usually the biggest houses in their villages—critics declared that only nine of them had accepted evacuees. By mid-August the Norwich town clerk was threatening compulsory billeting. Many of the evacuees arriving at this time had to sleep in rest centres while pressure was applied on unwilling householders. The trains brought more each week. Even Great Yarmouth, which had itself been an evacuation area until this time, was now expected to accept evacuees. By the end of August Norwich had absorbed 2,400 in city homes, and there was talk that 2,400 more would be coming.

Just as the pressures were becoming intolerable, government statements at the end of the first week of September suggested that flying-bomb attacks should end

107

within a fortnight. It was decided to suspend evacuation of organized parties forthwith. Those already evacuated were urged to stay in the reception areas until more houses could be repaired—about 870,000 had been damaged in London, as well as many schools. The evacuees, however, showed themselves anxious to leave their billets and go home, and within a week or so the trek back to London had begun. The *East Anglian Daily Times* reported on 13th September:

> The Cambridge train which arrived at Kings Cross at 12.30 yesterday was filled almost entirely by returning evacuees . . . Kings Cross received many evacuees from the Cambridge and Eastern Counties area. Fur-draped women with private school sons and fine suitcases contrasted with small urchins carrying gas-masks.

The villages of Suffolk, Cambridgeshire and Norfolk resumed their more placid ways.

Jeep rides were a popular event for children invited to a USAAF station. American Red Cross's Joan Smith had an overload of evacuees from London and other large cities who were lodged in the countryside surrounding Grafton Underwood.

Photo via Quenton Bland

CHAPTER NINE

Problems on the Farms

EVEN THE farmers admitted that the harvest of 1944 was a good one—the fourth in a row. A columnist in the *East Anglian Daily Times*, "Pightle", commented in April, that "it is abnormal for farmers not to grumble about the season, but really there are few complaints . . .". Nature was kind; the year began with favourable conditions for getting ahead with all operations on the land and, although something of a drought developed during the spring and frost damaged some of the soft fruit, prospects overall were good as harvest approached.

January produced abnormal growth of winter wheat. By early February spring oats and peas had gone in well and there was a good seed-bed ready for barley. Inspecting their fields in late April, most farmers saw that the oats they had planted during the last week in January were just showing in the ridges. They worried none the less: the spring corn seemed slow in coming through and fields and pastures looked rather bare.

By late May sugar-beet hoeing was in hand and this kept everyone busy for some weeks. Things still looked good in mid-July when a spokesman for the East Anglian farmers reported that the harvest would be later than usual, but this would give the grain a chance to swell and would level up the backward growths. Sugar beet, potatoes and roots were making rapid headway, and the prospects for winter keep were greatly improved. By the early days of August the *East Anglian Daily Times* was able to assert that wheat was one of the finest crops for ten years, the beet crop was estimated to be up to normal, barley was up to average and only the potato crops showed signs of being patchy, because of drought.

The harvest came on with a rush towards the end of August, wheat changing from the green to the full-ripe stage in a week, and well before the end of September crops had been safely gathered in most areas. The eastern counties escaped heavy rain which further north ruined crops left in the open after they had been cut in excellent condition.

Nevertheless, when the year ended the Norfolk NFU secretary, Mr J. F. Wright, declared that it had been a less profitable year than others during the war and he asserted that "many farmers have worked without net profit".

The remarkable wartime expansion of most types of farming had continued. Since 1939 the total arable acreage in East Suffolk had increased by 32,070 acres. Farmers there, checking their records for the ten months to May 1944 and making comparisons with the same period a year earlier, found they had produced fifty-two per cent more wheat and sixty-nine per cent more rye. In Norfolk a major reclamation scheme was completed: fifteen hundred acres of marshland between the sea-bank and the villages of Snettisham and Wolferton had been drained and planted with crops by the War Agricultural Committee. An agricultural correspondent of the *Eastern Daily Press* asserted that the stage had been reached at which "it is impossible to envisage a further big expansion of the county's arable acreage . . . It is generally agreed that farmers have as much arable land as they can manage with present labour supplies and machinery". In Essex not much above half the pre-war acreage remained as grassland, while wheat acreage had increased by twenty-five per cent, potato acreage by sixty-nine per cent and sugar-beet acreage by sixty-two per cent.

Farms in the eastern counties still carried large numbers of cattle: no fewer than 81,585, compared with 68,817 pre-war. These included 28,831 cows in milk and in calf. The number actually increased during 1944, and the keen demand for pedigree stock was one of the outstanding features of the farming year. During the six winter months to 31st March, 1944, dairy farmers sold 7,165,000 gallons of milk, against a target of 6,800,000 gallons[1]. It was Ministry of Agriculture policy at this time to foster dairy cattle and to use the price mechanism to discourage the feeding of bullocks, sheep and pigs.

Despite the increase in cattle many East Anglian farmers were convinced that Ministry policy was having a serious effect on the fertility of the soil. Their views were forcefully, and repeatedly, put by the *East Anglian Daily Times* agricultural commentator, "Lavengro":

> Practically every farmer of experience is saying that fertility is receding. Nothing but a general return of grazing cattle, sheep and pigs will tend towards the rehabilitation of the soil. The dissociation of folded sheep from arable farming, notwithstanding that they are absolutely indispensable for the light land, is inexplicable. It has been so badly treated that it now stands in needs of careful nursing . . .

Early in the year there were excellent reports of lambing flocks, with a heavy fall of strong healthy lambs; the only problem seemed to be the poor prospects for feed. In the farmers' view, the Ministry of Agriculture was working with the Ministries of Food and Supply to keep the prices of mutton and wool of arable sheep well below remunerative levels.

Certainly many flocks of sheep and herds of pigs were given up. At the Diss Lamb Sale in July the ten thousand entry of lambs and ewes compared with a pre-war average of about twenty thousand. The auctioneer, Mr Clement Gaze, was greatly worried at the extent and manner in which flocks were disappearing. Two were being dispersed in that sale and three more in the August sale a few weeks later. He would have had even less business in Diss if some old-established sales had not been abandoned during the previous five yars, at Kesgrave, Saxmundham, Halesworth, Beccles and East Harling (which had seldom had fewer than twenty thousand head).

The annual sale held under the Suffolk Breed Society's auspices at Bury St

Edmunds in August saw a good trade in Suffolk sheep—which was attributed to the formation of new flocks—but this did not make good the dispersals. Later in the year "Lavengro" was still complaining about the decline in sheep—"now so few that there is barely one arable flock where there used to be ten".

He was also a staunch champion of the horse on the farm. He showed contempt for the Ministry of Agriculture's vigorous efforts to encourage mechanization, referring to "the dictum of men who have never farmed for a living". After visiting the Ipswich Horse Show in September he declared that there was no immediate likelihood of Suffolk horses being displaced. His views were widely shared for there was considerable interest in Suffolk horses at this show and sale, with buyers from all over the country wanting working horses for their farms as well as breeding stock. "Breeders in the course of discussions on the future were not disturbed at the advent of the combine", according to "Lavengro".

To be certain of seeing a ploughman at work in the traditional way in the eastern counties, however, it had already become advisable to attend one of the ploughing matches that were organized to raise money for local hospitals, for the Red Cross or for the Prisoners-of-War Fund. These matches were very popular; 120 ploughmen competed at the opening event of the season at South Lopham in April.

A Norwich clergyman, the Reverend Willis M. Feast, put the cat among the pigeons when he wrote a short but provocative letter to the editor of the *Eastern Daily Press* in March:

> Our farmers in England today are bad farmers. Why? Because they have not used the machine as other industries have done. It is disgraceful that hedging and ditching, compost, root lifting, to mention a few obvious instances, have not been mechanised.

One farmer replied that this accusation reached "the giddy heights of bad taste" in view of the efforts the farmers were making. Men did the jobs better than machines, he declared, and they would need to have the jobs when the war was over. At this time there were about 250 combines in Norfolk, and some of the farmers who were making good use of them spoke up at a Norwich conference in May called by the County War Agricultural Committee to stimulate wider interest in modern methods of grain harvesting, drying and storage. Among the three hundred farmers present, however, the opposite view was widely held, and one of them expressed it thus: "Are we going to try to run the countryside with as few people as possible in it, or are we going to have a healthy countryside with as many people as possible in it? That is the fundamental question."

Another development was beginning that seemed likely to have profound consequences. There were plans to carry electricity into those parts of the countryside still without a supply, and a new showroom was opened in Norwich in March specifically "to foster the growing interest of agriculturalists in electricity as an aid to farming".

111

From September onwards things did not go so well on the farms. Bad autumn weather set work back. The biggest problem, however, was shortage of suitable labour. Most of Britain's regular force of agricultural workers had been exempted from the armed services, and they were supplemented as 1944 began by more than seventy-five thousand land girls. A third of these were employed by the War Agricultural Executive committees and many thousands more in the Women's Timber Corps or on gardening work. That left less than half the women in private employment on farms, and most of these were milkers. Farmers in general, and East Anglian farmers in particular, were still unwilling to accept that women could perform every kind of farm work.

From early June to September there were farm holiday camps in a number of Suffolk villages—Lavenham, Hundon, Mildenhall and Rougham among them——where young volunteers of both sexes lived under canvas and worked for thirty-six to forty hours a week for a shilling an hour (ninepence an hour if they were

Five land girls from a Suffolk WLA hostel hoeing the land of an independent farmer who was short of labour. The girl in front was in charge of the team, which had been fully trained by the War Agricultural Committee.   *Imperial War Museum*

Trying to encourage the public to spend their holidays at a farm camp with this advertisement, July 1944.

East Anglian Daily Times

Spend your holiday at a farm camp

You get paid for it and you ought to earn more than your keep. You'll have healthy work by day, fun and company every evening. And you'll be helping to feed Britain.

Write (over 17's only) for details of pay and accommodation to:

Your nearest Regional Organiser. Get his address from your Head Post Office.

This space is presented by *Boots* in the interests of food production for a healthy nation

BOOTS PURE DRUG CO. LTD.

under nineteen). From this wage they had twenty-eight shillings a week deducted to cover their keep. They hoed, weeded, planted, harvested, cut vegetables and picked fruit. Apart from their modest payment they received a railway voucher for a return journey at single fare plus free transport of their bicycles and—for 1944 only—a special issue of fifteen extra clothing coupons if they put in eighty-eight hours. The scheme worked well—Ipswich volunteers, who were organized in a "Land Club", put in a total of 3,500 hours' work during June, and the Suffolk Boy Scouts Association harvest camp, based at Long Melford, provided 5,389 hours' work on thirteen farms.

Other camps were organized for fruit and pea picking and potato lifting from July to the end of September, including a tented camp with marquees at Mildenhall. Cambridgeshire operated fourteen such camps, taking three hundred school-children every week to help with fruit picking, most coming from bombed areas of London.

The Minister of Agriculture warned in July that there would be no help from the army—"it has other work to do", he said. The county War Agricultural Executive committees supervised the labour arrangements, entering into contracts with the Women's Land Army, with land clubs and schools and various civilian organizations, and with parties of Irish immigrants. Even so, when the harvest was in full swing in mid-August there was insufficient labour. When, after a full week's work in September, there was still a great deal of corn lying out in the fields, the government was blamed. One of its offences had been to decree that Double Summer Time should be extended to 17th September. Farmers argued that young men in the harvest gangs who finished work at 5 pm BDST were "refusing to work beyond three o'clock by the sun"; and they did not want to work overtime because the extra earnings would have taken them above the figure at which they were liable to pay income tax.

Whatever the reasons, in mid-November many thousands of acres of sugar beet were still in the ground, and Lord Ailwyn told the House of Lords that sixty to eighty per cent of it would still be in the ground at Christmas. Some sugar-beet factories, he declared, were talking of closing down because they had no supplies. The Duke of Norfolk, Under-Secretary at the Ministry of Agriculture, explained that the potato harvest was being given priority because potatoes were more likely to come to harm if left out after the end of November. That needed another week or two, then he hoped more labour would be available for the beet and practically the whole crop should be lifted before the end of January.

Despite this assurance it began to seem unlikely that potato supplies would reach the Greater London area before Christmas, and the government moved in soldiers to help to riddle and load them in Suffolk, Cambridgeshire, Norfolk, Lincolnshire, Huntingdonshire and Peterborough.

Delays built up. At the beginning of December autumn cultivations were sadly in arrear and ploughing seriously behind on heavy land. Not more than three-quarters of the average acreage of wheat had been planted, and the farmers declared that little chance remained of getting it in. Still only just over half the sugar-beet crop had been dealt with, and it was proving to be a poor tonnage, with low sugar content. The *East Anglian Daily Times* commentator, "Pightle", offered this verdict on the year's farming:

> The year will long be remembered as one full of difficulties and extremes. Prolonged drought, continuing well into the summer, meant a general shortage of keep, with hay and stover crops much below normal, leaving us in a bad place for the winter. Harvesting operations were long and costly . . . Very little autumn corn has been planted, owing to the soil being unfit for cultivations. All land work is much in arrears, including harvesting of a very indifferent crop of sugar beet.

The labour difficulties were sometimes exacerbated when binders and other machinery broke down, for, in "Pightle's" words, "spare parts are the very devil to come by in these days".

the Felixstowe Young Farmers' Club, in aid of
The Walk, by kind permission of Mr. J. A.

Levington Drawing Match.   *East Anglian Daily Times*

There was one other important source of farm labour, but one around which intense controversy developed during 1944. The year began with over fifty thousand Italian prisoners-of-war housed in camps in East Anglia, and most of them had been employed on the farms. When the Italian government, having surrendered in 1943, went on to declare itself a "co-belligerant" of the Allies, prisoners-of-war in Britain were given the chance to enrol in an Italian labour corps.

This was organized on a military basis with Italian NCOs. The volunteers were issued with green battledress with "Italy" shoulder flashes and enjoyed better pay and treatment than those who did not volunteer. This development was announced by the War Minister in the Commons during May, and the first reaction from the eastern counties, voiced by one of its MPs, was anxiety that it might mean losing some labour from the farms because the Italians might in future be employed on a wider range of duties. The Minister replied curtly: "Quite likely." In fact about fifteen thousand Italians were employed on farms in the region during the latter months of 1944.

They were well distributed, often in camps just released by the Services. Thus a camp near Halstead, Essex, which had been built for the US army, became in the summer of 1944 the headquarters of "129 Italian Labour Battalion, Ashford Lodge", and five hundred prisoners-of-war moved into its fifty huts. Around it were

115

satellite camps at Bulmer, Borley Green, Liston Hall, Boxford and Stoke-by-Nayland, each with about a hundred prisoners.

During 1944 there gradually built up an outcry about the performance of some of the Italians, powerfully stimulated when nearly a thousand of them went on strike at one camp during the harvest period. Farmers who had been promised their services were immediately up in arms, one asserting that Fascists had stirred up the trouble. The strikers were put in strict confinement and part of their punishment was some meals of only bread and water.

At a Newmarket Urban District Council meeting on 30th October members were strongly critical of the amount of freedom allowed to the Italians and they sent a protest to the War Office. The subject was raised in Parliament several times during the following days, first by the Minister of Agriculture, Mr R. S. Hudson, who told Mr Somerset de Chair, the Member for South-West Norfolk, that there were about a thousand Italian prisoners-of-war working in Norfolk, and he was not satisfied with the output of some of them. Where complaints of unsatisfactory work or conduct were made by a farmer or the foreman in charge of a gang, disciplinary action was taken by the camp commandant, in accordance with the Geneva Convention. But the Minister added that several hundred more Italians were on their way to Norfolk.

In the Lords the Under-Secretary, the Duke of Norfolk, insisted that some Italians were good and others worked better when there were only two or three working as individuals, not in gangs. He conceded that there had been justifiable complaint about one camp in East Anglia, and said that the worst offenders had been put under sterner discipline.

Mr Somerset de Chair returned to the subject, using stronger language: "Those Fascists who boasted that they would march through the streets of Cairo are strolling about the streets of Swaffham, to the annoyance of the inhabitants", he said. The Norfolk executive of the National Farmers' Union called for Italian labour to be supervised by guards and foremen. Several speakers at its meeting alleged that the prisoners-of-war were unsupervised and did very little work, and in some places they wandered freely about villages and laid snares for game.

The War Office made a firm pronouncement on 24th November reaffirming the relaxed conditions applicable to Italians who had chosen to join the labour corps. Clearly referring to the stream of complaints, it declared: "As a result of recent experience, it has been found desirable to emphasize rules which have been in operation since privileges were granted to Italians who agreed to cooperate with us in the war effort." They were allowed to talk to civilians and to accept invitations to private houses; they were allowed to exercise within five miles of their camp or billet up to 10 pm; cycles provided by their employers might be used for pleasure, with the employers' permission; they might enter shops to make small purchases and might visit cinemas. They were not allowed, however, to enter dance halls and pubs, to use public vehicles when off duty, to enter any voluntary canteens or to make unwelcome approaches to civilians. The War Office said the public should bring to notice of camp commandants any abuse of these privileges.

The critics were not mollified. Lord Somerleyton told a meeting of the Suffolk County Agricultural Committee on 5th December: "The matter is a scandal in our district." He asked, "Can't you stop the food of those who don't work? No work, no food—that is reasonable. They are having it all their own way." The chairman said the committee was doing its best. Mr P. C. Loftus, the MP for Lowestoft, asked the Minister of Agriculture in the Commons to withdraw Italians altogether from Suffolk and Norfolk farms and to substitute more efficient labour; he declared there was growing indignation in the region. The Minister replied: "There would be much greater indignation and protests if I withdrew Italian prisoners."

At one stage during this controversy Mr Somerset de Chair suggested that German prisoners-of-war would be more acceptable than Italians. A rapidly increasing number of Germans were arriving at camps in Britain: six thousand in a matter of weeks after the D-Day invasion of Normandy, and by October a total of ninety-five thousand. In view of the harvest problems, commandants of the German prisoner-of-war camps were asked to submit lists of "reliable" prisoners —that is, those without known National Socialist affiliations—and about four thousand of them were sent to work on farms in East Anglia. Others were moved in later, as fast as suitable accommodation could be provided for them.

The Germans were more closely guarded than the collaborationist Italians. One of the earliest parties took over Camp 78, at High Garrett, Braintree, on 19th September after Italian prisoners-of-war had been moved out. Although hemmed in by barbed wire, some of them almost immediately attempted to escape. The military guards searched buildings and kitbags and made great efforts to find those responsible, but without success. Soon after, three German prisoners-of-war escaped from a camp at Colchester. The German prisoners had long and violent discussions as to whether they ought "to help the Tommies to win the war"[2]. They were paid a standard rate of three farthings per hour, paid in *lagergeld*, specially printed camp money which could only be spent in the camp canteen. They were provided with shoes, oilskins pullovers and gloves. One of those in the first batch, Hans Reckel, noted his impressions four days after arrival:

Work groups were formed, each with one sergeant-major, two *unteroffiziere* and 27 men. In open lorries, sitting on the tail-boards, we travelled to work in the mornings. On the way we met comrades from the American camp, who were transported in large buses. After a long journey through Braintree and Witham, we stopped on the edge of a large potato field. A foreman was already waiting for us, everyone received the usual wire basket, and then the great potato-picking began.

We were completely out of training and the work was mostly not easy, but we were basically happy to be able to prove our strength away from all the barbed wire, even if accompanied by armed guards. Although our backs got increasingly sore, we worked competitively; everyone wanted to do better than the next man. We drove each other on with words of encouragement.

117

Harvest time on a farm adjoining the runways of the USAAF base at Ridgewell.
Photo courtesy of Dave Osborne

At the beginning of the midday break we were allowed to take two buckets of potatoes to our resting place and cook them for ourselves over the tea stove. And in the evening we received permission to fill the empty food boxes with windfalls from a nearby orchard, so that we returned to the camp tired and knocked out beyond doubt, but fairly content. Content, too, was a gentleman from London who came to the field on instructions from his ministry and acknowledged that we were "very good workers". Later everyone heard it said that we worked 60 per cent better that our predecessors, the Italians.[3]

The greatest single cause of discontent among farmers was the government-fixed price structure for their produce. As 1944 began they were weighing up the consequences of a five shillings a week increase in the national minimum wage for farm workers, which brought the rate to £3 5s. This award had left the workers dissatisfied, as they wanted four pounds, but it set the farmers into uproar. The farmers' spokesmen and the Minister of Agriculture produced wildly different estimates of the financial consequences. When the Suffolk Executive of the

118

National Farmers' Union met at Ipswich on 11th January the chairman said that fourteen members of the executive had presented their accounts for examination, and on their farms the revised prices would result in an average reduction of their annual income by £350. The total acreage of the fourteen farmers was 7,267, so that the average reduction in profit would exceed two pounds per acre. The Members of Parliament for Sudbury, Bury St Edmunds, Eye, Lowestoft and Woodbridge attended this meeting and pledged support. When Norfolk and Suffolk farmers held a mass meeting at Diss three days later, however, the Norfolk NFU secretary. Mr J. F. Wright, argued for moderation in putting their case, and it was agreed to postpone action.

A backbench Tory motion tabled in the Commons expressed the view that farm price revisions had been inadequate for the great majority of farmers to provide for the payment of the increased wages, and that an unfair burden was thus placed on them. The House debated agricultural policy on 26th January, and the Minister claimed that gross farming incomes had risen substantially since 1940. "Experience shows that the changes in prices and costs [since 1940] have substantially increased profits", he insisted.

Whether this was so was debated vigorously in the columns of the *Eastern Daily Press*. The Minister had said that before the war a farm of two hundred to two hundred and fifty acres typically produced a profit of £250 a year. Henry Williamson, the author, wrote to the newspaper to set out his experience with a 235-acre Norfolk farm: 120 acres arable, eighty acres grass and thirty-five acres woodland. He employed six men, which cost him a thousand pounds a year in wages, and his other expenses totalled about a thousand pounds. His income was £1,618 from corn, £370 from sugar beet and £690 from livestock. After allowing for rent and depreciation, he said, his net profit was £170. This example unleashed a flood of letters from other small farmers over a period of weeks, saying how badly they were doing. One claimed to be losing three pounds per acre.

The Minister in his January statement guaranteed the wartime system of fixed prices and assured markets for at least a year after the war. The NFU noted "the conciliatory tone" of this statement, and the *East Anglian Daily Times* in an editorial comment thought the government position was acceptable, and called for greater mutual trust. The farmers' real anxiety, it argued, was whether after the war the experiences of 1921 would be repeated. The farmers continued to grumble, however, and "Lavengro" fed their apprehensions as he enquired: "After the war will it again be a case of cheap food at British agriculture's expense?"

Perhaps their real worry was the developing strength of the National Union of Agricultural Workers. Before the war this trade union had known hard times, in part a reflection of the general state of agriculture. During the depression of the early 1930s farm workers' wages had been reduced or hours lengthened, but from 1935 NUAW membership began to rise, nowhere more quickly than in Norfolk, Suffolk and Essex. At the outbreak of war the basic average wages being paid were

119

thirty-five shillings a week in Cambridgeshire, 34s 6d a week in Norfolk and Essex, and thirty-four shillings a week in Suffolk. Now, in 1944, they had moved up to £3 5s a week.

The union was displaying a new confidence. At its county conference in Norwich its president, Mr E. G. Gooch, proudly announced that 1943 had established a new membership record for the union, to which Norfolk had contributed two thousand new members. Its financial strength was greater than ever before. He appealed for a quarter of a million members by the end of 1944, and the two hundred delegates pledged that Norfolk would obtain its quota.

At another conference, in Saffron Walden, it was reported that membership in north-west Essex had more than doubled in the previous year. Announcing plans for a widespread campaign in the villages, a headquarters speaker, Mr A. C. Dann, said: "We have been much too quiet. Now we are going to shout as loud as the farmers." At its national conference in May, the NUAW drafted a new claim, for a £4 10s minimum wage for men and women at the age of eighteen. At the same time the union emphasized its commitment to the national effort, calling on Britain's food producers to back the efforts of the fighting men by making the campaign on the farms the greatest of the war years.

Edwin Gooch, President of the National Union of Agricultural Workers.   *Eastern Daily Press*

The union claim for a ninety shillings a week minimum wage was formally tabled and discussed at a meeting of the Central Agricultural Wages Board early in September. The farmers' representative argued that there had been no change in circumstances to warrant a rise. The unions countered that production on farms had increased by 120 per cent compared with pre-war totals, and that the current year's harvest would probably go down as one of the greatest in history, so that farmers would do well.

Consideration of the claim was adjourned for one month. The board met again on 4th October and rejected the claim, arguing that the percentage increase to agricultural workers during the war had been greater than in many other industries and that any further increase would be likely to lead to inflation. The union representatives requested the board to consider whether "a case for some increases" had not been made out, but this plea also failed.

The NUAW general secretary, Mr William Holmes, observed: "If anybody thinks that stabilising the wage at 65s. is going to keep people on the land after the war they are greatly mistaken", and almost immediately the union tabled a new, more general claim for "a substantial increase" in the minimum. The Agricultural Wages Board held two further meetings during November and, after ten-and-a-half hours' discussion, agreed by a majority vote to suggest to the county committees an increase of five shillings a week (to £3 10s) for adult male workers, with an extra penny per hour on the overtime rate. "Lavengro" expressed the view of East Anglian farmers:

> Costs are mounting up, while the returns for produce are declining in consequence of the land having lost much of its fertility. Following four remarkably good farming years, the portents are that less favourable farming conditions will for a year or so be experienced. Now farmers are to be weighted down with increased production costs in the shape of a further rise in wages, without any *quid pro quo* in the shape of better prices, so badly needed. It is illustrated in the increasing demands for bank overdrafts.

By the end of the year twenty county committees had agreed to the proposed five shillings increase and eleven counties were opposed to it. Those resisting included Norfolk and Cambridgeshire. In Suffolk there was deadlock and the differing views of farmers' and workers' representatives were being sent to the Central Agricultural Wages Board, which was to meet again on 10th January.

*

CHAPTER TEN

To the Frontier

BY HIGH summer the situation had been transformed. An increasing glow of hope suggested the end of a tunnel, and perhaps even that the war would be over before the end of the year. Churchill assured the House of Commons on 2nd August: "On every battlefront all over the world the armies of Germany and Japan are recoiling. In the air, on the sea, and under the sea our well-established supremacy increases with steady strides."

In France units of Patton's Third Army reached the Seine on 19th August, and by the 25th four Allied armies had closed in to the river and Paris had been liberated. The bulk of the German forces had withdrawn behind the "Siegfried Line". On the Eastern Front the Red Army, which had launched its main summer offensive seventeen days after the D-Day invasion of Normandy, quickly liberated Minsk, the principal city of White Russia, and was soon investing Warsaw. In Italy Allied troops had entered Rome two days before D-Day. In the Far East the decisive Allied victory at Imphal in June had ended the threatened Japanese advance into India, and by the end of July three Japanese divisions had been virtually destroyed as they retreated back to and beyond the River Chindwin, whence they had come.

The news on 4th September produced a particularly encouraging headline:

"FIRST 'CEASE-FIRE'"
Russo-Finnish War Ends
German troops withdrawing

From the British and American air bases in the eastern counties the bombers went forth daily to continue their raids on industrial Germany. In mid-September Bomber Command was returned to the direct control of the Air Ministry, and a directive of 25th September fixed oil installations and supply lines as the top priority targets for the RAF and the Eighth USAAF. At about the same time bomber groups of the US Ninth Air Force transferred to France: the 322nd left Andrews Field for Beauvais, the 391st left Matching for Roye, the 410th left Gosfield for Coulommiers and the 416th left Wethersfield for Melun.

During these exciting days people did not sit back to watch the unfolding drama. Everyone worked flat out. On the farms, as we have seen, all who could be recruited laboured hard to gather a record harvest. East Anglia's industrial capacity, such as it was, was also fully engaged.

Stradishall RAF station in 1944, with 75 Squadron Stirlings from Newmarket.
Photo courtesy of Earl Bedford and Jock Whitehouse

123

One unusual activity, directly related to the advance in France, took place on the Essex coast near Wivenhoe. Huge floating steel caissons, intended to seal locks and dock entrances wrecked by German demolition or battle damage, were assembled and launched throughout 1944 from marshland just above Wivenhoe Shipyard. Messrs Dorman, Long & Co. Ltd were given an order to construct over three hundred of them, and this involved the construction of an elaborate production site. Roadways, railways and reinforced concrete rafts were laid, covering three acres; launch-ways and a fitting-out dock constructed; electric, water and compressed air services and welding and other special plant installed; and twelve cranes erected—all within sixteen weeks.

A caisson a day was launched, towed down-river by a landing craft and handed over in the estuary to deep-sea tugs, which towed them across the Channel. In the event the caissons were not needed because Antwerp was captured virtually intact. Some were towed back to be dismantled and some remained in the River Colne for a considerable time. Production continued until the end of year, by which time about a third of the contract had been met[1].

In many different ways the war was brought close to those who remained at home in East Anglia. Regular appeals were made for blood donors, for example, and the ready response can be gauged by the fact that 689 people in Colchester gave blood in two days at the time of the Normandy invasion. There were well-displayed stories in the newspapers concerning young women who were the first from the region to come under fire in Normandy; they were L.A.C.W. Carter of Cambridge, a WAAF flying nursing orderly who helped to evacuate wounded from the battle area; and Subaltern Margaret Marshall, a twenty-six-year-old from Stoke-by-Nayland who led the first party of ATS girls sent to staff Montgomery's 21st Army Group Headquarters in Normandy.

After their victory in Normandy the Allied armies rapidly occupied the whole of France. Often they found that the Maquis resistance forces had taken over *départements* and towns before they arrived; this was the case in Paris and Marseilles. RAF and USAAF planes from East Anglian bases dropped leaflets to civilian populations and arms and equipment to the resistance groups in occupied Europe, and sometimes they dropped agents of the Special Operations Executive, whose job was to organize sabotage and guerrilla warfare in the occupied countries[2]. An RAF transport squadron at Rivenhall and US bomb groups based at Old Buckenham, Rattlesden, Snetterton Heath, Thorpe Abbots and Tibenham were among those that engaged in these operations.

An American–French invasion at several points along the hundred-mile Riviera coast between Nice and Marseilles was preceded by the RAF dropping a group of nine British parachutists into German-occupied south-western France. They were led by Major Andrew Croft, whose home was at Kelvedon Vicarage in Essex. For three weeks this group worked its way up the Rhone Valley until it reached Lyons, co-operating with the Maquis, reconnoitring German movements by day, ambushing them by night and dynamiting bridges along their escape route. The operation was highly successful in disorganizing the retreating German columns. Eight of the nine parachutists survived.

The only eastern counties battalion actively engaged in the advance from Normandy to the Seine was the 2nd Essex. After its heavy losses in Normandy, however, it had been reinforced with "a strange collection of many regiments and many still wearing their own badges"[3]. It became part of the First Canadian Army, which was given the task of capturing the heavily defended Channel ports. Cape Gris Nez, the nearest point on the French coast to England, was occupied on 29th August, and the seizure of eight cross-Channel guns ended the bombardment of Dover. Le Havre was invested and occupied on 10th/11th September. The Essex battalion, after clearing a section of the town on the 12th, pushed on to an area near Dieppe, acquiring some good stocks of wine and spirits in the process!

Such spoils of war occasionally found their way back to Britain—a little later the *East Anglian Daily Times* reported that Chelmsford police had taken possession of a thousand bottles of champagne, packed in cases, from a house in Manor Road. These had been brought from France in an Allied plane. The offence, it seems, was that no Customs duty had been paid, and some American airmen were questioned. The champagne was taken to Chelmsford police station and locked in a cell until Customs and Excise men collected it.

The 1st Suffolks and the 1st Norfolks remained in Normandy, training or making tactical moves, and as news of the dramatic events to the north trickled back "there was a little disappointment felt that they of the infantry, who had borne the heat and burden of the day, should miss the glory of its close"[4]. It was not long, however, before both battalions were called forward across the Seine, and by mid-September all three East Anglian battalions were in Belgium, poised for a new advance north-eastwards towards the River Maas (Meuse) and beyond that to the German frontier. Their progress by motor transport through France and Belgium was along roads lined on either side by thousands of burnt-out German tanks and lorries, and through flag-waving, cheering villages where they were showered with flowers, fruit and wine.

The progress of the Allied armies had been so rapid that they outran their supply lines. Antwerp, which had been designated the main supply port, was captured undamaged on 4th September, but the Germans held on tenaciously to both sides of the narrows giving access. A considerable combined operation was necessary to subdue the island of Walcheren and three weeks' minesweeping followed, so that it was 28th November before Antwerp's port facilities could be brought into use. Part of the minesweeping force from Harwich, which had already opened up Ostend, helped with this big operation in the Schelde estuary.

Montgomery grew impatient to drive on and to cross the Rhine at Arnhem. If this could be achieved, the Allies would outflank the main German defences and cut off the German army, still in the Pas de Calais. There was only one suitable

B-24 Liberators from North Pickenham drop supplies to troops during the Arnhem operation, 20th September, 1944.   *Imperial War Museum*

route forward, and there were two other rivers to be crossed before the Rhine, the Maas and the Waal. Four divisions took part in an airborne invasion of Holland—the biggest of its kind during the war—on 16th to 18th September.

That weekend thousands of people in the eastern counties watched a vast armada of bombers, transports, tugs and gliders streaming out towards the North Sea. On the Saturday night RAF Lancasters in strength flew off to hit airfields and attack a flak battery, and the following morning US Fortresses escorted by Mustangs bombed Nazi gun positions over a wide area. Then came the actual invasion. As planes and gliders flew towards the coast they were so low that the towing ropes and harness could be seen plainly. The glider fleet, which took over an hour and a half to pass, set out in two mass formations. The first was towed by twin-engined Dakota aircraft and the second by four-engined Stirlings.

An observer in the Isle of Ely wrote: "A massive air armada swept across the sky and filled it from horizon to horizon."[5]. In seven minutes an Essex observer counted 129 planes, then after an interval another eighty-one, and fifteen minutes

126

later several formations of forty. At one time the Brightlingsea Royal Observer Corps post plotted 1,500 aircraft in the air at once. The first of the towing planes returned flying solo after an hour-and-a-half and then the sky was once again alive with aircraft[6].

The story of the men who flew in these aircraft and landed on Dutch soil was one of the most heroic and painful episodes of the war. Part of the operation went well: American airborne troops captured intact all but one of the target bridges over the Maas, and a joint Anglo-American force captured Nijmegen and so secured the Waal crossing. But the German defence of the Rhine bridges could not be overcome. The first wave of the invasion—men of the newly formed First Allied Airborne Army, composed of British, American and Polish units—landed on the northern bank of the Rhine at noon on Sunday, 17th September in ideal weather conditions. Reinforcements followed in a second wave the following day. At

Advance on Germany. British and US Airborne Divisions dropped at Arnhem on the Rhine, Nijmegen on the Waal, and Grave on the Maas, while British Secondary Army forces advanced from the Mause-Escaut Canal into Holland. The line ═══ had been established by 30th September. The plan had been to spread out north of the Rhine, and to establish the line - - - - - from which to advance eastward into the Reich. - - - - - British line at 17th September. —————— German frontier.

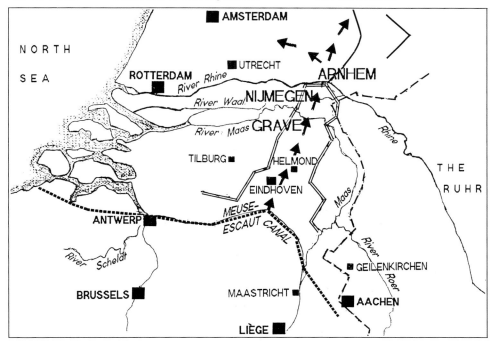

Arnhem they encountered fierce resistance. The Germans blew up one of the two bridges over the river and, after a battle lasting four days, overwhelmed the Allied parachutists trying to capture the other. With the remainder of the division in jeopardy, Montgomery ordered a withdrawal during the night of the 25th–26th, but only 2,400 of the nine thousand men got away.

Spectators in East Anglia witnessed some of the lesser misfortunes of this brave effort. A glider packed with explosives went out of control when passing over Aldeburgh, but by skilful effort by the pilot avoided crashing on land. An American bomber crashed on the outskirts of Norwich and ploughed its way, blazing furiously, through six bungalows. The crew and one resident were killed. An American fighter plane lost its tail over Colchester and the pilot, to prevent it falling on the centre of the town, tried to land on waste ground near Colchester United football ground. He cleared houses but hit a tree; the plane burst into flames and he was killed.

Coincident with the airborne efforts to capture the bridges over the three big rivers, the 3rd Division was given the task of forcing a crossing of a canal further south, near the Belgian–Dutch frontier. They did this successfully on 19th and 20th September. The Suffolks then took the Dutch town of Weert after a fierce battle, while the Norfolks occupied Helmond. Both battalions were given a rapturous reception by the Dutch. Afterwards they moved on to occupy positions only a few miles from the German frontier. The Norfolks found themselves under constant heavy shelling but the Suffolks fared rather better, only occasionally under fire, and those companies in positions near the river were able to enjoy a little quiet canoeing.

The 3rd Division was now holding the line of the Maas on the eastern flank of Montgomery's 21st Army Group front. It was not the same 3rd Division that had crossed the Channel on D-Day, for it had suffered ten thousand casualties, the great majority of them infantrymen in the rifle companies, and so a considerable turnover of men had taken place. More heavy losses now lay ahead. The Germans had maintained a bridgehead west of the Maas and during October both the Royal Norfolks and the Suffolks engaged in efforts to wipe it out. In a fierce seven-day battle for the village of Overloon and the small town of Venraij, the Suffolk battalion lost about a third of its strength in officers—one killed and ten wounded—and eighteen other ranks killed and 144 wounded, and the Norfolks suffered 211 casualties in two days, including five company commanders.

The battle took place in very difficult country of mud, ditches and sandhills, which had been heavily mined. Overloon was captured on the first day without too much difficulty. The next day—Friday the 13th—the troops moved towards Venraij, and the Suffolks and the Norfolks were two of the four battalions chosen to force a crossing of a watercourse called the Molen Beek, which blocked their path.

The Suffolks were held up for hours, soaked to the bone and freezing cold,

TUESDAY,

ALLIES FIGHTING ON GERMAN SOIL

S.H.A.E.F. REPORTS A FIVE-MILE PENETRATION

LUFTWAFFE JOINS IN THE BATTLE FOR REICH

175 ENEMY 'PLANES DESTROYED

DUTCH FRONTIER CROSSED : THE ATTACK ON LE HAVRE

S.H.A.E.F. stated last night that Allied troops are fighting on German soil. Yesterday afternoon General Hodge's First Army troops crossed the German border in "reasonable strength" about some miles North of Trier. They are about five miles inside Germany. Their entry into Germany was preceded by artillery bombardment.

The Allies have occupied Herve, ten miles East of Liège.

Yesterday the Luftwaffe joined on a large scale in the battle for Germany. They threw great formations of fighters—up to 100 in each formation—against 1,000 heavy U.S. bombers which attacked oil plants at Merseburg, Lutzkendorf and Misburg and the 800 escorting fighters.

The Luftwaffe suffered one of its greatest defeats of the war, and the worst it has ever known over its own soil.

The U.S. escort destroyed 116 enemy 'planes in combat and 42 on the ground, and 17 were destroyed by the bombers. Forty-eight of the bombers and 29 fighters are missing, but four bombers and about half the missing fighters are believed to have landed safely in France and Belgium.

The German challenge had been anticipated, and the escort of 800 was exceptionally large—easily more than double the number sent on similar missions of late.

The opening round of the battle for the Siegfried Line and for Germany has commenced, and the intention of the Ger--- ---he sky as well as on the land, is clearly ---

Headlines of lead story in *East Anglian Daily Times* of 12th September, 1944, "Allies fighting on German soil". *East Anglian Daily Times*

while efforts were made—unsuccessfully, because of the waterlogged ground—to get tanks across. Eventually the battalion crossed without tank support and under intense enemy fire, and in this day's fighting it lost not only its commanding officer, one of whose feet was blown off by a mine, but three rifle company commanders and forty-five others, killed or wounded.

The Norfolks fared better. They had two companies across Molen Beek by 5 am, they threw bridges over for the tanks despite heavy enemy fire, and by 7.30 am they began to advance. The first thousand yards were gained in the face of very strong resistance and before the end of the day the battalion had to be reformed into three companies because of its heavy casualties.

The 1st Suffolk was the leading battalion when the attack on Venraij began. Tanks had arrived and loosened up the battle, but there was still stiff German opposition. Their artillery concentrations were directed from Venraij church steeple until Typhoons roared in and bombed and set it alight. Venraij was occupied and cleared of the enemy by mid-day on 18th October after street fighting, and both Suffolk and Norfolk battalions were then able to rest and reorganize. Some men went on forty-eight hours' leave to Brussels.

Each battalion took a turn in garrisoning Venraij, after which the 3rd Division spent the remainder of the year holding a sector on and near the Maas further east. It rained constantly. In some areas snow lay eighteen inches deep. Montgomery visited the division's headquarters on 14th November to hand out decorations. During one of the quieter periods the 1st Suffolk sent Captain W. N. Breach with a small party to Roubaix in Belgium to search for the battalion's drums, which had been hidden there during the retreat of 1940, when the battalion had been compelled to abandon all surplus equipment. The Town Major delivered two of the drums in perfect condition and a third was found after digging at Watrelos.

The three drums of the 1st Battalion of the Suffolks being played at a ceremonial drill parade at Haecht. During the Allied retreat in 1940 these drums were hidden in Roubaix, concealed in civilian homes.
Imperial War Museum

Meanwhile, a little to the west the Essex battalion, with others, occupied the important town of Roosendaal on 30th October, then fought its way across the River Mark. After almost six weeks in the line without a break, in close contact with the enemy, the battalion moved back and some men were given leave in Ghent, Antwerp or Brussels. For the remainder of November the battalion continued to be involved in clearing the west side of the Maas, and at the end of the month it moved to an area of Nijmegen which had been badly damaged in earlier fighting. Almost immediately after its arrival there the Germans breached the dykes, and the area, which was below sea level, flooded. The Essex men moved into fortified houses and patrolled in boats, and they were in this unenviable position as the year ended.

While the East Anglian battalions thus saw out 1944 in quieter circumstances, not far to the south of them a desperate battle was taking place. The Americans had taken Metz and were poised to enter Germany; many felt that the end of the war

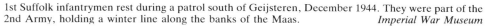

1st Suffolk infantrymen rest during a patrol south of Geijsteren, December 1944. They were part of the 2nd Army, holding a winter line along the banks of the Maas. *Imperial War Museum*

was at last in sight. The wild country of the Ardennes, however, had been left comparatively weakly defended, and the Germans concentrated twenty divisions there and launched an attack, aiming to recapture Antwerp. Their advance began on 16h December and they made good progress towards the Maas. For a few days the Allied air forces were unable to assist the ground troops because of terrible weather, but on the 23rd the Eighth USAAF applied its full weight and on Christmas Eve the Americans stopped the Germans' most advanced units three miles short of the Maas. The Ardennes offensive was broken, and the year ended on a note of optimism, with the front page of the last issue of the *East Anglian Daily Times* of 1944 headlined:

RUNDSTEDT'S WITHDRAWAL BECOMES ROUT AT SOME POINTS

Allied counter-blows gain more miles: enemy armour badly mauled
Germans may be on verge of 'major disaster'

The last phrase had been inspired by a communiqué from Supreme Allied Headquarters*.

Many of the inhabitants of Holland were starving when they were liberated and during the last few months of 1944 there was a regular cargo service from Harwich to provide relief. The headquarters of the Dutch Naval Command was at Parkeston Quay and so it was well placed to organize a flow of barges carrying food, clothing and hospital equipment.

The ground forces in the Low Countries were given constant support by planes operating from RAF and USAAF bases in East Anglia. They bombed rail centres behind the enemy front and Ruhr heavy industries, but there was no diminution of their assault on distant targets in the German homeland, with Berlin, Hamburg, Leipzig and Munich among the targets. They also kept the resistance movements supplied and dropped agents behind enemy lines. Flying Officer Arthur Dean, a Sudbury man, lost his life in August when trying to deliver three Dutch saboteurs to their homeland; his Halifax belonged to the 161 "Special Services Squadron", which conducted many such missions from Tempsford airfield in Bedfordshire. The Horham Bomb Group flew to Warsaw to support Polish troops during the uprising that began there on 1st August.

On one mission during September the 445th Bomb Group at Tibenham lost thirty aircraft in a day. In another, a little later, a Stirling from Rivenhall piloted by the station commander failed to return from a flight to Norway to drop supplies to the resistance movement[7].

Eastern counties skies were still full of planes, and some of them still suffered horrific accidents from time to time. In one of the Munich raids a bomber from Ridgewell crashed into a wheatfield on take-off and nosed down into a railway

---

*Later events were to show that the Germans had used all their reserves in the west and were desperately short of fuel.

cutting. Its bombs exploded, the pilot and co-pilot escaped with injuries, but seven other crew were killed[8]. In November an RAF plane crashed and totally destroyed the village church at Bawdeswell near East Dereham.

A new development was the "shuttle mission", with planes from Britain flying on to land in the Soviet Union. In the first of these the Eighth USAAF despatched a force of 114 Fortress bombers from Horham, Thorpe Abbots and Deopham Green, with sixty-eight escorting Mustangs from Debden and Bodney. They bombed a synthetic oil plant near Berlin, then flew on and landed at the Poltava base in Russia. Unfortunately, a Heinkel 177 shadowed them there and German bombers soon arrived and hit the base hard. Forty-seven of the B-17s, two C-47s and one Russian fighter were destroyed on the ground, along with much fuel, bombs and ammunition. Another shuttle mission was soon mounted and successfully fulfilled by seventy-six B-17s from Horham and Framlingham, accompanied by sixty-four Mustangs from Leiston. Their target was near Gdynia in Poland. There was a third and final shuttle mission during September[9].

Preparing bombs at dusk at Knettishall, Suffolk, for the coming day's mission.

Photo courtesy of Ian Hawkins

On the other land fronts great progress was made in the later months of 1944. In Italy the Allied armies were approaching the great northern plain of Lombardy by the first week of September. After the capture of Rome on 4th June the German Field-Marshal Kesselring had withdrawn in good order to the "Gothic Line", which stretched across the width of Italy just north of Florence and just south of Rimini.

The Essex battalion was among the forces moved to the centre of the Allied front south of the Gothic Line, and for seven weeks it engaged in stubborn fighting to advance to Arezzo, which it reached on 22nd July. Early in August preparations were made to assault the Gothic Line, but by this time the Essex battalion had been "bled white".

> The 1/4th Essex had suffered heavily at Cassino in March. It had been granted no rest after that gruelling test, and had been almost continuously in action ever since, under very trying conditions. Now, at the beginning of August, after almost four and a half months of battle, not unnaturally the battalion was tired. So when, with the prospect of yet another major attack ahead, the Brigade Commander . . . questioned its ability to endure another severe test in its present state, the Commanding Officer, very rightly, agreed that he could not guarantee it.[10]

The battalion was withdrawn for six weeks. Soon after it returned to the front in October, ready for battle again, it was transferred to Greece. There the Germans were in retreat and Greek ELAS (People's Liberation Army) guerrilla forces were endeavouring to take over the country. ELAS was regarded by the Allied governments as being under communist control and the country was seen as threatened by civil war. Troops were sent therefore to clear the guerrillas from the area of Athens and the Piraeus, and the Essex men found themselves engaged in this struggle, street by street, block by block, over Christmas. Their task was uncompleted as the year ended.

This military action was politically controversial, and a conference of the Cambridgeshire Federation of Labour Parties in December expressed itself "deeply shocked at the serious situation developing in Greece". Its resolution went on to express "abhorrence that British soldiers should be employed to suppress the progressive urge for self-government so much in evidence in the liberated parts of the country". A big crowd attended a Labour and trade union demonstration on Parker's Piece just before Christmas and unanimously demanded that the British government should reverse its policy, "to enable the Greeks to form a new representative government".

Another battalion of the Essex Regiment, the 5th, also fought in Italy during 1944, following up German forces withdrawing northward after the battle of Cassino and occupying ground that had been passed over by the advancing Allied motorized units. During the summer it was withdrawn and transferred to the Middle East.

Other East Anglians in Italy served in the 142nd Regiment Royal Armoured Corps (which had been the 7th Suffolks until November 1941). After the fall of

Rome this regiment took part in the drive northwards, fought the Germans in the Chianti hills south of Florence, and then engaged in a grim struggle on the eastern side of Italy. They operated in very difficult tank country, fighting from one small mountain ridge to the next as the Eighth Army tried to break the Germans' "Gothic Line". The plan was to advance into the Po Valley and then secure the passes into Austria, but winter descended and the Allied advance was brought to a standstill. Until 25th November the regiment remained in action, but then it was pulled back and its commanding officer made the shock announcement that it was to be disbanded, "due to a shortage of manpower". The men organized a bumper Christmas celebration in Camerino, a small town hidden away in the mountains south-west of Ancona, after which they were posted to continue their war with other units.

The progress of the war in India and Burma was surprisingly well reported in the British press. As we have seen, the Japanese attempt to invade India had collapsed by the end of 1944, and the British–Indian Fourteenth Army, under General Slim, had moved over to the offensive. The time had now come for a major Allied campaign to cross the Chindwin River and advance into central Burma to link up with forces which had been operating further north, near the Chinese frontier, under the American General Stilwell.

The 2nd Battalion of the Royal Norfolks was among the forces that engaged in this operation. It moved to a ridge about fifteen miles east of Imphal towards the end of July, by which time the Japanese were in full retreat. It spent some weeks patrolling as far as the river, in an area that remained fairly quiet. After moving back from the front for reorganization and replacement of men lost in action, the Norfolks joined in an operation which established one of three bridgeheads over the Chindwin early in December. After Christmas celebrations the Norfolks resumed their advance on 30th December, two companies transported on rafts down the river and the remainder riding in trucks, which occasionally refused to take the steep hills of the rough track and had to be winched up. Soon after lunch that day they left the hills and reached a level road into the plain, along which they advanced next morning. The prospects of taking part in a great victory lay ahead.

There were other East Anglian troops in the Far East who featured in no reports from the front. Their war was over, but they were never forgotten. These were the survivors of the battalions of the Suffolk, the Royal Norfolk and the Cambridgeshire Regiments who had become prisoners-of-war with the fall of Singapore. During 1944 they were scattered in camps in Japan and throughout the Japanese-held territories. Names of some of these prisoners-of-war were published in the regional newspapers, week by week, a few at a time, as postcards were received by their families. The messages were brief, usually: "My health is excellent. I am working for pay." Mr Anthony Eden, the Foreign Secretary, told the Commons: "There is no doubt that some of these communications are in terms dictated by the Japanese authorities", and he went on to say that the government had received "grave news" about their treatment. In many cases the health of prisoners was rapidly deteriorating, a high percentage was seriously ill and there had been some thousands of deaths. The Japanese government, he added, had withheld permission for a neutral inspection of the camps. They had not been allowed to know the number of prisoners held, nor had their names been communicated.

It was not until 17th November that a first comprehensive statement was made to the Commons. The War Secretary, Sir James Grigg, then reported that details of Japanese camps in Siam (Thailand) had been obtained from 150 British prisoners-of-war who had been on a Japanese transport that had left Singapore early in September 1944 and had been attacked and sunk. Survivors had been rescued by US naval forces and had just reached the UK. Sir James said:

> All that we have learnt from these men reveals that our prisoners have been true to the highest traditions of our race. To the relatives and friends of all the prisoners concerned our deepest sympathy goes out. It is a matter of profound regret to me that these disclosures have to be made, but we are convinced that it is necessary that the Japanese should know that we know how they have been behaving and that we intend to hold them responsible. We are collecting from the survivors every scrap of information they can give about other men, and this information will be passed on to the next of kin concerned as quickly as possible.

The Norwich MP, Sir Geoffrey Shakespeare, commented:

> This news will shock the civilised world and cause the deepest distress. Can any message of comfort be given to the relatives of these men? Is there any evidence that medical supplies or food and comforts have been reaching these prisoners of war?

Grigg only felt able to reply that constant efforts were being made to get supplies to them; he promised another statement later. This came on 19th December in these terms:

> In Siam, after the completion of the railway in October 1943, conditions did improve somewhat. These conditions are far below anything which would be regarded as reasonable for our prisoners of war in Europe. The men have, however, adapted themselves and become to some extent inured to these lower standards, while many of the conditions which caused such heavy sick and death rates in the jungle camps did not obtain in the rear camps to which the men were withdrawn. Consequently, there was apparently a very marked fall in the death rate, and on the whole the prisoners were enjoying fair health, and were in good spirits when the rescued men left Siam about July 1944.

On the war fronts the year ended with the Germans facing defeat on every front in Europe and with Japanese armies being driven back in Burma and her navy having lost control of the western Pacific to the Americans. Assuredly 1945 was to be the year of victory.

✳

CHAPTER ELEVEN

The Lights Go On Again

IT WAS another summer of "Holidays at Home". Despite the ban on travel to the coast, the seaside towns were crowded with visitors on August Bank Holiday. "More Ipswich people spent a day at Felixstowe during the weekend than probably at any holiday since the war began", the *East Anglian Daily Times* reported. It continued:

> Although officially closed to holiday makers, Clacton has had the busiest August bank holiday of the war. Many visitors came from London. In the rural parts of East Anglia whole families have spent a holiday in the fields, with everyone helping in the harvesting.

As in previous wartime years most towns organized their own week-long programmes of sports events, concerts, pageants and displays. The weather was some of the worst experienced during summer months in the twentieth century.

Colchester spread its programme over six weeks. It included everything from Handel's *Messiah* to Gilbert and Sullivan's *Trial by Jury*, and from a ballet company performing on Holly Trees Lawn to a War Workers' Athletic Championship meeting in the Castle Grounds. The events were promoted with enthusiasm and local pride: the Corn Exchange had "the largest polished maple floor in the county" and the Empire Cinema boasted "the brightest picture and the best sound in the town, a clean atmosphere and a staff of happy civility".

Bury St Edmunds staged its own, unique event on 1st August when many thousands packed the Abbey Gardens to celebrate Minden Day. There was something remarkably timely about this event, taking place in the year when, under Winston Churchill's leadership, Britain was emerging from long dark years of defeat and deprivation into a period of victory and confident optimism. The battle of Minden, which was being commemorated, had taken place in 1759. Then Britain had just found a new leader in William Pitt, whose firm leadership, enormous energy and strategic insight had turned the tide in a long-drawn-out struggle with France. Minden was a key battle in a year when, in the words of one of Pitt's colleagues, the church bells were worn threadbare with ringing for victories, and the Suffolk Regiment was one of six infantry regiments which inflicted a spectacular defeat on the French.

Bury St Edmunds now conferred the Freedom of the town on the regiment. For the first time ever the Borough Council held a formal session in the open air. An illustrated scroll was presented to the colonel of the regiment, Colonel W. N. Nicholson, by the Recorder, Mr Gerald Howard. Men representing battalions of

On Minden Day in 1944 the Suffolk Regiment was granted the Freedom of the Borough of Bury St Edmunds at an open-air ceremony in the Abbey Gardens. Here Colonel W. N. Nicholson, Colonel of the Regiment, is seen addressing the gathering after receiving the scroll. In the front row are: the Marquess of Bristol, the Earl of Stradbroke (Lord Lieutenant), Alderman E. L. D. Lake (Mayor of Bury St Edmunds), Colonel Nicholson, Lieutenant Colonel H. R. Gadd, Mr Gerald Howard (Recorder) and Mr Thomas Wilson (Town Clerk). *East Anglian Daily Times*

the regiment formed a guard of honour, the troops wearing their traditional red and yellow roses. Past members of the regiment and relatives of prisoners-of-war had an honoured place in a special enclosure, and units of the Home Guard, the NFS, the Red Cross, pre-service units and the WVS paraded.

In Norwich and Cambridge American forces stationed in those neighbourhoods joined enthusiastically in their ambitious Holidays at Home. In Cambridge the programme extended throughout the summer. A variety show on Christ's Pieces in July opened with "Moonlight Serenaders" from the ranks of the US army, and on the same day a big Anglo-American crowd at Fenner's enjoyed the finals of the Eighth US Air Force "track and relay" carnival. Watts' Naval School Boys' Band marched through the town a day or two later, playing sea shanties and sailors' hornpipes, and on the following Sunday the ATS Band and Pipers "beat the retreat" on Parker's Piece. So it went on, week after week. One variety show on Christ's Pieces was presented entirely by children, billed as "26 Little Starlets of the Future", and some of Britain's established theatrical stars came to town—including John Gielgud, who played Hamlet in a packed Arts Theatre for a week in August.

In Norwich fifty men of the USAF Liberator crews at nearby stations appeared

Parades and social events celebrated the Home Guard stand-down at the end of 1944. This announcement details the arrangements at Halstead, Essex.

Photo courtesy of Dave Osborne

Home Guard Stand Down.

3rd DECEMBER, 1944.

The 15th Essex Batt. Home Guard
will be holding their

STAND DOWN PARADE

on the FACTORY SPORTS GROUND, Colchester Road, Halstead, on **3rd December, 1944,**

The Parade will be Addressed by

The Commanding Officer & The Rt. Hon. R. A. Butler, M.P.

The Battalion will March through the Town at
12.15 p.m. led by the

BAND of the GLOUCESTERSHIRE REGIMENT

THE SALUTING BASE

will be established at the Eastern National Garage, High Street

THE SALUTE will be taken by

Air Vice Marshall J. R. SCARLETT-STREATFEILD, C.B.E.

accompanied by Brigadier R. W. McLEOD

'A' Coy. 15th Essex Batt. Home Guard

GRAND FINAL DINNER and SOCIAL EVENING

SATURDAY, December 2nd, 7.30 p.m.

At The Drill Hall, Halstead.

ENTERTAINMENT by the "HALSTEAD REVELLERS"

TICKETS **1/6**, including all Refreshments

From any member of the Social Committee, and must be obtained on or before WEDNESDAY, NOVEMBER 29th.

Dress—Clean Fatigue.

on the Carrow Road football ground in Stetsons and check shirts and (in the words of the local newspaper) "pitted their prowess against some of the meanest horses and the wickedest cattle in East Anglia . . . to show Britain just what an old-time cattle country gala should be like". Some of them had returned from a raid on enemy territory only two hours before their performance. Seven thousand people turned out to cheer their efforts.

People now began to feel that they might sometimes relax without having a guilty conscience. The end of the war was in sight. There could be no real doubt about that; in September the government confirmed it by raising the question of demobilization of the forces—it released some details of its plans for the period between the defeat of Germany and the defeat of Japan.

Some men up to the age of thirty-five would continue to be called up, but some in the services would be allowed to leave: men of fifty and over, and those who could work in such vital tasks as building houses. Demobilization would be on the basis of age combined with length of service, with two months of service equivalent to one additional year of age. To set them up again in civilian life, men would be given on release a suit, a shirt, collars, a tie, socks, shoes, a hat and a raincoat. Those over fifty would get eight weeks' leave with full pay, with additional leave related to foreign service, and they would then have reinstatement rights in their old jobs. The strictly limited numbers of tradesmen released would get only three weeks' leave and might be directed to any part of the country where they were needed.

Women in the auxiliary services would be released or transferred in the same way, except that married women would be given priority. The Ministry of Labour said it had ceased some time before to call up women over fifty for war work (though those born in 1893 had been required to register); now it promised that no woman over forty-five would in future be directed to work away from her home. The government added that general demobilization of the forces and of war industry would not take place until the total defeat of the Axis throughout the world.

These announcements were soon followed by another causing almost as great excitement: UK leave for men of the British Liberation Army would begin on 1st January. Soldiers who had spent the preceding six months continuously in any operational theatre would be eligible for leave. Every unit would have an allocation, and selection would be by "out of the hat" ballot. In fact some men arrived home on leave from Italy before the year was out—for example, on 2nd December Lowestoft gave an enthusiastic welcome to twenty-five-year-old Sapper D. Biddle, whose name had been drawn in the first ballot. A promise was made that all those eligible would have seven days' leave at home before the spring.

From September there came a spate of pronouncements indicating a run-down of war service. The Eastern Regional Commissioner, Sir Patrick Spens, stated that it was no longer necessary to keep the invasion committees in existence.

Then came a War Office announcement that the Home Guard would be stood down from 1st November, a decision that was not popular with many of the veterans. A correspondent of the *East Anglian Daily Times* complained that they were "being very shabbily treated by being prematurely sacked and deprived of their uniforms". In fact they were permitted to keep their battledress, cap, gas cape, anklets, boots and greatcoats, but simply as useful souvenirs. Tin hats, webbing, leather belts, ammunition, mess tins and water bottles were to be returned to central depots by the end of the year.

The Home Guard disbandment took place with much ceremony and *éclat*. Numbers had peaked during 1943, but there were still tens of thousands serving in East Anglia: in Norfolk, for example, there were 1,141 officers and 30,541 other ranks. Farewell parades were arranged everywhere, most taking place on the same day, 3rd December. This put a demand on available bands; Ipswich managed to field five service bands, Norwich had the band of the Dorset Regiment, Braintree had only the band of the Chelmsford Grammar School Cadets, while the Saxmundham men marched to the music of an amplified gramophone. In Norwich four thousand men turned out in full battledress; at Cambridge 3,500 paraded on Parker's Piece; in Ipswich two thousand marched through the town centre and past Cornhill; in Colchester over a thousand paraded on Le Cateau Barracks Square; and there were similar parades, great and small, in most places. Everywhere county and town civic leaders gathered and the salute was taken by a senior army officer who invariably expressed the thanks and admiration of the community.

There was much talk of comradeship, and hope was expressed that the spirit engendered during war time would be carried over into the days of peace. More than eight hundred Home Guards in the region were honoured for "meritorious service". Some officers were awarded OBEs—four between Norfolk and Suffolk; others became MBEs—eight between Norfolk, Suffolk and Cambridgeshire. For representatives of men in the ranks—three Suffolk sergeants and one private— there was a British Empire Medal.

Within a few weeks, however, came evidence that the Home Guard was not a focus of universal admiration. Delegates to the annual conferences of the county organizations of the British Legion in both Norfolk and Cambridgeshire and the Isle of Ely strongly opposed a proposal that former Home Guards might be admitted to Legion membership.

HM King George VI, accompanied by Lieutenant R. Bishop, Platoon Commander, and behind, Lieutenant-Colonel Bassett F. Hornor, DSO, OBE, inspecting a detachment of the 10th Norwich Battalion, Home Guard, on 12th October 1944.

In Cambridge one opponent, Major Jeeps, paid tribute to those Home Guards who had served on rocket batteries and other operational duties, but added:

> There was also the other section, which has done practically nothing. Platoon officers have had the greatest difficulty in getting some of these men, most from country districts, to parade at all. They are still having difficulty in collecting stores and equipment.

Another opponent, the Reverend F. F. Herbert, added the thought that the Legion wanted "quality, not quantity". Not surprisingly, the *Cambridge Daily News* received a letter observing that if this truly represented the feelings of Legion members, Home Guard veterans were best out of it.

Civil defence and fireguard duties were reduced in some parts of Britain from September, but it was mid-October before standby duties for part-time workers in Civil Defence in most parts of the eastern region were cut—from forty-eight to twelve hours in each four-week period. Even then some towns and rural areas were privately notified that they must not yet relax, namely Colchester, Lowestoft, Aldeburgh, Southwold, Leiston cum Sizewell, Felixstowe, Saxmundham, and many East Suffolk parishes in the rural districts of Blyth, Deben, Lothingland and Samford. Ipswich continued to be considered a vulnerable area until 20th December; then it was permitted to reduce the duties of part-time Civil Defence personnel, but only from forty-eight to twenty-four hours in each four-week period.

Fireguard duties were also reduced. Members of street fire parties had been permitted for some time to sleep in their own homes and to turn out only when there was enemy activity in their immediate neighbourhood; now the number required to be on duty at business premises was cut by half and small business premises were grouped together. This brought welcome relief to very large numbers of working women and elderly people—there were twenty-five thousand fireguards in Norwich alone.

In the midst of these relaxations the V.2 rockets arrived in East Anglia, causing many last-minute amendments of plan. In Colchester a partial relaxation of the warden's service was hurriedly countermanded. The Regional Commissioner warned a conference of Red Cross instructors at Cambridge early in November that East Anglia's ARP services faced another difficult winter. "Wherever the war in the air may be over, it is certainly not over in East Anglia", he said.

The run-down of Home Guard, Civil Defence and National Fire Service activity led to much nostalgic reminiscence among those who had served, and their memories were stimulated by the release of information which had previously been suppressed by censorship. The first statistical details of air raids on East Anglia during the years 1940 to 1943 were disclosed on 7th October, 1944. Only then was it revealed that Lowestoft had had ninety raids, causing 266 deaths and injuring 690. There had been 1,896 Alerts and 543 Imminent Danger warnings. Fifty bomb-wrecked acres of the town had already been cleared, and first-aid repairs had been done to 13,379 houses.

During these same years only twenty-eight of the 318 parishes in East Suffolk had escaped an air raid. Ipswich had been raided fifty-one times, but had had a thousand Alerts and eight hundred Imminent Danger warnings. Forty people had been killed and 542 injured, and 13,099 properties had been damaged. The total area of raid damage which had been cleared was eighteen acres. The *East Anglian Daily Times* summed up:

> Ipswich's story during the air raids can justly be said to be a providential one, and the town has been remarkably spared the destruction which would have been inevitable if the large number of bombs that fell not too distant in open country had found the densely populated areas of the borough.

West Suffolk figures showed 178 raids, in which forty-three had died and 130 been injured. "The people of the county have stood up to the onslaught from the air with typical Suffolk spirit, and the absence of panic in bombing incidents has been something to inspire pride", the paper thought. The figures for Norfolk (excluding Norwich and Great Yarmouth) revealed that seventy-eight had been killed and 346 injured.

Air raids of that kind were over and done with, and with the advance of the Allied armies the flying bombs and rockets could not long continue. With the end of Double Summer Time on 17th September, therefore, the government decreed that the blackout could be replaced by "half-lighting", except in a few special coastal areas and during raid warnings. Street lighting and car headlight restrictions were relaxed, and the railways were permitted to improve the lighting of railway stations and restore peacetime standards of lighting to the interior of trains, provided the opaque blinds with which most carriages were furnished were pulled down at night. Domestic properties were allowed to replace full blackout with ordinary curtains.

These relaxations were greeted excitedly in some towns—as in Cambridge, where the columnist of the *Cambridge Daily News*, "Robin Goodfellow", wrote: "Blackpool, with its peace-time illuminations, will have nothing on Cambridge in its pride in its new-found light." Under this stimulus:

> in some streets people stood outside their doors just at dim-out time and, as the lights automatically came on one by one [they were gas lamps], there was hand clapping and the singing of the opening lines of the popular song of black-out days, *When the lights go on again*.

At Colchester at the end of November, it was reported, "little children ran about in the High Street pointing and exclaiming at the unfamiliar lights".

While many towns immediately modified their blackout and sought permission for street lighting, others wanted a demonstration of the "moonlight" permitted. When they found that it meant fifteen-watt lamps on fifteen-foot-high standards, or the equivalent, some decided it would not be worth the cost involved. Norwich and Ipswich both took this view. Some who made the improvements were soon

When black-out restrictions were eased, the checking of lamps was a major operation. Here a Cambridge Gas Company employee is examining a street light.

Cambridge Daily News

dissatisfied. After conducting two inquests on pedestrians in a single week, the Cambridge Coroner declared that the town's gas street lighting created "pools of shade" and was treacherous to motorists and pedestrians. A police officer concurred when he added that it was "worse than the blackout", and the Chief Constable later told the Cambridgeshire Standing Joint Committee that "the whole lighting arrangements are a hopeless muddle". American air bases in the county were well lit after dark, and American vehicles used normal headlights. The committee called on the Ministry of Home Security to relax the restrictions on car headlights and to sort out the anomalies.

A King's Lynn resident noted: "The handling of this matter has been the worst example of bureaucracy gone mad so far experienced . . . Complete confusion in the public mind. The police are inundated with enquiries."[1]

Even while these relaxations were being authorized, however, the Minister of Fuel and Power, Major Gwilym Lloyd George, appealed for every possible economy in street lighting by local authorities because coal output had declined during the year. The three months' fuel ration for November to January for houses in the south of England was fixed at fifteen hundredweight and no one was allowed to hold more than one ton in stock.

For more than five years Britain's weather—a staple of everyday street conversation—was treated as a military secret. In the early days of the war it was decreed that fifteen days should elapse before newspapers might report on the weather; later the period was reduced to ten days; now it became two days that so, from mid-October it became permissible to print information about the weather "the day before yesterday" in any part of Great Britain.

The danger of German invasion having ended, East Anglian coastal towns were encouraged to try to restore some kind of normality. The ban on entry, which had applied to a belt stretching ten miles inland between the Wash and Lymington in Hampshire was lifted on 25th August. There was an immediate rush to the seaside. On the following Sunday crowds were queuing at Thorpe Station in Norwich two hours before the first train was due to leave. Great Yarmouth and Lowestoft were crowded. Buses from King's Lynn to Hunstanton were packed.

The areas opened were still subject to "regulation", which meant that the military was authorized to retain or to impose whatever local restrictions it considered appropriate. Certain small areas in East Suffolk remained restricted, and only residents holding a special pass were allowed in. Defence regulations continued to make it compulsory to carry identity cards, forbade the use of binoculars and telescopes, and imposed special hotel registration procedures.

The government organized the return to their homes of some of those who had been officially evacuated because of V.1 bombing, but it insisted that Great Yarmouth, Lowestoft, Ipswich, Aldeburgh, Southwold, Felixstowe, Leiston cum Sizewell and the Deben rural district (as well as London) were still unsafe. None the less, eighty thousand people returned to Great Yarmouth.

The army began to clear mines from the beaches and issued an assurance that it understood the public's desire to have this task completed as quickly as possible. It was not a simple one however; many of the mines had been moved by the tides, many were buried under several feet of sand, and some had exploded. No one knew just how many remained. The work was accompanied by a sombre warning: "Every care is taken to ensure complete clearance, but the probability of occasional explosions for some years to come must be faced." People asked if there would be compensation if they were injured, but there was no immediate response from the authorities. By the end of September about forty beaches had been reopened to the public, though access was still forbidden after dark[2].

The War Office met representatives of certain coastal towns on 8th November and advised them that they could begin to clear defence obstructions from their sea-front areas. Road blocks could be removed, but shortage of labour might mean that the job could not be done quickly so a priority list should be prepared and the most dangerous blocks removed first. The clerk to Felixstowe UDC afterwards reported to his council that they were free to remove six concrete pillboxes along the promenade and all other defence works except mines, and to do their best to make the sea front accessible and safe for the public. A limited amount of reinstatement

Demolition of concrete pill-boxes and anti-blast walls was a massive task. Here workmen with pneumatic drills are breaking up a strongpoint in North Hill, Colchester.

Photo courtesy of Mrs Hervey Benham

was also permissible, but this was dependent on the release of property by the military and prior approval of the cost, which would be met by the government.

The ban on place-name signs—including station name-boards—and on direction signs was revoked. Complaints were heard at King's Lynn that some sign-posts had been erected in the wrong places, giving false information. Permission was given to illumine public clocks again.

On the domestic front relaxations were announced month by month. In October the cheese ration was increased from two to three ounces a week, although the bigger ration of twelve ounces for agricultural and certain other heavy workers remained unchanged. The Food Minister, Colonel Llewellin, said in November that raw materials would be allocated for the manufacture of ice-cream, but he cautioned that it might be some time before it became generally available. The public's yearning for ice-cream, and the manufacturers' enthusiasm to satisfy it, was such that by 10th December supplies had reached three-quarters the pre-war level. There was no reappearance, however, of the familiar pre-war sight of salesmen on three-wheeled trolley cycles with loudly clanging bells.

There were improvements in supplies of household equipment and clothing. Local newspapers carried many classified advertisements like these in the *Cambridge Daily News* during November:

WANTED—Lady's Wellingtons, size 6. Also exchange gent's umbrella for lady's.
WANTED—Camp bed, good size, good condition. Also gent's suit, 6 ft 1 in.

Captain Charles Waterhouse, Parliamentary Secretary to the Board of Trade, promised an early improvement in supplies of prams, aluminium saucepans, carpets, nickel silver cutlery, electrical appliances, mangles and wringers and lawn-mowers—all things that had disappeared from the shops years before.

As Christmas approached, parents switched their attention to the hunt for toys. One Cambridge mother advertised:

WANTED—for little girl, from her Daddy in Italy, doll's house and large dolly.

The government promised that some toys would come into the shops, and also held out hope for a better supply of children's clothes. The President of the Board of Trade, Dr Hugh Dalton, announced that he had arranged for small quantities of children's Wellingtons to be supplied to traders, but only to shops in rural areas because "the mud is worse in the country". He added: "Natural rubber must be used. Synthetic rubber is no good, and natural rubber stocks are declining very rapidly."

Indicative of the problems of parents was the choice made by American airmen on the base at Ridgewell when they wanted to make a Christmas gesture of goodwill to the people of their neighbouring village. They asked the vicar to nominate two deserving girls who could be taken on a shopping expedition for complete new outfits of clothes. On 22nd December Molly, aged eleven, and Rowena, aged eight, walked the three miles from Ashen to Clare to catch a train to Colchester, accompanied by the base chaplain and a colleague.

They were not the only girls with cause to be grateful for American generosity. A collection of wedding dresses crossed the Atlantic as a gift, designed to bring a touch of glamour to ceremonies which would otherwise have lacked style in these days of acute shortage. They were loaned to brides who were serving in the women's forces, Civil Defence or Women's Land Army, or who were working as nurses. They could not be passed around quickly enough to satisfy all demands.

The many relaxations at this time and the hopes they encouraged released a tide of thanksgiving in the churches. The fifth anniversary of the outbreak of war was marked by a National Day of Prayer on Sunday, 3rd September, and a fortnight later there were special services throughout the country on the fourth anniversary of the Battle of Britain. Many of these services were linked to elaborate parades and ceremonies. Bury St Edmunds set a typical pattern: a service in the cathedral attended by a thousand people, including a great many service representatives, with the Mayor reading the lesson, followed by a parade of over seven hundred people with Air Marshal Sir Patrick Playfair taking the salute as

147

they marched past the Abbey Gate. There were men of the Royal Air Force, the Home Guard, the National Fire Service, the United States Army and the British Legion; women of the Auxiliary Air Force, the Auxiliary Territorial Service, the Red Cross, the Women's Voluntary Service and the Rest Centre Service; men and women representing the Civil Defence services; and youngsters of the Army Cadet Force, the Sea Cadet Corps and the Girls' Training Corps. Parades of this kind emphasized how men, women and youngsters of all ages had been drawn into uniformed engagement in the war effort. Even in the village churches there were groups in uniform and veterans of an earlier war wearing their campaign medals.

Nevertheless, the demands made on the lives of most people were being reduced and this fact, coupled with a conviction, now that the invasion of the Continent had succeeded, that the war could not continue much longer, gave a perceptible boost to morale. This was helped further when a government White Paper on 21st September announced one hundred million pounds a year of increased pay for members of the forces with three years' service and for those in the Far Eastern theatre. The increases ranged from seven shillings a week for ranks below sergeant after three years' service, plus an additional 3s 6d a week for each additional year of service; to twenty-one shillings a week for lieutenant-commanders, majors and squadron leaders, plus seven shillings a week for each additional year. Those in the Far East got similar additional payments as "Japanese campaign pay", irrespective of their period of service.

The men from the eastern counties held prisoners-of-war were never forgotten. From Norfolk alone there were about 1,500 held in German camps and nearly two thousand at various camps in the Far East, and there were an additional six hundred posted missing, whose families hoped they might yet be alive. Collections to pay for parcels to send to these camps evoked a generous response everywhere. The Earl of Stradbroke, Lord Lieutenant of Suffolk, presented a cheque for fifty-three thousand pounds collected in that county to the Chairman of the Red Cross and St John at the end of the year.

There was little sympathy, however, for members of enemy forces held as prisoners-of-war in Britain. Italians who had opted to collaborate with their captors were enjoying a large measure of freedom by the later months of 1944. They were allowed to talk to civilians and to visit private houses if invited, to visit cinemas at the discretion of their officer in charge and to make purchases in local shops; but they could not enter public houses or use public conveyances, except when on duty. As we have seen in an earlier chapter, they were widely criticized, and many of the critics wanted to see them under tighter discipline.

German prisoners-of-war aroused much stronger emotions. A few weeks after the National Day of Prayer a south London vicar appealed in his parish magazine for comforts for German prisoners who were in hospital in his parish. An Ipswich clergymen, the Reverend H. G. Green, vicar of St Nicholas, sent him a tin of rat poison with a note reading:

Having seen your tender-hearted request for comforts for the blasphemers of God and butchers of men, I herewith send a small comfort which I am sure they will enjoy. I am sorry the tin is not full, but a small dose will do the trick.

(This was the same clergyman who had testified back in the spring that a vision of the Crucifixion had appeared over Ipswich.)

Controversy rocked the diocese. Green told his congregation the appeal on behalf of Germans had made him very unhappy and he had thought it would be "a bit of a joke" to send the poison. The prisoners, in his opinion, were lucky to get the bare necessities of life:

These Germans have perpetrated vile acts of murder, terror and plunder, and their villainies beggar description. I have no doubt that people who make such appeals think that they are acting in accordance with the Sermon on the Mount and the teachings of St Paul; but I defy anyone to find me a single sentence in the Bible where I can be called upon to serve the enemies of God and man.

The south London vicar to whom the poison was sent passed the note to the Bishop of St Edmundsbury and Ipswich, Dr Richard Brook, who observed in a statement to the press:

Mr Green must not be taken seriously. He was trying to be funny. In any view, it was a poor joke, cheap and vulgar. He is entitled to his own views, though they are very different from mine. There is nothing I can do beyond telling him that, in my judgment, his action has been most reprehensible, and has brought discredit to the church.

We cannot know whose views most accurately reflected the majority opinion of Suffolk people at the time, but Mr Green told the *East Anglian Daily Times* that he had received 267 letters in one day and only a small proportion were against him. "I have received letters of congratulation from officers and men in the Army, Navy and Air Force, from doctors and from clergymen of all denominations", he declared[3].

Late in the year Prime Minister Churchill warned the House of Commons that the date of the coming victory could not yet be forecast. "I certainly could not predict, still less guarantee, the end of the German war before the end of the Spring, or even before we reach early summer", he said. "It may come earlier, and none will rejoice more than I if it should." Parliament passed the necessary legislation to keep the Commons in session for a further year—there had been no general election since 1935. Mr Churchill promised there would be one when the German war had been effectively and conclusively finished, and he pleaded that until that time there should be no break in the coalition or return to the party system.

✳

CHAPTER TWELVE

Post-war Prospects

O N 16th JANUARY 1944 nine people were killed at Ilford when a train from Norwich ran into the rear of an earlier train from Great Yarmouth. Among them was fifty-one-year-old Lieutenant-Colonel F. F. A. Heilgers, who had been the Conservative Member of Parliament for Bury St Edmunds since 1931. The resultant by-election on 29th February focused a political spotlight not only on this corner of East Anglia, but on what was rapidly becoming a national obsession: the debate about the sort of society to be created when the war was over. On the day the Bury St Edmunds contest opened, with the nomination of two candidates, the government was defeated by an Independent in a by-election at West Derbyshire, its second such set-back within a few weeks. The verdict of the press was that voters were "dissatisfied with the progress made with reconstruction and other plans of the present Administration". The Bury campaign, therefore, saw a tremendous effort by the government to stop the drift, with big battalions of ministerial speakers drafted in to support a strong local Conservative candidate, Major Edgar Mayne Keatinge of Westley Hall.

His opponent was an Independent Liberal, Mrs Margery Corbett Ashby. (The official party organizations—Conservative, Labour and Liberal—held to an agreement not to contest by-elections during the war.) When she arrived in the town three weeks before polling day she had no formal political machinery and her supporters had to start from scratch.

It was a lively contest, arousing great public interest. A Mass Observation commentator reported "a widespread view that Greene King run Bury"—it was certainly true that the brewery company was the largest local employer and that its influence in support of the Conservative cause was consolidated by the local farmers. Mrs Corbett Ashby's supporters declared that even before nominations were in the Conservatives had booked every hall in the town for the eve-of-poll, so that the Liberal was left to speak from a soap-box in the snow.

The local cinema showed a "Vote Conservative" slide between its feature films, and the Mass Observation man reported:

> One woman stood up and shouted "Take that off—you don't keep our advert on for minutes at a time". The manager came round and said "Oh, Mrs F——, you mustn't make a fuss". There were a lot of local boys there and they booed him and cheered her.[1]

There was a widespread fear that those who supported Mrs Corbett Ashby might be victimized. Miss Winifred Last attended one of the Liberal meetings and afterwards noted in her diary:

A countryman got up and asked if the ballot was secret, as most people here thought it wasn't, and he and others live in tied houses and might get notice to quit. He wanted it said and put in the press that it was secret.[2]

Despite assurances given, the Mass Observation observer concluded: "It seems quite likely that sufficient people refrained from voting from fear of victimisation to sway the result."[3]

The voting, declared from the balcony of the Athenaeum by the High Sheriff on 1st March, was:

Conservative	11,707
Independent Liberal	9,121
Con. majority	*2,584*

The opponents of government policy were pleased with the result and resolved that a "United Progressive Front" movement should be formed in the constituency, with a committee representing Liberal, Labour, Co-operative, Commonwealth, Fabian and Communist Party organizations. For the remainder of the year political interest remained high in the town. The Communist Party held regular public meetings in the Guildhall. Shock waves ran through other parties: Labour Party headquarters threatened to expel local officials who identified themselves with the United Progressive Front, and the official Liberal prospective parliamentary candidate—who had observed the political truce at the by-election—reasserted his claims to carry the banner at the post-war general election and repulsed approaches by the UPF.

After the poll Major Keatinge was carried shoulder-high through the Corn Exchange, but the *East Anglian Daily Times* reported a mood of restlessness in the House of Commons: "Members are asking when the government proposes to implement certain promises made on its behalf regarding postwar developments."

It instanced housing and education plans, which it thought were moving too slowly. Both candidates in the Bury by-election had agreed that housing conditions in the town were very bad and had promised action. A Mass Observation observer sent into the constituency reported: "The cheaper parts of the town are a maze of mean little streets of shabby little red-brick houses and small shops. In Bury it is said there is one bath to fifty houses." In this respect, however, Bury was typical of many towns in Britain.

The government did nothing to damp down discussion of post-war problems and prospects. On the contrary, it produced a string of policy pronouncements, and the re-housing of the people was a dominant theme. The programme of airfield construction was almost complete by the spring of 1944, and the government proposed that contractors should switch their heavy plant and machinery to the preparation of housing sites, laying down roads and installing electricity, water and gas services. The idea was that everything should be made ready so that, immediately Whitehall gave the word, building of houses could begin. Lord Portal,

Minister of Works, told the House of Lords that there would be sufficient plant to provide the infra-structure for the maximum number of houses that could be built during the first two post-war years.

That meant a hundred thousand permanent houses in the first year and three hundred thousand by the end of the second year, according to the Minister of Health in a statement to MPs. In addition there would be factory-built houses of "temporary construction". These would be of steel, and they were christened "Portals". A specimen was erected on Parker's Piece in Cambridge in November and attracted much interest. It had its critics, who argued that such buildings would create a "drab, dull appearance" in towns and who wanted only brick. A letter in the *Cambridge Daily News* signed "Ex-Serviceman's Wife" purported to put the opposite view, held by "people living in the congested and condemned areas of Cambridge":

> We exist in a dwelling that hasn't a single convenience, no outside building to garage cycles or anything else, no garden, and a sitting room floor that is under water almost

Housing became a major political issue during 1944. The government announced plans to supplement new permanent houses by factory-made steel homes, which became known as "Portals".

every time it rains. I personally would welcome and be proud of the chance to become a tenant of a prefabricated house, whether steel or wood.

The chairman of the Cambridge Housing Committee, Dr Alex Wood, declared that the United Kingdom would need four million new homes after the war, of which Cambridge would need eight thousand. It received Whitehall approval to build two hundred brick houses in the first two post-war years, and it was asked for two hundred "Portals". The council already had sites ready for one thousand and wanted to buy more land, but the government refused its approval.

Councils everywhere set their housing committees to work to produce estimates of post-war needs. Ipswich Town Council decided it would need five thousand new council houses in the ten post-war years to deal with the shortage, to relieve over-crowding and to re-house tenants from probable clearance areas. As a first instalment it resolved to build 112 houses on sites where it already had sewers and services in place, and to request seven hundred permanent houses as a minimum requirement in the first two years, plus 250 factory-made houses. Norwich Housing Committee also set its minimum post-war requirement at five thousand new houses, and asked for a thousand "Portals" and nine hundred permanent houses in the first two years. Great Yarmouth asked for 750 "Portals" and 350 permanent houses in the first year. Lowestoft Council prepared a scheme for a thousand in the first two years.

The smaller towns and villages also did their calculations and looked to the provision of the necessary land. Newmarket UDC selected Heath Stud Paddock as a site for a hundred houses; Eye Council agreed to buy land for forty houses; Clare RDC decided that it wanted eighty-four; Cosford RDC set the needs of its villages at a hundred; Deben RDC wanted 184; and Lothingland RDC fixed its target at fifty.

The government suggested that its scheme to switch airfield contractors and their equipment would be effective only for sites of five acres or more. To secure the necessary scale of work local authorities should plan collectively, grouping all sites within a radius of thirty miles, each project preparing for a total of two thousand houses. Norwich would be assigned a leading role in East Anglia, co-ordinating three housing areas: Norfolk, Suffolk, and Lowestoft and Yarmouth with Lothingland. On this basis the Ministry of Health thought site preparation could begin in June.

These proposals roused immediate and widespread opposition. Lowestoft and Great Yarmouth, the towns with the biggest bomb-ravaged areas, were among the most vocal critics. They saw the Ministry plan as a dangerous first step towards a system of regional government. They wanted the local authorities to be left to get on with the task with the aid of mobile labour and materials made available to them. The Mayor of Lowestoft, Major S. W. Humphery, was emphatic: "We don't want anything to do with the aerodrome contractors. We have seen quite enough of them and their methods of carrying out work in the most extravagant way possible." Cambridge Town Council also took the view that the scheme smacked of unacceptable "regionalisation", and this attitude was quickly adopted elsewhere. Site preparation did not go ahead as rapidly as had been proposed, therefore, and local authority delegates from East and West Suffolk and Norfolk were still at the talking stage in the autumn.

Housing for farm workers was dealt with separately. The Minister of Health, Mr Henry Willink, promised new homes for farm workers at rents not exceeding 7s 6d to eight shillings per week (exclusive of rates).

After being dormant for five years, the market in older residential property began to revive. Thousands of houses that had been requisitioned to billet troops and for other wartime purposes were soon to be released, and as early as January, 1944, one Ipswich estate agent was advertising "requisitioned properties for investment and future occupation". A Gothic-style house in south Norfolk with three reception rooms and five to seven bedrooms, plus five acres, was offered at £1,750; a Georgian house just outside Lowestoft, with three reception rooms, seven bedrooms and two bathrooms, plus a gardener's cottage and ten acres of land, was priced at £2,750; and an old-world house two miles from Woodbridge with three reception, seven bedrooms, three bathrooms, and three acres had an asking price of £5000.

Housing was the issue that most concerned the mass of the people, but aspirations went much wider. Post-war employment opportunities were passionately debated. A White Paper issued in May set out a plan for full employment and a higher standard of living after the war:

> Far-reaching measures aim at the stabilisation of prices and wages, mobility of labour—virtually no man will ever stand idle—raising industry to a peak of efficiency to secure overseas markets, elimination of "special areas", curbing monopoly evils . . . Rating and a measure of price control must be continued for some time.

The East Anglian region made its own considerable effort to position itself to take advantage of post-war opportunities. In Ipswich the town council set up a "Committee against Unemployment" and approved the establishment of a school of technology, which started with two prefabricated huts on land at the rear of Tower Street, housing a drawing office and workshops for carpentry, joinery and plumbing. The Suffolk Rural Community Council called a conference to discuss the future of small rural businesses, at which Lord Cranworth drew attention to the need for more youngsters to come forward to train as blacksmiths, carpenters, thatchers, wheelwrights and saddlers.

Ipswich's retail traders created a "Council of Retail Distributors against Combines, Multiple and Chain stores, Co-ops and bureaucracy". Its chairman, Alderman F. W. Warner, himself a trader, recalled a time when all the shops in Ipswich were occupied by private traders, living happily over their shops and giving personal individual attention to their customers. In 1944 there were 176 empty shops in the town, he said, and more were closing in face of unfair competition.

Just before Christmas the Export Group of Agricultural Machinery and Implement Manufacturers invited a party of potential overseas customers to visit two Ipswich engineering plants—the Orwell Works of Messrs Ransomes, Sims and Jefferies Ltd and the Foxhall Works of Messrs E. R. and F. Turner Ltd. Representatives came from Belgium, Czechoslovakia, France, the Netherlands, Norway, Poland and Yugoslavia.

In shops in the region products came on sale specially packaged in Union Jack wrapping and carrying "Buy British" labels.

Farmers gave much thought to their post-war prospects, and early in May a conference representing all sides of the industry produced an agreed statement on post-war farming policy for submission to the Minister of Agriculture. The Minister, Mr R. S. Hudson, brought in a measure to extend subsidies and offer cheap credit facilities, and that was seen as a small step in the right direction. He followed it up with an announcement of minimum prices for meat and milk, guaranteed for the whole output of farms for the following four years, and he promised that the payments would be "not less than those at present prevailing". This news was received quietly by the farmers, and the *East Anglian Daily Times* came to the conclusion that:

> Mr Hudson has gone some way to dispelling the habitual distrust of Whitehall that haunts many a farmer's mind, and to give cultivators of the land and rearers of livestock a measure of confidence as they face the transition period from a wartime to a peace economy. They have the firm promise of guaranteed markets and guaranteed prices. Every February ruling minimum prices will be reviewed and prices will be fixed for 18 months ahead . . .

Labour's post-war agricultural policy was expounded at a conference in Bury St Edmunds by Mr A. E. Monks, a union official who sat on the Central Agricultural Committee for England. His party, he said, believed the land should belong to the state, and a Labour government would acquire it by the issue of redeemable bonds on the basis of owners' valuation of their land for income tax purposes*. The wartime control and planning through the county agricultural executive committees had set the pattern for Labour's proposals for agriculture, he added, and he challenged farmers to say whether they were best off under a system of purely competitive sales or with some measure of control and marketing boards, as they had experienced during the war. One of those present, Mr J. Gibson Jarvie, a well-known right-wing voice, conceded that for the first time for twenty years the farmer was getting a reasonable price for his produce, but he insisted that his recent farming experience discredited planning and bureaucracy.

Mr J. F. Wright, the NFU Norfolk county secretary, challenged the Labour policy head-on:

*In 1945 a Labour government came to power and was in office for more than six years. It did not nationalize the land.

We must begin to plan for the early removal of much of the control that now obtains in connection with food production. The vast wartime machinery which has served a useful purpose during times of emergency must be swept away at the earliest possible moment, for the unfettered development of individual initiative.

The East Anglian fishing industry received special attention. Before the war Lowestoft had been the largest herring port in Great Britain, by number of boats registered and by number of men, but four-fifths of its steam drifter fleet and a third of its motor herring vessels had been requisitioned by the Services. It was anticipated that very few men returning from the Services would be able to re-equip themselves with boats and gear without assistance.

The Commons passed a Herring Industry Bill to provide grants and loans to help them, and the Minister of Agriculture promised that the Herring Industry Board would prepare plans for post-war regulation and development of the industry. The Members for Lowestoft and Great Yarmouth welcomed the measure, urging priority loans for nets, two-thirds of which had been lost, and arguing the importance of developing the Russian market for herrings.

Coastal towns faced other serious problems. Those that had depended before the war on attracting holiday-makers felt that their reputation as resorts had to be rebuilt from ground level. Felixstowe Council solemnly resolved to seek "residential holiday makers" rather than "day trippers", and it called for the railway line from Ipswich to be double-tracked. Southwold Council set up sub-committees to consider post-war reconstruction under eleven headings: recreational facilities, travelling facilities, housing, draining of the marshes, publicity, and so on. Lowestoft Council planned major reconstruction of the town, with a new civic centre, a new police station, a wider swing bridge, the elimination of the north railway station and a westward move for the central station.

In the shorter term the coastal towns from which the civil population had been evacuated looked for the early release of the hotels, boarding houses, private homes and other properties that had been requisitioned by the government, and their refurbishment and re-equipment. A deputation representing Great Yarmouth, Lowestoft, Clacton, Harwich and Dovercourt, and Southend saw Sir William Jowitt, Minister without Portfolio, who was responsible for this area of policy, and pleaded for special financial aid from the government. Jowitt visited many of the towns to see for himself. He recommended the Treasury to provide five million pounds in assistance, and also urged that the coastal towns be given priority supplies of beds, linen and so on. He considered the problems to be short term, however, and while promising help warned the resorts that they would have to take their place in a queue and would have to rely largely on their own labour resources.

These coastal towns that had been evacuated during the war had lost much of their rates revenue, and the government had helped them with hand-outs that were seventy-five per cent grants and twenty-five per cent loans. There was no intention,

Lord Jowitt said, to end the grants suddenly, but it was impossible to give a general undertaking that these sums would not be repayable. The Ministry of Health would consider each case on its merits.

The financial problems of the local authorities were mirrored in the experience of many individuals who before the war had traded, worked and lived in these towns. Back in 1940, when they had been urged to leave, a special Act of Parliament had granted a moratorium on the debts they left behind them. The government now argued that although early termination of this moratorium might create hardship its undue prolongation would create corresponding hardship for landlords and creditors.

So how were individuals to return, pay off their old debts and restart their businesses? Lord Jowitt suggested that "the larger people" would have to rely on their banks to help them over. He promised a Ministry of Health discretionary scheme to help the "small people". This would make interest-free loans to the local authorities, who would then be able to lend up to £150 to any individual to enable him or her to rehabilitate a pre-war business. The local authorities would charge a low rate of interest to cover bad debts, and would be responsible for repaying the money to Whitehall. The government recognized, however, that the lifting of the moratorium would mean that a large volume of debt could be enforced immediately, and so the Commons passed a measure giving power to the courts to reduce or remit a debt in whole or in part.

These proposals left a lot of people unhappy, and the MPs for Great Yarmouth and Lowestoft spoke up on their behalf. Creditors in their constituencies had suffered as much as debtors, they said. Elderly people who had once lived on rent income had been reduced to public assistance. Loans to individuals limited to £150 would be inadequate in view of post-war prices. Local authorities would find the tasks of reconstruction yet more difficult if individuals were granted remission of rates. Government grants and loans to local authorities should not be ended automatically immediately after the armistice. These were only part of their complaint. Shortage of labour was a major concern, they said, and the coastal towns wanted their own building workers back as soon as possible. Hotel bedrooms could not be opened because of staff shortage, and hundreds of thousands of visitors were likely to flock to the resorts and find no accommodation available.

Apart from a need for capital, traders returning to reopen businesses faced a maze of bureaucracy through which to find a way. Licences were required from the Ministry of Works to permit the reconditioning of requisitioned premises; licences from the Ministry of Food were needed by food retailers reopening pre-war businesses and by returning boarding-house keepers; licences from the Board of Trade were needed by many other ex-businesses wanting to resume their former activities.

These were the problems of the towns. In many villages in the rural hinterland of East Anglia the prospective post-war problems were of a quite different kind.

While electricity and gas undertakings were organizing town exhibitions and demonstrations of modern post-war kitchen equipment, in thousands of cottage homes there was not even an indoor water supply or proper sanitation. There were nearly four hundred country parishes in Norfolk without any public water supply; in this respect it headed the list of English counties. The West Suffolk County Federation of Women's Institutes announced in May that only twenty-nine of seventy-three parishes it had surveyed had piped water, and only thirty-nine had an adequate supply of any kind. People were carrying water to their homes in fifty-five parishes. In one parish of 217 houses, 117 were without any individual supply. In another there were nineteen wells for eighty houses. There were thirty schools with no water on the premises. Some houses drew their water from ponds. As for drainage, only thirteen of the seventy-three parishes surveyed had "a few houses with main drainage of a sort". The other sixty parishes relied on earth or pail closets, cesspits or tanks.

Attention had been painfully directed to these deficiencies because the first three months of 1944 were the driest for fifteen years. Rainfall during March was 3 mm in Essex (normal March average 34 mm); 9 mm in Norfolk (44 mm); and 5 mm in Lincolnshire (36 mm). Clare Rural District Council was told at its March meeting that wells never known to have given out previously were almost dry, and water was being carried considerable distances.

Unless these conditions were changed after the war, and quickly, they would make a mockery of talk of a brave new world and of the sweeping plans for reforms. The *Eastern Daily Press* was optimistic about future prospects:

> We are confident rural life will, in the postwar years, be equipped with the conveniences of modern science far more effectively than ever before. It is, for example, no longer a mere Utopian fancy to think of every village in England getting a clean piped water supply . . .

A number of rural district councils took preliminary steps to provide piped water when the war was over, but found the prospective cost a formidable challenge. Thingoe rural district provided an example; there it meant sinking three bores, laying about sixty miles of trunk main and creating three reservoirs, to supply half a million gallons a day. In the Blofield and Flegg rural district the estimated cost was nearly a third of a million pounds, and in the Swaffham rural district £147,000 at 1939 prices. Other areas could only contemplate short-term measures. In Clare rural district, where during July and August many wells and pumps ran completely dry and there was public demand that the council should "do something", the best that could be managed was the distribution of thirty-five tanks of four hundred to five hundred gallons' capacity, placed by the roadsides. Before the summer was out more such tanks had to be purchased, and the rates for the half-year were increased by more than six per cent to cover the cost.

How much consolation for folk with such problems could be offered by the Beveridge Report, with its promise of a comprehensive structure of social benefits?

In 1944 there were still hundreds of villages in East Anglia without a piped water supply and it was a common sight to see women carrying water in buckets from wells or streams.

This had been published in December 1943 and had captured the popular imagination, for it was seen as providing the essential foundation for the sort of society which the returning servicemen and women deserved. A Ministry of Health White Paper published in February 1944, dealing with the implementation of Beveridge, promised "free doctors, drugs, medicines, hospital treatment and other services for every man, woman and child", plus new health centres. The cost was estimated at £148 millions a year. Another government White Paper in September set out details of universal social insurance and a comprehensive economic policy for reconstruction.

Sir William Beveridge, the author of this historic document, became a Member of Parliament, elected to the safe Liberal seat of Berwick-on-Tweed, and he spoke at a public meeting in the Public Hall, Ipswich, during the following month. The local newspaper recorded that a "huge audience" gave him a great reception. He outlined his vision of a post-war society which would abolish want, provide full employment, establish peace by the rule of law agreed by the great powers and institute electoral reform.

Although these aspirations appeared to represent the public mood at the time, there were some who took a different view. The Economic League, for example, conducted a campaign in East Anglia on the theme that capitalism had "delivered the goods". "It must not be forgotten that the near and final defeat of Nazism is the result of individual and private enterprise responding to the urgent needs of the fighting forces", it argued. On Market Hill in Cambridge this message was heard by small crowds, but when the speaker moved to Bury St Edmunds he found himself addressing thin air. The league pressed on with its efforts to secure complete co-operation between management and labour, and retention of private enterprise in industry.

The Labour Party advanced the opposite argument and wanted to go beyond Beveridge. At its national conference in December delegates called on the leadership to fight the next election on a programme including public ownership of land, large-scale building, heavy industry and all forms of banking, transport and fuel and power. The executive tried to get this motion withdrawn, but it was carried by a large majority. One of the speakers, Lieutenant James Callaghan, the prospective candidate for Cardiff, advised men and women in the forces that they would come back to unemployment unless the Labour Party was elected and introduced a planned economy with public ownership.

Women's rights became an issue, and Cambridge was in the thick of the debate. National Council of Women members met at Newnham College to discuss "Women's responsibility in the postwar world", and at about the same time there were moves to form a Cambridge branch of the National Federation of Business and Professional Women's Clubs, eighty-two branches of which had been started in Britain since the war. In August the Transport and General Workers' Union—the biggest union in Britain—sent a prominent female union leader to Cambridge to speak on the subject of "Women Today and Tomorrow", and she told her audience that they should not relinquish the status they had achieved while doing men's work. Women, she insisted, would still have a place in industry after the war. The chairwoman wryly observed that women had achieved wartime equality so far as their work was concerned, but they certainly did not have equality of pay.

When the Mass Observation organization asked for assessments of women's prospects after the war, Miss Winifred Last of Bury St Edmunds offered this down-beat view: "A few married women will choose to go out to work, and keep a maid at home. The majority will prefer to stay at home. Others will be compelled to work to live."[4]

Another Mass Observation correspondent, William Stock, reported from his workplace in Chelmsford: "Discussion at lunch-time about the way ex-servicemen would be treated after the war . . . All agreed that it would be very difficult to get women out of jobs."[5]

Parliament had tried to make a modest start with equal pay earlier in the year by passing, by a single vote, an amendment to the Education Bill favouring equal pay for women teachers. Prime Minister Churchill insisted that the vote be taken again and declared he would treat it as a vote of confidence. The government then defeated the proposal, by 425 votes to twenty-three.

Many of the men still on the home front began to turn their thoughts to the resumption of sport. The 1943–44 season saw the first sign of a return to football. Norwich, which had fielded a scratch local team against a forces eleven most Saturdays, showed some impatience to resume professional football, but when the Football League made plans for the 1944–45 season it left Norwich out of the picture on the ground that it was too far off the beaten track, given wartime travel difficulties!

There had been no football at Portman Road, Ipswich, since the 1940–41 season. The Ipswich Town Supporters' Association collected seven hundred pounds towards the cost of repairs and renovations to the Portman Road ground and the chairman of the club, Mr Philip Cobbold, appealed for 150 people to take fifty-pound debentures to restart league football in the town. Two years earlier the club had been more than fourteen thousand pounds overdrawn at the bank. The chairman's family firm, the brewers Cobbold & Co. Ltd, had paid off most of it and the account had been cleared, and they now offered to write off half the sum advanced and leave the other half as an interest-free loan. But there could be no early return to serious football, Mr Cobbold warned, because most of the Ipswich players were in the services and would not become available immediately the war with Germany ended.

Colchester United had suspended its activities at Layer Road, but an army team—which usually went under the title of Colchester Garrison XI—had won a popular following, and had come almost to be regarded as the town's own team, drawing regular crowds of between one and two thousand.

As for cricket, the Essex County Services Club, fielding a side which included service cricketers in the county as well as actual Essex players, was formed at the beginning of the 1944 season.

Horse-racing was the sport least affected by wartime absences and restrictions, and the Newmarket Bloodstock Sales in 1944 suggested that the return of peace would see a fillip for the sport. Investment by owners broke all previous records. Mrs Florence Nagle set a new record price for a two-year-old at public auction when she paid fifteen thousand guineas for Carpatica, a filly by the Derby winner Hyperion, out of the 1,000 Guineas winner Campanula. The December sale ended with 508,207 guineas paid during the week for 669 lots, exceeding the previous highest total, back in 1928. Altogether the year's bloodstock sales had realized 1,042,965 guineas.

During what everyone hoped would be the last winter of the war, every town and village established a "Welcome Home" Fund to prepare for the return of the men and women in the forces. They debated what would be appropriate, services of thanksgiving, parades, tea parties and a long list of other possibilities. As early as

October Cambridge Entertainments Committee was making plans, and such was the enthusiasm in Saxmundham that it was felt that a committee of forty people was needed "to get the machinery in working order to celebrate the peace in the right way" (as the chairman, Mr M. F. Jennings, put it).

Apart from the rather grandiose plans advanced by government and community organizations, almost every individual had private aspirations on a more modest scale. A Norwich woman had . . .

> . . . no general expectations of peace and plenty and a good time round the corner. We can't hope for relief from rationing, coupons, and so on for a good long time . . . I am looking forward to getting domestic help and more petrol . . .[6]

A King's Lynn man wanted "full bellies and empty arsenals".[7]

The people of East Anglia were not entirely preoccupied with their own future prospects. As European countries were liberated by advancing Allied armies, it was recognized that many of their people were cold and hungry, and the European Clothing Relief organization was swiftly created. The government invited women to knit garments for suffering children, and the click of busy needles was heard in thousands of homes in East Anglia. The Women's Institutes distributed twenty thousand pounds of wool a month together with pins and patterns; Co-operative Guilds and the Women's Voluntary Service joined in, and village meetings drew up rotas of knitters. By the end of November West Suffolk WIs in seventy-five villages had dispatched five hundred shawls and 440 coats, "knitted in a delightful shade of pink, and really beautifully made", as the *East Anglian Daily Times* reported. Every item had a label sewn inside giving the name of the knitter.

The sixth Christmas of the war, when it came, offered a stark reminder that the rewards of peace were not yet within grasp. It was cold and frosty in East Anglia, there were acute shortages of money and materials, and the prices for new and second-hand goods seemed exorbitant. Shops had very few good toys, so second-hand dolls' prams changed hands at seventeen pounds, children's tricycles at fifteen pounds, Hornby train sets at thirteen pounds, rocking horses at ten pounds, and a toy motor car (at a Colchester auction) at seven pounds[8]. Five years earlier such prices would have been unthinkable.

The Ministry of Food allocated one pound of South African oranges per ration book over the whole of Britain and promised a boatload of lemons, with Norfolk and Suffolk among the first areas to have them in the shops; but they did not arrive in time. The Ministry declared there were enough turkeys for all, but in some places shoppers paid ten shillings a pound for them against a controlled price in the market of 3s 2d a pound. There were twenty per cent more Christmas puddings than in 1943, the Ministry said, and sultanas, raisins, dates, almonds and peanuts appeared briefly in the shops. The meat ration during the week before Christmas was increased in value from fourteen to twenty-two pence; and there was a little extra margarine and sugar, more sweets for children and an extra ounce of tea per week for those over seventy. But there was no extra beer, wines or spirits; a few who could afford it found whisky on the black market at five pounds a bottle.

United States servicemen in East Anglia again filled the role of Father Christmas, organizing parties for thousands of local children and performing countless good deeds. The British War Relief Society in America sent nearly two thousand toys and 2,040 boxes of sweets to Norwich for distribution to children in the elementary schools. Santa Claus arrived in a Fortress bomber at several bases, but at one Norfolk station attention was switched to his *departure*, waving from the pilot's cabin, and to the greater needs of children in recently liberated territory. Nearly 1,500 children were party guests at this base, and they watched excitedly as a Liberator bomber was loaded with fruit, candy, nuts, toys and gifts to be flown to Paris for distribution to French children. These gifts were contributed by officers and men of the station, and with them went Christmas cards and a book of greetings designed and made by the local English children.

At many East Anglian air bases American servicemen entertained local children at Christmas parties. Here US fighter pilots are seen with Wormingford youngsters.
Photo courtesy of Mrs Hervey Benham

They did not go without. The party at the US base at Ridgewell, Essex, was described by the chaplain there in his diary as . . .

> . . . the wildest I have ever seen. Picture 400 and more children pouring on to the base. The men have made friends all over this part of England—Essex, Suffolk, Cambridgeshire, Hertfordshire and Bedfordshire; they have gotten into the homes of hundreds of families, even in the cities of Cambridge and London. The children in these homes knew that a Christmas party was to be held. The men asked "Can we bring the children?" Could we say "No"? Kids were shoulder to shoulder, side to side, back to back, limb to limb. All the adults could do was stand there and either sigh or laugh . . .[9]

The diarist paints a comic picture. Bags of "cookies", full to over-flowing, were given to the children as they arrived. The contents began to spill out and soon they were all rooting about the floor, with much pushing and shoving, to retrieve them. In the midst of this confusion it was decided to hand out ice-cream cones. The children tried to hold their bags of cookies with their elbows while they ate the ice-cream. Some bit the pointed ends off the cones; soon everyone was skating on ice-cream. Then it was decided that Santa should hand out gifts:

> What an impossible task! All had the bag in their hands, while still holding the ice cream. Now they were asked to hold something else—their gifts. It was like a London blitz. I know now why the English are winning the war against Hitler. The English people "have what it takes".[10]

That comment provided a good summing up of the year, indeed of all the war years. The kids "had what it takes", and now they were getting rewards. The people had shown that they had the qualities necessary to survive and to hit back, and now they believed that they faced a future full of promise.

*

Operation "Manns". Night-time loading of food into an RAF Lancaster at an East Anglian airfield for the run to Holland. *Imperial War Museum*

Notes on Sources

The principal source for events on the home front has been the regional press, principally the leading county newspapers: the *Eastern Daily Press* for Norfolk, the *Cambridge Daily News* for Cambridgeshire, and the *East Anglian Daily Times* for Suffolk.

The regimental histories have provided the basic material for those chapters dealing with East Anglian regiments in action. Service files at the Public Record Office and some published autobiographical material has also been consulted, as indicated below.

The day-to-day experiences and thoughts of civilians living in East Anglia during 1944 are recorded in the Mass Observation Archive at Sussex University, and extracts have been quoted.

The standard reference books have been used for the national and international background: the various volumes of the official *History of the Second World War*, published by Her Majesty's Stationery Office, and Sir Winston Churchill's personal account, *The Second World War*.

Introduction and Acknowledgements

(1) H. P. Willmott: *June 1944*, pages 9–11 and 15. Blandford Press, 1984.

Chapter One

(1) Winston S. Churchill: *The Second World War*, Volume V, *Closing the Ring*, page 339. Cassell, 1952.
(2) Mass Observation: *Report on Bury St Edmunds*, Ref. MO2035.
(3) Mass Observation Diaries, Ref. S5205.
(4) Ibid.
(5) John F. Hamlin: *The RAF at Newmarket 1939–47*, page 10. Privately published, 1985.
(6) B. A. Stait: *Rivenhall—The History of an Essex Airfield*, pages 19–20. Alan Sutton Publishing Co., Gloucester 1984.
(7) Mass Observation Directive Replies, May 1944.
(8) Churchill, *op. cit.*, Volume v, page 373.
(9) Mass Observation Diaries, Ref. C5271.
(10) Mass Observation Directive Replies, February 1944.
(11) James Good Brown: *The Mighty Men of the 381st: Heroes All*, page 366. Publishers' Press, Salt Lake City, Utah, 1984.
(12) Ibid., page 364.

Chapter Two

(1) PRO: Ref. HO186/1640.
(2) Brown, *op. cit.*, page 381.
(3) Michael J. F. Bowyer: *Air Raid! The Enemy Offensive against East Anglia, 1939–45*, pages 302–305. Patrick Stephens, 1979.
(4) Brown, *op. cit.*, page 308.
(5) Ibid., page 389.
(6) PRO: Ref. HO186/1640.

(7) *An Historical Account of Air Raid Precautions, 1935–45*, pages 26–29. Cambridgeshire County Council, 1945.

(8) Noble Frankland: *The Bombing Offensive against Germany*, pages 72–73. Faber, 1965.

(9) Ken Merrick: *By Day and by Night—The Bomber War in Europe, 1939–45*, page 97. Ian Allan Ltd, 1989.

(10) Churchill, *op. cit.*, page 461.

(11) Merrick, *op. cit.*, page 97.

(12) Brown, *op. cit.*, page 403.

(13) Ibid., page 397.

(14) Ibid., pages 422–423.

(15) PRO: Ref. HO186/1639.

(16) Hervey Benham (ed.): *Essex at War*, page 65. Benhams of Colchester, 1945.

(17) Ibid., page 59.

(18) Ibid., pages 59–61.

(19) Bowyer, *op. cit.*, pages 302–305.

Chapter Three

(1) Colonel W. N. Nicholson: *The Suffolk Regiment, 1928–46*, page 171. East Anglian Magazine, nd.

(2) Colonel T. A. Martin: *The Essex Regiment, 1929–50*, pages 117–118. The Essex Regiment Association, 1952.

(3) Ibid., page 122.

(4) Ibid., page 122.

(5) Churchill, *op. cit.*, page 448.

(6) Willmott, *op. cit.*, page 14.

Chapter Four

(1) Benham, *op. cit.*, page 126.

(2) Stait, *op. cit.*, page 11.

(3) See R. Douglas Brown: *East Anglia 1943*, pages 135–144.

(4) Mass Observation Directive Replies, February 1944.

Chapter Five

(1) Mass Observation Diaries, Ref. C5271.

(2) Nicholson, *op. cit.*, page 75.

(3) Ibid., page 83.

(4) Willmott, *op. cit.*, page 71.

(5) Ibid., page 77.

(6) Ibid., page 75.

(7) Basil Collier: *A Short History of the Second World War*, page 412. Collins, 1968.

(8) Benham, *op. cit.*, pages 63 and 151.

(9) Willmott, *op. cit.*, page 66.

(10) PRO: Ref. WO 199/2544.

(11) Benham, *op. cit.*, pages 146–147.

(12) Ibid., pages 94 and 110.

(13) A. P. Herbert: *The War Story of Southend Pier*, County Borough of Southend-on-Sea, nd.

(14) Nicholson, *op. cit.*, page 85.
(15) Ibid., page 85.
(16) Mass Observation Diaries, Ref. S5205.
(17) Mass Observation Diaries, Ref. C5271.
(18) Brown, *op. cit.*, page 411.
(19) Benham, *op. cit.*, pages 62–63.
(20) Stait, *op. cit.*, page 31.

Chapter Six

(1) Quoted in Ian L. Hawkins: *Courage, Honor, Victory*, page 188. 95th Bomb Group Association, 1988.
(2) Mass Observation Diaries, Ref. S5205.
(3) Willmott, *op. cit.*, pages 63 and 66.
(4) Nicholson, *op. cit.*, page 95.
(5) Ibid., page 94.
(6) Martin, *op. cit.*, page 16.
(7) Nicholson, *op. cit.*, page 82.
(8) Ibid., page 82.
(9) Ibid., page 96.
(10) Ibid., page 98.
(11) Ibid., page 84.
(12) Ibid., page 90.
(13) *East Anglian Daily Times*, 3rd August 1944.
(14) *Suffolk Regimental Gazette*, quoted in the *East Anglian Daily Times*, 28th September 1944; see also Carlo d'Este: *Decision in Normandy*, pages 130–136. Collins, 1983.
(15) d'Este, *op. cit.*, page 131.
(16) Nicholson, *op. cit.*, page 102.
(17) Letter to d'Este, quoted in d'Este, op. cit., page 136.
(18) Martin, *op. cit.*, page 165.

Chapter Seven

(1) Martin, *op. cit.*, page 167.
(2) d'Este, *op. cit.*, page 153.
(3) Ibid., page 201.
(4) Ibid., page 252.
(5) Winston S. Churchill: *The Second World War*, Volume vi, *Triumph and Tragedy*, page 11. Cassell, 1954.
(6) Norman Scarfe: *Assault Division—A History of the 3rd Division, from the Invasion of Normandy to the Surrender of Germany*, page 109. Collins, 1947.
(7) Mass Observation Diaries, Ref. S5205.
(8) Nicholson, *op. cit.*, page 109.
(9) G. J. Scriven: *Called Up*, page 32. Published by the author, nd.
(10) d'Este, *op. cit.*, page 370.
(11) Nicholson, *op. cit.*, page 119.
(12) Brown, *op. cit.*, page 457.
(13) Benham, *op. cit.*, page 94.
(14) Mass Observation Directive Replies, June 1944.
(15) Martin, *op. cit.*, page 189.

(16) Scarfe, *op. cit.*, pages 130–131.
(17) Nicholson, *op. cit.*, page 123.
(18) Ibid., page 124.
(19) d'Este, *op. cit.*, page 431.

Chapter Eight

(1) Benham, *op. cit.*, page 68.
(2) Mass Observation Diaries, Ref. S5205.
(3) PRO: Ref. HO186/1640.
(4) Martin Gilbert: *Road to Victory—Winston S. Churchill 1941–1945*, page 810. Heinemann, 1986.
(5) PRO: Ref. HO186/1641.
(6) Merle C. Olmstead: *The Yoxford Boys*, page 42. Aero Publishers, Fallbrook, California, 1971.
(7) Brown, *op. cit.*, pages 361–362.
(8) Bowyer, *op. cit.*, pages 320–321.
(9) Mass Observation Diaries, Ref. S5205.
(10) See R. Douglas Brown: *East Anglia 1939*, pages 165–176, and *East Anglia 1940*, pages 25–28.
(11) Mass Observation Directive Replies, November 1944.
(12) Mass Observation Diaries, Ref. C5271.
(13) Mass Observation Diaries, Ref. C5271.

Chapter Nine

(1) *East Anglian Daily Times*, 22nd July 1944: Letter to the editor from Stuart Paul, chairman of the East Suffolk WAEC.
(2) Miriam Kochan: *Prisoners of England*, page 34. Macmillan, 1980.
(3) Ibid., page 34.

Chapter Ten

(1) Benham, *op. cit.*, pages 152–153.
(2) Stait, *op. cit.*, pages 40–41.
(3) Martin, *op. cit.*, page 190.
(4) Nicholson, *op. cit.*, page 124.
(5) Trevor Bevis: *From Out the Sky*, page 17. Westrydale Press, 1978.
(6) Benham, *op. cit.*, page 64.
(7) Stait, *op. cit.*, page 41.
(8) Brown, *op. cit.*, page 444.
(9) Olmstead, *op. cit.*, page 40–41.
(10) Martin, *op. cit.*, page 327.

Chapter Eleven

(1) Mass Observation Directive Replies, November 1944.
(2) PRO: Ref. HO186/1641.
(3) *East Anglian Daily Times*, 30th October 1944.

Chapter Twelve

(1) Mass Observation File Report No 2035.
(2) Mass Observation Diaries, Ref. C5271.
(3) Mass Observation File Report No 2035.
(4) Mass Observation Directive Replies, February 1944.
(5) Mass Observation Diaries, Ref. S5205.
(6) Mass Observation Directive Replies, November 1944.
(7) Ibid.
(8) Benham, *op. cit.*, page 84.
(9) Brown, *op. cit.*, pages 504–507.
(10) Ibid., page 508.

Selected Bibliography

Volumes in the official *History of the Second World War*, published by HMSO:

Sir C. Webster & N. Frankland: *The Strategic Air Offensive against Germany, 1939–45*, 1961.

H. St G. Saunders: *The R.A.F., 1939–45*. Volume 3, *The Fight is Won*. 1954.

Captain S. W. Roskill: *The War at Sea, 1939–45*, Volume 3, 1961.

Lieutenant-Commander P. K. Kemp, RN: *History of the Royal Norfolk Regiment* [Volume III] *1919–1951*. Norfolk Regimental Association, 1953.

Colonel T. A. Martin: *The Essex Regiment, 1929–50*. The Essex Regiment Association, 1952.

Colonel W. N. Nicholson: *The Suffolk Regiment, 1928–46*. East Anglian Magazine, nd.

Hervey Benham (ed.): *Essex at War*. Benhams of Colchester, 1945.

Michael J. F. Bowyer: *Action Station—Wartime Military Airfields of East Anglia, 1939–45*. Patrick Stephens, 1979.

Michael J. F. Bowyer: *Air Raid! The Enemy Offensive against East Anglia, 1939–45*. Patrick Stephens, 1986.

James Good Brown: *The Mighty Men of the 381st: Heroes All*. Publishers' Press, Salt Lake City, Utah, 1984.

Winston S. Churchill: *The Second World War*, Volumes V and VI. Cassell, 1952 and 1954.

Basil Collier: *A Short History of the Second World War*. Collins, 1967.

Carlo d'Este: *Decision in Normandy*. Collins, 1983.

Martin Gilbert: *Road to Victory—Winston S. Churchill 1941–1945*. Heinemann, 1986.

Miriam Kochan: *Prisoners of England*. Macmillan, 1980.

Ken Merrick: *By Day and by Night—The Bomber War in Europe, 1939–45*. Ian Allan Ltd, 1989.

Norman Scarfe: *Assault Division—A History of the 3rd Division, from the Invasion of Normandy to the Surrender of Germany*. Collins, 1947.

B. A. Stait: *Rivenhall—The History of an Essex Airfield*. Alan Sutton Publishing Co., Gloucester, 1984.

H. P. Willmott: *June 1944*. Blandford Press, 1984.

Eastern Daily Press.
East Anglian Daily Times.
Cambridge Daily News.

Index

A

Agricultural Executive Committees, 110, 111, 112, 114, 117, 155
Agricultural Workers, National Union of, 10, 119–121, 155
Agriculture, 109–121, 155
Agriculture, Ministry of, 110, 111, 114, 116, 117, 118, 155, 156
Air raids on UK, 28–30, 61, 142–143
Alconbury, 22
Aldeburgh, 49, 63, 100, 128, 142, 145
Alexander, General Sir Harold, 38
Amsterdam, ss, 89
Anderson, Sir John, 12
Anderson, Gen. Sam, 66
Andrews Field, 6, 122
Anglo-American relations, 2, 9, 42–44, 46–47, 50, 98, 138, 144, 147, 163–164
Anglo-Soviet relations, 41
Ashby, Mrs M. Corbett, 150
Ashby St Mary, 30
Ashdon, 18
Ashen, 147
Attlebridge, 22, 52
Auxiliary Territorial Service, 49, 98, 124, 138, 148

B

Baldwin, Lord, 10
Barker, Prof. Sir Ernest, 10
Barnwell, 40
Barrow, 50
Barton, Pilot Off. C. J., VC, 18
Bates, Cpl Sidney, VC, 91
Bawdeswell, 133
Beccles, 27, 49, 63, 105, 110
Beighton, 102
Benham, Sir Gurney, 10
Benton, H. J., 20
Bentwaters, 27
Berlin, 22, 24, 25, 26, 41, 69, 132, 133
Beveridge, Sir William, 158–160
Bevin, Ernest, 7
Biddle, Sapper D., 140
Bircham Newton, 24

Bishop's Stortford, 7
Blackout, 11, 143–144
Blofield & Flegg RD, 158
Blyth RD, 142
Boadicea, HMS, 80
Bodney, 133
Bomber Command RAF, 20–22, 122
Bombing missions, 20–27, 122; British public reaction to, 27–28
Boreham, 27
Borley Green, 116
Boxford, 116
Boxted, 22
Boycott, Maj. Charles, 71
Bradwell, 95, 98
Braintree, 28, 43, 95, 117, 140
Breach, Capt. W. N., 130
Brentwood, 63
Bridges, Frank, 20
Briggs, W. L., 41
Brightlingsea, 28, 63, 101, 127
Briscoe, Lady, 49
Bristol, Marquis of, 49
British Legion, 141–142, 148
Brook, Dr Richard, 149
Brown, Rev. James Good, 8, 15, 25, 26, 27, 64, 89, 99
Brownless, Capt. P. P. S., 36
Buckley, R. F., 104
Bulmer, 116
Bungay, 18, 30, 49, 105
Buntings Ltd, Messrs, 2
Burma–India campaign, 31–37, 135–136
Burnham-on-Crouch, 63
Bury St Edmunds, 2, 4, 7, 14, 18, 20, 43, 45, 48, 49, 50, 53, 64, 104, 110, 119, 137, 147, 150–151, 155, 160
By-elections, 150–151

C

Callaghan, Lieut. James, 160
Call-up, 139–140
Cambridge, 4, 7, 14, 15, 19, 30, 40, 41, 47, 51, 89, 93, 104, 106, 108, 124, 138,

141, 142, 143, 144, 147, 152–153, 154, 160, 162, 164
Cambridge Daily News, 8, 11, 24, 25, 37, 41, 50, 51, 142, 143, 147, 152, 166
Cambridgeshire Regiment, 135
Cambridge University, 9, 10, 28, 51
Canvey Island, 63
Carter, L. A. C. W., 124
Cassino, 37–40, 134
Censorship, 38, 89, 95–97, 101, 142, 145
Chelmsford, 3, 4, 5, 30, 63, 64, 67, 82, 95, 96, 100, 101, 102, 125, 140, 160
Chelmsford, Bishop of, *see* Wilson
Chesterton, 30, 42
Children in wartime, 43–47, 52, 102–108
Christmas, 147, 162–164
Churches, *see* Religion
Churchill, Sir Winston, 1, 7, 25, 38, 55, 56, 80, 97, 101, 122, 137, 149, 161, 166
Cinemas, 28, 64, 88, 137, 148, 150
Civil Defence, 2, 12, 18, 29–30, 40, 100, 142, 147, 148
Clacton-on-Sea, 28, 63, 100, 101, 102, 137, 156
Clare, 104–105, 147, 153, 158
Clary, F., 105
Clothes, 3
Cobbold & Co., 161
Cobbold, Lieut.-Col. John M., 10
Cobbold, Philip, 161
Cobbold, Major Robert N., 10
Colchester, 9, 10, 13, 14, 16, 28–30, 42, 52, 61, 62, 63, 65, 66, 101, 117, 124, 128, 137, 141, 142, 143, 147, 161, 162
Colne, River, 62, 124
Coltishall, 24, 102
Community Council, Suffolk Rural, 154
Consumer goods, 4, 5
Cooperative Guild, 162
Cosford RD, 153
Crabb, J., 107
Cranbrook, Earl of, 49, 50, 154
Crickmore, L. C., 20
Crime, 52
Croft, Maj. Andrew, 124
Cromer, 63, 102
Crosby, Bing, 2
Culford School, 10
Curtin, John, 10

D
Dagenham, 100
Dann, A. C., 120
Dean, Fl. Off. Arthur, 132
Debach, 27
Debden, 133
Deben RD, 142, 145, 153
de Chair, Somerset, MP, 116, 117
Dedham, 10
Demobilization, 139–140, 161–162
Deopham Green, 27, 133
Diss, 15, 18, 106, 107, 110, 119
Doolittle, Lieut.-Gen. James, 55
Dorman, Long & Co., 124
Dovercourt, 28, 89, 156
Downham Market, 22
Driberg, Tom, MP, 47
Dunmow, 6, 28, 30, 45

E
Earl's Colne, 6
Earnings, *see* Incomes
East Anglian Daily Times, 5, 8, 24, 28, 30, 38, 40, 51, 67, 88, 97, 101, 104, 105, 106, 108, 109, 110, 114, 119, 125, 132, 137, 140, 143, 149, 151, 155, 162, 166
East Bergholt, 7, 8
East Dereham, 133
Eastern Daily Press, 1, 2, 3, 107, 110, 111, 119, 158, 166
East Harling, 110
Easton, F. H., 106
Economic League, 160
Eden, Anthony, 12, 135
Eisenhower, Maj.-Gen. Dwight, D., 53, 55, 56, 66
Elveden, 18
Ely, 50, 126
Engledow, Prof. Sir Frank, 10
English, C. W., 42
ENSA, 2, 64, 88, 99
Entertainment, 137–139
Epping, 101
Essex County Standard, 10
Essex Regiment, 13, 34, 36–37, 38–40, 54, 58, 63, 69–70, 76, 79, 81–82, 90, 93, 125, 131, 134
Evacuation, 52, 102–108, 145
Eye, 27, 47, 49, 119, 153

F

Far East, war in, 31–37, 122, 148
Farming and Farmers, *see* Agriculture
Feast, Rev. Willis, M., 111
Felixstowe, 9, 49, 58, 63, 100, 137, 142, 145, 156
Finch, W. J., 52
Fingringhoe, 101
Fishing industry, 156
Flixton, 18
"Flying bombs", *see* V.1 and V.2
Framlingham, 16, 19, 30, 133
Fraser, Peter, 10
Fraternization, 50–51
Freston, 80
Frinton-on-Sea, 28, 63
Fuel supplies, 4, 52, 144
Fulbourn, 102

G

German prisoners-of-war, 117–118, 148–149
Gielgud, John, 138
Gimbert, Benjamin, 20
Girton, 47, 50
Glatton, 27
Gooch, Ald. Edward G., 10, 120
Goodwin, Lieut.-Col. R. E., 63, 81
Gosfield, 122
Gough, Lieut.-Col. J. G. M. B., 84, 94
Grant, Miss W. E., 46
Great Dunmow, *see* Dunmow
Great Saling, 95
Great Yarmouth, 14, 47, 61, 63, 98, 107, 143, 145, 150, 153, 156, 157
Great Yeldham, 18
Green, Rev. H. G., 148
Greene King, 150
Grigg, Sir James, 12, 63, 136

H

Hadleigh, 14, 45
Halesworth, 49, 63, 110
Halstead, 30, 115
Harris, Air Chief Marshal Sir Arthur, 21
Harvest, *see* Agriculture
Harwich, 62, 63, 80, 89, 125, 132, 156
Hawkins, Lieut.-Cmdr F. W., 80

Hawkins, Sq. Ldr Ron, 80
Health, Ministry of, 106, 152, 153, 154, 157, 159
Heeton St Lawrence, 102
Heilgers, Lieut.-Col. F. F. A., MP, 150
Hellesdon, 102
Hempstead, 5
Hemsby, 102
Henham Park, 17
Herbert, A. P., 80
Herbert, Rev. F. F., 142
Hitler, Adolf, 56
Holidays, 137–139, 156–157
Holland, *see* Netherlands
Holmes, William, 121
Holton, 14
Home Guard, 2, 138, 140, 148
Honours, 10
Hopton, 102
Horham, 22, 67, 132, 133
Horse racing, 11, 107, 161
Horsford, 102
Horsham St Faith, 27
Housing, 139, 151–154
Howard, Gerald, 137
Hoxne, 101
Hudson, R. S., MP, 116, 155
Humphery, Maj. S. W., 153
Hundon, 112
Hunsdon, 24
Hunstanton, 145
Hunter, Lieut. D. Lee, 33

I

Illegitimacy, 47, 50
Incomes, 12, 49, 112–114, 117, 119–121, 148, 160
Invasion plans, *see* Operation "Overlord"
Ipswich, 7, 10, 14, 16, 30, 42, 46, 47, 51, 52, 63, 80, 95, 100, 111, 113, 119, 137, 140, 141, 142, 143, 145, 148, 149, 153, 154, 155, 156, 159, 161
Italian prisoners-of-war, 50–51, 115–117, 148
Italy, war in, 31, 37–41, 122, 134–135, 140
Ixworth, 4

J

Jamieson, Capt. David, VC, 93

Japan, *see* Far East, war in
Jarvie, J. Gibson, 155
Jeeps, Maj., 142
Jennings, M. F., 162
Jockey Club, 11
Jowitt, Sir William, 156–157

K
Keatinge, Maj. E. M., 150–151
Kelvedon, 95, 124
Kesgrave, 110
Kesselring, Fld-Marshal, 37, 38, 134
King George VI, HM, 56, 64
King's Lynn, 48, 63, 93, 107, 144, 145, 146, 162

L
Labour & National Service, Ministry of, 7, 140
Lake, Ald., E. L. D., 43, 48
Langham, 24
Last, Winifred, 7, 53, 64, 104, 107, 150, 160
"Lavengro", 110, 111, 119, 121
Lavenham, 27, 112
Law, A. S., 105
Lees, Miss, 104
Leiston, 22, 49, 133, 142, 145
Little Chesterford, 19
Littleport, 20
Little Snoring, 22, 30
Little Walden, 18
Llewellin, Col., 146
Lloyd George, Maj. Gwilym, 144
Loftus, P. C., MP, 117
London & North Eastern Railway Co., 89
Long Melford, 113
Lothingland RD, 142, 153
Lowestoft, 49, 63, 107, 117, 119, 140, 142, 145, 153, 154, 156, 157
Luftwaffe, 6, 22, 28, 30, 61, 80, 133

M
MacEwan, Air V.-Marshal Sir Norman, 10
Maldon, 47, 63
March, 20, 28, 50
Marshall, Subtn Margaret, 124

Martlesham Heath, 9
Mass Observation, ix, 2, 7, 8, 28, 43, 89, 150–151, 160, 166
Matching, 27, 122
Matlaske, 102
McCaffrey, Maj. D. W., 84
Mendham, 10
Mendlesham, 27, 102
Mersea, 62
Metfield, 20
Mildenhall, 5, 102, 112, 113
Mine clearance, 145
Monks, A. E., 155
Montgomery, Gen. Bernard, 53, 63, 79, 80, 82, 124, 125, 128, 130
Morale, 5, 7, 8, 12, 148
Morrison, Herbert, 47, 48
Mountbatten, Admiral Lord Louis, 31
"Mulberry" harbours, 59
Mundesley, 102
Munnings, Sir Alfred, 10

N
NAAFI, 2
National Farmers' Union, 109, 116, 119, 155
National Fire Service, 12, 18, 19, 29, 138, 142, 148
National Trust, 10
Nayland, 16
Needham Market, 49
Netherlands, 126, 132
Newmarket, 5, 11, 12, 28, 46, 47, 49, 107, 116, 153, 161
Nicholson, Col. W. N., 55, 137
Nightall, William, 20
Norfolk, Duke of, 114, 116
Norfolk Regiment, Royal, 13, 33–36, 53–54, 58, 63–64, 69–70, 72, 74–76, 80–81, 85–94, 125, 128–130, 135
Norwich, 2, 7, 10, 13, 16, 30, 45, 46, 47, 51, 52, 95, 102, 107, 111, 120, 128, 136, 138, 140, 142, 143, 145, 150, 153, 161, 162, 164

O
Observer Corps, Royal, 61–62, 127
Old Buckenham, 124

Operation "Goodwood", 87–89
Operation "Manns", 165
Operation "Overlord", 22, 26, 53–78
Orwell, River, 62
Owles, Ald. and Mrs Allden, 105

P
Pampisford, 19
Parham, 19
Parkeston Quay, 80, 89, 132
Pathfinder Force, 22
Patton, Gen. George, 91, 92, 94, 122
Paxman's, 61
Peasenhall, 95, 103
Pickard, Group Capt. P. C., 22
"Pightle", 109, 114
Plane crashes, 15–19
Playfair, Air Marshal Sir Patrick, 147
Policewomen, 47–50
Portal, Lord, 151–152
Postwar plans, 150–162
Prisoners of war, Allied, 111, 135–136, 138, 148
Pryor, Grafton D., 46

R
Randle, Capt. John N., VC, 35
Ransomes, Sims & Jefferies, Messrs, 155
Ranworth, 102
Rationing, 2–4, 14, 52, 146, 162
Rattlesden, 22, 102, 124
Raydon, 14, 22
Red Army, *see* Russia at war
Red Cross, 111, 138, 142, 148
Regional Commissioner, 15, 28, 96, 140, 142; *see also* Spens, Sir Patrick
Religion, 7, 47, 147–149
Reynolds, Gordon, 17
Rhine crossing, 125–127
Ridgewell, 2, 8, 15, 18, 25, 26, 27, 64, 99, 132, 147, 164
Rivenhall, 6, 22, 66, 124, 132
Robertson, Maj. C. D., 49
Rocket bomb, *see* V.1 and V.2
Rockland St Mary, 102
Rommel, Fld-Marshal, 78
Roosevelt, President Franklin D., 1, 7
Rougham, 112

Rowhedge, 101
Rowley, Sir Charles, 49
Royal Air Force, 5, 6, 8, 9, 19, 20, 22, 24, 27, 28, 30, 55, 59, 61, 64, 67, 87, 90, 95, 98, 102, 122, 124, 126, 132, 133, 148
Royston, 7
Russia at war, 41, 122, 133

S
Saffron Walden, 19, 30, 42, 98, 120
Sainsbury, Frank, 105
St Osyth, 62
Salcot, 95
Salvage campaigns, 14
Savings, National, 13
Saxmundham, 49, 63, 110, 140, 142, 162
Sayer, Flight-Lieut., P. E. G., 9
Scarfe, Norman, 76
Scarlett, G. S., 106
Scouts, Boy, 113
Sculthorpe, 24
Sea, war at, 54–55, 58–59, 64, 66, 67, 69–71, 74, 80, 87
Seething, 30
Shakespeare, Sir Geoffrey, MP, 45, 136
Shelfanger, 15
Sheringham, 63
Skinner, Dr J. W., 10
Slim, Gen., 33, 135
Snetterton Heath, 124
Snettisham, 110
Social problems, 42–52
Soham, 20
Somerleyton, Lord, 117
Southend, 61, 63, 156
South Lopham, 111
Southwold, 30, 49, 63, 100, 142, 145, 156
Soviet Union, *see* Russia at war
Spaatz, Gen. C. A., 55
Special Operations Executive, 124
Spens, Sir Patrick, 96, 140
Spink, Rev. J. F., 106
Spixworth, 102
Sport, 11, 161
Stalin, Josef, 1, 7, 53
Stanstead, 105
Stansted, 27
Stilwell, Gen., 135

Stock, William, 3–5, 64, 67, 82, 96, 101, 160
  Stoke-by-Nayland, 116, 124
Stokes, Richard, MP, 27
Stowmarket, 16, 47, 49, 63
Stradbroke, 15
Stradbroke, Earl of, 17, 148
Stradishall, 5
Sudbourne, 101
Sudbury, 46, 49, 119, 132
Suffolk Breed Society, 110
Suffolk Regiment, 31–34, 36–37, 53–55, 58, 63–64, 69–76, 81, 83–84, 86–88, 93–94, 125, 128–130, 134–135, 137–138
Swaffham, 116, 158
Swainsthorpe, 10
Swannington, 98
Swanton Morley, 10

T
Taylor, Prof. Sir G., 10
Teichman, Sir Eric, 52
Temple, Dr William, 47
Tempsford, 132
Thames, River, 62, 98
Thetford, 52, 105, 107
Thingoe RD, 4, 158
Thornham, 93
Thorpe, 102
Thorpe Abbots, 22, 124, 133
Tibenham, 124, 132
Tilbury, 58
Turner, Messrs E. R. & F., 155

U
United States Army Air Force, 2, 8, 15, 18, 20, 22, 27, 30, 55, 59, 61, 67, 87, 95, 102, 122, 124, 132, 133
Upper Hellesdon, 16
USSR, see Russia at war

V
V.1 flying bombs, 95–101, 106–107, 145
V.2 rockets, 101–102, 142
Victoria Cross, award of, 18, 35, 40, 91, 93

W
Wages, see Incomes
Wallace, Nellie, 16
Walton-on-the-Naze, 28, 63
Warner, Ald. F. W., 154
Weather, 145
Weeley, 101
Welch, R. C., 20
Wenhaston, 40
West Mersea, 62, 63
Wethersfield, 102, 122
Whitlingham, 102
Whittle, Group Capt. Frank, 9–10
Wilburton, 51
Wilby, 15
Williamson, Henry, 119
Willink, Henry, 154
Wilson, Dr Henry, 12, 47
Wisbech, 50
Witham, 117
Witnesham, 106
Wivenhoe, 59, 63, 124
Wolferton, 110
Women in postwar world, 160
Women in war effort, 7, 8, 47–50, 61, 140
Women's Auxiliary Air Force, 49, 124, 148
Women's Institutes, 103, 158, 162
Women's Land Army, 112, 114, 147
Women's Voluntary Service, 7, 42, 105, 138, 148, 162
Wood, Dr Alex, 153
Woodall, Rev. Hugh G., 84
Woodbridge, 22, 45, 49, 63, 119, 154
Woodward, Lieut., 84
Woolverstone, 95
Works and Buildings, Ministry of, 14, 157
Wright, J. F., 109, 119, 155
Wright, Peter H., 40

	National and International	*Regional*
June	Allies invade Normandy on D-Day. Cherbourg liberated. Allied armies occupy Rome. Supply route to Imphal cleared of Japanese. Americans capture Saipan Island and inflict heavy losses on Japanese Navy.	First V.1 flying bombs reach East Anglia. Explosion in ammunition train in Soham station. Farm holiday camps opened. "Salute the Soldier" Weeks. Last Luftwaffe raid on East Anglia.
July	Attempted assassination of Hitler. Caen and St Lo captured. Leghorn, Siena and Ancona captured. Russians capture Brest-Litovsk and Lublin and cross Latvian frontier.	London evacuees sent to East Anglia—billeting problems everywhere. Sales show big fall in sheep flocks.
August	Eisenhower moves HQ from UK to France. Paris liberated; de Gaulle enters. Allied troops invade southern France and capture Marseilles and Toulon. Maquis liberate Bordeaux. Warsaw uprising by Home Army. Germans evacuate Florence. All Japanese troops driven from India. Red Army reaches east Prussian border.	Ban on entry to coastal areas lifted. Freedom of Bury St Edmunds conferred on Suffolk Regiment. Serious beer shortage. "Holidays-at-home". Good harvest yields.
September	Belgium and Luxembourg liberated and Belgian Cabinet returns to Brussels. US troops cross German frontier near Trier and pierce "West Wall". Unsuccessful Allied airborne landings at Arnhem. End of Russo-Finnish war. Liberation of France complete and French Provisional Government abolishes Vichy laws.	German V.2 rockets reach East Anglia. Civil Defence and fire-watching run down. Invasion Committees disbanded. Record prices at Newmarket Bloodstock Sales. Arnhem airborne troops fly over East Anglia.
October	Allies recognize de Gaulle's Provisional Government. Allies occupy part of Holland. Russians cross into East Prussia and northern Norway. Allied troops land in Greece. Bulgaria signs armistice with Allies.	New AA defences operational against rocket bombs. Beveridge gets enthusiastic reception at Ipswich rally.